Gordon Stewart is a musician, broadcaster and writer.

From early days in a Durham mining village, his educational journey took him to a school in Hampstead, then to Cambridge and a Modern Languages degree, and on to the Royal College of Music and a London University music degree.

As a pianist, he performed widely as a soloist and yet more as a partner of instrumentalists and singers. He knows the recording studio well, both as a performer and as a producer on the other side of the glass.

He was encouraged to work for the BBC and broadcast extensively in programmes for Radio 3 and the World Service. After a few years he joined the staff of Radio 3's Music Department, eventually becoming its Deputy Head. He's written, produced and presented hundreds of programmes, including six studio operas, one of which is now on CD.

His production of the first live music broadcast on radio of a concert from Leningrad, as it then was, gained a Sony Award for the outstanding radio music broadcast of 1986.

His professional writing, alongside the many scripts, includes programme notes for concert venues such as the Wigmore Hall and the Barbican, and a Third Leader for The Times.

Yellow Leaf is his first novel. He continues to write, both fact and fiction.

To my wife, Linda, whose love, patience, and advice have helped make this book possible.

Gordon Stewart

YELLOW LEAF

Gordon Stewart

AUSTIN MACAULEY PUBLISHERS™

LONDON * CAMBRIDGE * NEW YORK * SHARJAH

A CIP catalogue record for this title is available from the British Library.

ISBN 9781398475922 (Paperback)
ISBN 9781398475939 (Hardback)
ISBN 9781398475946 (ePub e-book)

www.austinmacauley.com

First Published 2024
Austin Macauley Publishers Ltd®
1 Canada Square
Canary Wharf
London
E14 5AA

My thanks to Mel Churcher for the information she gave me about what a newcomer might find out when being filmed for the first time. I found her two books, *Acting for Film* and *A Screen Acting Workshop*, invaluable sources, as well as good reading.

And to Maddy York for very valuable advice in the early stages of working on the novel.

"I'm leaving you."

"You're what?"

"Leaving you."

"I'm sorry, I don't understand."

"I'm lea—"

"Yes, I heard. Tonight? Now?"

"Yes – tonight."

"I had no idea."

"That's why I'm telling you now."

"I mean, I had no idea we'd got here," I said.

"I didn't think you did."

**

It was April 30th – just into the morning of May 1st. May Day. I was late back from the last concert of my short tour. Newcastle, Richmond in Yorkshire, Corby. An easy drive home. I slipped quietly into the house and there was Patti, sitting at the kitchen table, her coat round her shoulders, her car key in her right hand, her house keys on the table beside her handbag. At one o'clock in the morning.

As I came through the door, she had said Hi and asked, quite normally, looking up from the glass of milk she was sipping, "Good concert?"

"Yes. Went well – all three."

"That's good. Still on form."

"I suppose so. You're up late. Have you just got in?"

That had happened before with an overrun at the opera house for some reason. Occasionally. Maybe twice.

The half-drunk glass of milk and the biscuit crumbs beside it weren't usual, though, not even occasionally.

"Is something wrong?"

"You could say that. There's something I need to say."

I tried a laugh. "Is it so important that it can't wait until tomorrow?"

"Yes, it is."

And then there it was. "I'm leaving you." Gently spoken. Gently but firmly. Not looking at me.

"What? Why?"

"I want to live with someone else. Marry them and have children."

This 'them' thing? Him, her, them: what did that mean?

"Do you want to tell me who 'them' is?"

"Keith."

Who the hell was Keith? And the children? I thought she was being unfair...

"Why don't you want to have children with me?"

"Because you said you didn't want any."

"I don't remember saying that."

"You were very clear about it. Emphatic. Several times. Frequently at first. Almost vehement." Not quite so gently now.

I really didn't remember.

But I have to say it was possible, because of my parents' example....

"And so...this children with Keith thing...are you already underway with that?"

She really looked at me then. "I don't think that's a very proper question."

"Why not? I think it sort of follows on from what you said."

"I don't want to talk about it. But No is the answer, if you want to know."

I waited, but she had nothing more to say on the subject.

"Is that it then? You're going. Now?" I said.

"Yes," she said.

"Can I just ask – who is Keith?"

"He plays the trombone in the orchestra."

"In your orchestra?"

"Of course, in my orchestra."

She drank the rest of the milk and put the glass down.

"I'm off now," she said, and left, leaving a piece of paper with her new address and details of her solicitor. And the house keys.

**

I opened a bottle of whisky, a Christmas present from someone who didn't know my taste in alcohol. Prescient present.

I didn't want Patti to go. It had never occurred to me to think she would. We married when we were music students fourteen years ago, going on fifteen. Now she'd gone. Seriously gone. I walked around this place where we lived. Our place. Apart from the DVDs, there was no visible sign that she'd ever been here. Well, not to my tired eyes, enhanced as they were with the slug of whisky I was not used to. These last three days I'd been away had been spent very thoroughly. With a van in the street?

Perhaps she'd been moving her belongings out for some time and I hadn't noticed. Along with a lot of other things I hadn't noticed.

Had we not been talking at all? For that conversation to come out of nowhere?

I took my glasses off and cleaned them. As if I might see more clearly what had been under my nose…for how long? How long had this been going on? I poured myself another drink. Drink doesn't do my fingers any favours, and my fingers earn my living for me if there's a piano to play.

We were two busy people in the same profession, with different demands.

"I'll think about this tomorrow," I said. Out loud. It didn't do me any good, because deciding not to think about it was the same as thinking about it. So I thought about it.

Me, being vehement about not having children? I thought we were good as we were. But it figured. Neither of my parents had very parental characteristics. Both left me. And one another.

Wife leaving husband: did my mother leave my father? Or did he leave her? Looking for the latest models. Should it have been me leaving Patti? That had happened with one or two of my colleagues in the industry; in their fifties. Some of them were always looking for different models, and probably not noticing if they were different at all. Not me. I'm two decades short of them. I'd never looked at other women. It seemed that I hadn't been looking at this woman, either, or I might have noticed something. We were making love still. After all, it was only…only when? I couldn't remember. We'd both been so preoccupied.

Patti and I had been students together. She played the violin, and I played the piano, and we played together as a duo – played together and stayed together – what we did in music we did in life. We were in love. We really were. I believe that. We got married, although her parents thought she was mad, because they hoped she would surely find someone who wasn't a student. Anyone with better prospects. I didn't think my prospects were bad; a student pianist, yes, but good enough to have scholarships – several scholarships and prizes, and do well in that BBC Young Musician programme. I grant you that they couldn't have known that I actually did have prospects a lot better than many music students.

We were twenty. Fourteen years and some months ago. I hadn't wanted to let Patti out of my sight, in case someone else got her first. And amazingly enough for those days, we were both virgins. We were exceptionally devoted, had never looked beyond one another. We'd been faithful to one another ever since. At least, I had.

Those were fabulous days, just like a movie idea of what music students ought to be: no money, eating sandwiches, practising, standing room only in concerts, borrowing music because we couldn't afford to buy it, stealing it from libraries, or rather, paying the fine when you 'lost' it. I've still got some of those scores, with other people's markings in them. Living in one room, bed-sit, in a not-so-nice part of Clapham, with other music students, and a landlady who was straight out of Ealing Comedy Land and almost never at home, because she was writing musicals. She showed me a programme of one of her shows off the fringe of the Fringe. I've not seen her name since; maybe she changed it for commercial reasons.

All that had come to an end now. It had obviously come to an end some considerable time earlier.

Why? My time with Patti had got out of joint. We'd become like furniture in each other's rooms and not much more. I hadn't noticed what was missing exactly, and it was too late to try to find out. If Keith was a trombone player in her orchestra, then I dare say she saw more of him than she did of me on a day-to-day basis. I didn't want to think that she loved him the way she didn't love me, or that he loved her in some way I didn't know anything about.

What was I going to do?

I had never thought I would have to live without her. We were a couple, a partnership, we were used to one another. Patti clearly didn't see it the same way. It wasn't enough. Not for her. A trombone player had swept her off her feet and I was left.

I finished my drink.

Then I went through to play the piano. The only thing I could trust, my only true relationship? Quietly I played some Schubert – slow, thoughtful, painful, as he can be, and somehow able to come out of it. I wept. "When we two parted…in silence and tears." We learnt that poem at school and we thought it was something to do with the teacher who chose it for us. Now, what with Byron and Schubert, it was much too true.

I took another drink.

Was I just a piano-player now? Was that all I ever was?

I went to my bedroom. Our bedroom, it had been.

She had systematically removed her belongings while I'd been away. Keith must have helped. No, he couldn't have done that, Patti wouldn't have let him tramp around our place. My place to be. Keith? I'd never met him. Some extrovert brass player, fit and healthy with all that breathing to do. I was sure of that.

I looked in the mirror to see who it was she'd left. In the mirror, not in the soul – it was easier – to see if I could find the reason. At least, looking at the outward and visible signs of a man progressing quickly towards ex-husband-hood was a first step. I could leave the psychological things until later. I am still doing that.

My face. It was on the round side. Too much on the round side. My cheeks were round enough to deny my other features much of a look in. My hair was plentiful, but long, like a fading sports star, or someone on a panel show, and I didn't even wear it in a ponytail to make it into a statement of some sort. And although it's fair, it was dull and lank; greasy is the unhappy truth. I wear glasses. I've worn glasses ever since I was twelve, and they were heavy, unfashionable; why should I bother otherwise? I don't play the piano with my glasses. There was a general air of not taking care. I couldn't imagine her being attracted to a man who looked like this. She was still much as she was when we were first together. Pretty, if I can say that without putting her down. Back then I was pleased she was interested in me, even if I looked better then. I looked better than this. I think. Now I began to wonder if I would have warranted a second glance unless I sat down at a grand piano. Was that what had driven Patti away?

It was a long time since I had actually looked at myself in a full-length mirror apart from just before going on stage, so I stripped down, and looked at my body. I had put on weight while I wasn't looking. Nearly thirty-five, busy, a successful pianist. What did I expect to see? Certainly not what I saw. It wasn't very encouraging.

I looked older than I was. Not really, if you looked closely – no early wrinkles, but the overall effect was of a body on a downward curve. And an outward one, too. If it was physical beauty that Patti expected in me, then no wonder she left. I have a strong body, which I inherited from my father, who was a sailor. I have good basic musculature, well-shaped arms, in spite of taking no notice of them, except to make sure that I can get round the piano rather than look like someone brought in to move it. "Overweight" seemed the right word for what I saw – more than the beginnings of a beer belly, all the more insulting because I don't drink beer. For the purposes of my work, I looked well enough: clean, with short fingernails; tidy; when you play the piano for money you usually wear that sort of black or black-and-white clothing which stops people from looking at you very closely. People in a classical music audience don't worry too much about the way you look, as long as you can find your way on to the stage without doing anyone any harm. Some soloists look better than others, but some of the greatest pianists have shambled about on stage without damaging their careers.

I was just about to take a voluntary three-month pause from concerts and my little bit of teaching. I needed it: I'd been very busy – great for the career and for the income; but I needed time to learn new pieces, and check up on those I already played. The bicentenary of both Chopin and Schumann was a couple of years away, in 2010, and there was Liszt a year later. I had engagements. There was a CD under discussion.

There was time to do something about me. The one in the mirror.

Being overweight is not a good idea for a life on the road, with or without a wife, so I needed someone to bring me up to date. Three stone up to date, I reckoned, even four. It was a guess, since I had no scales then. Thanks to that forward planning, no audience was going to clap eyes on me for a while. Patti knew that, and I was sure that's why she had delayed until now. Until the middle of the night. You have to admit she had behaved well. Considerate to the very end, if leaving your husband unexpectedly is considerate at the very beginning.

Patti had gone

Patti had gone. I was alone. She was my wife, my friend – my only real friend, when I come to think of it. Now there was no one to talk to, to look to.

14

She had been everything I needed. Yes, I have acquaintances, through my work, people I am friendly with, neighbours I pass the time of day with, but my life is largely that of a traveller.

Patti had gone, and I don't believe she'd told me everything she felt about that. I had to make a new life just for me. Where to start?

Well, I could do something about my body, and see whether my mind would follow. Getting up to date was something that needed to be done professionally. I needed to find a personal trainer. Yellow pages? I didn't even try. Your average trainer is probably into six-packing, and press-ups and things, whereas I need to be careful of my hands, and the general wholehearted support they get from my arms and my back. Tearing around the keyboard in concertos is an energetic occupation, but unfortunately it's not the sort of exercise that produces a body to be proud of.

Someone had been recommended to me a couple of years back when I had been having a stressful time – a lot of travel, and not daring to say No to offers. The name was on my computer still, though I couldn't remember what it was filed under. I'd put it into a special file like Help-line, Emergency, Think-about-it-sometime. Something like that.

I found it under Personal/Trainer. But the friend who recommended him was someone who had just passed smartly out of my life, since it was Patti's brother. I didn't know if he was going to take sides in this affair, but I wasn't going to risk it by ringing him up. I could imagine a tricky conversation which I could do without.

Still, on mature thought, he'd been a good friend, when he was, so I decided to trust his judgement without speaking to him. I rang the training number he'd given me. It was answered by a slightly hoarse voice such as weight lifters often have, and I asked for Francis Macbeth.

"Speaking. Can I help you?" The Scottish voice was encouraging, though I'm not sure why – hard to place class-wise for an Englishman, maybe?

Francis was to come to me, and assess me, and see what he could suggest. I looked forward to that. I had made a positive move.

Getting the body into condition

When I opened the door, Francis was standing with his back towards me – wearing a puffy jacket, the hood pulled over his head. Less of him than I expected, but a sort of purposeful grace in the posture. Francis turned round and into Frances. A woman. Yes, definitely a woman. I wanted to ask a question or two, but I contented myself with, "I guess you spell it Frances." Why can't we be like the French and make a difference that you can hear: Françoise?

"You thought I'd be a man, didn't you?"

"Er, well…"

Frances had no problems – she was used to it; she looked like a woman and smelt like a woman. Prada, was it? She liked to be called Frankie, as in Frankie and Johnny.

"I wanted muscles that were fit for me, not to make me look like a wannabe Mr Universe. Men do that better. So this is what I look like."

She was Scottish, and she looked good. Better than I did, which wasn't very hard.

"Right, that's out of the way. Let's see what we can do for you."

In the event, the question of gender didn't come into it. We never got into a situation that was closer than was absolutely necessary for my development in this new direction. She stayed exactly as long as I paid for, gave no idea of where she was going next, where she lived, or who she was living with and how.

"You're not a special case," she said. "Definitely a mite too heavy, and you're looking unhealthy to boot. You need diet and exercise. Tell me about your version of those."

I explained. My long-term day-to-day diet obviously had to make plenty of energy to play in public, which takes rather a lot in a concentrated space of time, and certainly enough for brain-energy. And how to deal with funny meal-times in strange places.

In the short-term, I was to eat in a fixed pattern. Fixed by Frankie.

"Have you ever done anything like this before?" I asked.

"I have certificates. Would you like to see them?"

"I mean, worked with musicians before."

"Sure. I've got quite a few CCM people."

"Sorry?"

"Contemporary Commercial Music singers – pop and theatre people. The blokes like to get a bit of a six-pack if they can, a four pack if they can't." She laughed. "And they like pecs where they can be seen. I tell them it might not be good for their voices."

"Why?"

"Because…Lovely thick necks and less room for the voice-box."

"Is that true?"

"Not quite, but they need to know what the problems might be."

"Does that stop them?"

"No. I don't think their voices notice."

"Any classical musicians?"

"You'd be surprised. What is it you do exactly?"

"I play the piano."

"Oh right. Is that what you do for a living?"

"Do you work a lot with men musicians?"

"Yes, with a lot of men; they tell me they prefer a woman trainer, because we explain things better and we don't frighten them with the size of our biceps."

"You don't frighten me, you give me confidence…Can I just add that work-outs would have to keep my arm muscles free of strain? Not to mention my back."

Frances grunted.

"Am I asking something impossible?"

"Nothing is impossible. What I'll do is get rid of your fat and free up the muscles underneath."

She asked to see photographs of what I looked like before I got that mite too heavy. I had some which Patti had put in the desk. When I looked, I discovered she'd taken her own with her. How long had she been planning this thing she did to me?

There was one of me as a small boy smiling at the camera with not many teeth, and hair so blond it looked white. One or two of Patti and me together as students, although I was heavy looking, even then.

"Is that your wife?"

"Yes. She left. A couple of days ago." It seemed longer.

"Ah. I see. Good enough reason for a change in your looks."

She pointed to a picture of another couple. "And who are they?"

"Oh them. They're my parents."

"What do they look like now, if you don't mind me asking? It'll give me an idea of where your extra weight comes from."

"I've no idea. I've not seen either of them for years. And not much of them before they left."

"That's a bit hard."

"Maybe…but my grandparents were all I needed in the way of parents."

"They're good-looking."

"I suppose so. That picture was printed in a London paper. My mother was in a play at the time – one of three beautiful women in a solicitor's office or something. Translated from French. I think the word 'briefs' occurred in the title. Gran told me."

"And your dad?"

"He's wearing some sort of uniform. He was a sailor. He went back to sea."

"Your mum?"

"To Hollywood. Someone said he could get her into films. She believed him. Clearly. But she didn't seem to appear in anything. Or nothing that was ever exported. Probably the reason she didn't come back, if there is one. Ashamed of not having a career to show for leaving her lovely little baby."

"I can see a resemblance. You could end up looking like a mix. If you don't mind."

"I don't mind. I didn't put on weight just to punish my parents for going away. I didn't know them, for one thing. I didn't miss them. I really didn't."

That is the truth. It really is. Isn't it?

Diet came into it. Seriously. I thought fewer calories a day and a lot of water would be all that was prescribed. Calories don't put on weight: it's what they come with that does. Frankie said. But someone clever had been dreaming up menus that, until you looked at them closely, resembled normal food. My appetite had slipped away somewhat ever since Mayday, so it wasn't much of an effort to address the diet she chose for me to start with. I did it, though an omelette without egg yolks is something I've never got used to. She said she'd bring dumbbells, small ones, no biceps building equipment. Skipping rope, treadmill. She worked me hard and sensibly, taking my needs about wrists and elbows into account, and gave me a routine to do on my own every day. Almost at once I could feel the difference. It got easier to stick with it once the muscles I'd inherited from my father began to accept a trim shape. Frankie was not a cheap investment, but a good one, because she taught me how to move my muscles in a better way. Just what I needed to lead the life I lead.

At the end of our time together, spread out over three months or so, and dovetailed with my work on my piano repertoire, she said the only really positive thing she ever said to me. She looked at me with satisfaction and patted me on the shoulder.

"You'll do. Give me a call if you slip backwards. Better not to."

When I said Goodbye to her, there was a car waiting outside. A seriously well-shaped man manoeuvred himself out of the car.

"That's my man," she said.

They met like Greek statues intertwining. It was touching. I was envious; I didn't know anything about that.

**

That was the body. The hair wasn't a problem. You can hardly move for hairdressers who'll style you. And lighten up the colour a bit. My hair is fair, but I wasn't sure about the highlights until I saw them. They were flattering.

Then the glasses. I don't remember the time when I didn't need to wear glasses. I just needed them to see. I incline to long-sightedness, which means I can't play the piano at all without glasses: if I sit where I can see the music without them, I wouldn't actually reach the keyboard. Contact lenses were the answer – the throwaway ones that last a day, but you can actually wear overnight. Unfortunately I'm still not as tolerant of them as I wish. My heavy, long-lank-haired, glasses-wearing image must have been covering hidden assets, because the self-engineered makeover produced something rather different in three months. Something unexpected, like having a new suit of clothes, but one that replaces the skin. Permanently. Strangely, if I caught sight of myself in one of the mirrors in the house, I didn't connect with this person I saw. I thought it was someone else, someone I even wished I looked like. It's still like that, but not quite so bad. I suppose I ought to practise just gazing at my reflection, and moving a little to find out if I'm real.

The question was what to do with it. I wasn't intending to go and sweep Patti up in my arms and carry her off like a triumphant knight, a sort of Lochinvar come in from the West, was I? I hadn't done this for Patti. I'd done it because of Patti.

So, as they say in the restaurants, Enjoy.

**

Late in July I had an engagement for a music society in Yorkshire where I've played every year since my career began.

19

Mrs Phelps, the secretary, was picking me up at York station. She looked much the same as last time.

"Hello, Clara." I said. "It's a lovely day for the concert." She looked at me twice. And then again.

"Are you William Winton's deputy?" she said.

"I'm the only deputy I've got."

"You've changed."

"I'll admit the packaging has changed, but I'm the same musician inside."

"I can see the old you peeping through, now I look more closely. We didn't put your photograph in the programme because we know you. Or thought we did."

The concert was fine. Mozart, early Beethoven sonata, Ravel, and some Rachmaninov to end with. Mrs Phelps was happy.

"I had no more doubts the moment you started to play. Same sound, same clarity and feeling."

"I'm so glad you say that. Different weight makes you feel different."

"And look different. Can I say I approve? Perhaps you wouldn't mind posing for a photograph for our Archives. And you'll come again next year?"

No connection between the remarks, but if there had been I wouldn't have minded.

**

I got an email from my agent.

Email from *jane@curzprod.co.uk*

Will, my friend, I've respected your break, and I'm sorry things have changed for you personally.

I have a list of requests for your services, which I'll send separately, and some ideas from this office. The black and white CD you made earlier this year has done well, all things considered, by which I mean that it came out much too far from Christmas to make the effect it might have done. I'll try and get them to re-issue it – with a new cover. With a new photograph on it...

Let me explain: I had an email from Mrs Phelps in Ripon about your concert there. Great success. She was funny about not recognising you at York Station when she went to pick you up, which I didn't understand, until – great surprise— I looked at the attachment: a copy of the pictures they took of you for their

archives; one with her and a couple of other enthusiasts standing close to you.
Closer than usual, you might say. Yes, a great surprise. And new clothes. You
should have warned me. I think I'd better have a look at you. Soon.

Lunch tomorrow?
Luvya Jane

Agent lunch day

We met at a restaurant on a corner near the Barbican. Smart, modern, with a
menu guaranteed to provide something you could eat but not stand up pounds
heavier. It had the added advantage of being near her office in Clerkenwell.

Jane Curzon was looking very business-like, as she always does. She was
dressed in what my grandmother called a costume, by which I mean a suit.
Expensive. Formal hair, no wandering strands to be flipped back, discreet make-
up; all meant to show that she represents successful people, and that while she
likes to attract the attention of the customers, she doesn't intend to outshine the
people she represents. A bit like an old Hollywood idea of a career woman in
one of the films I watched when I was making my black and white CD. I like
her, but I never see her except on business.

She's done me proud, and I think I've done her pretty well too. Before I won
that international competition in Germany ten years ago, no agent was interested,
although I had come out of the Conservatoire bursting with prizes and laurels
and references as long as your arm. "Thank you," they said, "can you let us know
when you're playing in a major venue in London?" And I couldn't get a major
venue in London to give me a concert because I hadn't played at a major venue
in London. Pianists are two a penny, they didn't say, especially the ones with
prizes from the Colleges and Academies.

Looking back, it's easy to forget those two years between the hand-shake
from that Duchess or Countess or Princess, whichever it was the Conservatoire
had fished out of their pond to hand out degrees, and the competition in Germany.
I was married, Patti was picking up money as a freelancing violinist, I had a bit
of money from work at the Conservatoire, but we hadn't got enough to spare for
the cost of a ten-day visit to Germany for the Schumann competition. My
grandmother sold something and I rather think she went without a few other
saleable possessions; my grandfather would have wanted it, she said. I remember

her in such prayers as I say, because without her I might well have scraped around teaching more and not having enough time to practise.

My parents are divorced, I suppose, and living God knows where exactly – Mum in California, according to her most recent Christmas card, which was years-ago-recent. I have a very small pile of them somewhere; they never said anything, just 'All my love, Billy Boy' and a scribble which stood in for 'Mother'. No one else ever called me Billy Boy, and I don't like it. Work that one out. Dad is somewhere else, which always seemed to be changing; postcards used to come, when they did, from South Africa, South America: "Hi, son, thinking of you." He never sent me any money, and I guess he didn't have any. So the uniform he was wearing in the wedding photograph didn't mean much for very long. He couldn't possibly know what I'm doing, if he's in Uruguay or wherever. His cards came direct to the Conservatoire when I was a student, because someone must have told him I was studying there; the Conservatoire people knew as much about my relationship with my father as I did.

Gran had been there in the hall in Endenich when I won the Schumann Competition. Later I was able to buy her another necklace like the one she had told me she hadn't sold. It wasn't the same, and it broke the continuity in the family. But then there isn't much of that, is there?

Jane was in the hall too, and she put me on her books. With satisfactory results. She doesn't run a big agency: just Jane and changing help from trainees. At least, I think that's what they must be, because they don't stay long.

**

She was sitting at a table with her back to the door, looking at the menu until I kissed her cheek. She looked up.

"Right…let me look at you. Wow. I missed the full effect of your entrance. Could you pretend to go to the gentlemen's loo – or go, if you want to – so that I see you from behind and then walking towards me? Do you mind? For professional purposes."

I was a bit self-conscious about this, and I don't think I walked entirely naturally, putting my feet down more carefully than I normally do in normal life. I did tweak my careless-looking hairstyle a bit before returning, and put on what I took to be a catwalk face.

"Well now, so it's true. You've re-packaged yourself, or let's say, made yourself over. And spent some of your money on clothes. Very good taste."

I was glad she thought that, because I'd enjoyed myself on that shopping spree. Expensive shopping spree. But much less expensive than it would have been, because I could buy what I needed to update my professional clothes off a peg or two and not have to have them made for me with an elastic waist-line. Nowadays we're much less formal than in the full-on white tie and tails days.

We ordered. Just fizzy water as an aperitif, which shows you're trying to play the restaurant's game by having something they can really charge for.

"I'm a single man now, you know. As good as."

"Interesting. An in-between, I suppose. Neither one thing nor the other. You're still married, aren't you?"

"Maybe now isn't a good time to open that box of delights. Yes, I'm married, but on the fast track to a divorce."

"Ah, Patti's pregnant."

"No, she isn't. She said she wasn't and I believed her. I think she's playing by the book. It's her way of making it better for me. Or clearer."

"You're taking it very well, I must say."

"I'm not."

"But this new look of yours…"

"It's a protest march…You can't just accept things you're not sure you deserve."

We'd never talked about anything except practical things before. Trains and planes and hotels, mostly.

"Anything I can do to help, I will – Just ask."

"Yes, I will." We drank our water. The conversation ended there because the food arrived. Good thing about talking business over meals – you can change the subject or even sidestep it by calling the waiter.

The food was good. I was having two starter dishes, and that was all.

Jane chose her moment, so that she could say what she had to say next without having to chew at the same time.

"I couldn't believe you could turn out so well. You look quite stunning, which isn't, forgive me, how I've ever thought of you. Strictly as an artiste, you know, up till now. I had a sudden idea in the middle of the night after I got that photograph from Ripon, but I wanted to see you in the flesh first. Not so much of it as there was?"

"Indeed there isn't, and it cost me rather a lot – money, of course, and a whole marriage as well."

"I'm sorry, I didn't mean to be unkind."

"It's the truth, though. You mean you woke up the in the middle of the night to look at my photograph?"

"Not really. I thought that, if the camera hadn't lied, we could exploit your looks along with your playing, and make something to look at as well as listen to. A film. Short. It could even be based on your CD of black and white film music, and put in some stills or clips of the films.

"Second thoughts convinced me that would be expensive, because of the copyright. How about some popular piano pieces? With visual potential? You moving around; acting, you could call it."

"I'm not so sure. Cameras are OK for me as long as they're eavesdropping while I'm playing in a concert,– like Peeping Tom with a permit to view. They watch you do something you know how to do. But playing to them…? Inviting them in and 'acting' for them? I don't think so."

"No worse than making a sound recording. You do that for the microphone and the listener at home. This would be the same, but with a bit of dressing up, or whatever.

"We'd get you some good advice and direction. It's the post-production bit that matters most. No-one's going to ask you to do anything unlikely."

It could make a statement, I could see that. But I was doubtful.

"Do you think it will sell? It wouldn't be longer than half an hour at the most, would it?"

"This would be meant to be something new. Something special. Anyway, half an hour is a familiar length on TV. Some of their programmes last for an hour because they're padded out to make them last, with long introductions telling you what you're going to see, instead of just getting on with it, people walking from place to place. Haven't you noticed?"

"I must confess I don't watch very much."

"Think about it, and I'll see if there's some way we can get funding. We won't have to sell a million copies to cover our costs.

"I need some new pictures of you. If you're up for it, we can nip over to the Barbican and I can take some pics on my phone – casual poses to go with your new image. For me to send round so that there are no more mistakes like Mrs Phelps of Ripon nearly made. And then you can get some done by a professional with you pretending to play the piano. As well as more off-stage stuff, with outfits that show that *au fond* we are seriously relaxed in the serious music world."

I posed for her, having some fun, and incidentally getting to know Jane better in the course of it.

CD of film music

That CD of film music...Yes. Piano music from the films of the '30s and '40s; 'Black and White Notes from Black and White Movies', they called it. I enjoyed getting it together. It included Gershwin's 'Rhapsody in Blue' which is basic repertoire, and very useful on Saturday nights in a large auditorium. It wasn't written for a film, but Woody Allen very thoughtfully used it in 'Manhattan', which he shot in black and white, so it fitted. I had to learn 'The Dream Of Olwen' and 'The Warsaw Concerto', from long-forgotten films, and I'll most likely never play them again, but the rest of the music was straight up-and-down classics played or hinted at in films, or arrangements of notable scores, like 'Casablanca' and 'Laura'. The only serious omission was Rachmaninov's second piano concerto from 'Brief Encounter'. Deliberate omission – it would have taken over the whole project, for one thing, and I would rather make it a whole project on its own. When the time comes.

It's well recorded, glossy, and the CD cover is good, with a picture of me, I think, in the distance, playing the piano with spools of film all round me.

Alright, it wasn't intended for the serious market – more for the supermarket, but it's getting played on radio programmes that play classical music. So how can that not be a serious market? It got good reviews where you might expect them, and silence where you might expect that. Both of the free London papers welcomed it. With the booklet cover reproduced in smudges; the reels of film looked good, but the pianist – me – looked as if he'd been snapped by an amateur fan with an old camera. They both suggested that it would be a good stocking filler. I can think of better things to put in stockings, and it wasn't anywhere near Christmas (Easter was closer, having happened a couple of weeks earlier). I know Christmas seems to get earlier every year, but not that much, and you wouldn't sell many discs for Pentecost.

Life has to go on…

Meanwhile, there were the concerts to prepare. I had scheduled new items for the programmes I'd prepared during the three-month gap that Patti had completely emptied for me. I looked good…well, the best I could ever look; now I was having to learn how to be single again, and I couldn't remember what that was like.

It hadn't been hard to deal with my daily life. I was used to being on my own, if Patti had been on tour, which happened, though not very often. She was sometimes away playing in chamber groups without me. Or at least I thought so. Sometimes she went to see her parents. Without me. They approved of my success, but I don't think they ever really liked me. I wondered what they might make of the next man in line. Brass player. Keith.

I could manage the day-to-day things. Cooking, cleaning, I don't mind them. But music doesn't get into your fingers and brain via housework or cracking eggs. Practising was harder than usual at first – thoughts will run alongside sounds – and I had to make a rule that I would stop every time my mind wandered. Or rather, every time I noticed that my mind had wandered. It got easier, largely because I had disciplined myself to practise. And I am a quick study. I'm lucky that way.

Part of my reputation up till then was for being a bit of a whizz-kid, in the best sense of the word. It still is part of it, I suppose, because I can be impressive with quick fingers and strength and dazzle, and a heart. My work had taken me mostly down the broad highway of Romantic music, with a few diversions into other roads with Ravel, or Grieg or Prokofiev or Bartok.

Thank God for that, because it brought in the work. Being young often seemed to go with the music I played; Chopin and Schumann burnt themselves out, like Keats and Shelley and Byron – dying young, because they were fiercely intense, or going mad, or overworking or just ill. But hey! thirty-four was young anyway, especially for an unmarried, i.e. soon-to-be-divorced, person like me with no commitments, and no intention of going mad or dying of stress if I could help it. And I'm working on staying young in heart all my life.

All the same I didn't fancy going round the musical racetrack again and again, like a horse on speed. So there were always new scores on my piano… John Taverner, James MacMillan, Judith Weir…

Now was the right time to add something major – to stretch my mind, like my muscles. Time to climb the highest mountain, or one of the Beethoven range, anyway. There would be no need to feel scared, because his mountains give you a helping hand.

Beethoven? Late Beethoven. I'd played early sonatas, and the *Appassionata*, but I'd always been put off the late ones. Put off, mostly, by a teacher. In my teens, I started to practise opus 109. At the first lesson, my teacher got up and shut the book. "It's too soon for that," she said, "you'll need to grow up before you can deal with that." She didn't exactly pat me on the head, but it felt like it. Too full of grown-up thoughts, she said. Strangely, she let me learn Chopin and Rachmaninov, full to overflowing, almost, with grown-up emotions. I had my suspicions about her right from the start. Now, with the new free me released into the community again, I wanted to get back to the big boys; to the biggest boy. Be a Man, my Son, seriously.

Beethoven opus 109 it was: put it down on a CD, and that should perhaps show the world that I'm a new man, with intellectual potential as well, getting in there with the greats, and not afraid to meet Beethoven on his own terms.

**

The next day was my first day with Beethoven. E major is a warm key. First step had been completed – sight-read it a few times, straight through, take no attitude. Notice some things which will need special work. But don't sort them out now. Difficult to do, to be innocent, but anyone in the arts, I guess, must feel the same, faced with works which so many great artists have explored. But, come on, Hamlet and opus 109, you are living things lying in wait, dead, on the page until you lift them off. "Dormant" is a better word than 'dead'. Here I was approaching my new sleeping beauty, to give her the kiss of my life, once I had got through the thorn wood.

Good image? The frigid beauty, equals drugged, equals pricked by shuttle or pin, equals phallic, object. Doesn't one of the French versions of the story have it that the prince wakes her with a kiss, but only after a more tangible proof of his presence, unnoticed at the time by the sleeping beauty? Or did I make that up? OK. It's good for an analogy: a sleeping work of art becomes yours, provided you cut through the forest first.

I read some of Beethoven's letters again. I'm never sure how much the personal life of artists matters, except to them. Interesting, but maybe no more than gossip is. Does anyone in my audience want to know if I'm married or divorced? Or gay? Or the father of several illegitimate children? Would that make them appreciate the music more? All the clues they need are in the way I play, and my clues are in the text on the page.

I went out of my way not to listen to anyone playing my sonata when I decided to record it. I'm not afraid of hearing other people. They don't frighten me into making me conform to their ideas on how to play anything. After all, you don't get halfway through your thirties without having some belief in your own experience. But this was a time to be careful. Plenty of musicians have dropped out at this age. No longer young, not old enough to be revered. Be eighty and still prove you can move your fingers in the right direction, and you're OK. But coming up on to the sunny uplands of permanent success is a hell of a journey. It's better to travel hopefully than to arrive, isn't it? Not if you have listeners to consider. You do what you can, maybe push a bit if you have to, and get a good, loyal agent. Like Jane.

I didn't sleep well that night. Those thoughts about the sleeping beauty firmed up into dreams about Patti. I didn't want her to come to me in a dream, although it wasn't so long since she'd been beside me in our bed.

Our bed. This wasn't our bed – I had replaced that pretty quickly. I had to. With another double bed. I really didn't miss her – and yet – how could you not? I don't mean waiting at home or anything, not doing the ironing, checking my working clothes were regularly cleaned. Just being there. We were devoted. Weren't we? Obviously, we weren't.

Patti was a musician. Patti is a musician, although her new man might well override that, since I don't imagine that being in an opera orchestra is the same as being a soloist. A personal view, since I've not been in an opera orchestra. Let's just say it's different: hours of rehearsals, and having to bend most of the ideas you might have about the music to the demands of the person on the rostrum. No glamour to speak of and having to play longer than anyone else in the profession. Just because the operas take up more time, most of them. No wonder we lost touch. That isn't a rational remark. There are many good marriages among the players in opera orchestras. I don't go to the opera much, although I have been to a couple of Mozart operas and loved the music. That had nothing to do with why we grew apart. We lost the connection we had as musicians; we never made the time to play music together the way we did when we were kids – the violin and piano repertoire which we both enjoyed. I suppose I didn't take Patti's needs on board.

And she didn't take on mine. Perhaps no one could have done that, and now I was going to find out. How? If I didn't sleep well, it wasn't because of her, it was because of me.

The professional bit of life settled down well enough. I never had any doubts about that. I don't need to be married to play the piano. My career had picked up a lot when I won the international piano competition in Endenich in memory of Robert Schumann ten years earlier. It wasn't considered an important event in this country, that's for sure, and, to be honest, not much anywhere else. But there was a splash about it afterwards because the woman running it had a lot of money of her own, and she made sure she got interviews all over and took me along to some of them with her. An Englishman winning some European competition to which Russia and Hungary had sent pianists was a news item even if not many people had heard of the place. Not like the Leeds Competition, which I never tried, because I didn't want to be seen not to win it. I've made a couple of CDs, starting with Schumann's concerto from the competition recording. My CD of pieces by Chopin got a 'best newcomer' award, although I'd been a newcomer for something like five years when that came out. Quite an achievement, nevertheless.

What now? Going into a decline might be Romantic, but not practical, and I decided against having any fashionable psychotherapy. After all, I immerse myself daily in the emotional language of music, even when I'm not quite sure how the other emotional bits of me are working. I can't help feeling it is some form of therapy. Thirty years practising the piano, sitting alone with your fingers and other people's thoughts running through your head should help. I feel I know Schumann and Chopin and Ravel as colleagues. They found some sort of solutions to life in their music, so I follow them.

And now Beethoven.

**

My 35th birthday

September 21st is my birthday, and on my thirty-fifth my solicitor rang to say the divorce had cleared its first hurdle. That's what was supposed to happen. There were no financial problems. I didn't ask about the details. I wasn't asked to pretend to supply cause or just intent. Patti wanted no severance pay, though I'd been earning more than she had. Quite a lot more. It was not an issue for her, she said, since she was the one to give up. Her husband-to-be had a house, anyway. There were no children to think about, because he had none. That was the point. My legal adviser told me I was well on the way to being a free man in a few weeks. Lucky man, he said. I think he meant to be kind and show solidarity with me. It didn't help.

All the same, I set some money aside for Patti, without telling her. We'd divided up the possessions. Amicably. This house in Dulwich was mine. It still is. My grandparents bought it years ago when Dulwich wasn't so expensive, and they had left it to me. They had no other grandchildren.

Just for a while I desperately wanted Patti to see me, to see how I'd changed. Then I opened a bottle of champagne, in the middle of the day, just for me; and I toasted myself, for my birthday, and for the new man in my life. Me. Halfway through three score years and ten is as good a place as any to start again if you have to.

I had the new no-choice option of learning to be a bachelor, and there was certainly plenty to learn. Everything to learn. I couldn't wipe Patti from my past, but I was going to wipe her from my future. In due course.

**

Back to the Conservatoire

Three days after my birthday I went back to the Conservatoire. My old place. I've never quite lost the pleasant feeling of having the steps up to the main entrance under my feet, although I've been at the Conservatoire, man and boy, for about twenty-two years. Boyhood days at the Junior Con, growing up at senior Con, then on the staff. The only break was the year I spent studying in France. It's a whole heap of things to me: my past, and my present, and my umbilical cord to music itself. My holy art. My something like that.

It's a mess of a building. Modest classical ambitions in the form of some external pillars and a pediment, and Victorian details – fussy, pseudo baroque, but now fashionable. Inside, it's modern, so one way and another, the building could cover the styles a well-balanced musician needs. It's what the brochure says: "Sound turned into sight." That looks purposeful enough, although you could just as well turn it the other way round.

I was grateful when they asked me to do some teaching just after I left the place. I needed the money. But it's become harder as the years go by, harder to fit it into my timetable, and harder yet to give it the attention it needs. You can't just turn up and teach. Teaching is about developing the other person. It helps to show them your personal solutions, what you do yourself; and when you're in mid-career that's almost all you really have time to find out. But it's not enough. People have lessons in how to teach. I warned the Conservatoire authorities, but they said they were happy; they wanted young blood, and they no doubt thought I would teach what I'd just been taught, so I'd be like another branch on the old apple tree.

A bare minimum, and I regularly offer to give up altogether, because it's so little. But when I try to leave, they wring their hands. If they really do want an old boy on the staff, for continuity – well, I owe them something. And they understand it if I go missing once in a while. I'd missed the last term; not a problem, since all of my three pupils were post-graduates with no examinations to hurdle, and they were put with a couple of deputies who would give them a different view from mine. There's not just one answer to anything, especially in my world. They had now left.

As usual I slipped in, trying not to get involved too much. It's not hard. Being a pianist is not like being an orchestral musician, and even if pianists play in an orchestra it doesn't happen on a regular basis with most orchestral pieces. Practise alone, play alone, most of the time. Loners, however you look at it. You get the odd chance to play with other players – a bit of chamber music, but it's surprisingly little. Having a string quartet and a pianist at a local music concert costs quite a bit, even if you all take a lower fee. Of course, you can have more of a social life if you play for singers exclusively, but there might be a downside to that. I don't know, because I've not had much to do with singers.

I had four students, all new, and specially selected for me (I was told). Three were from abroad – two from Japan, with hands which seemed to have no bone structure, they were so flexible, and one from the West – an American. My Japanese were exceptionally able, but needed care, because they didn't have the English language at anything more than the level of how to get clothed, housed and fed. But they knew the usual musical terms; *Allegro* and *forte* went quite a long way – that, and a few well-chosen (appropriate is probably the word) gestures to go with the words. I had to talk to them, because if I sat and played to them, they were tempted to imitate. Disturbing, because I have a moral dislike of artistic cloning. They were married – to each other. I couldn't help hoping that they were going to turn out better than Patti and I had in that direction. Marriage direction.

The American was a special case in more ways than one. It's flattering if an American asks to come here to study with me. They reckon to have the best teaching over there, reasonably enough – Juilliard, Eastman, Bloomington – and if they want European teachers, they invite them to go and stay. They do much better out of it. One airfare can get them a multiple deal: several pupils for the price of one teacher. I'm not on that circuit yet, and Gary Gassman came to me because he was well travelled, and had heard me play in London and at one of my occasional concerts in France.

I asked him if he was a relation of the great Italian actor Vittorio Gassman.

"You're the first to ask me that," he said, "and it's possible, but I don't see my father much, so I've never got round to asking him." Another fatherless child. "My mother's current husband is a nice man, but obviously I can't ask him."

He looked like one of those guys straight out of an American magazine about wholesomeness. Perfectly printed. Jeans which had been meant for working clothes were now courtesy of some European designer. Shirts with cufflinks and initials on them. In some sort of blue stone. Perfect light tan. He was skilful, very much postgraduate material. Beautiful moments in his playing, beautiful pages, even, but there seemed to be a certain niceness, politeness, even, which surfaced from time to time, as if he wanted to please me. I would have to see how to deal with that. He'd come here specially, paid good money to come to study with me. A lot of money – foreign student money. I could firm up his piano technique, anyway, and play to his current strengths by giving him shorter pieces like *Valses nobles et sentimentales. Pictures at an Exhibition.* He should be able to play them, too. Then stretch him into longer tasks.

The fourth new student was a girl. English. Felicity Smith. Specially wanted to study with me. Because? I'd no idea. Fortunately she could actually play the piano, because she'd been very well taught. More than that, she had plenty of talent. You could hear from the first notes she played. She was almost eighteen. And going to be a real beauty. Was already a real beauty. Blonde hair, real and long; she looked like a model, un-made-up, as if she didn't need to be.

A potential problem for a new thirty-five-year old teacher, newly on his own. At that first lesson, we didn't talk much. She played and we tried out some technical things.

**

In my short lunch hour, I ate the apple and sandwich I'd snatched from Boots on the way in, after carefully reading the text on the package.

I spent some time looking at op 109. Looking, trying not to imagine it in sound, just looking for shapes and details with a cool head. What Beethoven was trying to tell me. Sound and fury turned into visual aids. Beauty and depth caught by the ink. It's like trying to interpret the Bible – is this really an accurate account of what those prophets and saints intended us to know? Which had not been put through the mill of other people's ideas of interpretation and translation? I wanted a new view, my own, me and Beethoven on an interactive call. I wanted the truth.

**

Lord Smith of Chislehurst

Lord Chislehurst caught me as I tried to slip out of the workplace.

Chislehurst is a nice, respectable place and deserves to have a Lord. Chislehurst's Lord was a second-generation entrepreneur – his father had laid the foundations of the family fortune by collecting rubbish. It turned more and more respectable, and the quality of the waste disposed of grew in value; and since out-sourcing became a requirement in various government areas, there was plenty of work. This lord had taken a surer pathway than his father by expanding his business empire, and giving some of the proceeds to one of those charities that calls itself a political party – I'm not sure which one, whichever one was happy to take money from the ground roots. In fact, he gave so much that he probably had some say in decision-making. There seems no point otherwise. So they made him a Lord after making him a Knight. In our profession, it's not usually the charitable giving that sets the gongs a-banging, it's being noticed by the people who make the lists, who seem to go to the opera and orchestral concerts. Which explains the number of singers and conductors who end up needing more space on the posters to accommodate their extra word.

While he was a knight, Lord Chislehurst was made one of the knights at the Round Table that passes for the governing body of the Conservatoire, and now he's leader of that bunch of non-musicians who keep an eye on us all – the Council. The great and the good who love music, and love meeting musicians. I'm not criticising them, because we need them.

I'd never met Lord Chislehurst, and had only seen him in the distance when he said a few words at our yearly graduation ceremony. If for some reason I had to be there.

"Noticed you were in the building, so I hung around in the hope of meeting you again. My meeting's not for a few minutes. Could we chat for a moment?"

I was rather taken aback by that 'meeting you again' bit. I hadn't recognised this man, so I'm afraid he got the smiling-in-the-green-room-Who-the-Hell-are-You? act.

He wanted me to sign my 'Black And White' CD for his mother-in-law, he said. That figured; she'd have been about the right age to have seen the films the music came from when they were released. I signed it, "Here's looking at you, Will Winton." I hoped it wouldn't smudge on the shiny paper, but he'd given me his pen to write with, so it wasn't my fault if it did.

Then he asked me about Felicity. Felicity? Felicity Smith, my new girl. She was his daughter.

"I specially wanted her to come to you, so I fixed it with the boss." It clicked into place. No difficulty there. The boss, the Principal of the Conservatoire, wouldn't have needed much persuasion from the Chairman.

Why me?

"Felicity was very keen to have lessons with you. I think she likes the idea that you're closer to her age group than the other teachers here. Maybe she fancies you, seeing you sitting among all those reels of film."

"Oh, I shouldn't think so." I should think not indeed. That was the old, fatter, me, disguised by the reels of film. "I may be closer to her age-group, but still far enough away. I'll teach her what I can."

"Has she got any talent?" he asked. For God's sake, I'd only met her for the first time an hour or so ago. "She's been well taught, that's for sure. And yes, she has talent." What else could you say?

He said something about meeting the family. His family. I said something about how nice and thanked him for buying the CD and hoped his mother-in-law liked it.

**

I decided to let music go hang for the rest of the day. I put in a DVD of 'Sleepless in Seattle', but the story of the two lovers who only meet in the last reel made me miss Patti. I switched to *"La Cage aux Folles"* instead, which she'd never wanted to see. Laughed a bit, fell asleep, resolved to spend the next day practising, of course, but also to write some do-me-good letters to fans, taking care not to send photographs, as I usually did, and talk to the agent.

**

The letters didn't take long.

I decided to home in on the last movement of opus 109 first. It's the goal, the dénouement: so, by knowing how the play ends, I could make sure everything is in place on the way through. Hindsight, brilliant vision guaranteed, no contact lenses necessary. No false notes. Wrong ones are another matter. In the long run, it's not very important for me which order you learn things in, because it all ends up being ground together in the windmills of your mind.

**

Glasgow concert

Glasgow for a concert on the following day. I no longer do the fly-in, play-the-concert, fly-out bit. I did that for a while after I won the competition; in those days they were asking me to play what I'd played to win my prize, and see if they agreed with the jury. Or what they'd seen me play on the TV programme that followed it. I was doing little more than reproducing. I was ten years younger too. It was exciting, more like a celeb than a serious artist: you've seen me on the tele, once, and by the way, I play the piano.

Now I was treated like an Artist – I was older and wiser, though not much – more serious, certainly. Opus 109 serious, though they didn't know that yet. Slimmer too, and better-looking, even I could see that. Play it cool, take it easy, take care of your hands and your back and your health. Work out on the workout equipment, but only selected exercises. Looking good was a new part of my persona, as much for me as for anyone, and I intend to stay that way until I get to be an old master and it won't matter what I look like as long as I can get there and sit down at the piano in a dimly lit hall and play from the music if I feel like it.

**

I had a dream about Felicity Smith. Well, not really, because at that stage I didn't have much more than a generalised picture of what she looked like. Anything blonde and young was Felicity. I don't usually dream about my pupils; I've not reached the old professor's level of salivation. I hope I never do. If there's been a relationship 'problem' with my students, it's been theirs; even in my earlier days the odd pupil would get a crush on me. It's like falling in love with your psychiatrist, with the person who's going to solve all your problems. We do well to practise the art of self-defence if the people we're teaching start switching on emotional lights or stoking up fires, and smoke starts to come out that has little to do with the music. Teachers are especially vulnerable, in both directions.

My colleague Silvio had trouble with one of his pupils, who complained to the authorities that he was pursuing her. Molesting. Over-physical in the lessons, she said. Poor Silvio, a good violinist and good family man with sei bambini, all with the same wife, whose wonderful mother had come all the way from home to live with them. I'm sure he was just showing this girl student how to hold the bloody fiddle; it was more than his life was worth to fish in the Conservatoire stream of talent; the lines of communication back to his home in Fulham were too strong. Not to mention to his wife's family back in Sicily. What he did elsewhere? Patti said she knew, and tapped her nose. Gossip, I thought then. I wasn't so sure now that I had an attractive student of my own. "But I'm single," I thought, with not much of an idea of what that might yet mean.

**

In Glasgow, the hotel I usually stay in had recently changed hands and changed image to go with it. Busier. Noisier. They had a fire alarm at 10.45pm, and we had to go into the street. The Glasgow rain had subsided into mist – not Scotch mist, which is rain, isn't it? All the same it was damp, and some people went on partying outside; cold air brings out the effects of alcohol, they say. Well, it was Friday night in Glasgow, and this was a rehearsal for Saturday night in Glasgow.

I managed to get some sleep, because I've got used to dealing with disturbed nights in hotels or even in the private hospitality which I now take only from people I already know. I'm not too keen on earplugs though I always take them with me just in case. I wonder if anyone has done any research on the long term effect of shoving those things into what is one of the most important parts of a musician's anatomy. An Ear, Nose and Throat specialist who's a neighbour of mine says that the smallest thing you should put in your ear is your elbow.

I moved to another hotel the next morning.

The rehearsal was OK. I've played Rachmaninov's second piano concerto with this orchestra before, and although the conductor, called Aaronowitz, was someone I hadn't met, we seemed to get on, though his English came and went, and Estonian isn't one of my languages, not even at a 'faster, slower, louder, quieter' level. He didn't speak French at all, which I am good at. As far as he was concerned it was plain Rachmaninov without too many explanations. If our views on Rachmaninov didn't quite coincide in the rehearsal, I would have had a word with the orchestra's leader, who could bend the conductor's performance in my direction. There's never much time.

I like the concert hall. Not all that old – Lally's Palais, it's been called because Pat Lally was the council leader who pushed it through. Trust the Glaswegians to make a joke of that. Good audience; it was Saturday night, and with the Unfinished Schubert Symphony in the programme and the 1812 overture with cannon overriding every other consideration, we weren't likely to have many empty seats.

The conductor Aaronowitz

I am a single man. I said it out loud to the mirror in my dressing room, although it wasn't absolutely true legally. I didn't have to go back to my hotel alone if I didn't want to. I'd got a day off before the next concert on Monday in a place near Aberdeen, and a local holiday up there. I thought. Scottish holidays are a mystery tour to a Sassenach like me. I'd planned a light leisurely meal somewhere, without Glasgow's famous, almost obligatory, chips; just me and me, quiet, alone with my thoughts and my diet. It wasn't in my head to look for company, because I'd forgotten how to chat women up, if I ever knew in the first place. Patti and I seemed to have been an item since the beginning of time, and we didn't have to advance and retreat, tease and compliment, except when we were making love, and then there was a sort of bypass to a foregone conclusion. I didn't want to think about that. Perhaps that was what was wrong, and her new husband-to-be would do it better than I do. Did.

In fact, I got company. The conductor. He suggested a drink and since we're told never to turn down the chance of making contacts and networking, I agreed.

I didn't know how influential he was in the Baltic States, or which direction he was taking in the rest of the world.

I went with him to the old-fashioned hotel where he was staying. Deep carpet, leather settees, coffee tables, standard lamps, old-fashioned luxury in a way. There weren't any people where we were; there was another bar with a higher noise level, but since we'd both spent the evening with the threat of simulated cannonry in our ears, quiet was preferable, unless you're looking for more company, if that's what he wanted. Someone was playing the piano. Music by Cole Porter, Gershwin. He was good. I play some of that music, too, but the temptation to put in lots of the piano things which Liszt could have written spoils the sense of it, and this man was better at it than I am. He sang a bit into the microphone, gently, worth listening to, but not intrusive. Not exactly a waste of a talent, but not an insult to it either.

Aaronowitz fitted into this situation. About fifteen years older than me, somewhat flamboyant, as in wearing a cloak, like Claude Rains in the Bette Davis film where Paul Henreid played the cello concerto. One of the films featured in my film score CD. And the long hair, which I'd recently discarded as being out of fashion. Looking at him proved I'd done the right thing. My short, slightly spiky hair was great and up to that minute. It made me look years younger than him, which didn't exactly displease me. All the same, Aaronowitz had something which I could see fitted the conductor image, that air that says 'like me or loathe me, but do what I tell you'.

Aaron – "Call me that," he said – surely had a wife somewhere, I thought, but she wasn't in sight, and he didn't mention anyone, or show me pictures of his children, which some conductors have done, as if to show they are just ordinary guys like you and me. Except I don't have any children. No noticeable wife any longer, either.

He ordered a bottle of champagne – typical for after a concert. "You can have whisky if you like." Champagne is better if you have to be travelling the next day, I find, although I don't do a lot of research. So, a quiet, gently fading, plush hotel with a quiet glass of champagne in one's hand. One glass should last long enough if I was careful.

Then we played professional musician games: Talking About Music. Or rather what we could begin to talk about in German, which we discovered we had a limited common knowledge of. I had learned a bit in Endenich, but not enough to develop subtle levels of conversation. His English was surprisingly better, too, once he wasn't in front of the orchestra. American soap opera English. Amazing what the Iron Curtain had been keeping from all those millions of customers. We switched to English, swapped dates, and dropped names. It's like a card-game in which the value of the cards depends on the status of the concert hall or opera house. I don't have the master cards yet, so I play with my cards close to my chest. There are no trumps, but the Brits can play a knighthood as a wild card. I don't mind doing this too much, because my diary is healthy, I have CDs on people's shelves, and I'm competitive only up to a point. Aaron hadn't reached that point. He was going to be the next Karajan, because there's a vacancy, though he didn't say it in so many words. Well, good luck to him, although it was a bit on the late side. These days the younger you are when you're setting out down the conducting pathway the more chance you have of getting attention.

We didn't touch on politics, so I didn't ask him what he'd been doing in the bad old communist days when you didn't succeed at anything without persuading the authorities you were on their side. He was alright, though the champagne loosened his tongue and released some very odd words from his wordbook. He was funny about the Eurovision song contest.

"But it's no worse than we are when we're being international." His American accent was getting more excitable as he went. So was his Estonian accent. Which, along with the pianist's '*I've got you under my skin*', and the champagne, began to make life seem a little less lonely for him. Unlikely, but less lonely. I gave up trying to follow him.

"I've got a concert in London in January," he was saying, and leant forward to emphasise his delight at that by patting me on the knee.

What was this about?

"You could be there? For charity. Because I'm not a famous soloist, I get no fee."

There'd been orchestral gossip about one of those soloists who had taken a very full fee for a charity concert, while the players did their work for nothing. It was probably false. I thought I'd decide later about whether to go or not. Probably not, considering the knee.

I was wrong about that. He went on patting me abstractedly because his attention had been caught by two women who had just come in. They really were like something from Central Casting Agency. Blonde, high-heels, aged sort of thirty, give or take five years, wafting powerful waves of perfume around the place – Samsara, which Patti sometimes used to wear. Alone, too, to all intents and purposes, though who knows who was waiting for them as they crossed the lounge, smiling vaguely in our direction. In any direction.

I wasn't interested. I may have been trying to celebrate my freedom, if that's what it was, but I wasn't going to do it with just anyone. My inauguration ceremony needed a bit more glamour than this. Otherwise I didn't think there was a hope I could make it. No second thoughts seemed to trouble Aaron. As I moved my knee out of his reach, he waved to the women with his other hand. The theory seemed to be, and I dare say it works very well where he comes from, that if you wave at a potential pick-up, there's bound to be someone else you could be waving at. It gives them the option of not responding without creating any embarrassment.

Stay out of this, I thought. Another half glass of champagne, a sandwich, smoked salmon, already ordered, and a taxi back to where I was staying. I had it all worked out, and a chance to play Brahms's second piano concerto with Aaron next season. He promised.

Aaron had entered predatory mode. He was halfway across the room. He was asking them to come and join us, and ordering another bottle of champagne as well. I felt nervous. What the hell was he doing? Two single women – single as far as this bar was concerned – they could have come from anywhere.

It turned out they were local. Glasgow with a sort of poshed-up accent and a touch of American. They seemed nice enough. But hanging around in a maroon coloured hotel in Glasgow on a Saturday night? Available to be talked to by an Estonian with long hair and an artistic manner, and a thirty-five-year old with shorter hair and a sad face because he's still trying not to think about the empty house waiting for him in London?

Now I had a problem. Did I want my first out-of-the-cage flight to be with one of these birds, assuming that they would come fly with me? I could see the women sizing the two of us up. I think they were rather torn. It's fair to say I'm better-looking than Aaron, but I wasn't the one buying the champagne, and making the running. Looks or money. And I wasn't sure that we were the sort of company they had been expecting. A couple of after-the-concert musicians, though they didn't know that, might not be the same as a couple of after-the-match football club executives with full wallets, and full stomachs, and perhaps enough drink in them not to expect much more than someone to take their money from them. I don't know – this is not my scene at all. And I had to keep in mind that Aaron was looking for something to finish Schubert's Unfinished Symphony somewhere other than on the concert platform. He needed an accomplice for that. All I could hope was that he was a quick operator, once he'd got his eye on what he wanted, and he would retire to his room with one or both of the blondes and leave me to eat and then go home. Please.

We never got that far. The manager (was it?) of the hotel appeared. Softly spoken. "Mr Aaronowitz, you're wanted on the telephone. It seems quite urgent. From Estonia, I think, would it be?"

It must have been well into the night in Estonia – I've no idea what the time difference is – and I guess Mrs Aaronowitz was checking up on Aaron, knowing that what was happening here was what was only too likely to be happening at this point after a concert. To be fair to him, he recognised the danger signal, and apologised, "I am so sorry…this might be a long telephone call…all the news from my own country, and…and…

"And William will pour you a glass, won't you, Will?"

This was getting worse. He left me with the two blondes. And I wasn't even staying in the hotel. Luckily, just as I got hold of the champagne bottle, I was saved. The night manager was still hovering very politely: it seemed that their taxi had arrived, and wasn't inclined to wait. Perhaps it was true. Let's assume that it was; anyway, they waved Goodbye and blew nice-to-meet-you kisses, and went.

Of course they were working ladies, working the hotel. It didn't need much experience to spot that. I've no idea what the set-up was, but I dare say if they'd gone straight from the entrance lobby to an upper floor there would have been no problem – in fact, that might well have been the normal arrangement – but coming into the social part of the hotel wasn't part of their remit. I was off the hook.

I had my salmon with a glass of champagne and listened contentedly to the pianist. All on my own. I said a word of thanks to him and I was into my taxi without Aaron making a return appearance. Mrs Aaron was obviously giving him an earful. Sitting in my taxi, I thought it was high time I got some sort of spin on what I was going to do about sex. I had no intention of spending the rest of my life in a state of nervous abstinence. But this sort of encounter on a Saturday night in Glasgow, or anywhere else, didn't seem to be the wisest way to jump on to the merry-go-round.

Back in my hotel, I turned on the TV. The programmes all seemed to be mildly pornographic. Oh God, I really was a newly created virgin. What on earth had gone wrong with Patti? I hoped she wasn't enjoying herself too much with Keith. That wasn't fair, and it wasn't my business any longer. I would have to think about some other way of pursuing love. In due course. And definitely without getting married again.

**

Aberdeen

Next day to Aberdeen by train.

"Never on a Sunday" is sensible advice when it comes to travelling by train. A train is normally a more relaxed way of travelling, and there's time and there's room, instead of being shepherded into a space designed for a battery hen, with close neighbours, and no room to move your elbows. I prefer railway stations to air terminals, if draughtier.

However, fewer people travel on Sunday, so it's the obvious time to shut bits of the network down for repairs of one sort or another. I'm not against the repair bit – it's useful to think the rails and overhead wires are going to stay where they ought to be. I still resent it, for no justifiable reason except personal inconvenience, but in my profession we're condemned to it if you prefer a central London drop-off point rather than face the Heathrow to London challenge. The journey was due to take two hours and thirty-six minutes, and there would be some sort of cold meal in the first class. The Scottish trains give you a better deal on that, or at least they did.

The sun was shining, and Scotland is a most beautiful place when it is. And when it isn't.

Beethoven was again in my thoughts. I was due to play his sonata in D minor at the concert I was en route for, and I got my score out and put it on the table, taking care not to invade the territory of the passenger opposite. It wasn't an issue, since there wasn't one.

I've given up feeling embarrassed about doing this. It can look as if you're seeking attention; some musicians make a sort of grunting noise when they look at music, as if their larynxes are interpreting it. I don't, and since this is my work, I don't care what people think, as long as I'm not in their way. This time I was aiming to look at the music with a fresh mind, for details that can get overlooked once you know a piece well. I expect actors have the same experience when they do Shakespeare. There are so many words we don't use in daily language. Or in Samuel Becket, where you might start putting in words to fill in the time before Godot gets there. I guess. I was looking for any details I might have forgotten. You have to be careful not to let your busy fingers bypass your brain, as can happen at the keyboard with surprising ease: you come to the end of the page and you haven't heard a thing. It can happen with words in books too.

Twenty minutes after we set out they told us we were being transferred to buses at Dundee. Repairing the line? Taking it up? Putting it down? They didn't say, but they promised us a packed lunch, downgraded from a cold meal, which would have involved plates. Still, there was an hour before then.

I went back to the beginning of the music. I guess Beethoven started at the beginning and worked through to the end, though you never know. I'd like to think he had the whole thing in his head when he wrote the first notes. Like Noël Coward, who wrote all of 'Blithe Spirit' in a weekend. Not quite like Noël Coward, of course. And I reckoned there weren't many people sitting anywhere at that moment reading 'Blithe Spirit'. Or Beethoven's seventeenth piano sonata.

Imagine a perfect sound, unfreeze the music in my head, without fingers. I set out in that direction…

"Sorry, am I in your way?"

She wasn't, but I was beginning to spread out over the table we were sharing, so I was the one in the way. She hadn't been there when we left Glasgow, because no one was, as I said, and because I would have remembered the way she looked. Perhaps she had just moved over from another seat…No, I'm sure she had.

I put Beethoven out of my mind, and looked out of the window. We'd stopped. Practising for the total stop at Dundee possibly.

The woman opposite rustled the pages of her *Observer*, obviously not reading them. Or even looking at the pictures. She was waiting. Then she peered round the edge of the paper and spoke. She was blonde, but more soignée than the two I'd avoided the night before – the hair swept up in a French pleat, I think it was. Good-looking. Very good-looking. Took a lot of trouble. In the best way. Thirty-something.

"We seem to have stopped."

It was true.

"I hope you don't mind, but I was at your concert last night. I wasn't sure, at first – I don't chat men up in trains – but when I saw the music, I was sure."

"Thank you for coming to the concert."

"I'm glad I did. I was at a loose end. And I must confess you weren't the first choice. That sounds rude; I tried the opera first, but they were doing Wagner, and they were full."

"Their loss. Our gain."

"Mine too. I loved it. Even the cannon going off. All it needed was some fireworks, and it could have been Guy Fawkes Night."

"Bit dangerous, fireworks. The Musicians' Union would never stand for it."

"I don't suppose the Concert Hall would be too keen, either. I loved hearing you play."

"Thank you again. Do you play, then, yourself?"

"No. Not any more. I started lessons when I was about seven."

"When did you stop?"

"About six months later." She laughed. "Mostly when you give up music lessons it's your decision. This one was my teacher's idea. She didn't need the work or at least not at that price. She was a nice woman, but honest. I don't think that happens very often."

"I think you may be right there…"

"The Rachmaninov was lovely."

"It's great music." I said. That's the best thing to say, because it's true. If you've done your job properly.

"It always affects me, and to hear it played for real – in a concert, in the flesh, so to speak – it's even more moving. I have to have a tissue handy at the end."

Well, that was good to know. I'm in favour of the audience being moved by the things which move me.

"I get very moved by music. It really gets to me. Like to my soul."

She laughed, in case I might have taken that as a confession.

"…if I've got one. And, if I can say this, you play it as if you have experienced the inner depths of the emotion in it."

That was nice; the right button for me.

"And you look the part – like a pianist you can look at as well as listen to…"

She was looking me straight in the eye. This was something I wasn't expecting. My motive for upgrading my appearance had been something to do with Patti, and then something to do with finding other relationships. It hadn't crossed my mind that it might seriously help my career in public places. I smiled gratefully.

And at least she'd made her comments about my performance in the right order…

"…though I expect a lot of women tell you that."

I held her gaze as long as I could. I didn't know what to do next, so I shrugged deprecatingly.

"Well, no, not a lot," I said.

"I hadn't wanted to interrupt you, because you looked busy, what with the music, and such… But I couldn't resist the chance to tell you. I'm Fiona Baker. I'm sure you'd like to put a name to an ardent fan."

I looked to see if she was wearing a wedding ring. That was an advance of a sort. She was, and a big looking diamond next to it. I decided it made no difference, though I wasn't sure what to. That, too, was an advance of a sort. If nothing else, it seemed a good idea to pay her more attention, as part of my conscious therapy on the way to a successful divorce. There was a look in her eye that suggested she liked admiration – either giving or receiving it. If she was flirting with me – chatting me up – then perhaps Beethoven could be left on the page for a little longer. She really wanted to hear me again, she said, so I told her about my concert the next day; the details of course, were somewhere in my bags. She gave me her mobile number, and I said I would send her a text to tell her what time the concert was and precisely where.

Then I had second thoughts. I wasn't sure about texting her. She was quite likely to have a husband and three children. But then if they all came to hear me play, there would be more in the audience. You don't turn the public away, especially for a solo recital, which doesn't always have the same draw as the concerto ones. What if she didn't have a family to speak of, and came alone? I should go for that, shouldn't I? Hope for it, even. I was nervous. I looked out of the window as we stopped at Stirling, and kept gazing in that direction, asking the odd question about Stirling and Bridge of Allan. She knew little about either.

"I'm English, you see." I had worked that out.

She read her *Observer* and fortunately didn't read bits out that she thought might have interested me, beyond saying that there wasn't a crit for last night's concert in Glasgow. Not on your national newspapers' list of must-dos, and much too soon, even if it ever were a possibility.

I thought I should be able to give her the slip when we changed into the buses at Dundee. It turned out to be a hopeless idea. We were told to go to the front of the station, where the coaches would be waiting for us. We went up the stairs from the platforms to the only noticeable exit. It was a sort of narrow passageway, not very well drained – wet, in fact. Passengers were wandering backwards and forwards, pulling their luggage, getting in each other's way. No one knew exactly where they were going, but people were following other people, whoever seemed to look like a leader, like a general election acted out on a concrete stage. No railway person was in sight. I'm sure the railway track was going to be terrific on Monday, but they had taken our money, and given us Sunday travel in exchange.

Dundee's frontage on to the Firth of Tay is going to be wonderfully indistinguishable from many another waterfront in the world but meanwhile the cement mixers were gathering, and cranes were roosting like vultures waiting for living people. Let's say herons, to be more aquatic.

Fiona Baker was my companion during this challenging time. We were fellows. We were united in adversity. We laughed at our inconvenience.

Sometime the shrugging had to stop, and fortunately someone's child escaped from parental control and looked round a corner and saw the coaches.

**

The train had been comfortable. The buses had been made to a different specification. Prickly plush seats, suspension suspended.

So much for shaking her off. I was going to have to be more devious.

I apologised for taking up a whole double seat with my music things.

"I must just get a chance to look through the music I didn't get round to."

"I hope I didn't interrupt your study on the train."

"No, no, of course not…"

"How do you deal with the music?"

I looked surprised. I read it…

She pointed up to the ceiling.

"Oh that." They were playing someone's idea of journeyman's music. A local radio programme, judging from the advertisements, offering sensational bargains (up to sixty per cent off – with years' long credit deals – just for me – or you – or you…)

Beethoven switched it off for me.

**

46

I was staying in Aberdeen, although the concert wasn't in Aberdeen itself, but in a place – a converted barn – where Patti and I had given a concert about fourteen years earlier. We were students then, but considered by the Con to be on the early slopes of the professional hills. It was a clever recital, it seemed to us: Handel, Beethoven's Spring sonata, Cesar Franck's sonata, and half a dozen Burns songs we'd cooked up into a sequence, some solo and others for both of us. With a carefully arranged encore of Gershwin songs up our sleeves. We liked it, and they did too. We were a married couple, and they were relieved, I think, to see that the wedding ring on Patti's hand looked real and blessed by the local registrar and not by the sales assistant in what was then Woolworth's. Otherwise it's possible that Mrs Eleanor Gordon, with whom we were to stay, would have put us in separate rooms.

Mrs Gordon was part of the local Gordon community. This was their country in the days of the clans, when they wouldn't have let other Scots, let alone the English, cross their boundaries. She was a lovely woman, a widow then, and still a widow, as far as I knew, unless some other clansman had taken her off to his castle, converted into a factory exporting frozen haggis to Scottish expats around the world.

She had taken to us like a godmother-in-waiting and since then she had kept us up to date with emails about the way the barn was developing into a real local venue (we're talking about twenty miles to the west of Aberdeen). The pictures on the website looked great. The barn now had appropriate mortar separating the stones, and no doubt binding them together at the same time. Sophisticated lighting system, audience space for about two hundred and something. A modern restaurant alongside, specialising in produce from local farms. Just the place to keep classical (and other) music alive and well. Mrs Gordon was running the classical part of the bargain, and she was eager to have us back. She knew that they couldn't pay our full fee, but she hoped that we would remember old friends. All written on good notepaper too, and not emailed.

We'd taken the booking two years earlier. Patti would have to negotiate time off from the opera company; agent Jane refused, in the nicest possible way, to have anything to do with it.

"I'll put it in your diary, just after your Glasgow concert, but I'm not going to get involved in the payment bit. What you are agreeing to do it for is well below your normal fee. I'm not a mercenary person, but I do have to make a living, and that means a living for other people. You couldn't live on this sort of money. Not any more. If you ever could."

She was right, but this was to have been a sentimental journey, something we needed to do, though I didn't see the significance of that then. Two years ago. Then, last year, Patti told me that the opera company couldn't spare her. There was a new opera coming up, specially commissioned from their new composer-in-residence (he lived in Hong-Kong, which proved to be a difficulty), and no NAs were allowed. So I wrote to Mrs Gordon at once to say I would do it on my own, if she would accept that.

She wrote back.

"Dear William, I am sorry that you will not allow me to relive the world as it was all those years ago – music is a good way of making the past come alive. But I understand. I always loved Patti's playing, but I must say I have not heard her recently, whereas I hear you on the radio and on my CD player. Please come on your own, and play us some Schumann of course, but anything else you like. The piano is a replacement. Not new, but good, and not big – a Steinway B, not an A. Our piano tuner from Steinway thinks it's lovely. We could give your joint fee to you alone, if that would be suitable; you could stay with me, to avoid expenses. I think the fact that you are a married man, and that there is a difference in our ages makes that perfectly proper. Anyway I don't have to look to my reputation. Give my love to Patti, and say how sorry we are…you will know how to put it. Best wishes, Eleanor Gordon."

I refused the accommodation, saying that I would stay in Aberdeen, at my own expense, because I had to be away early the next morning. In the event, that turned out to be a wise decision, because although I would tell her that I was now on my own, I didn't want to spend the time between performance and sleep dealing with her tact in not asking what had happened to us both.

I had chosen a quiet hotel in Aberdeen. More like an old-fashioned guest house, with a grey-haired landlady. Dressed in wool from top to toe as far as I could see. And probably where I couldn't see. The room had its own bathroom, which the old guesthouses didn't. Imagine queuing for the bathroom, and then sharing it with the person who'd just left it. There was a piano in the lounge which I was told I could use. People always say how wonderful it would be to hear a real professional pianist playing, and don't realise how boring the sound of someone doing serious practice turns out to be. It doesn't bore us, but then we're on the inside, it's part of our set-up. Some performers say they prefer rehearsing to performing because it brings them closer to the real thing – the music.

A comfortable night. Very respectable house, after all, and not much traffic.

I played the piano for half an hour in the morning, largely to please Mrs Mackay, who by the time I'd got through a couple of Chopin waltzes and Rachmaninov's C sharp minor Prelude was in seventh heaven, she said, but there clearly wasn't going to be an eighth. I was happy enough about that.

"It's like having Classic FM here in my house, live." You can turn Classic FM off, she didn't say.

My list of composers for the concert was standard enough: Bach, Beethoven, Ravel, Schumann, a touch of Chopin and Liszt for show, things to lure people away from their comfortable houses on a Monday evening.

I rang the mysterious lady on the train to get her and her family to come to the concert. Fiona. She asked for details of how to get there, because although she knew about the Barn Hall, she had never actually been in it. Was it alright if she came, and could she come back-stage afterwards to say hello again?

The concert at the Barn Hall

Mrs Gordon sent a friend to pick me up at my guest house and take me to the Barn Hall. He was a big man with red hair and a beard, who looked like an extra from a film about Rob Roy. We had no difficulty about making conversation during the twenty-mile journey, because there wasn't any. Companionable silence. Welcome.

He let me out of the car, and carried my case with my concert uniform in it into the barn. There's something about rocks the size of those in the walls that seems to connect you with the natural world. Sure, someone has hewn them into shapes so that they would fit with one another in a way that nature didn't intend, or she would have made them like that, and possibly numbered them as well. But they speak of the primal things at the centre of an artist's life, even when they've come through the heart and mind of Beethoven, or Mozart or Shakespeare. This place was a part of my early concert career. In the interval since we were last here they had updated it very successfully. Their own piano normally stood, locked, and tucked away in the wings, as far as you can tuck a grand piano away in wings of this size.

I said hello to Jim the tuner. He'd come up specially from his place in Stirling, a sort of central jumping-off board for most of Scotland. He knew all of the concert pianos in the north.

"You'll be alright with this one," he said. "Not young, but it's had a retread which made it like new. I wish they could do the same for people. I wouldn't mind being retrodden sometime soon. Good size too: these Model Bs are better than the bigger ones if you're out there playing on your own and not having to measure up to an orchestra in a large hall. Try it. I've nearly finished."

He was right. It was friendly, almost as if it might be your lover. Not new. Not stiff, like the new piano which the music society secretary pats proudly – "We've had I can't tell you how many coffee mornings to pay for this." Then it's like dancing with a virgin, who knows the steps, but not really what they're for. Better to get ones who've been round the block a few times; if you offer them your loving fingers, they'll let you do whatever you like. God, if I could do that with a piano, then surely…

I left Jim to finish off his tuning.

The dressing room at the back – one of two - was simple and tidy. There was a shower too. I tested it, dodging the surge of water which can't wait to get at you. This would do.

A voice called out.

"Mr Winton…William…"

I came out on to the stage. There wasn't a lot of light in the hall, but there she was, Eleanor Gordon, fourteen years on; I hadn't remembered much about her appearance until now, but she seemed just the same, triggering a memory or two which I suppressed. No point. She was tall. She was old-fashioned, in the sense that she was wearing the sort of clothes which were bought to last. Not quite the sensible tweeds syndrome, because there were a few jewels and scarfs around her throat. And she was part of our time.

"Hello, William," she said and did the side-to-side swinging kiss. "I'm Eleanor, and…" she tailed off. Of course I knew she was Eleanor, but she was one of those people who don't presume.

"I'm sorry she couldn't get away." She was talking about Patti.

"Opera companies can be difficult, I know. We had a singer due to come here who had to send a substitute because they were shipping her off to Germany or somewhere at the last minute. But orchestral players? Is she the leader of the orchestra?"

50

"Well no."

"I see," Eleanor said. "Ah well, you know your own business. She was a nice player, as I remember, a very nice player."

"She still is."

She looked closely at me.

"Let's go to the restaurant and have a cup of tea. Jim will be finished by then, and you can get your fingers round our lovely piano."

We had an amicable cup of tea in the completely modern restaurant – no hint of old farm property here – a good view of Scottish hills, with a supermarket roof in the foreground.

"We need that. Or rather we don't, but now that it's open we go there."

We talked about the view, and about the future of the barn theatre. I was the only classical thing for the next fortnight: otherwise they had a couple of films ("there's no local cinema, so we have to go into Aberdeen for the latest"), a couple of groups looking for the way to the stars, some folk music, a local choir extending its wings into concert conditions, a pair of actors free to read extracts from Scottish authors and play a scene or two from a James Bridie play.

"We're expecting a good audience. We put your photograph around a bit."

My photograph? The one with the glasses and the hair? She showed me the flyer they'd done a month ago. The Ripon photograph, doctored a little by the loving hands of my agent Jane. I could hear her mind working – no immediate money in it for her from this concert, but in future?

"I must say your recent photograph took me by surprise. I can see you're wearing contact lenses now."

"You can see them?"

"Well no, but you're not wearing glasses so I suppose you've taken the plunge. And you look very different. Toned, I think might be the word. Neater than I remember, as if your clothes are meant to fit. You used to look as if your appearance didn't matter and you could let the rest of the world go by, as long as there was a piano to play somewhere. And you do play beautifully." She laughed as if she'd said the wrong thing.

"This is the new me. A deliberate choice."

"You know, if a woman changes her appearance, it's quite likely there's a new love around the corner."

"My problem is the old love. You might as well know that there won't be any more duos. We've split up. It makes no difference to our careers. We hadn't

51

played a concert together for longer than either of us could remember, which was why we manoeuvred this one from you. Not that that was the reason we went our separate ways." I laughed, and she smiled. It wasn't funny.

"This was something of a sentimental journey, retracing the paths of fifteen years ago. But it's turned into something more like a voyage of discovery, and that's likely to be a long journey, as far as I can see." I stopped.

Eleanor said nothing. Poured some tea, which was the last drop from the pot.

"Would you like me to order more?" A good way of making an end of it.

"Listen, Will, you have a concert to do. If you want to talk about how you are, especially to an older woman who won't be seeing you again in a hurry; someone who knows nothing about you…It could be refreshing, and cheaper than a psychiatrist. I don't charge. Get in touch with me if you feel moved to do that. Come and stay and breathe the bracing air of Scotland. But now I'm going to send you off to get to know your current partner."

I must have looked surprised.

"Our piano."

"We're putting some sandwiches in your dressing room, and since you're the only person using it, there's a sort of comfortable chair for you to relax. And don't forget that the concert starts at seven. Country timing so that people can travel from far and near."

"Do they?"

"We live in hope, and we never check, because it's the best way to make sure that we're not disappointed.

"This is my mobile number if you need it." She went to pay the bill. A godmother figure to replace the absent mother whose face I could only remember from a photograph taken before I was born. What an unexpected thought.

It's not often that I have to hang around in the same place between rehearsal and performance at this stage in my career. Usually it's morning with the piano, afternoon in the hotel, with a rest if I feel like it, and a chance to go over my music in my head. This situation took me back to my early days, when the fee had to be spent carefully, and there was no hotel to go back to.

So I went for a short walk, more for the air than anything else, watching the clouds coming over the hills. I could imagine living here. Far from Patti territory.

There it was, what I was trying not to admit. I hadn't cleared Patti out of the space she occupied in my mind. I still missed her. How did I miss her? "Let me count the ways. To the depth and breadth and height my soul can reach, to the level of every day's most quiet need."

Not exactly what Mrs Browning meant. But she knew a thing or two, that woman, and that's what I had to come to terms with. Some female company was necessary. Patti's behaviour had left me seriously confused. Had she been hiding from me? Or had I just not been watching carefully enough? I had never in my life pursued women, and they had never thrown themselves at me, or if they had I had been looking the other way. It's not good to feel you're a failure at something quite so basic.

The sandwiches were fine. Recent meat had obviously been recruited for them. Someone had the sense to realise that thin bread would be better for sitting at the piano. I was alone, too, which was good. Jim had said the piano was good, and he was right. He'd stayed long enough to hear my opinion, and to check that my ears and his were in accord about the tuning. And then gone back to Stirling.

I splashed my face with cold water, changed, and washed my hands several times. It sometimes takes me that way. Then I sat down and looked at my programme, rehearsing the change from composer to composer. It's not a problem, really, because the moment I put my hands out ready to play the next piece, the music changes the way they feel. As if a spirit was entering them. Not a good explanation, but I can't think of anything better.

The barn was very nearly full. I wondered what it had been like when the cattle were there; contented cattle, chewing the cud, or giving milk; not unlike a performer. I like these far-from-the-madding-crowd venues, as long as some of the madding crowd comes through the turnstiles.

I gave them a Bach prelude and fugue. Audiences who come to a mixed recital often seem to regard the great man as a warm-up, something for us to get our fingers going and for them to clear their ears and minds of what they were thinking when they arrived. But Bach is where I go when I want to be in the presence of someone who knew humanity from end to end. Someone who could sparkle and think, argue and feel. When I was playing the intimate and sweet-tempered prelude in F sharp at my play-through, I'd become aware that its two voices supplement and complement each other until they tie the knot at the end. Of course it wasn't written to prove that marriage is a good institution unless it goes wrong. I let its own version of harmonious co-existence, extraordinarily rich to be coming from such small means, override my own defects.

My Beethoven sonata has a nickname. 'The Tempest'. He didn't call it that but the story goes that he told someone to read Shakespeare's play when they asked him about it. And Chopin's Study which they call the Winter Wind. Schumann remains a magic place for me to go since I won that Schumann competition, so I played his 'Carnaval', a kaleidoscope of characters, including thumbnail sketches of two girls, his current one, and the eight-year old who would grow to be the love of his life. The gallery of characters in Ravel's *Gaspard de la Nuit* is something else: a water nymph who teases, and a goblin who creates mayhem, and between them a dead man hanging from a scaffold. Then Liszt's version of a waltz from Gounod's 'Faust', and an improvisation I'd planned (but not written down) on a couple of Bothy Ballads, just to fit the locality, though how many of the audience were deeply local apart from Eleanor I could only guess.

After the concert

There was a bit of clapping where there wouldn't be any in London, between movements in Beethoven, though I'm sure it wouldn't have surprised him – audience manners have changed a lot in two centuries. Applause is approval, and a form of love, and I was grateful to get some practice in the second direction.

When I'm on tour, I don't get many friends coming round afterwards, just a few people of various sorts, like the ones who say they always knew I was going to be a success, having heard me when I was a teenager on the BBC competition programme. There are always one or two autograph-hunters, and now there seemed to be more than usual – perhaps my new look made them want to see me close to, do you think? And then there are the ones who say, "You'll remember me…" And I don't. I smile and say, "Of course." I know other performers who say, "No I don't." And yet others who are only nice when famous people come to the dressing room. That's not a problem I face very often. An occasional mayor or councillor. I'm happy to see people and do my best to recognise them.

I did my hand shaking and scribbling on programmes, had my shower, which was useful rather than luxurious, and got comfortable in jeans and the new sweater I'd bought online. It took much longer to get into than I expected, because it fitted much more tightly than I'd been used to – not unflatteringly so, when I finally got into it. I was ready to talk to Eleanor, having waved to her at the end of the concert.

I wondered where Fiona and her family were, with some disappointment. No sign of her at all.

Eleanor was there, looking like a proud relative.

"I feel a little protective about you. I well remember when you came and did one of your first concerts here. One or two others have come back, and it's nice not to lose contact, to know how they're doing, the people we helped, if you know what I mean: a concert is a help at the right time. Don't let it go too long without letting me know what you're up to. I'm sure I'll see your name here and there, and if you come to play with an orchestra in Aberdeen, you must be sure to let me know."

"Of course. I wish I could stay longer now, and I wish I was staying with you instead of going back to Aberdeen. But I have to be off early tomorrow, you know."

"Then let me give you a lift."

We were walking out into the hall and towards the vestibule when I spotted Fiona. Alone, except for the man who was going to do the locking up. She was sitting in a chair talking to him; she was wearing a short skirt, which he was noticing, and there was no family, which I was.

Eleanor took it in quickly.

"Company?" she murmured.

"I don't know," I lied.

She laughed.

"Of course, you're on your own now, aren't you?"

This was a bit tricky. It's true, but I liked this woman I was talking to and I felt slightly embarrassed because Fiona did look much like a female version of the other company Chaucer's Wife of Bath had enjoyed in her youth.

"True. But I don't advertise it. This is someone who asked me if she could come to this concert when I met her in the train yesterday. I have to say that she didn't look like this then."

"Maybe you have this effect on women? I can see how it might be."

That made it easier.

"I don't know. I'm just out of the box, you know."

"Wicked man. I'll leave you. There's a local taxi which could be with you in five minutes. I'm not sure that you'll need that."

"If you still want, when I come to Aberdeen next, may I stay with you?"

"The offer still stands."

We walked on. I realised I couldn't remember Fiona's surname, and I was going to have to introduce her. But…

"Hello. I'm Eleanor Gordon. I think you're waiting for my captive pianist."

"Fiona Baker. Hello."

"You're not a native Scot, I can tell. In spite of the Fiona." Eleanor made it sound very pleasant. And Scottish.

"I'm afraid not. There are a lot of Fionas all over the place. I'm just one of them. Part of the oil influx."

"You'll be giving William a lift in that big car I can see through the window. Look after him. He's a precious talent."

"Yes, it's mine. And I will look after him. I'm a careful driver."

Eleanor kissed me. "Bye. Take care. Be brave. Being alone is no bad thing, once you're used to it," she whispered. And went.

**

Fiona's was a big car indeed, and it was good to sink into it – Raymond Chandler got that image right.

"I've no idea what artists do after concerts. You might well be wanting something to eat. Any restaurant you'd like to go to?"

I had no idea what the eating scene was like in Aberdeen. Modest food, and not much of it, was what I wanted. Our eating patterns are difficult enough as it is when we're travelling.

"Just leave it to me," she said. And since I was already doing that, I did. That skirt looked even shorter behind the driving wheel.

It was only about a quarter of an hour to her house in a nice outskirt of the city. Some trees, some driveways. This was oil territory, where you used to need a fortune to buy a house. Probably still do.

"Come on in. I thought you might like a relaxing drink here rather than wherever it is you're staying."

I told her the name of my guesthouse.

She laughed.

"You won't get a drink there, unless you smuggle one in with you. It's just one shaky step away from an old-fashioned temperance hotel. Your landlady is well known at the sharper end of the reformed church – a speaker, and hot on drink and sex. Well, hot, meaning cold like a cold shower."

That was the start. I muttered something – I did have to go back there later…and I had to make sure I wasn't too late, because I didn't have a key.

She took no notice.

A very nice house. A lot of money had been spent on making it look glassy and glossy and yet comfortable. Quiet lights, and soft music which came on with the light switch.

"D'you mind the music? I can easily turn it off if it reminds you of work." It was harmless enough, strings slithering from chord to chord, the sort of thing that players in London do in recording sessions with no rehearsal, and minimum fee. Patti used to do that when the opera house was shut. Perhaps she was playing on this one.

I looked around for signs of alternative life. There were none I could see.

Such thoughts occurred as Fiona disappeared and returned, bringing a bottle and glasses and things on plates. Smoked salmon, predictably, and champagne. Some biscuits and cheese, local, I think, although I didn't look too closely.

She poured me a glass and disappeared again – I was to make myself comfortable. I noticed she had my CD with the film themes on it. Fortunately she wasn't playing it, though that sort of thing has happened before, as if people think I want to hear myself all the time; it's like playing games of patience – alright as a last resort. Seriously last.

It was a good champagne and I had to remind myself not to drink too much. This counted as new – champagne and fair acquaintance. But I was flying back the next morning and intending to go to the Conservatoire to teach later in the afternoon and on into the early evening.

There were only two glasses, although it looked like a marital house. No sign of a husband except in the form of a wedding ring, and certainly no elderly mother and father, no sign of children.

Wait a minute, I thought, I'm a virtual bachelor. I'm alone, I'm nearly single, I'm available. Let's see what happens.

When Fiona came back, it was clear what she had in mind. You could see she was alone in the house. What she brought with her was not someone else. Just something else. A complete change of atmosphere and a complete change of costume. Her hair was loose, let down, and seemed almost to have a life of its own – purposeful, as if Medusa had been to a hairstylist in the King's Road and traded in the snakes for gold.

Her hair wasn't the only thing that was loose.

Something more comfortable was what she'd slipped into, and clearly more comfortable to slip out of, and perfumed, and somehow what she wore touched enough of Fiona to suggest what she would look like without it. I looked, and drank her health silently. And mine. I was trying to be a big boy now. For Goodness's sake, thirty-five, and I could do as I pleased. I didn't look at her closely, but caught myself peeping. Come on, Tom boy, you're too old for peeping. She leant over to recharge my glass. And it wasn't just the scent she was wearing that sent out the message that she'd slipped into this garment and little if anything else but some high-heeled shoes. Mules, could they be called? Hard-working animals unable to reproduce themselves. Was that the message?

She didn't sit next to me, but opposite, smiling, listening to the music, and smoothing her clothing. She was a married lady, and that left something to be cleared up. It seemed unlikely, but I needed to know that some hunk was not going to come through the door straight from an evening with the boys after rugby practice, and happy to talk to some tabloid about the state of classical music. Or the local Provost, if that's what her husband was, returning from a Council Meeting convened to vote extra money for the arts.

She brought it into the conversation, the explanation:

"It's great you came round. I get left alone a lot, what with my bonny Charlie on his oilrig." Wow. That seemed safe enough. You don't accidentally come home from an oilrig, unless you have to be rescued from it.

"I don't get a chance to talk about art and music much…"

It didn't look as if she intended to talk about art and music much then, either. It was getting late. But she got up, and got my CD, and asked me if I'd sign it for her. There was something about the way she opened it, and the way she flicked the cardboard stuff out of it as she sat down next to me, just to make sure I spelt her name properly. And mine too, I dare say, because by then I was no longer certain of my handwriting.

"I think the idea of this music for films is lovely. They're before my time, of course."

"They were before my time too, but they arranged special showings when I was doing the recording."

"Don't you find music really puts you in the mood for what happens in the film?" Not a real question, but I answered it anyway.

"I guess that's why they put it there, and some of it has a life of its own."

"Yes, well, I meant that, of course. And can I ask what sort of life of your own do you have, up there on the concert platform? Is it as exciting as it looks?" Her voice was getting lower. Not that I couldn't hear her.

"I'm certainly on my own up there."

"And afterwards?"

"I unwind. I have physical exercises. This is a physical job, playing the piano."

Not the wisest way to put it, but it happened to come out that way.

"I can see that. But after the muscles have been dealt with?"

Her tone of voice was interesting.

"We get used to unwinding mentally. Joking, accepting praise, that helps."

"Are you married?" An innocent question, but one I hadn't been expecting, out of the blue like that, especially as it seemed too confrontational. For me.

Hell, I thought, this is a path I must go down. I needed this, more than she did, probably. In a different way, because I had to go on, forget Patti. Forget why our marriage ended, if there ever was to be a reason. I had, God forgive me, to prove myself, and I thought it might be now.

"No, I'm not married." It was a white lie, but a near-truth. She sighed. It felt like a door opening.

Fiona reassembled the CD and snapped it shut. She was very close, very perfumed, very warm, and, as I said before, clearly, under that sort of silky wrap thing, not very clothed. A peignoir, was it? Something that started life as a gown to put on while you did your hair. And maybe undo your hair, let your hair down…which she had.

She gave up waiting for me to do anything; I was clearly not living up to my image as a travelling professional bachelor, the artist who lives for love, while still living for art. She kissed my cheek, turned my head and kissed me on the mouth.

What was that like? It wasn't what I expected. What I needed was to start with a chaste kiss, and then, well, and then I could begin to experience this new thing called love, unreflecting love, love without love. She took my breath away, and half my mouth with it. For some reason, I had turned her full on, without intending to, at least not quite at such pressure. Her husband the oil-rigger clearly came home with enough testosterone to light a beacon, and she had got into the way of producing female hormones to match. Moreover, she wasn't used to keeping them to herself. And I…I responded, rather modestly, rather surprised to discover that I could respond at all. She broke off to say, "My God, you are fabulous, gorgeous, and you kiss like a prince."

That wasn't a bad start, especially as I didn't seem to be the one who was doing the kissing. I was learning what the rewards were of the way I now looked, although I'd done it for Patti. No, as I said before, I did it because of Patti. And here I was with Fiona. She hadn't discussed what she thought we should do, but there wasn't much doubt. It seemed more a matter of where and when. When was now, and where…

She didn't actually pull me to my feet but she indicated that standing up was a preliminary to the next stage, at which point I found myself with her in my arms, and my hands on that silky material which seemed to slip over her flesh. What could I do but follow her upstairs to the bedroom, picking up my champagne glass, because it seemed more sophisticated, and with a faint feeling I might need it to play this new role in my life.

We didn't talk. In fact, come to think of it, there hadn't been much talking since I arrived. What was there to talk about? I couldn't help wondering. She began to undress me. That is, to pull my sweater up. Pulling someone else's sweater off over their head is not an elegant activity, anyway, and this undressing thing hadn't been part of my marriage; we just got into bed, as we did every night we were together. This was that on-line sweater, a size too small for me, the one I had trouble getting into. It was clear that I was having a hell of a lot of trouble getting out of it, especially as my arms weren't cooperating at all.

"Come on, Billy Boy," she murmured, "give me a hand." The last person to undress me had been my grandmother, and a long time ago. Suddenly I felt nervous and somewhat ridiculous. And certainly not sophisticated enough to make some manly joke about it. Mixing my grandmother up with Fiona wasn't making me comfortable. And 'Billy Boy' … how had she hit on that unfortunate reminder of my mother's Christmas cards? And 'Billy' which no one else but Patti called me? Her absent husband – I knew he wouldn't come back, but could I measure up? I thought I'd better keep touching Fiona, or she might touch me more experimentally, and I certainly wasn't ready for that. In fact, there was a growing knot of anxiety in my stomach, which another swig of champagne would do nothing to alleviate, and the energy which had been beginning to make itself felt began to evaporate. Like a gentle *diminuendo* at the end of a Chopin nocturne. The Chopin comparison was particularly discouraging because I remembered that in Chopin's famous relationship with George Sand, the sex bit went out of their affair rather soon, and she became a sort of mother to him. Though how anyone can know the truth in those days before investigative journalism I don't know. Turning Fiona into my grandmother, whom I loved deeply, or into my mother's Christmas card, into Patti even, or Chopin's surrogate mother, wasn't the best foreplay, and maybe that was something I would have to look into, before going to the therapist I didn't intend to go to.

There was something else, too. My eyes were uncomfortable. I was beginning to be desperate to take my contact lenses out, and I couldn't remember where my glasses were. Back at the guesthouse, maybe? Somehow the situation was deteriorating, and it was important that this first time was right.

It hit the ground when Fiona said, "Listen, Billy, there's only one way to get you out of this thing you're wearing. We need a pair of scissors. Give me a minute or two to get my sewing basket." Fiona with a sewing basket? And 'Billy' again?

That's when I knew there was no way I could go ahead. I couldn't do it. What the hell was I going to do with this eager and impassioned lady, except pray for lightning to strike, or her husband to come home? No, not for her husband to come home. I had to leave. I wasn't going to do my reputation as a great lover any harm, because I didn't have one, and Fiona wasn't likely to talk much about what we didn't get round to doing.

So I left. I had run downstairs, had picked up my coat and bag and was out of the front door before she came back from rummaging about in her basket. I hope she wasn't too disappointed. She certainly had been ready to go, and I know I should have handled things differently. But I hadn't.

I picked up a taxi quite soon, in fact very soon. The driver nodded as I got in. He knew the address I gave him.

"You'll be just in time," he said.

"In time for what?"

"She closes up at midnight." I hadn't checked. "And you'll be lucky to have got away so quickly," he added, looking at the bedroom window, where the curtain was showing extra light. I didn't ask him what he meant exactly, but I wouldn't have been entirely surprised if he'd said, "I know this house well," like the cabdriver in that wicked French film *La Ronde*.

In the event, Mrs Mackay was still up. I rather think she had rollers in her hair under her turban, which didn't go with her Presbyterian style of dressing.

But she was nice enough, asked about the concert, and pretended it was her fault that she hadn't asked how late I was going to be, or given me a key. She showed no surprise when I asked her for a pair of scissors. We fixed a breakfast time. I went to my room and cut myself out of my chain-mail sweater. With some snack-like things to eat and a drink of the water she had left for me in its Spring bottle. Much better for me, really.

One day soon I needed to come to terms with things, but at that point the only time I really knew where I was emotionally was when I was sitting at a piano. Is that how poor Sviatoslav Richter was when he played the piano by candlelight in the Festival Hall? In a magic circle? Ten fingers in place of a life? Well, it was something to frighten myself with. I didn't – don't – want to end up like those sad people in Dante's Inferno, who couldn't relate to anything at all and were left between Heaven and Hell for ever because they couldn't commit. And couldn't even decide not to commit to anything. I could see it happening to me.

Of course, I didn't sleep. Not surprisingly, all things considered. I know I can rationalise what happened: a woman running at a high temperature, no doubt deceived into thinking that all performers are performers in all senses of the word and faced with…an inexperienced man, shy, even. But how could she have known that? I wondered if I ought to get some help. Was I still that plump man, with unattractive glasses, who couldn't see himself through other people's eyes or even in a mirror through his own contact lenses?

**

So, having got up early, I had a couple of hours to while away in Aberdeen. A fine city. I decided to go to a bookshop and browse. I found one which looked modest and discreet. I decided against asking where to find a book or two which might help me, especially as I didn't know what sort of book might help me.

I took the precaution of wearing dark-glasses and a folding hat I put in my pocket if the weather looks uncertain. What with that and the coat I was wearing, I was close to looking like your man in a raincoat, but I thought I looked anonymous enough for my purposes. I don't see why we can't be open about our needs, especially if there are books on the subject, but I didn't seek advice, I just looked on the shelves. Not 'medical', I thought, because if there's something medical wrong with me, then a doctor would be the best for that. "Health" seemed a better bet, something about a happy sex-life in marriage, or outside of marriage, would do. There turned out to be several, from pseudo-moralistic ones, written by religious people, to versions of the Kama Sutra in full thirty-two bit colour, with matching DVDs. I took something in between, with chapters on kissing and undressing and what to do first, and positions, tastefully drawn rather than photographed. I felt safer with those, because I didn't want to speculate on what the real-life models did for a living beyond hanging around studios waiting to be persuaded to perform the act of love-making in which the camera was a willing partner.

Then I thought a bit of mild pornography might be a good testing ground, to see whether I – well, to see whether…

With a bit of hunting around and looking over my shoulder – Tuesday morning was quiet – I found a book with a mix of drawings, reproductions (let's say reprints) of paintings, and some photographs of both sexes, sometimes doing things, sometimes just looking – that is to say, looking out at the world with the sort of expression that might come from thinking pornographic thoughts…It was a French book, no text to speak of, called *Volupté*.

I took my two books to the sales desk. Feeling a little embarrassed – feeling a lot embarrassed, but also feeling incognito, as a man in a raincoat might anywhere in a bookshop. I turned back at the last moment and found two paperbacks by former winners of one of those awards books get. I thought that would make it look as if the two other books I'd really come to buy must be part of a general improvement project.

At the desk, the girl (of course, it had to be, didn't it?) looked up when I put my pile of books down to be checked.

"Oh, Mr Winton," she said, "can I say how much I did enjoy your concert last night? The Schumann especially; you made me think of Claudio Arrau, if you don't mind the comparison."

How could I mind the comparison?

"You have no idea how much that means to me," I said. "What you said. He was a great man."

"Shall I put these books all in the same bag?" she asked.

"Er, all these books? There should be only two. The novels."

"Oh," she said, "there are others here." She looked at them without curiosity. She obviously saw quite a few crossing the counter. They wouldn't have them on sale otherwise, would they?

"No. They're not mine. I don't know how they got there."

"I suppose they must have been there when you put your books down." She scooped them up and put them behind the desk.

"When are you next coming to Aberdeen? We're called the Granite City, but that doesn't apply to our ears, you know."

It looked as if I needed another role model. Don Juan, as in Byron? My Byron book of selected poems just gives a selection from his longer poems, so I went back to the shelves, but they didn't have a copy of the whole poem, only of the first four cantos.

I still haven't read the novels. Nor do I know whether she believed me about the books. But I did order a copy of Don Juan, complete, with over five hundred and fifty pages, on the Internet, when I got home.

**

After Aberdeen

There was a patch of quiet time, and just as well. I went twice to the Conservatoire. It meant the lessons I gave were rather close together, but with experienced students that's no problem. I have to pack them in if I'm going away. I've had an occasional last minute replacement call for a concert. One was because a brave pianist had gone skiing with his family, which he's done all his life, but this time he fell over and stretched a muscle which was already stretched as far as it was meant to go. That doesn't happen much – pianists mostly take care of themselves, some more neurotically than others. I don't go so far as not to shake hands in case my opponent is an arm-wrestler, but I usually take his forearm in my other hand to spread the load. And I maintain my personal keep-fit-and-in-condition routine. We have to take our bodies as seriously as athletes, though not in the same way – we expect them to last longer…I keep up with the things I learnt from Frances-Frankie.

I could see that Gary was showing signs of that obsessive nature that sometimes happens with eager students. He was practising almost to danger point. He had to be encouraged to take it a bit easy, or, God help him, he would have too narrow an approach to life. And what was worse, there could be muscular problems lying in wait.

Felicity Smith was getting some sort of balance. Intense, well prepared, but with a smile like Emanuelle Béart, who played the violin in one of those French films; *Un Cœur en hiver* was it? A beguiling mixture of serious and light-hearted. Interesting that I didn't remember much about her looks after our first meeting. Surprising, with hindsight. She must have been eighteen, and it's a terrible shock to think that people so many years younger are now grown up. Still, it was a good time for her to be taking her music seriously.

Maybe meeting her formidable father gave me the impetus to see how much like him she was, or wasn't. "Formidable" may not be the right word – I'm sure he's just one of those people who buy property and rubbish in equal quantities, spot a hole in the market and fill it appropriately.

Lord Chislehurst obviously didn't think it was a risk to put his little girl into a place stacked out with potential musicians who are also potential misfits like me, and whose main talent is to blow, finger, stroke, or hit. OK, so he was the chairman of the place, but did he know that music can draw you together so that you get common feelings which aren't your own, but Mozart's or Tchaikovsky's? Dangerous at times. Should he have trusted his girl to a nearly divorced man like me? Divorced men are men with a past on the loose. I wonder what he'd have done if I'd seduced her. For that matter, I wonder what I'd have done if I'd seduced her. Rephrase – tried to seduce her. I'd never tried seducing anyone. Where do you start? "Where've you been all my life?" "Well, for half of your life, waiting to be born." Better just to teach her to play the piano. Then send her on to the Juilliard School in New York, or to Henri Samain, who had taught me in France.

**

Beethoven was coming on fine.

Opus 109.

The nuts and bolts – marking in fingering, making a few scribbles if I think I've found something I want to remember – had been done. The framework, too, had been settled, while keeping everything flexible for further discoveries.

The last movement is a theme and six variations, a way of going over the same territory several times, looking at it from different angles. I had to find the way of making each individual part count, and yet merge them into a complete inevitable whole. Six voices singing different tunes from the same hymn sheet. I looked out my copy of Pirandello's 'Six Characters in search of an Author'. The title is intriguing, and suggests the sort of searching I was facing. I had plenty of time to read; there was no one to talk to, and my non-working evenings were free. As air. Practice and thought, and reading and occasional outings, alone, to the theatre. A lot of people live like that, very happily. It has advantages, once you look for them, as Eleanor Gordon told me.

My 'Six Characters in Search of an Author' were 'Six "Me's" in search of Me'. It didn't take long to read. And it didn't help me personally, since I couldn't decide which character I was, or, like Pirandello's people, know if I was real or acting.

**

I played in the Home Counties. A music club not too many miles from Bletchley. Very nice, modern, real facilities, and, more important, a lovely piano. It used to belong to Frederick Jeffries, who was one of my teachers, who has gone to the great keyboard in the sky, as he used to call it. "Fredgie" was how we knew him, because that was how he'd been known since about 1930 in his preparatory school; it's hard for a boy with a nickname to grow out of it. It could well have accounted for his unfailing sense of humour. He used to say he'd played in every music club in the country – once.

The piano had been beautifully restored, and like a lot of those pianos from the 1920s, the tone is round and warm, and the keys can respond. Slightly posh audience, but not the sort that won't clap for long in case they spoil their hands for playing bridge or handling a gun. Bach to start with – Fantasy in D major, Chopin's second sonata, Debussy's Images. Rachmaninov Preludes to end. I really let myself go in the Rachmaninov, letting my own emotion take over, and there were tears in my eyes. It got a bit scary, and there was a sort of loss of control which I think Fredgie would have noticed, if his ghost is living in the soundboard.

It didn't make me happy.

All the same there was rather a lot of applause at the end and a couple of wolf-whistles. I think that's just the new way of showing appreciation for musical achievement rather than an invitation to extra-musical pleasure. Afterwards more autographs than I've ever signed before. I smiled a lot, and scribbled 'love from William…' until no more programmes appeared in front of my nose. I know they'd listened to me as well.

Drive home – no problems. I used to come back by train. Last time I was on the last train there was a fight, and I'm not too keen to go through that again. It got dealt with very quickly, but all the same, my hands got frightened in case things got out of hand. All about someone objecting to someone smoking. That's what keeps me off last trains, not because I think that someone will recognise me, because they won't.

**

The film begins

I have to hand it to Jane. She is an agent with imagination, looking beyond the normal thing of arranging recitals at the Wigmore Hall and other halls, or rattling the cages of the people who put on the festivals in Edinburgh or Aldeburgh.

Email from *jane@curzprod.co.uk.*

Will, dear. Decision time. A small, but respected company, Pythagoras Records, wants you to record a CD for them. I told them that you were occupied with Beethoven's opus 109, and they welcomed that. It's short, obviously, and they suggest you run some other major work beside it, but not more Beethoven. Any ideas? Recording early next year. A good bolt from the blue, don't you think?

Jane

I didn't need much time to sort that one out. It was just what my career and I needed, one to help the other along the way.

Will@williamwinton.uk

Of course. I had been thinking along those lines almost without knowing it. The other piece would be Schubert's late sonata in A major. Maybe not recorded so often.

Will.

Next day she was back to me.

from *jane@curzprod.co.uk.*

They have grasped that with enthusiasm. Just give me precise details.

And I have another point.

Do you want to keep on going as you are, busy, that's true, with this new CD on line, working with orchestras, with the odd Prom thrown in, or do you want in addition to be a trail-blazer in classical music, and change its face for ever?

67

Of course the film I suggested won't make any difference to your solo career, you know. You're not going to be Liberace. ....And it's you that have to make the decision.

I've been putting together a proposal, and looking for finance. Details to follow. Think about it. Seriously. J

I hadn't given the film idea a thought.

A film – with all that visual stuff? Followed up by inevitable appearances on chat shows? Was it really her view that you don't exist as a force in the arts unless you can go and sit alongside a Personality or two, share a few funny incidents, made up, if necessary, promote your latest book or recording or whatever, and, in my case, play something?

Did I really want to enter that maze?

**

Then she rang me. Personal touch, to make sure I didn't delete the email.

She expanded on her idea. Music and visuals. Not too complicated, but expensive-looking.

"I want it to be – how can I put it delicately? – sexy."

"I don't think I'm sexy, not delicately even."

"They can fake anything these days," and she laughed unnecessarily.

"I've no idea what you mean."

"Oh come on, it's just a word. It means you must look your best, smile a bit, and smoulder a bit – look like the music you play a bit. We'll get someone to give you some coaching, and you'll be surprised. It'll be bits and pieces of your favourite things. Automne by Chaminade, Rustle of Spring. Liebestraum of Liszt. You know. Encores, bonnes bouches."

"But it will be me as I am, won't it? Not air-brushed into the dustpan of anonymity?"

"Clever remark. No, we'll get it all shot from weird angles. Bit of art among the hype, and good music. Not all that long. About half an hour at most. Be like Liszt – a showman in the best possible taste?"

I wasn't looking to the publicity that might come out of this new project to define me and put me on the map. Nevertheless it could just be the shot in the arm I needed in my life. Fill a glaring emotional gap. I said I'd think about it, which she thought meant I'd do it, and she proved to be right. There would be no difficulty about getting backing, she said, because there's a market for this, and I would be the first one in it, as far as she knew. She hadn't researched that much, because you can find all sorts on YouTube.

I insisted that it must be released in tandem with the serious Beethoven and Schubert CD.

**

Doubts about Keith

Life went back to normal. The questions went unanswered. Had I become too careful? Was it possible that having a wife was my way of being a virgin for ever? I didn't mean that really, because of course we had sexual moments together. Or at least that's what I thought we did until she left. I think I may have said that before. A career, doing pretty well, a useful agent, and a wife to take care of my human emotional needs. That's what I had, and it was enough for me. And Patti? I'd failed to understand her. Failed to understand much about young women. Women in general. Just took, without giving.

Behind it, the same question. What was her new man like? Did I know him? Had I met him? I did the ultimate stupid thing. I googled the orchestra he played in. Several pictures of the whole orchestra, posing on a stage. I could make out the brass section, but I couldn't even see which instruments they were holding.

Then I found it – section by section – holding instruments as if they were trying to deflect the camera.

I didn't know whether to be pleased or sorry at what I saw. The brass section. He played the trombone, so he must have been one of the three in the picture. Pleasant enough guys, good lighting on the instruments, and on them, and not one of them the drop-dead gorgeous man I thought he would be.

I'd suspected that was how it was. Which made it worse.

**

Chislehurst Family Party

Meanwhile, life as normal, as I said before.

69

With a slight change. My divorce became absolute on the first of November. It didn't seem to make any difference now that I'd grown accustomed to the idea. I'd not been playing around, if you're not supposed to do that 'while you're waiting', though I doubt if it mattered in this case since the only chance that had come my way had been bungled.

It was a reminder that I had to get a move on, and what? Find some way to get up enough steam to have affairs, or find whatever it is that propels you into them. Giving and taking, without destroying the women involved. That's it. How do you do that?

**

Lord Chislehurst had meant it when he said, "Meet the family."

An invitation – "Just a few friends, who would love to meet you with no music, that's a promise." – arrived on very stiff board in a thick envelope. At least, the days have gone when the rich and lovely would have asked us round as performers, spoken to us kindly, and then expected us to play for our supper. I won't play for nothing now, except for charity, and charity isn't the first thing that comes into your mind when your hosts have a house in Chelsea and another in the wilds of Surrey, and no doubt will have one on Mars when it proves possible to breathe the atmosphere.

Lady Chislehurst, whose card it was, hoped I might be free on November 5th.

"Fireworks after drinks and things. Rather short notice," she said.

It was, but my diary is usually free of dates on November 5th every year. I make a point of not competing with other people's fireworks. Yes, I was free, and it interested me to see more of the background of Felicity, the Chelsea Émanuelle Béart, who would be there. I texted my acceptance and went.

**

What with his housing schemes, not to mention the Olympic stadium to come, Lord Chislehurst was very prosperous.

Very prosperous indeed, judging from the house in Chelsea. I try not to be impressed by wealth, although I know that in our industry we've always had to rely on the moneyed classes.

Composers had to live in their households as servants, or give lessons to their daughters. Say nice things and collect the money. If Lord Chislehurst's father had set the pattern for making money as opposed to inheriting it from those ancestors who'd annexed the common land, then I have some respect for him.

Lady Chislehurst was more of a lady than her Lord was a lord. He wasn't quite like Squire Western in Tom Jones, but there was a bit of the spade-is-a-spade about him and certainly there were few frills. She was elegant, carefully preserved, beautiful, even, with a gentle, pleasing, voice to round it off.

Felicity looked different at home. Young, of course, but sophisticated. Our relationship here was social, not master and pupil. Perhaps we should always meet our pupils outside, in safe circumstances.

She expanded to fit her home. The very expensive simple dress looked French, but the necklace wasn't. It had nothing of the French couturier about it. Dutch diamonds, Hatton Garden setting? Quite another girl, and quite a girl too.

Their ravishing house was just off the King's Road before it turns left and then right. Modernish, ostentatious and tasteful at the same time, with the sort of results you can only get when you get someone else to go over the interior for you. Full of wealthy style. I'd like to say that somehow it didn't join up: that it was a just a collection of items rather than a programme. That's me being defensive, and it wasn't true. Everything was real, and nothing looked as if it had arrived with a book of instructions. Certainly not the pictures on the walls.

There weren't too many guests. I sidestepped my suspicion that, after all, the Chislehursts didn't know too many people who were dying to meet me. Still, the dozen or so that were there were enthusiastic enough.

My Black and White film CD had sold a sprinkling of copies.

"Brought back those lovely days," said the old woman who was Lady Chis's mother, her face wrinkled, but still handsome.

Lady Chislehurst herself was called Myriad – no, not Miriam, though I wondered if her mother had a cold at her name-giving ceremony, or was as deaf at the name-giving as she was now when her deaf-aid wasn't plugged in.

Her son-in-law had seen to it that she'd been wired for sound, and she made no attempt to hide anything under her hair, or in her ear. She had a small microphone which you had to speak into, which meant that she knew she had your undivided attention. It was like talking on a mobile phone, except that the respondent was there in front of you. And you didn't have to raise your voice, because the technology was the latest money could buy. Technological money.

She mentioned the music I was playing on the CD in passing, but used it as a vehicle to go for a journey down memory lane; that's a risk you take when you tie music to external images. It was a calculated risk, and reminded me of the one I would have to calculate about my film-to-be.

The old lady soon ran out of memories of James Mason and Merle Oberon. "That film about Chopin and George Sand was not black and white like the title of your record says; it was in Technicolor, you know," she said, tapping me playfully on the arm with what would have been a fan a century ago, but was in fact one of those fork-and-spoon combinations you get at buffet parties, only this one was in silver, solid silver, no doubt. She was beginning to ramble a bit, so I didn't tell her that James M wasn't in the Chopin film; it was enough for her just to be thinking about him, even implying that he had been her lover. You never know, but I think her thinking was wishful. Anyway, she was right. 'A Song to Remember', the Chopin film, wasn't represented, and I only know it because it's wonderful nonsense.

Myriad Chislehurst swept me off. I was sure by now she'd put on this small party to have a look at the man who was teaching her daughter.

"You mustn't mind Mother. She really did listen to your CD. We plugged her in directly, and she couldn't avoid it. That sounds rude, but I don't mean to be. She looked very happy at the time," she murmured through clenched teeth. I thought at first that the clenched teeth had some significance. It turned out it was her way of talking: when she smiled she showed perfect, secure teeth. "And I loved it every time." She looked round the room to check.

"How do you find Felicity?" she said.

"Just turn round and you'll find her; she's at your elbow." Felicity had come to ask me to do something.

"I know you're not going to play a solo because we don't do that to people, but would you play a Schubert Marche Militaire with me? Just for fun; it doesn't really need practising, does it? As long as I remember to count, and they'd be thrilled to see me playing with you. Playing a duet with you."

Interesting correction and perhaps not significant, but her eyes danced with the thought of Schubert, or something. I cleared my throat as a way of saying yes.

When she went off to get the music, another version of her took her place. A bit older, and more experienced, from the look of her. Disconcertingly.

"I'm her cousin, in case you're wondering why we look alike. I'm Barbara, and Uncle George is my uncle."

"Uncle George?"

"Uncle George Smith – Lord Chislehurst. Married to Myriad. That really is her name – and everyone from the vicar downwards thought someone made a mistake. But no, my grandfather was a poetic soul, and Aunt Myriad was a late baby, as you can see from Grandmother over there, and he thought she brought them a myriad of blessings. She's survived her name pretty well, apart from her teeth."

"How do you mean, her teeth? I thought they looked alright."

"Ah, you see, you did look. They are alright. But she clenches them. Defence mechanism, Mummy always says. You don't know my mum, her sister, and believe me you need some sort of defence from her."

"Oh, is she here?"

"No, and it's not that sort of defence you need. There's just me, and I don't play the piano, by the way, or anything but games, and then only some. Lucky Felicity."

I agreed she had talent.

"I don't mean because of her talent, though that's nice for her. I just mean lucky Felicity."

I was getting the hang of this now.

"Suppose I ask you what games you play, would you tell me?"

"When this little party's over, and you've been inspected by the aunt and uncle to make sure you're decent enough to teach their daughter, we could go on somewhere?"

It was a short question, but Felicity came back with the Schubert music, clapped her hands and said we'd play the first Marche Militaire without repeats. Barbara went on to the back burner and stayed there. I didn't want to get entangled with the Chislehurst girls, even if they were in-law girls.

We played the march. I didn't mind the smattering of conversation while we were playing. It's sociability music, and you don't have to listen to it as if it's a symphony by Mahler.

Nice polite applause.

I asked Felicity about the paintings.

"It's terrible, you know. I almost take them for granted like posh wallpaper. Though some are so valuable we have to have bars on the windows. And burglar alarms all over the place. Still Daddy would insist on that anyway. Go and look at the Picasso. It's over there."

"You have a Picasso?"

"Yes. I used to tease Mummy that Daddy married her just for the Picasso her mother had. Maybe from Picasso himself. It's a nice thought. Until I saw that she didn't find it funny. He married her because she was beautiful, which she still is."

There were a lot of good paintings on the walls by serious artists, some unknown to me.

The Picasso was different. I was looking at it when a heavy aura of expensive perfume surrounded me. You don't wear perfume like that if you don't expect to be noticed, and I love women's perfume.

The voice that came out of the cloud was low, but on the point of laughing.

"You don't suppose it's a fake, do you?"

"I don't think so," I said, without looking round.

The voice modulated into a hand on my arm. "But how can you tell? All Picassos look like fakes."

I looked round.

"That was a joke – I couldn't afford the bars on the windows, let alone a Picasso. Does it look like anyone you know?"

"Oh come on, it's a Picasso."

"Naughty…once you know the signs…"

"Teach me."

"The nose, the eye, the ear, could remind you of someone in this room."

"I think there might be quite a few who would pass that test."

"You're joking again. Look over there, the one with the deaf aid, Myriad's mother – it's her painting, and she says she posed for it."

"Is that possible?"

"Yes, if you mean she was alive when he was still painting. And she may well have been around when he painted it. But the big question is, did she pose for the painting, or did she pose to get the painting? Subject for a novel. He gave it to her. The painting, I mean."

"Has no-one ever quizzed her on the subject?"

"You could go and try shouting the question into her deaf aid. That should stop the room in its tracks. She might well tell you. She likes attractive men, because whatever is wrong with her ears there's nothing wrong with her eyesight."

"You sound as if you know her well."

"No, but you don't need to, to know that."

"Why does it hang here? She's not the live-in mother-in-law, is she?"

"She lives next door, with her own staff to look after her and her needs – some of them."

"She doesn't mind being parted from her souvenir of Picasso, I suppose."

"She probably has other ways of remembering him. Or wants us to think that. She's very well-marbled."

"Sorry…?"

"Has them all. She reads what I write, and tells me what she thinks about me; that's refreshing if not always welcome."

I looked at her. "I think you might have the advantage of me, here."

She was good to look at, as well as smell. A little older than me, maybe. Loose hair, but not too long. Her appearance obviously meant a lot to her, but she didn't seem to rely on it to create herself.

"I'm William Winton – Will usually, unless in France, where I'm Guy."

Was I trying too hard?

"I play the piano for a living."

"You play like a man who plays the piano for a living. I write books for a living."

"Ah…"

"And you don't read books."

"I do read books. I'm a traveller, and stay in hotels. I do read books but I don't keep up the way I think I should. I read books in French to keep my French up, but they're usually classics. I've been reading Balzac recently."

This was true. I hoped that might end that line of enquiry, because I felt a little guilty about not keeping up.

"Interesting. Which one?"

"*Béatrix*."

"Ooh…I thought I was the only one to read that. Based on Liszt and George Sand. Loosely. I think it's a mistake to write novels which have real people in them. How would you like it if I wrote a novel about you?"

"It depends on what you said about me."

"The great thing is to start with a bit of the truth and then make it pure fiction…"

"So – let me guess – you write novels."

"I wondered if I'd been too tactful in making that clear."

"So, should I have read you?"

"No. Not my novels. They are extremely well written but with a particular market in mind."

"You don't mean…"

"No, I don't. They are romantic novels. Might be set in Hungary, or anywhere else I might have been for a holiday."

"And the next one is about a pianist in a rich man's house, teaching his lovely, but very young, daughter?"

"Not my style – too near the truth."

"I beg your pardon?"

"Don't get me wrong. I just mean the teacher-pupil thing is always tricky. Keep away from that."

"Exactly how I feel. Too young. Too close to a powerful daddy."

"You would do well to look to an older woman. You've been around a bit yourself, I would guess."

She couldn't have said a kinder thing. An innocent like me at large in the wicked world projecting an air of experience. Yes, that would be me, some day.

"Not your novels?"

"I'm sorry?" She looked surprised.

"You said I wouldn't have read your novels. You write other things? Poetry, perhaps?"

"If only. Criticism in the Literary Journal."

"That's impressive. If you tell me your name, I'll make a point of reading some."

"Debbie Watkins – Deborah Watkins in the Journal."

"Don't you find it hard to be a serious writer and then criticise how others do the same thing?"

"Well, it's not the same thing. I don't write stuff anyone would want to criticise in print. Something to read on the train, or on holiday on a beach."

"Even so? We don't usually do that in our profession. We could discuss things with our pupils, with other musicians. But not for public eyes or ears."

"It's quite usual for us. We try to be fair, and not cruel. Not like the drama critics or film critics who don't write plays or make films. But then we would all say we're only telling the truth, so help me God."

"For money."

"Naturally. Not a lot."

"Ms Watkins in the Journal, and…"

"And…?"

"In your bodice ripper novels?"

"Oh not much ripping goes on there. It's all very willing. After a time. Or not, sometimes. It can happen quite quickly, if the time is right. And the signs."

"What sort of signs?"

"Oh, you can tell."

"In a novel, I can understand that, because the author plants them. But in real life?"

"It can be easier, sometimes."

We left that there.

Someone came and filled our glasses again.

I caught sight of Felicity's cousin Barbara watching me. I looked away in case there were signs there too. How nice to be pursued, if that's what it was. How awkward if all the signs were coming on at once. Like Piccadilly Circus with all the lights at green.

"So your popular novels are anonymous?"

"No. I use a man's name."

"Doesn't that put women off?"

"What makes you think the readers are women?"

"Aren't they?"

"I don't know. I haven't done any research. But I think it's safe to think they are. My publishers sell me to them as the man who writes about such things – getting into bed at the other side. It excites some people."

She looked at me. Was I one of those people?

"Are you going to tell me your trade name?"

"No name."

I was having a productive conversation. We were standing. The drink helped. She looked at me over the top of her glass from time to time – over a glass darkly – which seemed provocative. I was learning. The perfume helped. So did the talk, into an area I didn't normally invade. I mean the literature bit. Also that other area.

She changed the subject. "I know something about music, you know. I've been quite close to it for some time."

She looked round the room, and pointed across to a tall slender man with old-fashioned horn-rimmed glasses. He looked as if he'd popped out of a box marked '1930s prototypes'. There was something familiar about him, but maybe that was why.

"That's Gilbert May," she said.

I knew about Gilbert May; he was a contemporary composer who wrote serious music, not much performed, but worth listening to when you could find it, and television incidental music, much performed, and good. His TV music sounded as if it came from an artist, rather than from a computer which generated stuff that just does the same bit over and over again, and can be stopped anywhere without anyone noticing it. Except for people like me, who find it hard not to hear it draining the meaning out of the programme.

"He's a good man. I must talk to him. Maybe he could write something for me."

"That could easily be arranged."

"He could write me something romantic, and witty – just the thing for an encore. If he would accept a little commission like that."

"Oh, I'm sure he would."

"You're as sure as that?"

"Yes. He's my partner, you see."

Silence. Except for the sound of a door banging shut. It opened again.

"Would you like to come back with me? We could talk more and I have some nice brandy."

"But…"

"Oh just with me. Gil and I are free spirits."

"You mean he doesn't mind if you take men home with you?"

I added: "I didn't mean that to sound as if you make a habit of it."

"Why not? As it happens, I don't. But we have what is called an open marriage, except we're not married."

"Mightn't he be there?"

"How do you mean?"

"If I came back with you?"

78

"You mean I should come to your place?"

"I don't think that's a good idea."

"You mean you have someone there too?"

"There might be."

"But it doesn't worry you if you don't go back there?"

"No. Not everyone who might be in my house is part of my life, you know."

All of this was true. I knew perfectly well there would be no one there, apart from the ghost of Patti, and that was fading at last. All the same I wasn't taking anyone else back there until I planned it.

Debbie was looking at me rather closely. Writing another chapter of her book?

"Oh, Gil doesn't mind. We have separate quarters. He's often writing his opuses well into the night, and I don't do that sort of thing. I'm not George Sand with the coffee and the cigars."

She really looked into my eyes this time. "I think we could have…"

I didn't find out what we could have, because the real fireworks started. I don't like fireworks – the explosions hurt my ears. But these were expensively scheduled to stay where they were – outside, but where we could see them from the drawing room windows, and not have to crane our necks to see where they'd gone.

"No point in paying a lot for something all of London can see," muttered Lord Chislehurst. If I have to watch fireworks ever again, these are the ones I'll have. Catherine wheels and Roman candles, not at all like the ones I remembered from childhood. Imported from God knows where, and full of colour surprises; the finale was a fair representation of the Picasso I'd just been looking at.

Debbie found Gilbert May for me, and I asked him if he would write me a piano piece.

"I'm very flattered, I love writing piano music, but mostly I don't get asked. I'm not sure I can programme it just now, unless you could put up with something like the music I'm writing for Howells."

Howells, who was that?

"It's a new detective series, set in Aldeburgh, lots of pebbles, and the sound of the sea and no Benjamin Britten."

"Yes, please do it when you can, but soon would be good. Something I can slip into a programme unannounced, except by me, verbally. Audiences like that; talking to them shows them we're human, not just mechanics on instruments.

Then after that maybe something more serious? I've got a broad repertoire, but I don't get into the twentieth-first century often enough. When the Chopin and Schumann year is over. After 2010. Perhaps we could meet and talk about it?"

We parted, leaving me with the problem of how to leave this place with his partner, in such a way that he didn't notice.

"I'm not going to be home tonight," he said to Debbie.

"At least not until late. I've just run into an old friend, and we'll be having a drink or two."

"I'll be in bed I expect," Deborah said, and he didn't say, "I expect you will."

They had got it worked out. And there we were.

"There you are, William Winton. The open marriage door just opened wide. Have you got your car?"

"I don't do drink and drive."

"Neither do I, but it's not far, and I'm a good driver."

"Are you sure?"

What sort of risks was this woman prepared to take?

I said my goodbyes, with the odd kiss. Felicity's cousin Barbara was insistent about that. Maybe I should have been going with her, but I looked at Lady Chislehurst and knew I'd made the right decision.

I didn't see Deborah leave, so maybe no one noticed we were going at the same time.

She was waiting outside, standing by a splendid car. I saw why she wasn't concerned with the law, because this one had its own driver. Maybe she had called it up during my procession round the guests, and it wasn't her own.

"This isn't my car, you know. I just have an account with a local firm, and a pretty fair idea of when I'll be leaving."

And not alone, I suppose. But that wasn't fair. Just because she'd picked me off a tree at a party didn't mean she went down into the woods every day of the week with a basket on her arm.

**

The house was a successful author's house. Those paperbacks, or eBooks, were doing well.

There was even a garden, small, but large enough to have a sort of summerhouse.

"Don't be deceived by that," Deborah said, "it's an all-purpose house, where Gilbert writes his music, sound-proofed, and where he sleeps, as often as not. As in tonight, if he comes home."

There were books all over the place. Neatly on walls mostly, but some on chairs.

"Do you ever read for pleasure, if you're always reviewing them?"

"Do you ever listen to music, if you're always playing it?"

"Touché. But I enjoy it, and yet can notice things about it which other people might not, without that getting in the way."

There had to be some way to get from this book-chat to what I hoped we'd come here for.

"Would you like a coffee? The coffee that I might have invited you in for."

"If it's the same coffee that you might invite me in for, yes, I'll settle for that."

I was getting a bit vague about this situation. Was she just asking me back for a coffee? What happened to the brandy? Was this going to be a long-term strategy situation? I hadn't planned on that, and frankly it wasn't what I wanted. Deborah had given every sign at the party of wanting a clear-cut situation, and that was what I wanted. Desperately. I know those signs, I thought. What else could they mean?

After a minute or two, I followed her into the kitchen, which was easy to find, since there were sounds coming from there.

"You don't mind if I watch you making coffee?"

It was an extraordinary kitchen. Not big, but you wouldn't have to do much to cook there. It looked as if there was a button to press for every stage of making dishes. And probably serving them up too. Deborah looked exactly the same. She hadn't slipped into anything comfortable like the oilman's lady in Aberdeen. She didn't seem to have any plans on the subject.

I watched her. Good enough to look at close to. And just the thing for a man like me – like young Don Juan with Donna Julia – a dream come true. Without having to hide under the bedclothes when her husband comes in. The coffee came in a small cup. Quite strong, like a Wake-Up call.

We sat at the breakfast bar, on chrome and leather bar stools, the sort you have to remember not to lean backwards on. We looked at each other.

"I don't often drink coffee late. Only if I'm driving back after a concert."

"What an exciting life you must lead."

"Like writing successful books. And criticism. Yes…"

"Don't forget we're writers first. Words are what we do. We are looking for the truth all the time, but we have to make it readable, even when we're criticising other people's writing."

"My most recent crit, from a local paper, went something like 'at least if you don't want to listen to him, you can watch him'."

"I wouldn't mind that."

"I didn't mind either."

"I meant I wouldn't mind watching you."

Smiling time. Easy to do.

"I meant watching you play. It could be quite fascinating."

Ironic smiling time.

"It was interesting to see you with Felicity. She's desperately in love with you. You know that, don't you?"

"It's my job not to know. It's not uncommon for pupils to believe they are in love their teachers. Up to a point."

"But it's the body language. She was so happy to be sitting next to you, hoping your hands might touch as you played your little duet."

"I didn't notice." That wasn't true. But I had switched off the current that lit that part of my brain. It wasn't off now.

I took her hand. "I would like us to touch hands in our little duet."

"So we shall."

She freed her hand and put her fingers between the buttons on my shirt.

"That's nice," she said.

"Yes, it is," I said, and ran my fingers lightly up her arm.

"I think we should go somewhere else. Kitchen floors aren't made for bettering one's acquaintance. They're too hard, and the fan comes on if the temperature gets too high."

She led me up through the house. Carpet everywhere, warmth everywhere.

The bedroom was feminine. No Gilbert traces to be seen. Their arrangement went as far as the furniture.

I embraced her as I walked into the room behind her. She leant back, into me. Soft, not fleshy, but not like a person who thinks about kilos.

She put her hand over her shoulder and touched my head. She turned round, and kissed me. Not on the mouth. On the cheek and put her hand inside my shirt again. From there onwards, there was no sense of anything but the present, no thought about anything but the physical delight which created and released tension. For the first time for years, the bed was a place for pleasure rather than a place in which some pleasure might happen. She was made for love, as she might have described it in one of those novels she wrote. She made me take my time. Something musicians do by nature – but I wasn't making music here. Maybe she would write something about making music together in her novels, but without clefs, expression marks. I had never been caressed like this before, and it was easy enough to respond. This was a body such as I had never known. Her skin was soft. *Dolcissimo*, responsive to the fingers, things a pianist enjoys. And…

After the dots…the conversation…very tender, low-voiced.

"You mustn't go to sleep."

"I wasn't."

"You were very quiet. Even breathing. Danger sign."

"No. Extreme pleasure doesn't need words. Or sleep. I'm too pleased to sleep."

She kissed my cheek. There had been no kiss-kissing, I noticed.

"You must go. Gilbert and I don't do overnights. It was a mistake we made once in the past. The next morning was not good. For anyone. Let alone the poor woman he had with him."

"She…"

"She didn't know what to talk about while she ate her bowl of muesli. I knew her too, which made it slightly harder. In the normal way, socially, we could have talked about television programmes or something like that, but somehow in the kitchen with the imprint of one of our beds on her face, it sounded false. I grabbed my cup of coffee, and disappeared. We made a rule."

"Let me just say that I would love to stay on, and sleep beside you. An extra pleasure, to share a bed with a woman like you. Except there aren't any women like you, are there?"

"You know the right things to say, too. But a rule is a rule."

"I can see it's wiser."

"Can I watch you dress? I'd like to see how you cover yourself up. Take your time. I'd like to remember it. Undressing was part of something else, not a lot of time to notice very much. Dressing tells me more about you and your body."

"Is this something for your next novel?"

"Saucy man. No. Maybe the one after that."

"Saucy you. I suppose you have to try things out."

"I don't do much research, if that's any consolation. I don't do affairs. Casual is the horrible word for it. Suggests far less than it is."

"It didn't feel casual. Very meaningful."

"You are a fantastic lover, you know. It almost seemed like your first time, in the sense that you wanted everything to be just right." She hadn't noticed anything had she? She had more to say.

"You know your part, or should I say role? You respond quickly, no prompting needed."

"That's nice to know."

"And yet I get a sort of feeling that you needed this in some sort of way."

"Did I cry? Say something I shouldn't have at an important moment?"

"No, and if this sort of neediness is something which goes with your love-making, keep it in the script. It's very flattering. As if what I have to give you is the answer to a question."

"Perhaps I should practise until I'm perfect at it like a Rachmaninov study."

I moved towards the bed.

"No, no. Tempting though you are, I am not changing the rule of the house. I'm sorry in a way about that, because you're real. Hello and Goodbye it is, but believe me, you'll be a memory."

"And you – need I say?" I smiled at her.

She changed direction.

"How long have you been alone? Without a wife?"

"What?"

"How long have – "

"Who told you I was divorced?"

"No-one. You don't wear a ring, but you have a scar on your left hand."

I looked.

"I can't see one."

"No, but I could feel one. When I held your hand. The ring that's not there."

"You don't write detective stories, do you? Agatha Christie's Miss Marple with a different angle."

"As in horizontal? I don't do the old maid thing. Not yet, anyway."

"You are an amazing woman…"

"You miss her?"

"Do I miss her? I think I miss Me more."

"This Me is better."

"How do you know?"

"Because this Me couldn't be better. Trust me."

"I think that may be temporary, something to do with what you and I have been doing. Nothing could be better for a man out of quarantine. Fifteen years of it."

"And no straying during all that time?"

"No. It didn't occur to me. Nothing occurred to me."

"Old habits die hard. She left you, didn't she?"

I didn't answer.

"She was missing something if she didn't appreciate you. Quite apart from the sex."

"It was never like this. You are something special. You made me feel as if what we did was the conclusion of a longer courting period. As if you and I had known each other before…before we…"

"Perhaps you're the one who should be writing my books. It has something of the style."

"There's no copyright on what I just said. I'll have to buy all your new books to see where you quote it. And look for me."

"You won't be there. Some things I don't use because I don't want to share them, and you're going to be one of them."

I was dressed by now.

"Will I see you again?" I murmured, shy.

"No. It's not that you don't please me. You do. But I don't run risks by getting involved. For several reasons."

"I understand that. I do."

"And I think you're vulnerable. You must go. But come here a moment before you do."

She kissed me. Properly. For the first and only time.

"You look nice all dressed up. As you did all undressed up…"

We laughed.

I got a taxi. And was happy. Yes, leave it there. Go hunting? No. But look for the signs, all the same, and don't try to replace what's past.

The next stage in the film

More details about the film arrived from Jane. Preliminary thoughts for me to mull over and react to. She would see to setting up a possible company, and finding a sponsor.

Email from *jane@curzprod.co.uk.*

It's to be a real film, involving you in all aspects. In other words, not just you at the piano with different angles, from inside the instrument, from a distance, of fingers bouncing around, and a few photogenic flourishes of the wrist. Like you see in a concerto broadcast, nice enough for live TV, but nothing more.

So we need visually-oriented music, pieces which composers took from nature and such. You will be seen playing, but also you'll be seen in natural surroundings, walking, watching, thinking, looking like an artist. Glossy images. There will be help at hand, in the form of an acting coach, as well as a director anxious to make his name as a visual and artistic commodity, and go on to greater things. By which I mean feature-length things. (By which I guessed she meant films with plots and Oscar potential.)

Rustle of Spring, the Raindrop Prelude by Chopin, perhaps the Flaxen haired girl – pieces that suggest pictures. Shouldn't be hard to make up to half an hour or so…And half an hour is what we're aiming for, just to confirm our earlier discussion. Six or seven at most, some perhaps beginning with the music and a blank screen and patterns, for say that Ave Maria prelude by Bach. Well not the Ave Maria Prelude, because that's in Disney's Fantasia, *isn't it?* (It isn't – the Ave Maria involved is Schubert's) *And others where the visual bits would lead into the music. In the case of Autumn by Chaminade, which I know you play as an encore – in autumn – we would have you out in the falling leaves, walking through, kicking a few up, with an autumnal face. That sort of thing.*

The director's called Josy, thinking along those lines. We'll think of a title, not too explicit, but not deceptive either…

Having said which, I have to point out that your appearance is going to be important. There's no point in doing this otherwise. In this case only, of course. We're aiming to sell this as a complete package, and we will expect you not to put on weight, (in fact you might take another couple of pounds off), to keep up your work-outs, not grow a beard, or shave your hair off, though we might put a few extra blond streaks in, not get chicken-pox or start shaving with some new herbal thing. Part of this is a joke, but quite honestly this film is going to cash in on your appearance, now that you've got a proper one. Let's face it – and I think you should face it too, Will – you're now a good-looking man. No-one I know of has done this before. I don't count those people straddling their instruments who look as if they're going to give you a really good time until they pick up their bows and start to play. With a bit of luck, we could make some money which will free you to do all that serious playing and studying you talk of from time to time. And as you say, we'll make sure the serious, serious, seriously serious CD comes out before the film does. Beethoven and Schubert sonatas, you said. And some other things to make up the length if necessary. It depends on what space there will be and how long the sonatas are in your performance. CDs seem to come with various lengths – the length of Beethoven's Ninth Symphony was what they were aiming for, they tell me on the web. Less music, cheaper disc. We can get some ideas from Pythagoras records, who'll be promoting you; after all they should know all about the music of the spheres, as their Greek namesake did.

Let me know your thoughts. Be open, and willing.

There's an enquiry for you from Knutsford, by the way, and a return visit to Richmond, in the old theatre there – nice dates.

Ciao… Jane…

There it was. I looked at my face in the mirror. I don't usually look at my face in detail. My eyesight means that I don't really see what I wash and shave, all I need is the general direction in which to move the razor. If I want to see my face in detail, I have to wear glasses or, as I did this time, contacts.

It was thinner than it was. My face. Rather even, and more or less the same on the right as the left. Quite a generous mouth, good teeth, shaped brown eyebrows, and hazel eyes, sometimes green and sometimes brown depending on something which I haven't yet worked out. Yes, an even face, regular, like my mother's in her photograph, which she no doubt thought would stand her in good stead when she shipped off to California. She must be around sixty now, and she may be playing someone's mother in a local soap. I hope so, because as far as I can tell, her looks didn't bring her anything more tangible than a continued absence from home.

And I can't know whether my sailor father still sails the oceans blue. He could well have settled down somewhere and produced many half-brothers and sisters for me to meet. My parents' wedding picture shows them to have been the handsomest pair you could hope to see outside of a publicity handout, which to some extent it was. I can't criticise them, because I don't know them, but it seems likely they relied too much on their appearance, and not enough on what they could do for each other otherwise. I seem to have inherited the second part of that. Somewhat.

To my horror on that November day, through my lenses I thought I saw some faint razor-burn.

From *will@williamwinton.co.uk Jane – you're my agent, and I'm impressed by this music of the spheres thing – and I thought Pythagoras was the man who squared triangles and created musical commas.*

I know this is a problem you don't have, unless you've been deceiving me with your beardless lady act: I think I've got some razor burn – just a faint reddening on my chin. Advice, please, the name and number of some skin person with credentials. W

After I sent the email, I realised that this wasn't razor burn at all. And probably not entirely cosmetically approved of. Hah.

I also thought I saw a grey hair just above my ear. Or was it blond?

Follow the music film road. Or not? I had no one to ask. No teachers, no parents, no Grandmother. No wife. I had to go conditional. What would they have said? Mother, no doubt, would say go for it – use the looks I bequeathed you. Dad would say go for the money, I imagine. Patti would shrug, and say, "Make your own decisions, Billy, and then you won't have to blame me. I mean, you won't have me to blame." Teachers would say, "Don't touch it; go on ploughing the furrow of the developing artist. Your best years are ahead of you, when all the work and experience you have will slot into place."

And Gran? What about her? She had brought me up, and she would have expected me to think about it seriously. "Ask yourself some questions and answer honestly."

Hard enough. I am a serious musician. The world is changing. Audiences are getting older, according to the research. If people don't go out so often, why not go into their homes in person? In my person. The customers who buy this might well not be the ones who come to concerts. Or maybe, if it works, they might be persuaded to. Anyway, this product will be an artefact – something which isn't just a concert on film. My conclusion? As long as you stay true to yourself and to the music, you should be alright.

I thought Gran was right. Honesty wouldn't do any harm.

Emails

To *jane@curzprod.co.uk*

OK. Let's talk, and I promise not to eat more than I normally do.

Beethoven's opus 109 it is, with a Schubert sonata in A major – the late one, so it's two late works. The one I want is in the catalogue as D 959. It will be a short CD, maybe over 60 minutes, but I could put in some other bits and pieces to make it up. See what Pythagoras think. See if they've got an angle, Ho Ho. They're the record company after all.

But overall I need to know more details about the film. I won't just do anything for the camera. I'm a properly brought up man, with only one divorce to my credit.

Will

To *will@williamwinton.co.uk*

One divorce makes you an interesting proposition, and available, which ups your market value. It increases your newsworthiness when you appear in the film world. This will be a mix of classical music and image-appeal. After all, you look good, and if we play to your looks and accidentally turn you into a sex icon, well, I think you can deal with that. That's a joke, Will. If people sigh while you play, don't forget that you're making them listen to music. Oh, and don't forget they have money to spend.

P.S. Maybe it's important no-one should ever find out why *you're divorced. Keep them guessing.*

Bye-Jane.

To *jane@curzprod.co.uk*

Hi-jane. Do you *know why I'm divorced? I don't.*

Thanks for the reassurance about my looks. I was beginning to get conceited. And basically, Jane, I'm rather shy. I feel best sitting in front of the only faithful love of my life, the black and white notes on the piano. Ouch. Pretentious, too. And not quite true. WW

I took out the last seven words. I must keep my secrets.

Another email to Jane Curzon:

To *jane@curzprod.co.uk*

Timetable time. We have to line up dates for the Beethoven and Schubert, and provided all is OK, I am persuadable about this film. Can I meet the director? I must build in a holiday – somewhere to get a little gentle tan, and wash the London pollution out of my hair. Do you know a good hairdresser for the highlights, whatever? Can we try some out first to make sure my hair doesn't go green or anything? I would happily appeal to the Green Party, but not via my hair.

Will

Email from Jane Curzon

To *will@williamwinton.co.uk*

Leave it to me. Just keep thinking, and practising, and leading a good life.

By the way, I want to use your contact with Lord Chislehurst's daughter for sponsorship, because I think it looks very hopeful. But I'll wait for your OK before I get in touch with him. Don't have your hair cut until we've met Josy.

Jane

To *jane@curzprod.co.uk*

Ideas are happening. Tell me more about Josy. A surname, for example. He or she? I've made that mistake before. What sort of age? Names of films, or any work, and I can have a look on the web.

Will

A couple of days later Jane got in touch again.

From *jane@curzprod.com*

Josy is definitely on board for you. Josy, pronounced Jozey, is a guy, real name Jozef; I showed him your pictures, played him your film CD and he can't wait. Did I say he's wanting to use this as a way into big-time movies? But before you begin to feel like a staging post where they change the horses, don't forget that people on their way are often more interesting than the ones who've got there already, and the sort of things Josy's been doing are very good. He wants something with a bit more…how shall I say?…style, class, to show his adaptable nature, and then it's the States for him.

He wants to make it like a-day-in-the-life-of-, with the music running in your imagination, coming out of near-reality, and into a twilit world…I'm not putting it well, largely because I'm not sure what he's talking about. Better leave it till you meet. First session at my office – no lunch or anything like that; eating distracts Josy, because I think he might have dyspepsia, but don't say I told you that. Even an ulcer. And I don't want you putting on weight with an office lunch. This Friday? 2.30. I see from your diary that you're free, that you have a concert on Saturday in Liverpool, but it will still leave you time to catch the train. I'll have the ticket here. Come casual. I'll leave it to you and your wardrobe. But wrap up against this November weather.

Jane

That hurt, the bit about knowing my diary. There's almost nothing in it except what she puts in it. That's not normal, is it?

From *will@williamwinton.co.uk*

OK, done. I'm a bit worried by the fact that Josy's expecting to get more stylish, classy business. Does that mean he hasn't any? What sort of films has he been making? Documentaries? Student movies? Do you think I should see one of Josy's products? Have I seen one of Josy's products? Do they have titles? Does he have another name, or is he a one-name man? W

From *jane@curzprod.com*

Not necessary to see Josy's product. He'll convince you, believe me. Second name is Cherkavinsky, so you can see why Josy is best, at least for now. Never have a name no-one can remember. Agent's rule Number One. And he made documentaries on the mainland of Europe before he started the film shorts business.

Jane

Josy

Josy thought his reputation should bring in some finance, though he clearly didn't know the British system. She'd mentioned Lord Chislehurst and my connection with his daughter. How did she know about my connection with Lord Chislehurst, indeed? Jane, of course, being an agent, knows everything.

Josy? Josy, by any reckoning, was one hell weird. My musician friends can often be slightly off-centre, and I'm used to that. But basically, we're a practical lot. Even writing music is practical with all those notes to write down, whether you use a computer or not.

Josy was a completely new experience. I know there are film directors who look like executives, but Josy was a mess. No idea of dress sense, not too many visits to hairdressers or to men's counters in Boots. If any at all. He was somewhat incoherent, even if you make allowances for the fact that English wasn't his first language. I'd always trusted Jane as an agent, and I believed her when she said Josy had made amazing documentaries and short movies to split your head open, in whatever country he comes from. Somewhere in Middle Europe.

He had suggested he get us a showing of his best movie. Full-length – very full-length – and on a low budget. Not much happening, and the actors aren't actors, just people living their lives in some bit of non-touristy Europe, where you watch the crops grow, if they do. Jane managed to head that one off, but found part of one of his sheep sagas for me to see quietly at home. More important, she said, was that he'd made ads, too, for cat-food. So that's what the short movies were about. I don't suppose there's much tradition for that sort of thing if you live in one of the emerging democracies. He could get as much work as he wanted doing what he did. He told her. And here he was looking to do something to show he wasn't limited to peasants, or things to put in bowls for cats. That seemed to put me somewhere in between.

When we met, he chatted for a while, mostly about himself, and then walked round me, asked me to take my jacket off, inspected my waistline, got me to walk around him, made me look into his eyes, which were blood-shot in the most spectacular way. He wanted to smoke, but Jane wouldn't let him. He threw me a few thoughts: how would I feel to be a drop of rain, or a flame of fire; what did it feel like to be a note on a page of music, living with other notes, some of which were exactly the same? I think notes enjoy being in the company of other notes, but he didn't wait for any answer. He felt he could find some good angles. An acting lady he had in mind would help – not that I didn't have ideas of my own, I was to understand, but to sort them out. The acting lady was busy just now coaching some American actress to speak good Cockney. I wouldn't have to speak, except with my fingers and my eyes, but I would need to have some thoughts in my head, he said. Doesn't matter what they are, he said, just any thoughts will do. Not music, though, because that would be too vague. I tried to explain that music isn't vague, but somehow it got lost in the talk about money. His money. I didn't listen.

Continuing activity

I went to play in Liverpool. The Grieg piano concerto, my grandmother's favourite concerto. I don't play it very often, but it has everything an audience can want for a Saturday night in mid-November. For all the other days of the year too. An opening flourish, tunes, and enough soul and glitter to thrill the audience as well as your own fingers. Some pianists won't learn it; it's too populist, or they remember Eric Morecombe's unforgettable television interpretation in his performance with André Previn, preserved for ever in archives; but it lies in my fingers, and in my heart, and I've always done it. Eric's ghost fades quickly if it ever appears at all.

It went well. The weather wasn't good, though, and the audience had got slightly wet, even those who'd come by car. I like the hall: "sensuously curved" is how it's been described, and it makes you feel that you can reach everyone in the audience. They liked me, and I played an encore – a showy piano version I'd made of a couple of popular songs. It doesn't quite work, because the styles get mixed into a lumpy sauce, but I thought of Liszt and his arrangements of Schubert songs, and George Gershwin and his piano concerto, and threw myself into it. It was Saturday after all, and it sent them into the bars with a light step.

After the interval, I slipped into a seat in the auditorium, anonymously (change of clothes) to hear Sibelius's Fifth Symphony. If I can, I go to hear orchestral music, live, and without having to start playing at the next cue.

The lengthy journey home on Sunday by rail gave me a chance to comb through my list of possible items for the recording. Some Liszt who left a treasure trove of pieces with appeal and good visual titles. Fire Dance? By Manuel de Falla. And some Bach. There had to be Bach. And whatever visuals they could make out of it. Make them do some work. I didn't know who 'them' would be, apart from Josy.

Making a short list of short pieces isn't really very hard, and it didn't take long to make. Cutting it down would take longer.

I sat for a while and thought, watching the rain on the window. Gran's favourite concerto and an empty house to go home to. In the past, if Patti hadn't been there because she was out for a rehearsal, or even, I suppose, out with Keith, the atmosphere felt as if it had recently been used, and not left to get idle. There used to be substance in the space, traces of movement, or something. I did my best not to think about it. I looked around, and didn't see anyone I fancied talking to, much less fancied. That was a step in some direction other than backwards.

Sunday papers are something I wish I had more time for, although just to pick one up seems like a minor hazard, they weigh so much more than they cost. Something for everyone. Why not? It inevitably means that some of the supplements seem to be meant for somebody else, so when I'd bought one at Lime Street Station, I'd left chunks of it behind in the shop. I get my news from the radio, because I find you get more for the time you spend than you get from anywhere else. I don't have much idea of what most of the politicians in charge of our destiny look like. They don't usually appear after any of my shows in the group at the dressing room door. Even if they are the current Culture Minister, who might well be passing through on the way from a football match to another ministerial appointment. "Thank you, Prime Minister, for giving me this portfolio; I am indeed honoured to be your choice; and I would like to add that if there were any other way in which you felt I might serve my country, please don't hesitate to call on me."

The local MP doing a surgery day in his or her constituency does sometimes turn up, and is always welcomed.

'THE IMMINENT DEATH OF CLASSICAL MUSIC'. Headline. Classical music had seemed alive enough to me the day before in Liverpool, but you have to read this sort of thing, in case the journalist knows something you don't. This man thought that it's the question of the age. The age of the audience. The group that cares is getting older, and the new one isn't coming along behind. The forty-year olds who used to progress to classical music as they left their wild youth are now reluctant to give up dreams of eternal youth, and stay faithful to the old pop stars of their youth. It must be a consolation to look at them and think how young you look yourself.

Much as I hoped it was just newsprint fodder, it confirmed my decision to do the film. Maybe, when my time comes, I can join the other fading stars in the twilight world of fond memory. Bringing out new tracks which seem to run between the same terminal points, and with luck photographed through the mists of time.

I found a copy of the manuscript of Beethoven's op 109 online. It needs deciphering to a degree, but to a publisher used to seeing this sort of thing cross his desk it no doubt seemed clearer than it does to an untrained observer some two centuries later. An indescribable mess of ink early on, and shortly afterwards what look like visible signs of impatience. In other places, things were crossed out, chords reduced to one note, simplifying the texture. It is remarkable how this notably messy writing could be the expression of a very clear vision. It's almost as if he's trying to bypass the look of the score and communicate the sound to someone on his wavelength. Of course, Beethoven may have corrected anything that wasn't what he wanted at the proof stage.

I couldn't go on waiting for ever – you can miss the tide. It could be that actors can only really get their heads round all the subtleties in Hamlet when they're seventy-five, but it doesn't look very good if you need a stick to get round the stage. What we get from young men or women is a double supply of youth: their own, and what's written into the part. Opus 109 is a work for all ages. A masterpiece, but not a forbidding one. Schnabel and all the other old maestros have nothing to fear from me, except perhaps, that I am alive, and I should be playing it live for a few years yet.

Schubert's late sonata that I was pairing it with on the CD is, like Beethoven's, one of his last three. It's closer to me emotionally, because there's something about Schubert's confused way of life that seems to go with mine. It wasn't his bad experience with money, which wasn't my problem, or the chaos he lived in, or having had to share a room at one stage with a poet friend who was a depressive and eventually took his own life. Just the emotional thing. He rose above it – through substance, shape, reason, and his extraordinary modesty. When he wrote this piece, he'd enrolled for a series of lessons on how to improve his skills in writing music. When it came to the point, he had only the one lesson, because he'd gone by the time the second one was due.

**

Fixing Felicity's back

The Conservatoire work was rolling along nicely. When I explain things to students, I learn something about myself. Using words is hard, because words are chains to link thoughts and feeling together, or keep them locked apart. I have to find useful ones and, as much as I can, explain through music.

I saw Felicity Smith for the first time since her father's party. She made no reference to it, except to say how nice it had been to play a duet with me.

"I learnt such a lot being alongside you. The sheer concentration that comes off you when you play – that's something a young girl like me doesn't have."

"You'll get it, though."

I wondered whether her father was going to put any money into the film thing. She didn't mention that, and I didn't think it was fair to use her as a spanner to wrench cash out of her father.

It's likely that she didn't know anything about it. She was, reasonably, more concerned with the music she was learning, and that's what I got paid to deal with.

But even music which on the face of it is abstract can lead you where you don't want to go. The first movement of Schumann's G minor sonata is marked to be played 'as fast as possible'. But later, in the last bit, Schumann tells you to play 'faster', then 'even faster'. Not very logical. Felicity had a possible answer.

"Do you think he means you have to feel something that's absolutely the greatest thing you ever came across, and then somehow…there's more and then there's more. Like falling in love?"

"That's how falling in love could be, I suppose."

"That's how it is for me."

She looked ready to say more, but I changed the image.

"Or it could be like eating a box of chocolates, I suppose. Once you start you just keep on."

"I don't really think so. Love and chocolates. Are they the same?"

"Up to a point, in terms of what they can do for you." Both were denied me just then. Diet and absence of reasonable opportunity. I had to say something to get out of this ridiculous corner I'd been painting for myself.

"Maybe that's a subject you should discuss with your mother."

"Love and chocolates. Mother's told me all she's going to tell me about them. Enough to keep me out of weight trouble, or what the Victorians used to call 'trouble'. But not out of emotional trouble."

I shunted her back into playing the piano, which is why she'd travelled from Chelsea, and abandoned the talk about love and chocolates. Schumann asking for more and then more remains an interesting problem.

I had a more important problem to deal with. Practical. Hands-on practical.

Felicity sat well at the piano, but had a curious trick of bending over the keys as if she were trying to make more emotional contact with the keyboard. It makes playing harder. She needed straightening up, and I needed to do it. I had to make an issue of it, because there would be muscular pains waiting for her in the future if she didn't put this right.

But how the hell do you touch young girls sitting on piano stools without them texting their friends? Or the newspapers? It's bad enough for us piano teachers and worse for the ones who deal with breathing, like the woodwind teachers and voice teachers. Bring back the cane. The one you use to poke your pupils' backs or feet, as they did in ballet classes.

I told her that making music is physical, and tiring. That you find the easiest and most effective way of getting things to work – time and motion research.

"I know this," she says. "I'm sorry that I forget. Perhaps I should wear a Basque corset?"

What on earth was that? I didn't ask, because she giggled.

"Do I bend it too much, or arch it, do you think? My back?"

What on earth was she up to? Fortunately the Conservatoire, like most music colleges, has two pianos in its piano teaching rooms, so I sat at the other piano and showed her how I was taught to sit.

"Of course, I'm a man, and our weight is distributed differently, and it makes a difference. Do you want me to send you for some lessons with a woman teacher?"

"No I can learn all I want from you; I trust you."

I took off my jacket to show her how my back remains poised, easy, active, and ready to move.

"Can I touch you, to feel the way the muscles in your arms are, when you play?"

No, she can't feel the muscles in my arms, or anywhere else, and I need to answer.

"It wouldn't help, you know, because my male musculature isn't exactly the same as a female one."

I told her to have Alexander Technique lessons, which have helped many a musician, and for which the Conservatoire has a specialist teacher.

But somehow the whole thing felt rather out of hand. It had everything to do with playing the piano and nothing to do with playing the piano at the same time. I was feeling wholesomely physical. Unwholesomely physical.

"I'm going to straighten you up while you're playing. Is that OK with you?"

So I straightened Felicity up while she was playing. That seemed to be a fair compromise, and it diffused the situation. For her. Not quite for me. Touching her was…I didn't quite know what to make of it. Certainly not pure teacher and pupil. But equally not predatory male and desirable female. Because I wasn't at that stage. Not yet, and feeling that I never would be. Depressing, really. The incident with Deborah had been a welcome relief, but I had been on the receiving end of that – not the huntsman, more a willing prey. Why did she only do one-offs? Not fair.

My relationship with Patti seemed to have been my escape clause. Is that what was making me nervous? While we were married I didn't look at other women, that's for sure, and it's also fair to say that they didn't look at me.

Now I looked at them, and some looked back. What next? I wasn't sure. Felicity was very attractive. Nice to straighten up. Did she shift my attention from her hands to her…well, to the rest of her? Of course not. We were dealing with Schumann, who wrote this sonata for Clara Wieck over a period of eight years, during which he was falling in love. With her. I think I shall give up teaching.

I did my best to listen to what she was playing. My automatic pilot light heard a couple of wrong notes, and the odd tied note which was played twice. So that's what we dealt with. She was eighteen. The age of consent had been well passed. For her, at any rate. She was self-possessed, well-guarded, both by her parents and herself, and talented. She was also rich, or would be, unless there was some Chislehurst son squandering the overflow of Lord Daddy's money in nightclubs in the East Indies.

What's more, I had to be careful not to try to find in this eighteen-year-old the eighteen-year-old I found in Patti all those years ago.

It still nagged me: why Patti really went. We didn't discuss it, she and I, either before or after. Was it because I didn't let her move on? Her new husband (they must be married by now) didn't know her as a young girl. He knew her as a thirty-five-year old. And I didn't.

I spent a brief moment – a serious one – considering whether to go and get counselling. The Conservatoire had a counsellor, a nice woman, smart and sophisticated, but the last thing I wanted was a woman counsellor, and this might not be the best place to find what I needed, especially as I don't know what it was I needed. This was something between me and me. And music. I stayed on after Felicity's lesson and did some practice.

Next steps

There was an email waiting when I got back.

From *jane@curzprod.com*

We're in business. We've got some funding from some invisible trust 'devoted to the popularisation of serious music' set up by some woman not long dead. It seems she gave you a sort of bursary when you were a student? Her will wasn't properly written up but her even more invisible relatives decided that this was the sort of thing that she would have liked to do, rather than leave it to cats, and they are that rare thing, comfortably off and wanting to do some good. And they don't like cats.

Lord Chislehurst's interested too, and will pick up the shortfall, as long as we can produce receipts and keep it within reasonable bounds. It's in Josy's interest to bring it in on budget, because of where he's looking for the future.

Can we talk about items? He'll need to vet them for pictureability. I know that's not a word, because my computer's just underlined it, but I can't think of a better one. So write them up a bit, to give him a chance to visualise them.

Jane

I was committed. A good idea? Logical? Maybe not, but now it was someone else's problem too.

I looked at my list. An obvious one. 'Fire and Water' a working title, maybe. The 'Ritual Fire Dance' by Falla, and Chopin's 'Raindrop Prelude'. I knew it wasn't written as a description of rain, but people know it more than they know Debussy and his 'Gardens in the Rain'. 'Flaxen headed maiden' from him. They could surely find some blonde model to fill in for her. Liszt's Will o' the Wisp (*Feux follets*) should give some light effects. If Josy really wants to do a morning-to-night effect, we could have Bach to start the day, and Liszt's *Liebestraum* for bed and bitter-sweet dreams. Mme Cécile Chaminade's idea of autumn, *Automne*, which has leaves on the outside and a storm in the middle.

From *jane@curzprod.com*

Will, my dear one, things are happening. I've been looking carefully at your diary, and I am assuming that – how shall I put it? – since you are currently not married to anyone, you are by and large available. I've scheduled a couple of possible dates for recording the music for the film, and a week for the filming itself. Josy promises to get it done in that time. We need some rain for the Chopin's prelude, but there are ways of fixing that if global warming sends us a non-stop heat-wave in January. The spring and autumn shots will be faked because realism is not the issue.

Ellen Manning is to be your coach, and I've also pencilled some dates with her. One soon, so that you can come to terms with what you have to do. She'll come to your place because she wants to get to know the real you. I hope you don't mind, but I told her a bit about you, because you're just a man who plays the piano to her, and she'll want to give you a real going over so that you get aware of yourself and learn which are your best expressions and angles. You know. You can practise looking in the mirror, meanwhile.

I want to schedule the Beethoven/Schubert recording before the filming. That should give time for the two things to come out within a short time of each other – the CD first, then the film.

Does that look possible?

Let-me-know…Jane

From *will@williamwinton.co.uk*

I will make love to the mirror. As for finding the real me, I rather think I've left it around in little shreds wherever I've been. Talk soon. Will

Beethoven was living up to his reputation; movements one and three were going to be alright, in a condition to take impulsive thoughts. The second one wouldn't deliver; an angry scherzo one minute, a theatrical one the next. In a way, it's back to basics: I have to see him as a Titan, like Kronos. That's what I tell myself.

But if I got doubtful, I went to the Schubert sonata; he adored Beethoven, but in his own way, and he makes me weep at times, and smile with happiness too.

**

Life was busy. Getting the two sonatas up while keeping up with Chopin's Polonaises and Liszt's concert studies for their bicentenaries takes time. Fortunately my habits at the piano are good. I can practise for hours, if I want to, thanks to clever teaching I had when I was a kid, and I don't get tired. And I do a lot by just looking at the music. Music scores are pictures of music. Coded pictures.

I did some experiments with the mirror. Really looked at what my face tells me. Did I look different after my fireworks on Guy Fawkes night? I couldn't tell, because I didn't know what I really looked like before. Just thinking about my fireworks brought something into my eyes that I rather liked the idea of, quite apart from other sensations which I turned away from quickly.

Ellen Manning

Ellen Manning. Acting coach. In jeans and T-shirt. A lively face. Dark hair, curling slightly. Attractive? Was that the word for her? Something more, because you would want to look at her twice, and want to see her looking back at you.

"I'm Ellen. Ellen Manning. Your new acting coach."

I can't say I was feeling very relaxed about this. I'd spent my life working in a clearly defined area as a performer, and I'd become rather skilled at it. Once off the piano-stool, I was in a new performing country, and I was worried about how soon I would be found out. Inadequacy was something I was currently sensitive about. Still am. Especially if the decisions are being made behind my back, which was what had happened with Patti.

Just before my new instructor arrived, I'd changed what I was wearing a couple of times. It turned out that I'd settled for what she was wearing: jeans and a sort of loose top.

"I've never had an acting coach. I didn't know how to dress for this session."

"Working clothes like the ones you have on now." Small pause. She went on...

"You look younger than I expected."

"How old did you think I'd look?"

"I don't know. Successful classical pianist...I don't know anyone to compare you with. Perhaps I thought classical musicians lead a sedentary life."

"You thought I'd look sedentary?" Understandable. It's easier to play some instruments sitting down. Like the piano. But even the ones you can stand up to play are better played sitting down if you're going to do it for any length of time. I think musicians are as active as the next woman or man when not actually playing for a living.

101

"I'm thirty-five, going on thirty-six, and that's no secret, if anyone wants to find out. I won a competition nine years ago, and the papers said I was twenty-six then. You can't keep your age out of sight after that. I think I used to look older than I am, and older than I look now."

This was awkward talk. Slightly stretched awkward talk, as you might to a new doctor, perhaps. But the tone was light-hearted enough. Two professions crossing.

"But Ellen, you look younger than I expected. That's because you are younger than I expected. I thought you'd look like someone who specialises in rich vowels, "How-now-brown-cow" stuff, and have diamante spectacles on a gold chain dangling on your ample bosom."

"I can do the brown cow stuff if I'm asked to."

"You do this sort of thing for a living? You look good enough to be an actor, and yet here you are showing other people what to do."

"I am good enough to be an actor, but I like doing this too."

"Which is what?"

"Coaching actors. You sometimes see our names on the credits at the end of a film."

"I never watch long enough to see all of those. Who made the tea? For example."

"Very important all the same. Everyone is needed for something. All those technicians, for a start."

"We don't credit our technicians in concert programmes. The piano tuner, for instance."

"You couldn't do your job without them."

"I know. The only trouble with that is that we don't usually know until the day who's going to do it."

I liked the look of her, and the sound too.

"How do you coach actors? Or, why do you coach actors? I would have thought you engaged the ones that fit, and let them work it out for themselves."

"You do, and that's what they do best. But they sometimes need a bit of help from outside."

"Like when they've got to do a Geordie accent? Or the Brown Cow?"

"Sure. And a voice coach's ears lurking out of sight of the camera can be a big help. Making sure people remember to breathe, because sometimes it's easy to forget, would you believe? There's too much else going on."

"Will you be reminding me to breathe?"

"If I need to."

"I thought it was something we do naturally."

"We're not exactly doing a natural thing when we're performing, are we?"

True enough. I'd never thought of breathing in connection with playing the piano, but maybe I should have. Touching base?

"What else? How do I start? How many sessions will we have together?"

"Usually it's not many in a situation like this for a film; one session is not unusual."

"You mean I have to learn everything I need to know to carry a half-hour film on my own? In an hour? Now?"

"Not exactly. This isn't a normal case."

"I'm glad about that. My agent told me I'd have several sessions with you and she'd already pencilled them in. I thought for a moment there we were going to pencil them out."

"Not at all. This film revolves round you."

"That's what I thought and I'm not entirely confident about it, as you might imagine. Lots of tricks with the cameras, and then the things you do afterwards. That's what I'm relying on."

"You play the piano brilliantly, they tell me."

"How can I answer that? I play well, and I'm honest with the music I'm playing; it seems to please the people who listen to me doing what I do."

"And you look good."

"That's kind of you to say."

"It's true, and being honest about the material is important."

"I can play, I can look good, as you put it, but looking good is a stationary activity. I'm going to have to look good and move at the same time. I've no idea how to do that."

"Yes, you do. You're doing it now. We harness that up. Join it up. Connect."

"How many hours will that take?"

"Well, we have an agreement, your agent and I, that you should have as much time with me as you need. I'll also be around during the shoot and the post-production work. We will be a team and there will be cross-overs so that anyone can have an input."

"Don't you have unions that forbid you to do cross-over things? My former wife played in an opera orchestra and there were rules about who was allowed to do what. Obviously within the orchestra it was limited by the notes on the pages in front of you, but there were grades about whether some of the music qualified as a 'solo'. For which you get more money. On the stage, you could only move scenery if you were engaged to do it."

"We don't need those rules. We'll be a tiny ad hoc outfit."

"How many people?"

"I'm not entirely sure – not more than ten or so, I'm sure."

"What? So many? For a little film with only one character?"

"Even for a little film with one character…for a TV drama you could have a team of a hundred and fifty or so. And a major film would need hundreds."

"Scary."

"You're part of the team too, of course. We're all in it together."

"All of this for ME?"

"Yes, without you this wouldn't happen."

"I knew that when I said I'd do it, but now that it's getting closer…"

"You can do it. We'd never have got this far otherwise. There'd have been a reason to drop it. We have the backing for the project, which means that you and I will have as many sessions as it takes to make you realise how simple it is to fit in and reach your true potential. I'll be there all through the filming, as I said."

OK, so I was an actor.

We moved on.

"Can I ask if you've ever done any sort of acting? School play or something? Shakespeare for A level?"

"Yes, I did. I had a scholarship at a local boys' school. They did a Shakespeare play every Christmas term. When I was fourteen, I got the part of Maria in Twelfth Night. My voice started to change during rehearsals, and it sometimes flipped into a potentially male sound, and back again. I played her in glasses, because I couldn't see very far otherwise. Then when I was seventeen, I was Henry V, without glasses, because I was solid and could project the words. By then we'd started having girls in the sixth form, and there was no question of playing the French princess, although my French was very good by then. Not even her maid Alice. I would have made a lot of the last line of their scene, it's meant to be rude."

"How would you assess your performances?"

"On a scale of one to ten?"

"Ha. In your own words."

"It was some time ago. My Maria was rather ambivalent, because of the voice, and I played to that, since I didn't look anything like Sir Toby Belch's woman of choice. Henry was different, but I think it must be difficult to play him as anything but blokeish, even if I couldn't see much without my glasses…but there was never a problem with that, because I was the King, so everyone got out of my way."

"Sounds like a good line to follow."

"Grandpa used to say that he wished my poor mother, who longed to be a film star, had got as much talent as I had. However, the idea of going to RADA was never floated."

"How did you rehearse? Do you remember? You worked on the text and the subtext?"

"What I remember is that there was really only time to learn the words and understand them as best you could and then say them to the right person."

"Right. What did you think of the performance as a whole?"

"I don't think you could go wrong. We didn't interfere with the story and undermine the historical setting, the way I've seen since. We had to rely on each other and what we had memorised. For us that was terrific, it fired our imagination. We trusted Shakespeare, the way I trust Beethoven."

"It's a good way to begin."

"Good. So where do we start now?"

"Would you mind standing up?"

Ellen walked round me, as Josy had, looking at me all the time; I felt like a slave in a Roman marketplace. She thought the camera would have no trouble seeing me in the round.

"Now down on the floor, on your back, knees up."

"Could I have a cushion to put my head on?"

"That's allowed." She found one.

"Thumbs on waistband, rest of hand on your belly – abdomen if you like, and breathe normally, as if you were asleep."

"How do I know what I breathe like when I'm asleep?"

"Breathe as if you're going to sleep."

I tried.

"This is tidal breathing. Just breathe when you need to – just ordinary breaths like you do to stay alive."

We did more of that. I relaxed.

"Stand up now. Carefully. Sometimes men leap up and then feel light-headed. And you're too big for me to catch if you fall."

Then more exercises to find out where the tensions were and learning how to release them. I had no idea that breathing was so easy and yet how much I had to learn about it.

"You might well find this useful before you go on stage to play in a concert."

"Even at the piano, I guess, when I'm playing."

"Now some actor workout things to be done sitting down."

Harder. Much harder, and I didn't do very well. Those things which mean going inwards and bringing out what you find there.

Quick first-thought reactions to her words. That shouldn't really be a problem; you can even edit them if you're sharp enough: 'Light – dark. 'Cold – warm'. Nothing surprising, unless you want to be. 'Shakespeare: Marlowe'. 'Keats: Shelley'. 'Bach: Handel'. (She'd been looking at my programme, a good sign.) 'Chopin: George Sand'. (That caught her out a moment, and she went back to familiar tracks.) 'Father – son'. 'Mother – that could have been 'son' again, but I'd used it up on 'father'. Silence. What did 'Mother' mean to me? Even in a word game? Perhaps that's what went wrong with my marriage. Patti as Mother as well as Wife? Ellen watched me being silent.

I said, "Grandmother."

Pause.

"I've a list of your music. It starts with a piece called Autumn. Would you play it for me.?"

So I played *Automne*, Madame Chaminade's little piece, written for a good pianist, since she was a virtuoso pianist herself. Ellen liked it.

"And your face doesn't switch off either. Acting for films is delicate. Almost nothing. No Keystone Cops. Let's feed in some more things. Here's a line from a poem to get you going. 'My days are in the yellow leaf.'"

"Nice. Who's it by?"

"Lord Byron. I think the one line will do – one image should be enough. Yellow leaf. For autumn."

Sounded OK to me. I said it a couple of times and played the opening.

"That gets you into it. Now let's try something else. Kick ideas around, looking for things to turn corners."

"I'm up for that."

"Let your imagination off the hook."

We stayed with Autumn. "Play the last minute or so…then do a sort of warm down from playing…use words, sounds, gestures, whatever you like that keeps the mood and then brings you back home."

'My days are in the yellow leaf.' I thought of colours and autumn leaves, and I played the last bars. I looked at my hands for the last chords, slowly took them from the keyboard, straightened up, but with my head still bowed.

"Storm's over…air's cooler…drops falling from the leaves…breeze is still quite strong, *et m'emporte de ça, de là, pareil à la feuille morte."*

"What's that?"

"The last bit? A few lines of a poem by Paul Verlaine. *'The wind blows me me here and there, like a dead leaf.'* Came into my mind."

"It looks unhappy."

"I look unhappy, you mean?"

"Well, both. Like autumn, you could say. Now keep the thought, say that again or something like it – but whisper or mutter your English thoughts, then speak the French."

I started.

"Wait…needs the last moment or two of the music."

It worked again. I felt I was putting different strands of myself together. Weaving them, you might say.

"I could do a couple of lines before the music starts…"

"As in?"

"Les sanglots longs

Des violons

De l'automne.

"Sobs and music…"

Ellen got me to say the poem to myself. It's short, but covers a lot of ground, because the last verse is about an angry wind. Then I had to say it to her, trying to tell her something, although she didn't speak French, to make her understand the feeling behind it. Then I had to say it to her while playing the piano. Then to think it, without saying it, while playing the piano. Lovely games, full of growing sensual melancholy. I mean 'sensuous' of course.

"That would work in the final cut, mixing the words and the music. Josy would love it, since he's from somewhere in Europe, where they always like French films. I think."

"Debussy's Flaxen-headed girl prelude was based on a poem too," I said.

"Try that out for your homework," she said.

"I will. I promise."

"And if you could make a recording of you playing all the music and send it to me, with a few details, then I can get used to the sound.

"I need to be off now to report back to Josy, and tell him how you're doing."

"That sounds daunting."

"It isn't. We're looking for the ways to use your qualities to make a film which would be truthful, and add those things which only vision can add to music. We're a team, remember?"

I didn't tell her that I'd made sure that for the most part the music would stand up to whatever they liked to do to me. Almost. I hadn't seen Walt Disney's artists' ideas in *Fantasia* for nothing.

She left. I looked out my book of Byron poems and spent an hour trying to find the quote about the Yellow Leaf. I found what I was looking for eventually. The second verse in a poem called '*On This Day I Complete my Thirty-Sixth Year*'. Suspiciously right for me, although there were still some nine months to go. When I read the rest of the verse, it was clear why she said we wouldn't need it:

"*My days are in the yellow leaf:*
The flowers and fruits of Love are gone;
The worm – the canker, and the grief
Are mine alone…"

A bit too close to home, and I wished I hadn't discovered what it could feel like to be the age I was. I didn't want any invisible worms eating away at my bed of crimson joy, if I ever found one.

But Byron did something better for me. My second-hand *Don Juan* that I bought from a bookseller that I never met arrived. I read the first pages, and laughed twice. That did it. For the moment anyway.

**

I recorded my music and sent it to Ellen. I spent some time looking in the mirror, the second full-length mirror I'd just bought.

Patti took one of ours with her when we split up our goods and chattels. I disposed of the other, kept only my shaving mirror. Imagine – I didn't want a mirror in which she might have left her image. Of course I'd then bought a full-length replacement for professional reasons. I have to see myself as an audience might see me. And now I needed another mirror. So that I could see myself if the audience was in the round.

My place, my grandparents' house, was still in the process of being done over. Patti and I had started to do that a couple of years earlier, when we felt established financially. By this stage, we had done the bedroom – that was an irony in itself – and the bathroom, which was luxurious with two wash-basins, His and Hers, or, as it worked out, Mine and Mine, and a circular shower against the wall – that is, almost circular, more like a D shape, so as not to make the place darker. Quite a large D, because those were my heavier days. My latest thinking was to leave the rest of the house as it was. There was a room large enough for my piano, with double doors to another for rehearsals with other players if I'd a chamber music date coming up.

Now that I was learning to live as a bachelor, I didn't have to consider anyone's taste but mine, and this was the house where I'd spent a lot of my childhood. It still breathed something of my grandparents' air. Less and less of Patti's.

My books were coming back into the drawing room. They'd been piled up in the second bedroom, because Patti had pictures, which thankfully she'd taken with her. I hoped Keith liked them.

**

Liszt's concert study *Feux-follets – 'Will o'the Wisp'* – was on my film list. It needed a public airing before the recording. My concert programmes are all delivered and printed up in advance, but I decided to play it as an encore after the Liszt concerto that was scheduled for Hull later in December. *Feux-follets* always goes down well, even though many people don't know it. It's witty… Will o' the Wisp' is shooting lights in music, with shooting fingers to match. Quiet ending as the marsh lights disappear. A couple of moments before the applause arrives.

Beethoven made me anxious

Beethoven was making me anxious. It happens sometimes. The first careless moments of rapture meet reality head on. I had the notes, I was following the instructions in the score, the second movement had let me into its secret, and the last was growing in the right way. It was the first movement that was still hitting me with doubt. It starts serenely enough, maybe asking a question, if you like to put it like that, but then there's an interruption to the flow, as if this just isn't saying all Beethoven wants to. A new tragic interruption cuts across the path, just the way it had in my own life. That's how I identified it, and how I identified with it. But surely all the parts had to go in the same direction, and just then it had begun to look too much like a maze with nothing but dead ends round the corners. My fingers knew their job, and they gave glimpses of where I might go, but they weren't yielding up any unity. I needed to take a pace backward. I was trying to personalise some of these moments into those from my own life. Nothing wrong with accessing personal feelings, and nothing wrong with reacting like that as you listen, but is it a good idea to use them to drive someone else's piece? Rather than finding out what's going on without burdening it with your emotional problems?

I played it half a dozen times, without listening to myself. Played it at any old speed. And left it to mature by going and getting a cup of coffee.

When I came back, I played a prelude in B flat by Bach, which interrupts itself in mid-flow as Beethoven does. Yes. So this isn't just Beethoven and me occupying this hold-up; it belongs to other people too, who aren't living out their disappointments through someone else. I needed to come in through another door, try to speak Shakespeare as if Samuel Becket had written it. It's not a bad exercise, as long as you know what you're doing. I tried playing Beethoven as if Liszt had written it, Liszt at his showiest. I went for some glitter, played it faster, showier. Of course it didn't work, but it wasn't meant to. It was meant to clear my mind.

My pupils and their problems...

My pupils were doing well. They were getting more of my time just then, with a couple of extra lessons. Make-up lessons they're called, with no make-up except what you come in. My Japanese students, Horace and Michaela (which was how they wanted to be known in English) wanted to do two-piano work together. Their conscientious teacher was making them learn solo pieces, studies and such, to give them more to bring to the keyboard when they sat at two pianos. It's harder to make a career if you need two pianos for your concerts. It's alright if all you do is glide around the major concert halls in the world, where there are two good pianos on site. But when you're in the country, away from the major cities, you're lucky to get one good piano. That's when you access the wonderful things written for four hands intertwining their music on one keyboard. Duets.

Gary was talking about going in for a competition, and I put him on hold. I didn't think he would win, but it shouldn't do him any harm, as long as he was patient with the jury.

And then there was Felicity. I gave her extra time, because – oh yes –because I enjoyed working with her. She was like a lamp that lit up. She stimulated me; by which I mean she asked questions, questioned my answers even. That's a proper student-teacher relationship, not 'tell me what to do and I'll do it'. Give them the facts, and let them make up their own minds. With some advice.

She mentioned in passing that her father had told her he had some project involving me – filming, she seemed to think. She was obviously very curious to know more about that, but I wasn't playing this game, even though she did drop a hint that she might like to come and watch. And that if Daddy was putting up some of the money, how could I object? She didn't exactly say that, but it was there.

There was no way that was going to happen if I could help it. I hadn't given it a thought, but I wanted as few people as possible watching me make my first steps before the camera. I'm not unknown to the camera, but all I'd done was treat it like a wandering eye. I'd never done filming before, and I would rather be alone with my mistakes. Apart from the crew. I told her she could come and turn pages for me when I recorded my Schubert and Beethoven CD. That dealt with that.

Josy Calls

I had a call from Josy; he wanted to come round to see me in my native habitat. At least, I thought that's what he said. I was prepared to believe his English was improving daily, but the telephone is not kind: it emphasises words at the expense of meaning. It didn't help in his case that he was overlaying his accent from wherever with an American one.

He reckoned he had a slant on the whole thing. It turned out to be the one Jane said it was. Morning to evening, everything linked to the clock, like a Book of Hours.

The twenty minutes of his film that Jane had found for me on the net didn't show more than twenty minutes of sheep chewing or being herded a bit. It looked good, if short on action.

Then he appeared.

I'd got back rather late the night before from a concert in Reading. Mostly Chopin, but for the last encore I played *Automne*. One of the women came round afterwards and told me that her grandmother had played it to the composer herself, Mme Cécile Chaminade. It's always interesting to get a direct line to a composer, especially a dead one, so I asked her what Mme Chaminade had said to her grandmother. She had smiled and said, "That was lovely, darling," in French.

Josy was settling in to London life, he said. The money from the trust fund behind this enterprise had given him confidence.

"I like your new look," I said. He did look different. On the way, perhaps. Cleaner, certainly. And he was making inroads into English.

I started with a polite question. "How do you like London?"

"I just love it. It's special." New friends, and maybe some admiration for his film…the hair had a sweeter-smelling disorder, and so had he.

"I just like love your house." Different company, new vocabulary already. New grammar too, or lack of it.

"We could come and film you here, to make everything real for the fantasies that take off in the music to make a contrast."

Not possible. I wasn't going to tidy up my studio, or the bedroom; and I wasn't aiming to share my bathroom with anyone at the moment – certainly not the general public.

"No, it wouldn't work. I have lovely neighbours and I am very careful not to disturb their lives with my practice. I regulate it. I am soundproofed as far as I can be. Seeing even one movie camera coming in, with someone to work it, would mean they might feel their privacy was being de-privatised. Sorry."

"Tell me about your life in this place."

"Not much to tell. I'm a reconstructed bachelor. Quiet life."

"Apart from the girls." He laughed. Definitely different company.

I ignored it. It wasn't his business, and if that was what he wanted to think, he was welcome.

"I just love the music – this music you've chosen."

"You know it?"

"I do now. Your lady Jane sent me recordings."

No doubt by all the top pianists of the last fifty years. I hoped he wasn't going to expect me to be Ashkenazy and Rubinstein and Gina Bachauer rolled into one.

"But they don't look like you. Some of them are dead, and some were women, so that would be hard." He laughed.

"Now, what do you do in your house?"

"I'm a pianist."

"I know that. I read my contract." He was a joker. "I mean, how do you live?"

"I have to practise – keep in trim at the very least, and learn new pieces."

"What do you do when you are not practising?"

"I'm away quite a lot. I'm lucky enough to have a good career, and a good agent. I read. A great deal."

Josy looked at the books.

"I see."

He didn't inspect them.

"And…"

"I watch television a little. I watch films sometimes. I sit and think. I listen to music on Radio 3. I keep notes for a diary." I decided to qualify that last remark. "Just a note of how my concerts went." I didn't want him thinking I was going to write my memoirs. It might alter our way of talking to one another.

"Nothing very exciting, really." I ended, in case he might be disappointed that I wasn't wilder.

"Maybe not…but it's you: a good simple, straightforward life, like the peasant farmers in my last film." The idea of being close to the earth pleased me. "So, what do you do when you get up?"

"What?"

"I need to know. We do a day in your life – like reality TV, you know. Explain a little more for me."

"Right. Shave and shower, breakfast. Some exercises for my muscles, and I play the piano. First thing I play each day is some Bach. It's a habit. It activates my brain, and it does my fingers a bit of good too."

"Exercises for your muscles?"

"Yes. I'm going to use them, so I limber up."

"We will make your house in a studio. A false house. I want to show you as an ordinary guy, in ordinary circumstances, doing the ordinary things you do, then taking off into your imagination. Having dreams while playing the piano."

"What do you mean by 'ordinary circumstances'?"

"You know – like anyone."

I could try to do that.

"We start the day with you and Bach. Bach would be cool and clear like water on a summer's day. Bach is the German for a stream, you know."

I did know, but I don't think of Richard Strauss as a bunch of anything.

"Like the water you would dash on your face after shaving."

"I hope we don't have to be too realistic," I said.

Then he thought that the whole thing could work as a film within a film. I would watch the tele at breakfast, and see myself playing; the image would become reality, while remaining imaginary, as I watched myself on the screen, and drifted into my own thoughts. Something like that. Maybe I didn't quite understand what he was getting at.

He thought some improvisation would help.

"You must go on working with Ellen. I really trust her Sense and Sensibility," he said.

That cheered me. Josy read Jane Austen. But it turned out that he just knew the title of the film.

He got me to play the piano, and listened, as well as looked. He said he was relieved I didn't suck my teeth, blink, breathe heavily. How many musicians had he seen?

And that was it, for the moment.

First scenario

Josy sent me my scenario. I was to be seen shaving. Then I was to open the window and inhale the studio air as if it were fresh with lilac blossom. I don't have lilac in my Dulwich garden; I would have to imagine the night-scented stock grown every year so that, coming home after work, there was fragrance to welcome us. Me, I mean. A few gentle early morning things, stretch, yawn, walk through the door. In the background, until the music starts, there will be a gradual fade-in of natural morning sounds – the street outside, water running into the basin. Like the beginning of 'The African Queen', he said. Wasn't that the film with the noise that turned out to be a congregation singing a hymn?

"I'm not quite sure about that. And what will I be wearing while I do this?"

"Oh yes. Well, we decide on that later…"

"Right," I said.

I was supposed to catch sight of me playing Bach on the huge television screen.

"I don't have a huge television screen. I live here alone."

"Is not important – it's not important – it will be brought in special. Specially."

Me in some early morning clothes watching me playing Bach in some special early morning clothes, on screen. Then they would film me walking around, feeling at home, amused by the sight of me playing.

"Then you go to the real piano. And play. We cut from you playing real to you on TV screen."

I made a non-committal noise.

"Trust me baby. I want you to get the feeling of your own place, like being at home here."

Then I would be seen finishing a cup of coffee, then the fire and rain, and the autumn leaves, then…well, we would improvise, invent as we went.

I wasn't sure how this would work, but he was the director, and he had a reputation for making films that covered a period of several days, if not months. It could well be that it would work for half an hour. In a mock-up of where I lived.

**

Now Beethoven wouldn't let me go. The music goes round and round. It's there when I wake up. When I go to sleep. In this case, it was welcome, because at last Patti came into my mind less. She was still coming back to hurt me; I was still blaming myself, and not her…

But the thought was beginning to grow that I didn't really do her wrong, as Johnnie did to Franki. I just got her wrong. I know it takes two to make a divorce, but I couldn't blame her, or her new man. It pained me to realise that the man she married, and who was scheduled to be a very good father to the children we didn't have, was – is – just ordinary. I wondered what she'd have made of me, this new me? Would it have just been the old me, tricked out differently?

At any rate, my feelings were still alive. Perhaps waiting for the curtain to go up and the show to begin. No, that's a muddled thought. I was beginning to make myself look at people with a 'view to a possible relationship' like the people seeking partners in the papers. All the same, I wasn't intending to commit anyone to another life sentence with me, because marriage should be about loving, not a long-term insurance against falling in love again. Poor Patti. Poor me.

The sessions with Ellen promised to do something or other.

Session two and an exterior

"Have you had the time to do some more work?"

I had thought about it a lot, researched on Wikipedia to find connections behind the music, if they didn't get too far-fetched. Even if they were. Looked at my face as often as it would let me.

My recording of the music was ready to play.

Ellen had other music on her phone.

"Shall we dance?"

"Naturally. The immediate point being to…?"

"Let's dance, and you can guess."

Was I supposed to take her in my arms? No, she started to dance on her own.

She choreographed me, just by the way she moved. That was something in itself, something else. Almost like a workout: on the spot releasing, tensing, doing what unformulated dancing can do. No lessons or books of steps, like the ones my grandparents had. Quickstep, fox trot, waltzing in reverse, samba, even.

Interesting. I hadn't danced for some time. A four stone heavier time. My new body liked what it felt. Most musicians have a good sense of rhythm which gets into the whole system. They don't necessarily express it with dancing. What I expect from the muscles that get turned on with this amount of movement needs some thought. Who am I? How can I show that? It seems a good way to find out. Twist and turn, stop and start, stretch and contract, slow down, get faster, manic even.

Ellen was somewhat breathless. "You really surprise me. Did you like that? Did it release anything?"

"You could see."

"Suppose you dance on your own. Just for you. I'll not be here. Not even watching from a hiding place. I'll walk in, be interested in what I see, and you will make me join in, just by the way you look, by the movements you make."

"I'll try that. Have you got a track that starts, like me waking up, then whatever…surprise me."

116

"Something close enough. Remember you have to make me want to dance with you."

Ellen set the music going. It was a slow beat. I closed my eyes and went with it. I didn't see her leave the room. I turned about, no mirrors to watch me. Stretching, growing small, opening up, preening, strutting – then suddenly the music changed mood completely. Reaction a bit slow, I thought; Ellen opened the door, coming in, surprised, curious, "What's he doing on his own like this?" All by gesture in rhythm, dance inviting an answer. "Waiting for you." Exhilarating, making a small drama out of social dancing.

Ellen stopped the music.

"Do you come here often?" she said.

We laughed, because we had made contact with no specific meaning or purpose.

"To this moment, you mean? To this feeling of release? Not like this. Coffee?"

We took a break.

"We arranged to have some time free this morning, if the weather was good, which it is."

"You have a plan."

"It's called 'into the woods'. Some external shots for our library. Rob is on his way with his roving camera to take us out to Burnham Beeches, where there are still enough autumn leaves on the ground in late November to be walked through."

"Do I have to wear anything special? Do you want to inspect my wardrobe?"

"I leave that to you. Jeans and any sort of blue sweater that will keep you warm. And waterproof trainers."

"No problem."

"Before you change, I've another exercise now that you've limbered up. Walking."

"Walking?"

"Sad walking. Autumnal walking about the year that's past, the winter that's coming. Here's another track of music to put you in the mood. You probably know this song…'Autumn Leaves'. It seems appropriate."

Ellen sensed my hesitation. "Something wrong?"

"No…no…I know it well." I wouldn't go there, from choice, there are too many emotional traps, but these confused feelings are ones I must confront, and lighting this fuse could be a way of defusing them. She went on.

"Yves Montand. The leaves are being swept up, along with regrets and memories. These are emotions that the leaves remind you of. Let them invade your whole body, and then control them. There may be some hope, because they are things in the past…I don't want to prompt you, so I'll leave you to it."

It turned out to be easier than I expected, because I knew this road, and I didn't go very far down it. Just enough to make my walking hesitant, intermittent.

**

Rob was our Director of Photography ("cameraman" to me, but I was going to learn about job descriptions as I went along). He had his four-wheel drive, and drove us to Burnham Beeches, in search of leaves. Yellow leaves. Byron's leaves. Prévert's *feuilles mortes*. The sun let out occasional rays, as if to photograph them for springtime, Ellen said.

It was light enough to get some images but not enough to make it look too jolly. *Automne* has black notes enough in the music to suggest that.

Ellen got Rob to spread some of the leaves around from the piles which some hard-working keeper had amassed.

"Is that such a good idea, when I'm a law-observing pianist?"

"Oh, Rob'll put them back," she said. He can't have heard her, because he didn't.

I walked among these leaves, picking my way, sometimes looking down, sometimes up, while Rob filmed me from a distance, then on a re-run from close to, as I walked towards him. This was my first moment of acting for the camera, but with the setting and power of the song in my mind, my fellow workers seemed to think it gave me a resigned, nothing-else-will-happen look.

The middle part of Chaminade's piece is stormy. We had to think of something which would go with that. Rob showed me how to kick, as in kicking a football. Embarrassing, because it was something I hadn't done since I was about eight years old. I defend that by thinking that professional footballers maybe haven't played the piano much since they were eight. I did it, not by being the footballer I wasn't, but by being angry and taking it out on these leaves that had died, turning round, punching the air, punching anything I could think of that seemed wrong or unfair. Therapy among the trees.

Rob borrowed my trainers and did some close-up footwork, making me hold the camera. I held it as steadily as I could. He was noticeably more expert than I was, both with a camera (it was his job) and with football-kicking leaves (it wasn't). He did a few dives around in a long shot. By then, he was showing off. They were likely to be completely wasted because this wasn't me, not even in a long shot. He was good, and any thoughts I harboured about impressing Ellen receded. My left and right leg control is best exercised using the pedals on the piano, or driving a car. Basic male instincts were reviving, because I didn't enjoy being outdistanced by Rob.

Then we had to stand off camera, all three of us, and breathe in relays, so that there was misty breath about the place. Otherwise people would think you never left the studio.

Rob dropped us back at my place.

Ellen stayed on to develop a few thoughts on the Raindrop Prelude. Not Chopin's title, but the repeated notes could well suggest it. I tried to deflect Ellen from real rain by suggesting we could use an Edith Sitwell poem, 'Still falls the rain'. I looked out my copy. It's a beautiful poem...

"Blind as the nineteen hundred and forty nails Upon the cross."

Those 1940 nails are about the blitz on London. To be read again and thought over again and remembered again. But not for us at that point.

Or for Chopin.

Verlaine's poem with the line '*as it rains down on the town*' was written in prison, or at least about prison, so that had the wrong overtones too.

It looked like being real rain – and I'd have to get used to the idea of getting wet. And think about a reason why.

More emails

Email to *jane@curzprod.com*

Acting training is going alright, just, and I'm relying on the untold skills of camera work and retakes and editing to get me by. The public is supposed to be listening to the music, as well as watching. The Raindrop Prelude, though, begins to look as if it's going to involve rain. Real rain. Me going out in the rain. ON PURPOSE. It's something I avoid for health reasons. Please deal with this, and include insurance in my fee, and maybe have trained medical help standing by. It won't be enough to tell me that you got a badge for First Aid at school.

Will

To *will@williamwinton.co.uk*

Trust me. Ellen is pleased with you – thinks they already have some great footage (footballage, even – thought you were very adaptable about that) and she thinks your face will shape up nicely, with some really usable expressions. She thinks you are really photogenic…one of those people the camera will love…

Cheer up. It will be great. I will intervene if the rain gets heavy. With an umbrella. Singin' in the Raindrop Prelude. You know…

When the time comes, I intend to be there for you.

All best Jane.

To *jane@curzprod.com*

It's nice to know I'm loved, even if it's only by a digital camera.

By the way, can you let my employers know that I want to record some extra music, just in case they want something during the credits at the end? Two little Songs Without Words by Gabriel Fauré which I do as a final encore to send the customers out happy.

I'm glad you'll be there at the filming. But can you guarantee it? What about your other artists?

Will

To *will@williamwinton.co.uk*

I'll manage. Don't get jealous. I admit I do two-time you with others; after all, if you were my only artist, I'd have to take more of your money as my commission, and much as you love me, I don't see you agreeing to that. Do you?

Two points…

We have a new recording producer who will look after the recording of the film music. A very clever young woman called Victoria Baldwin, greatly recommended by Steve Hamilton, who did the sound for your film CD – remember?

A vague plan for October next year:a festival somewhere in Italy, I can't remember where, but prestigious. You will be one of the featured artists, along with Kerri Burston, who's an opera singer, former winner of a big American *prize for the best performance by a newcomer in the US of A. I don't know how long ago that was, but it still figures large in her CV. Couple of concerts each with a chamber orchestra, and then a shared concert: i.e. you will play and she will sing at the same time, well, only sometimes at the same time… She's a real star-in-the-making, her agent says, with publicity pictures to prove it. I don't know how old they are, but they can't be that old, can they, or she would be a star NOW, wouldn't she? Heard one of your concerts a couple of years ago and loved your playing. She'd heard rumours about you, and I had to send pictures of the New You. She wants to use you because she wants someone on stage with her to look good, and she wants the audience to believe there's some chemistry between you when you appear together., She's eager to meet with you, as the Americans say. Give it a whirl. Lots of dosh. She has a protector, it's said. Think it over. And be careful – from all points of view. No point if you end up needing a protector to protect you from her protector. Jane*

I wasn't as desperate as that, I didn't think.

**

Organising the school concert

Felicity asked me if I would go down to her old school to play.

The sooner the better, really. Could we do it before Christmas?

I could. Sometimes concert dates thin out then, as the local demand for carols gets going; some of the big halls go over to pantomime, or ballet, depending on their public.

"It's very short notice, isn't it?"

"Well, yes, but…well, I was going to play on my own, and then I sort of thought it might be really nice if you came and played too. There'll be a good audience – it's dinner and all that – happens each year, with a different sort of slant."

Her father had something to do with it, and if she didn't exactly mention the bit about him putting money into my *Fire/Water* project, she could well expect a quid for Daddy's quo. Some music scholarship fund would benefit, and would I go and play for a fraction of my usual fee plus a magnum of champagne. I think they had a pre-conceived idea about my private life.

They were going to charge a lot for the tickets, because they were having a chef to cook the dinner. For this sort of thing, I usually find it easier just to send a donation, rather than turn up and be sociable at the dinner before I play, which can take a long time, depending on the number of courses they think the ticket is worth. I know that's better than hanging around outside with the servants as musicians had to in the bad old days – as I did in my own student days of playing at "Dinners". I agreed for ten per cent of my fee, but on condition that the playing would be after the preliminary drinks and before the eating, which meant I could be a social asset at the meal (I don't hold my knife like a pencil and don't talk with my mouth full). We would both play, Felicity and I. No problem there. And I would tell them how much music means to any sensible school.

She had Chopin ready to play, and that would give her a chance to shine. For me, one or two dazzlers with the cocktails, and then a duet or two – Dvorak's dances are good, and you don't have to do all the repeats...

It was a stop-over job, and I needed to make sure there was nothing in the diary for a couple of days afterwards. The business of being what people expect you to be – an artist, charming and maybe a bit peculiar, with one or two stories, not about colleagues – can be exhausting, even though I am, of course, naturally charming and just a bit peculiar. The school had excellent guest accommodation, Felicity said, and it might well be so, considering the sort of parents who send their girls there. For fees I could only guess at.

I talked to the Principal (the Headmistress, I suppose in other times) and the Chairperson of Governors. They professed they were thrilled, although they thought it rather short notice, and they could have advertised it more if they'd known. I wasn't too sure that my name would have made all that much difference, since it was the event that mattered. It was a fund-raising dinner for the scholarship, part of the run-up to Christmas. Just after the school play and the night before the Carol Concert, with an exhibition of some of the girls' paintings and sculptures, or other artefacts, making a sort of Arts Festival. Good for the girls, all likely to go into the higher reaches of education or marry into money, and either way good for their development. It also meant that the parents who might have to come from a distance could have a day or two in the London area, and do some pre-Christmas shopping and theatre-going, once they'd seen the school play.

More work for the film

Meanwhile there was Ellen and more limbering up. Josy had been looking at what we did in Burnham, and he'd detected a touch of self-consciousness, even in the way I walk. It wasn't a problem in the bits we'd done, because it's the leaves that matter, and the odd swing of the leg that wouldn't get near the goal in an under-11 match could be disguised. Rob looked fine in the distance, and could almost be me, and would be by the time the mists come swirling in – mists and mellow fruitfulness, you know, she said. The mellow fruitfulness sounded intriguing, but I didn't think it meant anything more than a bit of Keats to throw into the ring with Paul Verlaine. And Byron's Yellow Leaf or leaves.

Self-consciousness, which I could well understand. All I do in public is walk on to a stage, bow, sit down, stand up, bow or wave, or applaud the audience, or the orchestra if I've been playing a concerto, shake hands with the conductor, if there is one, and the leader of the orchestra, and walk off again.

I had to get more physical.

Leg-stretching…

"It'll do you good, what with you spending all that time on a piano stool."

I was good at standing on one leg and pulling my other leg up behind me.

"I actually do work out," I said.

"Sure you do, but how often?"

"Well, I'm in a busy playing patch." The truth was that I hadn't got round to anything for a few days.

Ellen gave me a set of exercises to do at home, every day, to go with my Frankie collection. To give me more choice, to put me in control. She gave me some back movements too, rumba ones from side to side, and one involving pelvic flexibility which put some others into my head. She changed the subject.

"I'd like to come to the session when you record the music, if you don't mind. Two days are booked in January, Jane told me. She said you wouldn't need that long, because you are quick."

"That's the easy part. I'm not so sure about the rest of it. It's got to come out right for me, or I'll look at my contract to see if there's an escape clause."

She looked at me. "Don't worry. You'll be OK. And I'll be there."

She kissed me. And went. That was nice, disturbing, and probably unwise. I wished she hadn't done it. As it turned out, she never did it again; her thoughts must have been running parallel with mine.

This wasn't part of the scenario with Patti, no unexpected kisses there. We had been settled people; created by nearly fifteen years of safe sex, by which I mean no special thrills, just comfort for two. Comfort for one, apparently, and getting safer all the time by being more infrequent…And the action with the lady in Aberdeen – Fiona? – there was something about her kissing that killed desire. It was an expression of her own passion, rather than an invitation to anyone else's. I think that's what that was. And only one kiss with the writer, Deborah. Afterwards.

What about Ellen? She knew more about me than I knew about her. I thought she might have a boyfriend. An actor, or someone who wrote plays. Or just someone. I hadn't liked to ask, and I wasn't going to rush out of the house and call down the street after that kiss…maybe she was just being friendly. But I liked the idea that she wanted to come to the recording. Even if it was only as part of her work, looking for ideas to talk over with Josy.

The filming place

Email from *jane@curzprod.co.uk*.

The studio for the filming is not a studio but a location. I'm told this is absolutely normal, which is why they thought they could try filming you in your own house. So it's not a studio as such, it's an old Victorian village school in Kent. Cut off by a new main road from its natural hinterland and its source of children. Replaced some time ago somewhere else by an up-to-date version, probably now needing updating itself. As schools do.

It's been bought by a couple who had a corner shop in the village. I spent quite a lot of time in it when I was staying with my aunt along the road from them. Their place became very interesting to a posh supermarket. The village itself has become a sort of halfway suburb between London and the Chunnel.

They cashed it in for a good price, so the rumours say, and bought the school, which had meanwhile been a sort of hostel which failed.

Colin and Kate are making it over for themselves: their home with maybe a B&B business and certainly a separate long-term renting unit in what used to be the children's lavatories. Suitably de-odorised. The money from our project will let them complete the works. To date they've got the upper floor set up as two bedrooms. See attachment for further details.

J

Attachment: Note on the recording venue.

The ground floor was the main assembly hall for the school, more or less as it was on the day the school closed…we're talking small scale. They used to divide it up into two classrooms with a space between the two of them. There's a playground cut into the side of the hill behind the school, so small that it looks as if the children would have had their playtime class by class; and two solid brick-built buildings which were the lavatories – one for the girls and one for the boys – running water, and not just the water which runs down the hill which the school was built into. There was a roof between the school and the outhouses to keep the little ones dry if they needed to be excused. It was rotting, so there isn't one now. I've checked up with the unit who'll do the filming. It's a temporary company put together on the advice of Lord Chislehurst, who knows about these things. And there is plenty of space to do the shoot. A special team will be assembled by Rob, whom you know already – the expert cameraman you played football with among the leaves. What helps is that no sound will be recorded here, because all your playing will be pre-recorded, and although there will be a real piano for you to play, that won't get in anyone's way, or else that would make the whole thing more complicated...

NB 'complicated' = 'expensive'.

The place is quiet, but not exempt from aeroplanes heading in towards Gatwick, or noise from traffic, including some farm vehicles, or an occasional horse – there are stables just up the road. So there could be the odd moment when a microphone pricks up its ears at the sound of hooves. Not, as I said, an issue.

My friends, by the way, are taking off for a visit to their daughter in Canada in February. Perfect for us, but maybe a bit cold for them.

Lord Ch. has OKed the money and his unit thinks it will work well.

We can go and have a look at it together if you like.

Jane

PS It will still be January for the sound recording.

This was going to be a new experience for me, in a field with considerable potential in the anxiety area, so I welcomed the idea of going to look at the place beforehand to take some of the edge off that.

Email to *jane@curzprod.co.uk.*

All sounds OK to me, if someone's opinion who knows absolutely nothing at all about the system is of any value. I have to add that it seems very money-consuming. I hope a) that there's enough money to cover it and b) that I can deliver whatever is needed in the way of talent to justify it.

125

I leave the financial worries to you, and my contract too. I don't want to lose money, that's all. Or to miss the chance of making money if, as you said in one of your persuasive moments, it could free me up to do some special projects of my own. And to continue to pay the costs of my hair-styling.

And yes, let's go and look at your friends' place. Together. A date? Will you drive?

With an anxious sigh,
Will

An email in quick reply from *jane@curzprod.co.uk*.

Will, my dear one, rest assured. Lord Chislehurst is not only a rich man, he has wide contacts and much experience of financial matters. He expects to make money out of this, even if all you were to do was sit at the piano and let the camera look at you for half an hour. He will get the technical people on some sort of contract which will cover them for their studio work, and then for the post-operational stuff. I suspect with a low immediate payment plus bonus built in if it's a success. Which he believes it will be. He can always sell his Picasso, if there's a shortage of cash.

Just keep smiling. And teaching his daughter as brilliantly as you do with all your students.

And mark those February dates in your diary, as I already have.

Lie easy, and sleep well. There will be a team to support you. And remember that what you do so well is at the centre of this: you play the piano, just believe in that.

Jane
PS You look good too.

Answered with another quick email from me:

Is it widely known that there's a Picasso in his house? No wonder he has so many bars on the windows – Picasso serving a prison sentence. By the way, Lord Chis doesn't own the Picasso; it belongs to his mother-in-law. But I daresay he has other resources. I will take your word for it.

Can I see if Ellen could come too on this trip, if she's free? She might give me some ideas of what to expect. She knows the way round this filming business, and I don't want Josy at this stage, unless he knows a lot about old school buildings. Which doesn't seem likely. And Ellen is my coach, although we will go in your car, since you know the way! William

**

We went down together, the three of us.

We followed the road towards France. The hills begin to rise to the left of the motorway. Our school road looked unimportant although it has A status, and Jane drove straight past our destination. Satnav time.

It looked like a village school, Victorian, solidly built to last.

No thin walls here. A nice garden in front, with a solid double door entrance.

Colin and Kate came out in response to the crunch of car wheels on the drive. They hugged Jane.

"How long is it since we last saw you? You were a little girl then and you haven't changed a bit. Well, perhaps a little."

"You're the ones that haven't changed."

"Come on in, all of you. William and Ellen, it must be."

We got a sight of the garden at the back stretching up the hill.

"We inherited the vegetation – you can't get plants to grow that high and look so fertile between signing the contract and moving in," Colin said.

"It's nice isn't it?" Kate said. "We're still getting things done, which is why we're letting you in for your project. We intend to use the rent you'll be paying to get on with the rest.

"The ground floor is continuous; there were two classes here. Infants, you know, and wooden and glass foldable doors to keep the little ones apart and make a corridor down the middle. As you can see, this is now just one big space.

"The girders are to keep the upstairs where it belongs. This will be two living rooms and an entrance hall. The back of the hall is already made over into a roomy kitchen, with a downstairs cloakroom. Lovely old stairs – there must be some trees missing up there on the hill – to take us up to the headmaster's old living quarters. We've done that part into two bedrooms and two bathrooms. We can camp out to eat, but not to sleep."

Colin took us through the back door, waving at the kitchen as we passed by.

"This is the way out to the garden, which is up there beyond the little playground. It'll be where we sit out to eat when the weather plays into our hands. Not a lot of sunshine, but lots of light and privacy. Over there, on the other side of the play area, are the lavatories. We'll add to that, and make a unit

127

which we can let. Water and some sort of local drainage is already supplied. You are very kindly going to equip some of that as a bathroom, I believe, complete with shower and basin and hot water, which fits in very well with our plans for the work. And you have generously agreed to make that over to our specs for us when you've finished with it."

Jane had obviously assured them that there was money in our kitty. Lord Chislehurst's money. I don't know if the cats' trust fund had been sidelined anyway, so that if there was any profit, it would all go in his lordship's direction.

"As you can see, work's begun on that. The local plumbers are in there breaking things up and fixing other things."

Kate had made coffee.

"You'll be wanting to have a look at your working area, the classroom area."

"It's a good size for a single character movie, isn't it?" Ellen said.

I had no idea. "Certainly we can get a piano in. And there'll be some furniture to make me look at home, won't there?"

"There'll be some pieces, I imagine. Brought on when they're required. There won't be a lot of room, what with the lights and the cameras, and the green screens which will be used for CGI."

"CG…?"

"Computer generated images. Scenery put in afterwards. They could be quite big."

"So I could be anywhere. That sounds a bit daunting."

"Don't worry. You'll know what you're supposed to be looking at or not looking at, if it's behind you. It could be action shots. And we won't dress you in green, or you'll disappear."

"Right." I obviously infused the word with anxiety.

"There'll be no problem. You can do this, after the exercises we've been doing."

"If you say so."

"You'll have people around you, keeping out of your way when there are takes, of course. When there aren't, they'll be moving about, fixing lighting, camera angles, making sure you look the same from shot to shot for the retakes."

"Where's the control room going to be – with the screens for Josy and you to monitor my behaviour on?"

"There isn't one. We'll all be in this same school room together. This is the way it would have been if we'd done it in your house."

"Right."

"We'll be looking after you, believe me. Tender, loving care for our principal asset. Our only asset."

"It all depends on me."

"You'll do just fine, Will. Be excited. Be a new man."

"Perhaps I need some more intensive coaching. How about tomorrow?"

We agreed on lunch and then intensive coaching. Seriously intensive coaching.

More thinking time

I spent time chasing ideas and thoughts about my pieces.

How do you put Debussy's blonde girl on to the screen? The girl with *cheveux de lin* was a Scottish girl in Leconte de Lisle's poem. I can think of Debussy's music as a love-song, because that's what the poem is. The man talking to this beautiful blonde girl, with her cherry-red mouth, her long eyelashes and her curls, is a huntsman, out to find deer, partridges; he forgets all of that at the sight of her. The music is her portrait as he falls in love with her. I'll work on that.

Another lover in Liszt's *Liebestraum*. It's not short of meanings you can put into words since it began life as a song with a poem. Complicated meanings, because Ferdinand Freiligrath, who wrote it, was a complicated man. He had radical ideas which didn't suit the people in power, so he spent a long time in exile in London.

He's giving us good advice. You must seize true love when you can, and treasure it; take care not to hurt your partner's feelings, since that's the way to destroy it. As if I didn't know. That has a sharp edge to it, and you can feel some of that in the music. The dream itself is more like that time between sleep and waking, when you don't know whether you're thinking or dreaming.

You have to inhabit Liszt's fingers to find the *Feux follets* in the other piece of Liszt in my collection. The picture here is of a phenomenon I've never seen – methane gas catching fire in marshes or wherever there's rotting material to produce momentary lights. Their German name, *Irrlichte*, literally means 'lights that lead astray'. And their English name belongs to me: Will o' the Wisp, with me as a goblin.

The German story of the Pied Piper of Hamelin gave me a clue. Not the Browning poem we read at school, but the German folk version. This Piper with his Dudelsack negotiated a contract to get rid of the rats infesting the town of Hamelin by leading them a dance to their death in the River Weser. Once he'd done that, the good citizens thought they spotted a way of getting out of this deal they'd made with him: Oh, come on, the rats would surely have left anyway, given time. Big Mistake: they were mixing with the wrong guy by not paying him. He paid them back by playing his happy tune to their children and leading them to the edge of the river where the Irrlichte were will-o'-the-whispering away, luring them into the river. Enticing, menacing, subtle, since it wasn't the lights that caused the tragedy but the councillors wanting to keep the council tax down. Some good images to access there.

This all went on to hold when Ellen arrived.

She moved my new mirrors and put one against the window, where there was light for me to see myself. She put the other in a less obvious place, for me to catch sight of myself when I thought I wasn't in a mirror.

We did some quick work, loosening-up exercises, which Ellen did alongside me. Then some dancing, with music we made ourselves with nonsense syllables.

Quick cold lunch. I have time and space to cook now, and I do read the food supplements, sometimes, looking for ones which seem to have less calories, which means I can strip the ingredients down to the ones I've heard of.

I took this break as a chance to try to change the direction of our relationship.

"We've been looking at me. What about you? Don't you think that might help us to work on me if I know more about you?"

She told me a little. Ordinary background, she said, though ordinary isn't a word I like. School in Bedford, followed by art college, ambition to be an artist. Somehow the paintings didn't attract attention.

"Could I see one of them some time?"

"They're wrapped up in brown paper. The ones I've kept. I don't remember what they're like. I'm too busy doing other things."

"Perhaps you've got a major work of art maturing there under the brown paper."

"If only…I think not."

"Do you still paint?"

"No. Not really. My fingers itch occasionally."

"Would you like to paint my portrait?"

"I would like to be able to do that, but you're not my sort of subject."

"Should I be insulted?"

130

"No. I think I'd try to put too much into the canvas, because I know that what I see now was going to change the moment I'd finished the brushwork."

"I notice that you look at me in different ways."

"How?"

"One's the professional one. How to get the best out of me for the sake of the project. The other's more direct as if…well, I don't really know…"

She thought for a moment.

"I think I'm trying to work out how you can deal with the emotions that come out of the music, and yet organise them to fit the marks on the page. They seem so prescriptive."

"They're not instructions on a tin. They don't inhibit us, or all performances would be the same. You do have to hit the marks. But that still leaves a lot of options. You can bring out details, you can bend the time, the rhythm, because you're going with the flow."

Back to the mirror.

"You don't spend much time looking in mirrors, do you?"

"What makes you ask?"

"I don't know – it's almost as if you don't really want to see yourself."

I shook my head. "It's true. Maybe it's wearing contact lenses. The way I look has never had the slightest impact on my life. Looking at my image is a new experience for me."

She went on looking at me in the mirror.

"Does something bother you?" I said.

"No. I think you look great. But you sometimes look as if what you see in the mirror isn't what you expect to see."

"Doesn't that happen to everyone?"

"Could be, but you're sort of the other way round. In my case, I don't find that I look as good as I wish I did."

"Oh no, not you. You look wonderful. If I may say that."

"Why not? We're trying to be honest in what we do."

What did she mean by this 'we're trying'?

"What d'you mean 'we're trying…'? Are you talking about you and Josy?"

She laughed. "No. I'm talking about you and me."

OK. I gave the boat a little push.

"Well then. If we're talking about you and me, can I ask for a bit more about you? We didn't get very far."

"William…You'll find out about me. Some time. If the time comes."

Boat grounded.

"Don't let this get to you. I am paid to do what I do with you. I have to deliver you in a state fit for purpose. If it worries you that I know more about you, it may be because, to be honest, you've told me probably more than you need. In this film world, you have to look into your own experiences, but no-one has to know what they are, except you."

"Have I made a mess of it?"

"Of course not. But we need to get back to work."

"Right? So…?"

"The Ritual Fire Dance. Spanish music. Gypsy music. Yes?"

"From a ballet."

"Fire. Means?"

"Warmth. Burning. You don't have to know much about the story, but this is a woman playing with fire. To exorcise the ghost of her dead husband. So that she can move on."

"Are you watching from a safe distance or are you identifying with her?"

"As in exorcising the ghost of my departed wife so that I can move on? If I make this personal, then I could end up looking guilty."

"And?"

"I think it's too soon to go there."

"Actors have to do this for the purposes of a film…"

"And I'm an actor. Let me play the opening bars…"

Buzzing trills, strong rhythmic music, not always loud, to burn a ghost up. Not to warm yourself with your memories.

"I'm the man creating the fire, making it work for other people, and a bit for me."

"Play again…make the strength in your body visible, stand up, keep the mood, and move around. Let's change the way you stand. Spanish dancing figure, arched back – not too much – stretched to full height, use your shoulders. I'll finger-click, clap my hands in my own version of the rhythm, dance too and you must react anyhow you like."

We began. Quite different. Letting my body be loose enough to do what it wanted.

"Eyes wide open, drive me away with your look. Not personal, professional. You've been hired to cure this poor woman of her delusions about her life. Be angry if you like because I'm not getting the idea, then be gentle at times, pity me, but never forget the reason for the flames."

I enjoyed this, not because I felt that I was good at it, but because I could go with the feeling in the music.

"Listen to your recording of the music and move to it when you're on your own. Secretly. Look in the mirror sometimes."

"Now a new exercise.

"Close your eyes, and listen to me: I'm going to move around making a gentle humming sound and you have to follow me, eyes still closed."

The first time it didn't work at all. I stood up with eyes closed, quite sure I knew where I was, and floundered, of course. The second time I laughed in anticipation. Next time I made sure it worked; I caught up with her, pulled her close, and still with eyes closed, made to kiss her. It didn't happen.

"That's lovely, Will, just in the mood, and that I'm-going-to-kiss-you expression is going to be fabulous on screen. Can you keep that in mind, so that you can reproduce it to order?"

I looked at her, and she gave me the ghost of a flirtatious smile. Conspiratorial, in a situation where there was no conspiracy. Given the time and the place, we might try it again, it said. Perhaps she just meant we'd keep it in reserve for the filming.

She left. Almost at once.

For now, the Ellen-William relationship remained within the bounds of commerce. She was being paid, I was being paid, although no one had mentioned a fee. Royalties, of course… And that escape clause? right of final approval? I still hadn't asked. So we met professionally and maybe the undercurrent of attraction between us was engineered and meant to turn me on to the point where I could be a visual package, while being sure not to muddy the water by getting closer than was necessary. That hint that things might yet get on to an emotional footing was designed to bring out something in me that the camera needs. I was being lured into the trap of falling in love with the camera. Not with Ellen.

This wasn't love. I'm just a man who's still unclear about what it is. Taking pleasure in someone else's nearness doesn't have to be love. Was I coming to believe it had something to do with sex? The Kraken wakes…although I hope the outcome will be more successful in my case than it was in Tennyson's poem.

**

133

The school concert

Down to Felicity's school.

The accommodation was pure luxury, too much pure luxury, including a whole new guest wing, donated by some Sheikh pleased to have somewhere to stay when visiting his daughters. This multi-father could probably have stocked the school out with his girls, all quite legitimate where he came from.

The Principal made quite a story of it. She was totally unlike the St Trinian's Ronald Searle Headmistress type. Confident, stylish, smart, probably a better businesswoman than a teacher. All part of the new management culture. Meeting the parents on their own level, but with a PhD in something. No doubt from the 'right' university, since the cleverer girls at this school would go to Oxbridge and you couldn't have anyone from anywhere else directing the pupils.

Dr Jerome took me to my quarters. They were of a hotel standard beyond anything I can afford to stay in.

"This is where we put our girls' parents. And our distinguished guests."

"It looks magnificent."

"Double bathroom, which you won't be needing, but at least it gives you a choice."

"It's impressive."

"We're terribly happy to have you here."

I didn't have time to find out anything more about Dr Jerome. I had a concert to deliver, and although occasions like these don't make me particularly nervous, I don't treat them lightly. I explained that I needed to look at the piano and rehearse with Felicity and Dr Jerome remembered that she had other arrangements to see to. Edge-of-flirtation conversation wasn't what I wanted to practise at this moment.

This was the sort of not-too-serious date where I thought I could try out some of the things I'd been rehearsing with Ellen. Years of tradition have built up a convention that when you play you should do nothing to take attention away from the music. With Ellen's schooling, I realised that showing nothing is a body language just as powerful as showing something. The deadpan face, the controlled body, is a bit like Buster Keaton in the silent movies. The man to whom things happen, rather than the man who initiates them. But not yet on the level of my new ideal, Donny Johnny. Loosening up my professional behaviour would be no bad thing.

Everything went according to plan, except there wasn't really a plan. Felicity was good, from the first notes of our duet version of Handel's 'Queen of Sheba', who arrived in style. Feet were tapped, the drinks, clutched for the most part in bejewelled hands, were put on hold until the end of it. Applause was generous, slightly muted in the case of those with glasses, but about right for a fund-raising activity, where the money slows the circulation down. Felicity looked good too, ripening into maturity. She was at that age when women can show their arms as they play their musical instruments. Men, who have muscles to show there, are not expected to display them. She was draped in a Grecian style, very flattering, like my very own Galatea. At eighteen, she was matrimonially eligible, and if her father had his eyes on the aristocracy, he'd want to keep musicians' hands off her...or any hands, come to that.

She did her Chopin Nocturnes with a delicacy Chopin would have loved, and a standard of playing few, if any, of his pupils ever achieved. I scampered round the piano in some Liszt, then played Debussy, and the Ritual Fire Dance. Felicity played a couple of Gershwin songs which she'd never played to me, with a nice feeling for them – it don't mean a thing if it ain't got that swing, and she had. Our final Dvorak duet was noisy, and everyone clapped, well aware that if they clapped too long there would be encores and basically they wanted to eat.

I felt free to experiment with the subtext in the fire dance and with Debussy's girl. The Lady Principal said she had no idea how much acting came into playing the piano.

"You made me feel a quite unprincipled Principal in both of those pieces," she said. "I always thought of that flaxen-headed girl as Scottish heather. Mais ta jeune fille has red blood and a warm body."

It looked as if I might sell one copy of the film when it came to the point. I noticed she was wearing a wedding ring, which these days could mean anything; and by being a Dr she bypassed the Ms or Miss or Mrs Thing. Perhaps she was like a nun, wedded to her calling. She didn't look like one.

They all made a fuss of Felicity: a star in the making, she might be, they thought, and they asked me about that. Well, you don't make predictions about such things, if you have any sense. Too many imponderables. But you can be positive while remaining vague without putting anyone down.

"She has serious talent, and if she's prepared to drop everything in favour of a career, at least at first..." Delivered with a certain wistful sincerity. They liked it.

135

The usual thing, lots of smiles for me, and with a predominantly female audience, only slightly modified by husbands and fathers, the rest being at office parties, no doubt, I enjoyed the sort of success that almost any male might enjoy when showing off in front of women.

I thought that if I'm going to make money out of this upcoming 'Water-fire (whatever)' film, I'd better start putting in some spadework in the PR direction. I was interested in everyone I was introduced to, asked them questions about their daughters, and answered questions about how much practice I did, and how often I go to the United States and Europe. They seemed on the whole more interested in the US than Europe, although several confessed to a second home in France. Or third.

I told them about my next concert in Lyon, and allowed myself to think about the happy student time I'd had there. And No, I wasn't married, at the moment. And No, I wasn't between marriages, because I wasn't intending to get married again unless someone very special appeared. And yes, it must be very hard being married to a musician, what with them being at home so much. Or away so much. And yes, I enjoy working with Felicity, and didn't she play the duets well, too, and yes, we did practise them, didn't it sound like it? (The last bit didn't get said.) Yes, I do look after my health, No, I don't take vitamins, and Yes, my hair is cut in a stylist's shop in Kensington, doesn't it look like it? (Which also didn't get said.) No, I don't recommend anyone to take up my profession; I don't want too many challenges, do I? Which I did say out loud.

Carriages had been ordered for 11.00, but I made my exit, to renewed applause – wasn't that nice? – at about 10.30. Dr Jerome shook my hand very warmly, wondered if she would see me at breakfast (breakfast here? with all the girls?). She explained that she took it privately in her quarters. I didn't ask how early one had to turn up for that breakfast, and murmured instead that I had to be off betimes and I would just make myself some early morning tea and examine the biscuit tin in my wonderful accommodation, and look forward to our next meeting. She kissed me on the cheek three times; her French education had been thorough.

It was good to get back to my room, kick off shoes, slip out of jacket, undo shirt a bit.

There was a knock at the door. I wondered what I'd left on the piano.

It was the music for the duets. Brought back by Felicity.

She had loved her evening. She'd been pleased with her performance, just enough displeased with a detail or two to show she had a critical faculty in operation, and didn't feel that the praise heaped on her by her old school music teacher, and the teaching staff in general, had turned her head. Going back to earlier instructors can catch you out: jealousy is not unknown in teachers. "You used to play with such natural feeling, before you won that competition/went to that teacher/got to be so successful/went to live in London. Now it all seems a whisper artificial, as if you're playing everything for the fiftieth time. You know what I mean?"

Felicity wasn't subjected to that.

I offered her a drink; an infusion seemed the right thing. She refused, and I think that was just as well. She had to go back to her mother, and I think that was just as well too. She had been thrilled, she said, and couldn't thank me enough for helping the school.

"Thank you for letting me play duets with you in front of a real public. You've no idea what I learn from that, and how much it lifts my playing beyond my wildest dreams. And for letting me play on my own account, when you could have played what I played with much more understanding and sheer basic talent."

She was on a high, and I was the object of her worship. I was very heady too, given the classical dress and the drapery. I reminded myself why I was here. For Music. A Scholarship.

Felicity clearly wanted to say something else.

"I know it's not really the time, but I do want to know what my chances are. Coming back here makes me the big fish in the small pond. But this is an old-fashioned place in a lot of ways, and quite a lot of the girls will be looking for good marriages.

"Money and family still mean a lot here, I can tell you. And Daddy has reasons. He's a great father, and a self-made man. A good marriage for his only daughter is on his list of must-haves. So I thought you might like to know that they're looking around for a possible husband for me."

"Not just any old husband I assume? Not someone else's."

She laughed. "Well no. Rank and Station would be nice, I guess. Nice little commercial package. It's not uncommon."

"Well, I have to say it's not something I know anything about. You sometimes get ambitious women marrying conductors in the hope that they can make them lose their critical faculty when it comes to how their wives sing or play the piano."

"I suppose it's just possible that Daddy might go for other sorts of proof of quality. Like success in business, or the theatre, or the music industry, even…"

What exactly did she mean by 'music industry, even'?

Time to change the subject.

"You played excellently tonight. Just the right thing for the music, especially in this setting. The future is – well, the future, and that'll declare itself eventually," I said, sounding the way an agony aunt ought to sound. But her talk made me realise how far I'd come since Patti went. Unmarried, and marketable. And getting more uncertain, and just a little afraid as well.

I went out of my way to repeat what I said about how well she'd played, and that I was proud to be her teacher. There's room for a lot of good people in our profession, even if they have to fight their corner.

"Have a good Christmas, and keep practising. I won't see you tomorrow morning. I'll be off early because I have a meeting in town." Which was true.

"And now you'd better go back to Lady Chislehurst."

I didn't feel good. I didn't feel bad. I had done the right thing.

**

Christmas Day

December went past quickly enough

More working sessions with Ellen, and on my own. I went to Hull to do a concert with an orchestra which was theoretically amateur. Virtually every person involved had been fully trained, but gone into a non-performing part of our sector, usually teaching. The Liszt concerto I was playing was admirable from us all, and I played the wild Will o'the Wisp piece as an encore, with a not very practised joke in my introduction identifying myself with the main character. I stayed on to hear them play William Walton's First Symphony.

Life slowed down towards Christmas Eve.

Christmas Day itself started very badly. By lunchtime, a terrible gloom had settled. I opened the present I'd given myself, and I didn't like it. I hadn't taken on board what it would feel like to be on my own on Christmas Day; I just hadn't given it any thought. Patti and her parents had always been part of it; it was tradition to go and eat too much and inhale her father's cigar smoke and watch an old Morecombe and Wise show and several old movies and do the big crossword in the newspaper. I have no family of my own now, except a cousin or two in the north, and although we send each other small presents, thanks to my grandmother's encouragement while she was alive, and thanks to her memory now she's gone, we wouldn't for a minute think of setting a Christmas pudding alight together. I can't count my mother and my father.

I took myself to St Paul's Cathedral where the music was good. I don't often feel lonely, except a little when other people are conspicuously enjoying not being alone. But the carols brought a lump to my throat, and I even wondered what my abandoning mother was up to. I'm not sure I ever want to see her again, quite apart from the fact that I'm not very likely to: I'm much too old for Billy Boy things. Not exactly the ideal thought for Christmas Day. I left before the end and the onset of more thoughts.

There was a message on the answerphone, which I hadn't been going to check. Ellen. They were having an unexpected party – her brother had come home from some business trip to one of those countries where they don't have Christmas and don't have drink either, and there were a few others who were hanging around with no families or had quarrelled with their families, or had families a long way away and couldn't get home for Christmas because they had a show in London. Media, entertainment people. She didn't know what my plans were because I hadn't said anything, and if I wasn't here I was to forget it. Upshot, going round to someone's top floor attic flat in Islington; bring a bottle, and anything you might have been going to eat, and bring a friend if you like, but one only. Casual, but be warned, we do party-pieces at Christmas.

I wasn't sure. Of course, I was pleased to be asked. But what were Ellen's friends like? Actors work with other people much more than I do. On the other hand, I had been to a couple of Patti's orchestral binges, and they were OK. And there was always Ellen. With a partner?

In fact, it was fun. I got a rare taxi, at Christmas Day rates.

I took my Christmas dinner with me: a platter of cold seasonal meats, liver pâté, some reasonably fresh fruit, a pack of French cheese with biscuits. And the magnum of champagne they'd given me at the school, which had been sitting in my garden shed, so it was cold-ish. It was suitably large.

It was a good investment. We danced with no one in particular, and sang a few Christmas Carols which I played on a keyboard set up with a jazz backing sound.

The party pieces had a time limit. Just as well, when you've got media people who can't help doing auditions, and loving the sound of their own voices. My party piece is an imitation of Cole Porter singing 'Miss Otis Regrets'. I think Cole Porter's voice was better than mine, but I play the piano better than he did, so it works out even. That took them by surprise, because no one thought a concert pianist knows what it is Miss Otis Regrets. For ten minutes after that, I was a star, until someone mimed and danced to Kiri Te Kanawa singing 'I Got Rhythm'. He was part of the stage crew at some London theatre and clearly used to lugging weights: it had to be seen to be believed. There ain't nothing like a Dame, but I'd like to see a Dame pretending to be a man with muscles.

Then we played charades. Not since I was nine had I played charades. And these weren't played the same way. We played them properly at home – silently. Here, with actors all around, we were expected to improvise dialogue There were about twelve of us. Everyone had been properly introduced and some names remembered, but not securely attached to anyone, some forgotten. One of the men had been an actor at his university, but had decided not to take it up, he let us know, in spite of some fantastic offers, because he had chosen another sort of fantasy world to live in; he was a financier in the City, trained as an economist. He organised his team brilliantly, taking the star role, and battered us with subtleties. The word for his group was 'polyurethane'. They had fun with the Beggar's Opera, and the man who bent forks, and Macbeth, not mentioned by name of course, from the Scottish play. The trouble was that when they did the whole word it was like an elephant in the middle of the room.

Our word was much more subtle. Ellen suggested 'indistinguishable'. It split up well: Indies – as in West or East – Sting – well, bees came to mind, but one of the actors suggested Sting, the singer, a bit of a dead one for me, but who was I? 'Wish' and 'Able' would finish it off. The wish one fell to Ellen and me. This was easy: we'd been spending quite a lot of time improvising; it's what she was encouraging me to do.

First, "Indies" had two explorers quarrelling about whether they had got to India or not, while I played 'East is East and West is West' on the keyboard, a sure sign of my grandparents' taste in popular music, and unrecognised by anyone else there. An actor called Jolyon, who was in some Chekhov play, did what I am told was a credible whispered imitation of Sting singing 'Every breath you take/Message in a bottle'. Then came 'wish'…We hadn't worked this one out in detail, but the scenario was two people sitting in a car driving somewhere.

We'd agreed not to use the word very often, and it's funny how hard it is to avoid a word when you have to. We gave the impression that we were eloping, each leaving a lover behind. "You're the one I've been waiting for, and now I'm going for it, pulling up the road behind me. All the same, I wish you would drive more slowly". Then I pulled the car up, opened Ellen's door. "Here you are – you're home. See you next week at the same time – I wish." We ignored the last syllable.

We were quite pleased with that, but it went on rather long.

The other team got the word in one, even though we tried to hide it by using as many long words as we could think of, and wrapped it up by all doing the same thing, so that we were indistinguishable from one another…

Jolyon came up to me and asked me right out if Ellen and I were lovers.

"How do you mean?" I said.

He said, "How do you think I mean?" and it began to sound like a lead-in to a row. Or a fight, even.

I said, "No." It was the truth. Unfortunately the truth must seem to be the truth as well; it's no good on its own. He didn't believe me.

"There was something going on in your improvisation which came over loud and clear. You know each other too well."

"Ever heard of acting?" I asked him.

"Yes, now you come to mention it, I have, because that's what I do. Acting."

"I know. So you should know."

"Come on, acting is what I do. What you do is play the piano. I never met a musician who could act yet."

Ellen came up and put her arm through his.

"You have now. He's having lessons to do a solo film based on the piano pieces he's playing. I think he must be doing very well, if he convinced you that we have something going on beyond what you do when you work with people."

Clever. I didn't want to believe her. But I watched her with Jolyon. He looked very convincingly like her boyfriend, but perhaps he was acting too.

I sat and played the keyboard. It had a sort of piano touch as well, and a pedal on the end of a piece of wire. I played something very slow, and then I improvised with some of the interesting sounds it would make. It had an automatic rhythm setting, which worked very well with Chaminade – Autumn with a blues beat, just right for that season.

Then this girl came up and wanted to hum along, so we did 'Autumn Leaves', and she sat on my knee while she sang what she could remember of the words.

It spoilt the pedalling, and some of my chances to reach the keyboard, but it improved the way I felt. People were dancing, the way they do when the music is quiet, two men were playing chess, and after Autumn Leaves I did my best with some boogie-woogie. It dislodged the Autumn Leaves girl. We'd reached the end of our relationship. Then Ellen took her place beside me. "Play something serious," she said, so I played a lively Bach Fugue in G minor, and people danced to that, which was perfectly possible, and Ellen didn't. She stayed close.

"Where's Jolyon?"

"He's gone; he's got a matinee tomorrow and it's a rather physical show he's in."

"It must be a strange production of Chekhov; on ice, is it, then?"

"No, he's not the Chekhov man – he's over there. Jolyon is in a pantomime in Dartford. And before you start looking like a classical artiste who plays on the South Bank, pantomime is an art-form that existed before Mr Bach got his first church job."

"I wasn't looking like that, "I said. "I was looking like a guy who is pleased someone has gone. Let me play something just for you."

Making things up on the spur of the moment is something I do to amuse myself, but not in public, where you have to organise what you're doing and give it a shape. I'm no Chopin, but then who is? I used Ellen's name as a rising shape on two notes, and worked it into a soulful sort of declaration of interest. I looked at her, but she didn't return my look, keeping her eyes focused on her glass and saying nothing. When I stopped, she turned to me – her expression was very far away.

"You make it very difficult for a woman when you do that, make something for me before my very eyes, you know."

"Ears?"

"Yes, ears…"

"Don't you want me to make it difficult? It's Christmas, it's nice here, the people are nice, you are nice, and I am nice. What more could you want?"

"I don't know. Something that either means less than you just played, or something that lasts longer. I don't know. We have a working relationship, and I still think it's best that way."

"It wouldn't get in the way of that," I said. "I used to work with my wife…" and I stopped.

142

"Yes, I know," she said. "So it would get in the way, for two reasons. Keep playing."

I went on with just a few finger patterns over a bass. Automatic pilot again by now.

"One is the work. It's better to keep a cold spotlight shining on the product we're in if we want a result."

"We're not making Gone with the Wind," I said.

"Yes, we are. Just a little bit of it, if you like, even if it's commercial. And it's part of each of us, blown together by the wind."

"You're getting sentimental."

"No, it's true. You don't make things which are meant to last for ever in a different way. I mean from the way you make the ones that are meant to be temporary. You just let it be an accident."

"And the second reason?"

"Is that the work we are doing is slowly uncovering you…"

"I wish."

"That's from a charade. We're loosening up your thinking and feeling so that you can show the real you on screen for thirty minutes or so. Sure, Jane and Josy hope your looks and your playing will sell this right across the market. But however much you dress it up, and however you might be sold, it's still you. The you who's coming to the surface when we work together."

"Don't you think it might come to the surface more if we…got involved?"

"It might. But it might not. We are temporary. Just as long as the contract specifies."

I stopped playing, and felt more unhappy than I could ever remember. I hadn't come here for a Christmas love affair. I came because of the loneliness of being on my own. I suppose that made some sort of sense. What made me sad was that this woman, the object of my softening affections, seemed possibly attached to some serious actor appearing in a pantomime. And maybe I didn't want to recognise that I was on the point of wanting a real human relationship. Or maybe something on the way to it. A staging post.

My new problem, which I really needed to think about, was that all I was doing was sitting back and letting the relationships seek me out. Just waiting for the partners. What is Women's Lib about, after all, if it's not for us to be the hunted as well as the hunter? And not to mind which you are. But so far only two. What sort of record is that?

"Kiss me, at any rate," I said. She kissed me. Someone may have seen, but there wasn't much to see, because the soft gentle kiss she gave me was indeed so soft, so gentle, so warm, and so pure that although I tried to make it turn a corner into something more, it didn't.

It was a token of friendship only – she wasn't refusing anything, and she wasn't offering anything either. That way lay danger, if I began to care.

I looked round for the girl who had sat on my knee. That was a desperate move, and a waste of time. She'd got rather closely linked with someone dressed all in black. It could have been anyone, a dummy, even. It was getting late, and time to go. I had no pantomime tomorrow, but I did have a concert in Wales on New Year's Eve, and discipline was calling. Christmas is just a day like any other, once you've done the church bit, if that's what you do, and now I felt as if it was over, like any other.

I tried to slip away unnoticed, a bit intoxicated with the drink, some of it my own champagne, but Ellen was there.

"You're a good man to work with, don't forget that. The things that are worth having are worth waiting for."

"Even if they never arrive."

"Even if they never arrive," she repeated. "No-one is rejecting you, remember. Just settle for being a man who once was married, and now has a life full of things to do. I'll see you in ten days."

And she gently pushed me towards the stairs as I said, "Tell your brother what a great party it was…" I'd never met Ellen's brother.

**

Work, Wales and practice

New Year came and went. In Wales. It was one of those concerts in which there was a mixed bill, the Litolff scherzo and Saint-Saëns's second concerto. Lots of notes to play, to dazzle listening ears, and yet make sense of, so that it doesn't sound like a mechanical piano. Plenty of wit for the concerto's scherzo – Dance, little lady, think of Mummy wherever she may be in Hollywood. The whole show was topped off with some real fireworks outside, after the orchestra had deafened everyone with the cannon in Tchaikovsky's 1812 Overture. Twice in one season, for me, but I was insulated in my dressing room. (One day someone is going to use that burst of gunfire to offload a real bomb, like in Hitchcock's '*Man Who Knew Too Much*'.)

A few weeks earlier I'd had an email from Agent Jane to say that a former fellow-student of mine, David Probert, had been in touch to ask if he could have my home number, because he was a cellist in the orchestra in Wales, and wondered if we might meet. She was checking. I remembered him with pleasure; we'd played sonatas together and even a couple of trios with Patti as the violinist.

I rang him. After the usual well, well, what a surprise and it's been a long time hasn't it routine, he asked me if I'd like to stay on after the concert with him and his family (wife and children) and mother-in-law. The mother-in-law came with a big house in Radyr, a village now joined on to Cardiff. Thanks to her wealth from well-chosen ancestors, the place was divided up admirably, and my room would be with its own bathroom. Helena, his wife, played the viola, but because of the children had decided to teach privately, so that her lessons could be scheduled around her willing duties as a mother. I didn't recall her from my student days, which wasn't surprising, because she'd studied in Manchester.

"I expect you've booked in for two nights at the hotel in Cardiff, one before and one after the concert. If you're happy to leave the booking as it is, which gives you somewhere to go between the rehearsal and the concert – we're doing a morning rehearsal that day, as you no doubt know – then you can come back with us for the New Year."

I went by train, and checked in at the Jurys Inn, where they found me what they promised to be a very quiet room. It was.

I looked for David in the rehearsal. I've a traveller's memory for faces. Names don't always come to mind quickly, but our post-concert visitors usually say who they are. In fact, he looked just the same. Wearing glasses now, slender, as he always was, with what I always thought of as a good cellist's shape in that he looked as if he'd been born with a cello in mind. There's a theory that our bodies tell us which instrument will suit us.

He had a different problem.

"You really do look different. When I saw the posters, I thought you had got the opposite of a Doppelgänger, someone who didn't look like you but was passing themselves off.

"We're looking forward to socialising, after the concert, and maybe even some music-making, if you feel like it, after the ball is over."

The atmosphere was good, the audience was good, a Happy New Year feeling hung around the place, and I played an unfinished piece by Liszt which I finished with my own hint at Auld Lang Syne with a welter of notes.

We were out of the hall pretty quickly after the concert ended.

David's car was one for a married pair of string players, good access from the back for a cello.

"I'll just need to move a couple of the children's remains; I mean things they've left behind after Christmas."

"How many children?"

"Two. You'll meet them, because they're ten and twelve, and qualify for Midnight Chimes."

"Are you having a party, then?"

"Not really. Just us. And a couple of neighbours. I'm pleased you could join us."

"Nice for me. I don't get many family opportunities. In fact, any at all."

"You have no family? Brothers, sisters? Seems a bit unfair."

"I've never known anything else."

"And no children."

"No. It wasn't part of the plan. And it's probably just as well, since we're divorced now, Patti and I."

"I heard you were divorced. Things get around."

"Well, I suppose it's OK, if it's the truth. Saves the embarrassment of having to think who to tell."

"You surviving alright?"

"I'm getting used to it. No alternative, really. And I'm busy enough not to brood about it."

Not exactly true.

David is a very nice man, very suitable to be head of a family.

"I'm a few years older than you, so maybe I'm settling into my middle years comfortably."

"I remembered that – about you being a bit older because you'd been to university before coming on to the Conservatoire. But 'middle years'? Prime of life to come. You enjoying the orchestral scene?"

"Very much. We get good concerts, and regular audiences. We're even recognised in the streets like an old acquaintance. We do outreach programme into the local schools, getting the students to play instruments. It's a good life."

146

"You make me rather envious. I can't do that as a pianist, though."

"You must get a lot of compensation from being a soloist."

"Yes. Yes, I do."

We were at the house now.

It was impressive. Late Victorian, with wings.

"Crazy, isn't it? I don't think too much about what it was built with. Bricks and stones bought by profit-making mines and works. But mother-in-law Gwyneth is generous about it; she's put aside accommodation for students, or for musicians with short-term contracts with the orchestra, or the opera. Carefully soundproofed, so that they can practise without everyone hearing their personal problems, if any.

"We pay our way for what we use. The children have a great time, because there is ground around it, enough for whatever games they want to play or train for. It works."

Helena met us. She was warm in her welcome, both for David and for me. In that order. Slightly pang-creating. Is this what I could have had?

It was about quarter past ten. My room was comfortable, with that passing-through comfort that a hotel room has, except that there were books on shelves and pictures on walls that seemed at home.

I changed into my casual clothes and went downstairs. David was already there.

"We're lucky, we've got plenty of room. This is the sitting room, where we'll be suppering – all cold, but as much or as little as you like. And a music room through here with a good enough piano if you thought of playing something with us."

"I'd like that. Not a lot to choose from for piano, viola and cello, though, unless you've got some hidden treats."

"We have a solution for that."

"One of your children a prodigy?"

"No, though they both have instruments; we have a secret source which goes with the house.

"Come and meet the children and have something to eat and drink."

The sitting-room was on a Victorian scale; a high ceiling with a candelabra, which might have been the original gas one, with only one other sign of grandeur – a big fire-place with a mantel-piece, whatever you call it, with mirrors in it duplicating the family ornaments and pictures. A couple of side tables set out with food. And glasses.

Laurence and Abigail, in order of age, looked up from their chessboard. Chessboard. And waved before Laurence said, "Checkmate. My turn anyway. Abby won last time."

"Do you play chess?" Abby asked.

"Not officially. I know the rules. But I wouldn't know how to apply them."

"We play at school. In matches with other schools. And sometimes win."

Children. Clever children, friendly. Yes. That was something I'd never thought of. And wasn't going to think of now. Not yet, if ever…

It was a good evening, bringing in the New Year or not. The piano was an old instrument. With a Victorian look, but not a Victorian sound.

Food and drink were good. We were joined by Gwyneth, who arrived carrying a violin.

"Now we have a quartet. And a couple of our neighbours are from the orchestra, so we can enjoy bits and pieces. Not all with piano."

We made music. Took a break for the sound of the local church's bells, hoped the New Year would bring us and everyone whatever they hoped for or needed. Gossiped, of course, demolishing a few well-known names as we went. And made more music.

I didn't notice the time we went to bed, but I was happy.

I got an afternoon train back to London, not busy, because it was a public holiday.

I rang David to thank him and Helena for propelling me comfortably into 2009.

"I really enjoyed the music."

"We did too," he said, "and I wanted to give you something to think about. We have a regular quartet in the orchestra, and we do the odd concert in the quiet times…as it might be next August. Would you like to come and play a couple of quintets with us? We get a good audience, use a hall at the university, good piano. Not much of a fee, because the seats are deliberately cheap. Food and accommodation thrown in. I don't need an answer now, but do give it a thought."

"I don't need to. Just suggest a date or two. I've a quiet time after the Prom I'm doing, and then little until early September."

Yesterday had been good, but I was missing the company, being part of a family, such as the one I might have had, with children playing chess. Leave it. Forget it. Put it out of your mind.

I wanted to do nothing for the rest of the day. Just watch tele or DVDs. Tele had nothing for me, which is often the case, unless I channel-hop. And I didn't fancy any of my DVDs again: I'm totally against watching '*Brief Encounter*', because it might fill my mind with images which are too precise for the next time I play Rachmaninov's concerto. I love Celia Johnson as an actress, and I'd like to be like her as an actor because she shows so much about what's going on behind the façade; but the concerto isn't in the right order in the film, and that bothers me a bit. It's not something you can watch with the sound turned off, either. And Noel Coward's other film – '*Blithe Spirit*' – is funny, but I'm not too keen to look at anything with a plot which involves the first wife coming back from the dead. '*The Philadelphia Story*', full of witty lines, is about a couple getting married to each other again after their divorce…why do people think divorce is funny?

No escapology then, I actually did some work. I practised the piano. And maybe because I'd been distracted, I began to see my way into bits of the sonatas I hadn't seen before. I let it happen, and listened to myself like a stranger. Beethoven had been working on me without my knowing it.

Schubert was giving me more and more. I was a pianist-turned actor. Not just one actor playing Hamlet, but a whole troupe of actors playing the whole play, having to find out how they talk to each other, and how to play all the characters at the same time. So I tried playing bits as if I were Polonius at the front of the stage, not behind the arras, and Hamlet and Queen Gertrude speaking to one another. The last part of the slow movement was like Ophelia singing in her madness, with comments from those watching her. Then I listened to it as if it were an ensemble in an opera. How can you have all those different thoughts and put them down on ten lines drawn on a piece of paper? Because they depend on each other.

So the day ended well enough, after all.

**

Email to *jane@curzprod.com*

I hope everything is on cue for the bits we're recording next Wednesday. Piano tuning, sound producer. Who is it going to be? Is it Steve? Or are we not in his league for this project? Let me know. Will

Email from Jane to *will@williamwinton.co.uk*

Dear Will. Everything couldn't be better. You sound a little worried, but don't be. Becky is the technical woman. Yes, the piano is being brought in from Steinways; it's one you've had before, and Martin will be there to bring it to your taste.

I don't like to say it, but you obviously don't remember my email about recording the music for Fire/Water. We've got a very bright young woman producer, Victoria Baldwin, Steve's assistant, and tipped for the top. Already has a Cambridge degree in music, but is practical too, Steve says. Specialist in piano recording, and going to be better than he is at it, he says. OK? J.

Of course it's OK. But I felt less easy-going than usual, for some reason. New departure. I was worried about the piano. Who'd been leaving his fingerprints on it? There are still some Russians about who were brought up under the old regime going round factories – can the piano be heard over the machines?

Recording the film music

Getting to Cricklewood, where the music studio is, was time-consuming; train and underground and bus with a first change at Elephant and Castle. That place still looked as if they have it in mind to do something some day but the plans have got stuck in the printing-machine. Surprising bits of London are beginning to look like this, after the brothers in New York crashed: "To Let" signs on some of the buildings I passed on my way to London's Barbican Hall among the new ones being built with cranes threatening retribution from the air. It gave me some little pleasure to see the mighty financial giants tremble because their own beanstalk might be as fragile as the one in the story. But not much pleasure, because when you earn money as I do, from engagement to engagement, you need to put some away to look after you when your fingers are outstripped by your brain. Those Brothers and their mates deserve some special gift in my will, if I can think of something suitable to make them remember me, and the millions like me.

I had only half an hour's sound to put down in the session, but I find recording tiring. You are your own audience, as well as a performer. You go and listen to playbacks, you're delighted it sounds as good as it does, and then wonder if you couldn't have done it better. You're doing what you can to make it worth listening to more than once, or else why make a recording at all? It's a special art form.

I was expecting a studioful of women – four, anyway. Ellen, Felicity, Becky, the technical woman, and the new person, Victoria, as the music producer. And maybe Jane as a fifth, unless she had to be with that American woman who wants me for the concert in Italy. I had leapt into this female world, which I suppose had been there all the time, except I just didn't notice it while I was married.

Ellen sent a message to say that she thought it better not to overload the place with people giving advice, especially as she didn't know anything about playing the piano. I was disappointed out of all proportion, but she was coming in the next day.

Felicity was there.

But there was something I had to do first: the practical thing of getting to know the latest woman in my life: Victoria, the unknown quantity of a producer.

Becky, who would operate the desk, was someone I'd worked with before. She introduced us by waving the cable in her hand.

"Hi, Will. You remember Dr Baldwin?"

I didn't. Had she told Becky we'd met before? I didn't think we had.

"Dr Baldwin? Of course, you're Victoria. It's good to meet you, and especially someone who comes with a recommendation from Steve."

"I know you were hoping you'd have Steve for this recording, but believe me, I'll do my best..."

"I'm sure that'll be fine. We all have to move on some time, and Steve's doing something else, I guess."

"He's in Prague at the moment. With a conductor who refuses to make a recording without him. You know how performers get..."

"Some. It's as well we don't all feel the same."

Practical musicians can get a bit suspicious of working with people with doctorates. We feel they've got an advantage over us. Honorary doctorates are OK – they may well mean you're fortunate enough to know the people who hand them out.

"I didn't mean that. About performers being difficult," she said. I knew she didn't, and I know that investing in an orchestra costs a lot more, so you send your best people. Anyway, I know what I'm doing.

"So, about you…You've been doing the postgraduate training thing at one of those universities that make people doctors who do media studies?"

I actually meant to be rude.

Victoria behaved splendidly. I could tell she wasn't pleased, but kept the atmosphere calm. First lessons in the recording studio. Make friends with everyone. Keep the artists on an even keel. We are supposed to get a good end product. Together.

"I did extra postgraduate training in sound technology, because I've been recording anything that makes a noise since I was a child. My dad was a BBC studio manager in the days when they were properly trained. He said. My doctorate is from Cambridge, I'm afraid. In music. Beethoven – the piano music, you know."

I apologised.

"I'm a bit nervous." I wasn't, but it was the best thing I could think of to say, because I thought I'd better make up for what I said before. I smiled with as much of a wrinkly, friendly face as I could manage.

"I wondered what a woman who doctored in Beethoven should look like."

"Oh? How should I look?"

"Just the way you look today. Good. And confidence-inspiring."

She smiled.

"Martin's in with the piano. He asked if you'd look in when you arrived."

"I've brought one of my students to turn the pages. I hope you don't mind. If I need them turned." I introduced Felicity, trying to think of a way to let them know that there was money coming with her, and nothing else, but how could I do that?

"Oh," Becky said. "We've taken the music desk off the piano because I thought you wouldn't need it."

"Fine. I don't need it. In which case, Felicity can just sit in with me."

Victoria intervened.

"No. Let her come in here with us, and we'll be careful about what we say."

Martin had done a good job on the piano, as always. He tunes my piano at home, and always has since I could afford to buy my own Steinway. He was going to be around, because a piano can start to go out of tune the moment the tuner leaves it, especially if the piano has been shipped in. Temperamental things pianos. The microphones might notice.

The studio was quite small, but not as small as some of the places I'd been in when I started my career. Then it was small projects for new labels, and you'd turn up to play in someone's basement.

It's good to be in a proper studio to record. If you rent a concert hall to do your recording, the control room is usually some way away, if not actually outside in a van in the street. Personal contact recedes into the distance and you're talking to a disembodied Big Producer over a loudspeaker. "Will, that split note in bar 56? Could we cover that, do you think?" That's OK, when it's said gently in your ear. Coming out of a loudspeaker it sounds like a verdict. It gets easier when you know the producer. I was with a new one. At least in this case, Victoria had only to take a few steps into the studio and she could be a comrade sharing my performance with me.

Even so, it was a little while into the session before we started to warm towards one another. What if she thought this was a pretty down-market thing we were doing? A film, a prostitution of the noble art of music. Not my view, just a short visit to my encore cupboard. The fun-bit after the serious work had been done.

Victoria had another job on her hand – getting on with Becky. I got the distinct impression that Victoria thought she could have done it herself. You might think it's a luxury to have two people or more laying the sound down, but it's not, even with only one instrumentalist. Pianos aren't easy to record, because the sound comes out all round at different levels, and a lot of it from underneath. Becky knew how to get the best sound, that special sound which is yours because it belongs to your own body. I have learnt to trust that, because microphones never have my ears. They hang around in places some distance from where I'm sitting. With a less skilful balance, you get percussive sound, like the hammers are justifying their name, or else a mushy sound as if you've got a slight cramp using the sustaining pedal.

While I was making my own discoveries about the piano, Becky moved the microphones, often by an inch or so; one off the end of the piano and one looking at the middle of the piano; there was another one up in the space above. I like to know where they are, and even find it a help to play to one I can see.

They seemed happy in the control room after twenty minutes or so.

"Come in and have a listen." Victoria said. A good sign. And no doubt part of the protocol they teach on these advanced courses. Make sure the artist can't complain afterwards. All the same I can't see myself suing my producer or a sound engineer – it would be like cutting your umbilical cord before you were ready to live on your own.

I listened. "The quality is great. But I need to get into it more. I sound a bit tense. Even to me, and I'm the one doing the playing."

"Probably. I wonder if you could afford to take the projection down a bit; play for a girl, or guy who's in the room with you – not the one sitting here behind this desk. The one who'll be watching as well as listening."

I knew this, but I didn't mind being reminded of it.

"One of the BBC continuity announcers used to say 'Play to your mother'" said Becky. "Talk to your mother, of course."

Fat chance with my mother.

I didn't answer that one.

Victoria said: "We can turn the volume down, naturally, but it's much more about the Stanislavski circle of concentration, you know."

"Sorry, tell me again…"

"The Moscow Arts Theatre director, Stanislavski. Three circles of concentration. This is the first one: the personal one that barely goes beyond you."

"Perhaps I ought to ask Ellen about that."

"Or you can ask me." She smiled. Very nicely. This woman was ahead of me, but at least we'd left the confrontational mode behind.

I had at the desk a woman who had Beethoven at her elbow. That was good. I began to feel more comfortable. She was on my side, as all producers have to be: if they go home with no product, they end up with no job. All the same, there are producers who can't help trying to run the show. Svengali without a Trilby. Wanting to hypnotise me into giving the performance that they would have given if they could have played as well as I do. One of my Conservatoire colleagues had walked out of the studio in the middle of a recording, saying, "OK, if that's what you want, play the bloody thing yourself." At least, that's what he said happened, although that wasn't the adjective he used, if you believe him.

It was working well enough, but I felt something was missing. I hadn't been exploiting the things I'd been researching to look interesting for the cameras. I accessed them and there it was. the right trigger for this music. I played Liszt's

Liebestraum dreaming a dream of love about someone. And after that, Bach with activity for the fingers in the prelude to one of his English suites, full of glittering life and brilliance, was music to show how much my mind was involved as well as my feelings.

Liszt's Will o' the wisp is hard, as you might expect from a transcendental study. It's a showpiece, and meant to be. He added the title later, but I like to think he had the subject in his mind from the first note. The music has grace, sweetness, however momentary, and I wanted to make sure I caught every aspect in the recording. That was the one we spent most time on.

Chaminade's Autumn piece is likewise a study, a French concert study. I like to lighten it up a bit in the stormy middle section, so that it doesn't take off down a middle-European torment route.

The rest of the programme made its own individual demands but yielded themselves up more directly.

No one knew about the two 'Songs without Words' I wanted to record for the credits, if needed.

"No problem," all round. Nobody knew them, but they loved them.

I hadn't used Felicity at all, but I wanted to make sure that she would take a good report back to her dad, so I made a point of explaining the odd thing. I think she was overwhelmed anyway. The sheer mechanics of it were enough to do that.

"I hope you've got a sort of idea of what a professional studio is like. Bit boring otherwise."

"Oh, I loved it. I really loved it."

Having thanked the supportive regiment of women, I gave her a lift in my taxi.

I was too exhausted to talk much, and really just wanted to be on my own. She was OK with that.

Once at home, a shower, a cup of camomile tea, and bed. It was half past seven. I slept for three hours, then took some soup. There are times when I wonder about recording. Music is here and now, the future turning into the past. When you're trying to preserve the moment by recording it as it goes by, you make an object out of it, firm it up, like a picture or a sculpture. Stop time in its digits. But at least it means that at some time in the future I'll know how I sounded at this age, and felt like this about what I'm playing.

I definitely needed a quiet night.

The speech

The music had all been recorded on the first day. The second day could be devoted to the two poems, which might or might not make it into the final film, but which should help me get into the atmosphere. A new experience. The first time I'd ever recorded my voice on purpose. Just been recorded in the odd interview.

Becky was there, with a table and chair and my new intimate friend for the day, the speech microphone. She'd brought an older-type: a vintage 1930s one, a tall hexagon shape on a stand of its own.

"It's a ribbon mic. It doesn't take in sound from the sides, so it's as if it's listening to you alone. Very good for the voice. Let's give it a go, and see what you think."

I counted to ten in French, spoke my Verlaine poem, and went in to hear the playback. To my surprise, it sounded almost the way my voice does inside my head. As if my thoughts were speaking.

Ellen arrived in time to hear it.

"Don't you sound good? Tender and sad, like autumn itself, with a touch of agony towards the end."

"Thank you. Nicely put."

"By the way, Josy is fixing to come in."

"I'm not too keen to have him direct me in these two poems."

"Don't worry. He won't do that because I told him we would be starting at midday. He just wants to hear whatever's ready, to see if it gives him new thoughts."

We settled down.

"I've printed out the poems you sent as an attachment. I don't speak French much – a little from school, and a hint of the sound from the films I admire. You speak French, so you must tell me where you need retakes. I'm going away now, and you can start to record any time you want. Feel free."

I smoothed my paper out, and looked at the squiggles I'd made on it. Tried to remember what I meant by them.

The red light came on and my voice didn't. I swallowed instead.

"Remember to breathe…" Ellen said gently. I swallowed again. And did some breathing practice.

I read *Les sanglots longs* by Verlaine. It didn't come out as it did when I was trying the microphone. Not at all. I did it again at once.

"That's good. Lovely. I'm coming in."

So what wasn't so good or lovely?

"D'you know, you're just like all of us when we start."

"Is that supposed to make me feel good?"

"Of course. You've given a lovely imitation of someone reading a French poem, but trying to sound as if they're not reading."

"Oh, I get it. Any ideas?"

"Have you?"

"Look for details – of colour, individual words?"

"Yes..."

"And then forget about them?"

"Yes, let's try that," and read the last verse about the wind...

It was better.

"Just one more thing...Am I right in thinking this is a very dense poem? Give it more time. Say each line, and then ask yourself a question to which the next line is the answer. In French if you like. You know: the long sighs...who is this that's sighing? And so on. It will overload it with meaning, but something will remain behind when you read it all again."

It took time, and it worked.

And there we were, ready to deal with the flaxen-headed Scottish girl in Leconte de Lisle's poem who gave Debussy his starting point. I'd edited the poem, leaving out the hunting, shooting and fishing lines, and concentrated on the girl.

Ellen got me to do it a few times with no comment.

Then she came into the studio.

"What did you think?"

"I thought it was alright," I said defensively. "But" (afterthought) "could I say it directly to you? Not through the glass..."

"Right. Why not? Becky, can we just put the machine on and let it run?"

She sat opposite me.

"Remind me, what does it mean?"

"Word for word?"

"No, what's it about?"

"The way you look, and what that does for me."

"OK Bit more detail now."

"Your mouth asks to be kissed, your hair to be touched; love is calling to me; please don't say No – that would be cruel – and don't say Yes, because I would rather find the answer in your eyes, on your lips."

"Now say the poem to me here and now."

I did.

"You've got it off the copy," she said. "And you looked into my eyes all the time."

"What did you see?"

"You. Telling a girl how much you love her, and looking for words beautiful enough to say so."

"Did it mean anything?"

"It meant exactly what it should have meant."

There was no more time for this hopeless byplay, because Josy flew in with Victoria and we had a complete playback, music already edited and words roughly edited. He was happy.

"I don't know much about music, but that seems visual to me. Plenty of loud and some soft, stimulating and smoochy. (Interesting word for him; where did he get it from?) Not a lot of tunes to remember, but then you don't expect that with classical music."

Victoria couldn't let that pass.

"These pieces have got so much personality you could cut them in pieces and sell them by the slice – without images. That's what we want, isn't it, Josy?"

"Yeah. Right."

Ellen said, "We need to go on thinking. How to fit in with what Will's done, and make something no one has ever done before. We don't want to illustrate the music, certainly not like a cartoon. We'll use Will as the central image as much as possible."

"Yeah. Right."

I took that as a sign of approval. It was in his hands anyway. He was the one who would have to make the money being spent on this venture look good.

His English had got yet better, and he surprised me...I looked at him more closely. Yes, strange, a bandanna, and I thought that was a tattoo I glimpsed on his hand. On both hands even. Or maybe they were scars from years of toil, like the peasants in his films. This man could be roaming the plains of central Europe and I dare say he'd done that, because I still hadn't asked where he was from.

Maybe he understood the will o'the wisps in the Liszt piece better than Liszt did. Had seen them, even.

"You must not get tired," he said. "You must not look tired."

Did I look so tired now that he said it twice?

"You need to look just the way you look now. We'll do as much preparation on the sets and lighting before we get you in. We'll get used to finding the right angles for you. I want the whole thing to be fresh."

"Do you think I should look at some of your commercials to find out more about what you expect? I hadn't thought of that."

"Don't think of it." "Don't do that." Two voices at once.

"Be yourself. If you aren't, we could just as well get in another hunk and teach him the keyboard." His girl-friend-dictionary was doing good work: a 'hunk'?

Meanwhile I was happy with the recording I'd done. Short pieces aren't easier because they're short. They need sharp definition; you have only a small amount of time to say anything you want to say. Like a bit-part player making an impression as a star. Stealing the picture.

He said there had to be more sessions with Ellen. Yes. Clearing things up.

Bringing in Victoria for the CD

Email from Jane: *jane@curzprod.co.uk*

Will. It sounds absolutely great – they sent me a CD of the rough edit. I think the sound is real, sensitive. I'll work out a few more adjectives for the press release when the time comes. How did you find working with Victoria? You could have her for your Beethoven and Schubert, if you see what I mean. Advantage of a 'new' producer, and a photogenic one too. We could add a picture or two to the publicity and the booklet.

Steve could be available, but he's got a whole series with an orchestra: every last note written by César Franck and his Schola Cantorum. No, they can't possibly do that, there are so many of them. I've no idea who will buy it, but some distant descendant of somebody is putting up the money. He could fit you in, but you might do better with someone who would devote themselves to you. If you see what I mean again. You know how easy she was for the film recording.

How about meeting her for lunch to get to know her better? I could be there too, to give it a bit of edge.

Lemme know. J.

Email to Jane Curzon:

We got on fine. Good ears. Good brain. Good rapport. Good appearance. All we need is a good lunch and feedback from that.

Fix please. You keep my diary. Nothing else is going on just at the moment that isn't in it.

Will

**

I found Victoria easy to get on with. That awkwardness I'd conjured up at the beginning of our association had completely gone. A Beethoven girl, who would take time over the sonata, and talk about it and maybe teach me something about it.

Lunch. Italian. Because I can choose from the antipasto dishes if I'm not up for a main course.

Jane and I got there early: we had some possible dates for the CD. She had some more distant dates to talk over. To Germany in March next year for a 'former winners' concert as a late follow-up to the Schumann competition all those years ago. His piano quintet with a German quartet I'd never met before. I'd heard them on disc, and they were great, so I wanted as much time to rehearse with them as possible. I don't get the chance to play chamber music often, and I was looking forward to the concerts in Wales later in the year. What would it have been like to live in the nineteen-twenties when you went to some rich patron's house after a concert, and played chamber music for the fun of it? And listened to the young English composer Rebecca Clarke telling Ravel's fortune in Tarot cards...

Jane had been my agent for going on ten years. She always says she'd got me marked down as a potential client even before I won the prize and got some attention in the papers. I'd like to believe her. She has standards; she's a good musician in her own right. She was a student at the Conservatoire just ahead of me – I played Poulenc's flute sonata with her in my first year. She was good.

When I signed up with her, I asked her what she'd been up to since then.

"Why didn't you become a professional flautist?"

"Oh…too many people learnt to play the flute in the turbulence created by James Galway and his golden flute. Remember him? Quite a lot of that gold turned into base metal in other people's hands. It made much more sense to get work for other people than to sit around waiting for the phone to ring, with my flute on my lap and my lips pursed ready to blow. Strangely, I don't miss it. I still go and play in my daughter's school concerts."

"You never told me you were married."

"I'm not, and my partner is a woman, and yes, it is my child physically, though Lizzie is the other real parent, as far as upbringing is concerned."

Victoria arrived. Yes. She was dressed like a lady who lunches. Wearing a colourful jacket with a black skirt, a necklace. Her dark hair had, I suspected, been looked after in a smart hair salon. It seemed to my ill-informed knowledge of women, that she intended to look womanly. How old-fashioned can you get? Me, I mean. Yes, I did look at her legs. Good. She was wearing high heels. How did she know about that?

We ate wisely and well.

Jane had to go early. Agents keep on their toes going around to get more work for us.

Victoria and I were left. It was tell-me-about-you time.

"University degree in music. You know, where you work out how music is put together and try and write it the way they did in the sixteenth century. Good discipline, and at least it makes you respect composers. You must have done some theoretical training like that."

"I didn't have as much time as I would have liked; somehow there was always a keyboard waiting for me to bring to life. That's my excuse: it just sat there, daring me to play it. I felt like a ballet dancer, who can't miss a day or it would show."

"Hard work."

"I suppose so, but it pays dividends. If that's what you like to do."

"Do you ever wonder what you'll do when you give up playing in public?"

"No. I could go on for ever as some pianists do – eighty years old and they can still play. I've seen some who could hardly stand up at the end of a concert, and yet had played like a thirty-five-year old. Depends a bit on your genes, like everything."

"Like everything," she said. "So what else is in your genes?"

That was rather a sudden switch.

"I don't know, really."

My genes. DNA? My wandering father? My mother, who would do anything to be a success in films? Clever, adorable, Grandmother? Solid Grandfather I didn't get to know very well before he died. I recognise something of all of them in me. They were the only family I knew, and now they have gone.

"I don't know, really," I said again. "We might find something out when we start to film. Or start to record Beethoven."

"Will you have me as a producer? Not wait for Steve?"

"Yes, I want that. It'll be a first for both of us. Beethoven together."

"First time in the studio, but not the first time Beethoven. We played his Emperor Concerto together, you know. That's when I first heard you. You came to do it with the University orchestra. I played the drums."

I didn't remember much about that. Anything about that. I said something that fits any situation.

"I would have been happy to have the rehearsal go on for longer. Not because of the way you played your drums."

"I had practised. You have to hit the right one, and hit it in the right place. At the right time; lots of counting goes on." She laughed. "We'd had a big argument about how 'authentic' we could make our performance sound on modern instruments. The way Beethoven might have heard it in his inner ear. We were very serious music students in a university music department. It sort of spilled over into your rehearsal."

"But it went alright, didn't it?"

"Oh sure."

"I'm glad, because I did special homework for that concert. There's a place in Kent where they have a collection of historic pianos, and I went to give the Emperor Concerto a spin on the Conrad Graf piano there. It's almost the same age as Beethoven. The Emperor's Old Clothes. You get a different sound in your ears, and a different feeling in your fingers."

"Could be why we found it so easy to play along with you. That and the fact that you were someone who had such an air of success."

"I'm not quite sure what you mean by that. Success – like shallow?"

"Just like big, sensitive, yet with no doubts about thinking and feeling in public. Even those of us who'd been in various high-flying youth orchestras felt good about it. I still remember that, though it must be five years ago."

"Probably more."

"It was something of a challenge to think I'd be working with you on this project. But somehow you're not the person I expected."

"How do you mean?"

"You look different. Completely different."

"Good. I tried."

"That's not really it. You're much more approachable. There was something preoccupied about you. You didn't relate to us much, as if you weren't interested in people. We talked about it afterwards; you know, the academic post-mortem. 'What have I learnt from this experience?'"

"Maybe I wouldn't have accepted the date if I'd known you were going to do that."

"I don't believe that. You'd done some homework, as you said. We thought your playing was fantastic, but we didn't get much idea about the human being beyond the music. A musician, yes…Oh, you can imagine the sort of thing that got said."

It didn't seem likely that I could, because such things hadn't crossed my mind. How was I different, apart from being able to get into clothes with a waistline? Had divorce shone a light into the recesses of my soul?

"You were sort of plump and wearing glasses, and your clothes were crumpled, a case of premature middle-age…Talk about a make-over…"

"So, what did you write about my Beethoven in your thesis? No, don't tell me."

"No…well…" She stopped.

"Now you're teasing me. I hope."

"Well, you had a reputation for speed and a technique to leave most of the others in the lay-bys."

"Ouch."

"But true. And you can get away with more in-your-face playing in the Emperor concerto. The outside movements, anyway."

"You're making me nervous."

"But…"

"But?"

"I thought, from behind my drums, that you brought us to life. I won't say that I played my drums as never before, because I'd never played them in a real concert before. Or since. But you had a real hold on the whole thing. A touch of poetry, if that's the word, in the slow movement, and I didn't play in that, I just listened."

"Thank you."

"Strange. I wanted to tell you at the time, and now it's like telling someone else. As if the person inside you in that slow movement had come outside for me to see."

"That's a nice thing to hear."

"It's a nice thing to say."

A moment of musical intimacy. Maybe something more than that, because there were subtexts, if you wanted to find them. As Ellen has shown me.

"How about making a sort of test recording of the two sonatas at my place? It might save time in the studio." I said that.

"That might be a good idea: I can get a hold on your take on Beethoven. And Schubert. Look, I'll bring my own portable system. It's good."

I actually have good recording equipment. But we left it at that. Woman in late twenties, ambitious, sensitive to music. I didn't need to take any of her ideas on board, but I'm not fixed in stone. Beethoven and Schubert are more important than I am.

We made a date for a couple of weeks ahead.

**

I went home and played through opus 109 complete with no pauses. To see if I'd got the whole shape in my head. It worked, not perfectly, but it was getting better. There are some sounds here which were unusual in his time – on his piano even. People used to say it was because he was deaf and couldn't hear the result of what he wrote on paper (that notorious mess) by playing it on his instrument. It was up to me to make it sound like what he heard in his head. As far as I could. I tried it again – no thought, just let it happen, let it run round the track under its own steam. Let my fingers lead me to Ludwig and let him take me over.

They'd warned me that when I'm doing my film actor thing, there would be a lot of short takes. Actors have to learn how to pick their characters up in a second. Out of sequence. A series of short truths. Momentary truths, even. So I tried it with Beethoven, stopping and starting, then playing it out of sequence, picking up the feeling as quickly as possible. Interesting. Exciting crossover techniques, learning how not to stand still.

Getting closer to the filming

Next day a session in the afternoon at my house with Ellen, Rob and Josy. My living quarters were being re-created in the studio…well, not exactly, more like the idealised version an estate agent would dream up if you were selling your house. All the same, my mentors came to watch me walking around. Where do I sit, how do I sit, do I have any personal habits which would photograph well. Or any which definitely wouldn't.

It made me look closely at the place where I live. Over the last months I'd reinvented my appearance, my mind-set, and finally I'd begun to reinvent my home. The result was a bit bare, apart from my books, so my little bronze statue from the Endenich competition has been promoted to a central spot among the odd pictures and ornaments from my pre- or post-Patti period. With a light of its own, like a spirit watching over me. Junk, but I don't mind junk like that.

Rob took pictures. "It doesn't have to be exact, because there may not be too many people who know what your place is like. But we think it should help you to feel at home when we're filming you."

"Anything that helps. Important first thing is that you need the right size of piano."

"They come in many sizes, is that what happens?" Josy asked. "I don't know about pianos."

I went over to the piano and patted it.

"This is Model B. Perfect."

I lifted the lid and put it on its long stick.

"It looks pretty inside. With all those gold strings," Rob said.

"Brass really."

"That row of black things?"

"Dampers to stop the strings vibrating when you don't want them to."

I played a bit of Liszt.

"They jump up and down. Dramatic. Good visuals. What do people want to see? On television?"

"They want to see what you've just seen. And my fingers playing the keys. Best way for that is from above. If you get a camera up there."

"One looking inside, one looking down."

"And we need to see Will's face," said Ellen.

"Ellen's been working on my face. And if you stand in the bay of the piano, you can look straight at me."

"Thank you. I've taken pictures. Seems like we need three cameras which could be on site before you start each section of the film."

"So, we have seven scenes to film. Start each one with the piano, set up before we begin. You in your costume – your clothes for the item."
That's what they settled for.

In the salon

They'd arranged a session for me with a make-up lady.

"Make-up?" I asked her when she rang me.

"What you need for the camera. Check your finger- and toe-nails." Toenails?

"And look at your eyebrows maybe."

"I don't want to be a prima donna, but is this necessary?"

"You're going to be in close-close-up and everything has to be right. It won't show."

"What's the point of it then?"

"Put it this way: it would show if you didn't wear any."

No answer to that one. We made an appointment.

So there I was in a salon, run by Maria, a woman who not only does media people, but also the public people; even some of the fringe-beneficiaries of the royal family. And politicians.

With Marty, male make-up man, partner of Maria, the lady who was supposed to be doing it for me.

"Sorry about that," he said, "but there was this film came in suddenly. The star threw a wobbly about the man they'd engaged to do her face. About the only thing she could throw, although she's playing some big heroic Roman woman. Or is it Greek? It's about the Amazons, and I don't mean the internet shop."

He must have meant she was playing Penthesilea, who had only one breast, because she had the other one cut off to make it easier to dispatch arrows from her bow to kill more men more accurately.

"Right, let's have a vada at your eek. Mmmm…Not bad," he went on.

"Sorry. What was that you said?"

"I just like some of the old camp slang. My clients find it fun, but I'll skip it if it means nothing to you."

He inspected my face.

"The eyes are fine. You must get plenty of sleep, or it's going to show, whatever they do with the lighting. And no naughty behaviour – or least not more than usual; it shows if you're not careful." He smiled. He might have saved himself the bother. There was no sign of naughtiness on the horizon.

"You can bathe them in hot water with a face flannel, and then splash with cold. Lashes might be curled a bit more, but they're long enough. A little colour on them, too. Tweak a few of your eyebrows out."

"You're not going for an ambidextrous look by any chance, are you?"

"Course not. But you need to look like someone made you up. Like an advertisement for music. That's what it says on my work sheet. That's the basic look."

"There's more than a basic look?"

"Well, it says here: fire-dance, sleeping in bed, raindrops, which will mean you'll sweat and you're going to get wet."

I said nothing.

"We could just lighten the skin underneath these eyes; you've not got bags, not that you can carry anything in, but a hint of purses…maybe. Skin's OK. Ever tried designer stubble?"

"No. I don't fancy looking as if I'd got up too late to shave. How do you keep it always at that same needing-a-shave length without it turning into a beard?"

"Use an electric razor. Easy. Butch effect. You know: 'I've got so much testosterone that it keeps bursting out on my face.' Lovely."

"I think we'll leave that one out."

"How do you shave?"

"Shaving cream and a four-blade unit in a razor." Marty took a sharp breath.

"Ever cut yourself?"

"Well, no."

"Just take care, like you're shaving for the first time. It's not a horror movie – you mustn't turn up with scars."

I promised.

He noticed hairs at the bottom of my neck. "They'll need neatening. In fact, I'd better see the rest of you. A bit of instant tan may be what you need."

"I'm not intending to undress for this film."

"You wouldn't be the first to say that, and believe me," he said, helping me off with my shirt, "you never know with these things. What starts out in innocence can take a steep downward curve. Or upward, if you like. You just never know. My oh my, what have we here?"

"What do you mean, my oh my?"

167

"The hair," he said.

"I had it cut the other day, and I like it," I said.

"No, not that. Though I must say I've seen better styling."

"It cost enough."

"Beside the point. Still, if that's what they want you to look like…"

"What d'you mean, then?" I knew perfectly well.

"Your other hair – that stuff – it's not fashionable at the moment."

"It's nothing to do with fashion. It belongs to me. It grew when I wasn't looking."

"Of course it did."

"So?"

"People in your position in the Noughties are shaving it off."

"What position is that?"

"Making films, whatever. Going for the statue look…clean lines, just skin."

"Oh come on! You can't take this away from me. I feel safe behind this hair. I haven't seen my chest in full for years."

"Please yourself," he said. "But your director might like to have it off." He actually giggled. "Too many Carry On films. He might not think it's artistic."

I thought this was turning a bad corner. What had my hair to do with playing the piano? I'm not as hairy as all that. I don't look as if I've just swung in from a branch in a jungle.

"You're going to be in close-up, you know. People will see you close to. This is a film."

"I hadn't really thought."

"You need educating. Haven't you seen any pop films?"

"Maybe a bit of one by accident. It's not my line of country."

"Some of them are very raunchy. You won't be doing that, of course, because you're legit, and some of those artists will do anything to be noticed. All the same if you want big sales, using your body a bit won't come amiss."

My hair is fair, a little darker on my body than on my head, but he thought I was too thick on the chest, and reluctantly I let him skim it a bit. But I didn't like it. It felt part of me. He also thought my natural skin colour would do.

"Not that I can do much about it," he sighed.

By now, I really felt like an object, something to be looked at and judged. It wasn't exactly unpleasant, just disconcerting. Was I playing with danger? Not with Beethoven and Schubert to back me up. I don't take my shirt off to play them. I took a taxi home as fast as I could to try the Schubert sonata; there's something about the opening bars which seems like a connection between the body and the soul. I can't have one without the other. Composers didn't hide it.

Sir Gregory offers me a job

The Principal wanted to see me. He'd left a message on the phone.

He wanted to know about Felicity. Lord Chislehurst had been in for a meeting, and talked about the concert at her old school, though he hadn't been there personally. Sir Gregory had been the Principal for twenty years, and never spoke to me when I was a student. It was only after I left, after I won my prize, that he knew my name. Once I'd got that Schumann statuette, it was as if I'd risen from the sea like whichever God it was. Or was it a Goddess? It was. Aphrodite. So I was a male version, complete with waterproof piano.

"You're doing a wonderful job with Felicity Smith," he said. His voice had a sort of public-speaking quality that suggested he wanted something from me. I was intrigued, because I didn't see how I could help him. He had his knighthood, and you would have thought that was enough for any man. It must be something to do with Lord Chis. I had an interest there, didn't I? Hadn't he put up most of the money for my film, if not all? Sir Greg surely didn't know about that yet.

"Yes, indeed you are, a really wonderful job. She's one of our rising girls. Bit of a problem for her, do you think, being the chairman's daughter? Imagine how careful the students have to be when they talk about him."

He folded his hands over his stomach. It surprises me that an organist like him ever puts on weight – you would have thought that the business of playing the pedals as well as the keyboards would be like being on an exercise bike.

I couldn't imagine that any student would want to talk about Lord Chislehurst.

"I don't honestly think they have much of a problem with that. I doubt if many of them know. I'm sure Felicity doesn't tell them. The young men might be keeping their eyes on her, which wouldn't surprise me."

The Principal looked at me rather carefully. I could see he was not too keen on the idea that I might find her attractive. I went on:

"She seems a very balanced girl, and musically experienced, and well able to deal with problems of that sort. I'm sure that if students have any criticisms of the Conservatoire, they wouldn't try to get to Lord Chislehurst through Felicity. I'm sure they'd come and tell you. With an appointment, of course."

Sir Greg laughed, while he thought of something to say. "Of course they would. The door's always open – with an appointment, as you say, just to make sure they don't all come at once." He laughed at the unlikelihood.

He straightened his tie for some reason. Drawing up the drawbridge, maybe.

"They should definitely talk about Lord Chislehurst, though. He does so much for them. He's brought so much to his role at the helm. Tireless in our interests, and in maintaining our standards."

Did he really talk like that naturally? It sounded as if he were answering questions in an interview or writing an obituary.

"Oh, yes, he's done a lot," I muttered that. "He's very generous with his hospitality, too."

That seemed to throw Sir Greg.

I went on. "It's a beautiful house he has in Chelsea; and the pictures…"

"Yes, the pictures." His face was meant to be muted in recollection, since it was obvious he'd never been there.

"That's not the reason I asked you to come in. As you know, it's our centenary and a half in July. A hundred and fifty years since the charter was sealed, and I'm planning to conduct our orchestra at one of the major London halls, and then take it on a mini-tour – Liverpool, Edinburgh, Cardiff – to fly the flag. Show off our most distinguished past pupils, too. You know. Dame Evelyn Knight will sing the Strauss Four Last Songs, and I wondered if you would play a concerto with us."

"Had you not thought of using present day students? Fly a recent flag?"

"It's not so easy, you understand. In fact, damned hard, you understand. Whoever I chose there would be a lot of ill feeling. And if it were Felicity Smith…well, you understand."

He was determined that I was going to understand. He was right in that respect, certainly. Choosing Felicity would be a total disaster; she was a first year student, and there were other talented young pianists who would feel passed over. This was his best way out. The only people who would suffer would be the poor students in the orchestra, who would much rather be getting themselves holiday jobs to earn a bit of money than working their socks off trying to sound like a young Berlin Philharmonic to promote the Con's image. And Sir Greg's too.

"I'm delighted to be asked, flattered to be thought of as an illustrious alumnus. But what about Brian MacArthur? He's a very distinguished clarinettist, great member of staff, too. He'd do you a superb Mozart concerto."

"Possible choice, but I wanted someone younger, who's caught the imagination of the audiences, and who would look as if it doesn't take so long for our training to pay off. Evelyn shows how our training can set you up for a long and very distinguished career, and a Damehood. And I believe she's thinking about retiring."

I told him I was interested in principle, but that he'd have to check with Jane Curzon who kept my diary. I didn't say that I knew she would ask him for a decent fee. There was a limit to how much I was prepared to do for nothing. Especially for Sir Greg who, as I said, had somehow not noticed me when I was a student. Though it's fair to say he hadn't noticed many of the others either.

**

Email from Jane Curzon to *will@williamwinton.co.uk*
Will, dear friend, I must apologise. I can't get to be with you for the filming. I've to sort out a problem with replacing one of my clients who's fallen ill. My thoughts are with you, but not my umbrella for a rainy day. J

**

I met Ellen for lunch the next day. Briefly. A business meeting. I told her about my experiences with Marty the make-up man.

"You look good."

"You look even better," I told her, which was true. Looking at her more closely, she seemed to me to have taken that extra bit of trouble about her appearance, which I hoped she meant for me.

"That's beside the point. You're the one on camera."

"I feel very naïve in this world of yours," I said.

"Don't put yourself down," she said. "You've been a good pupil, the way you've been cooperating."

"Thanks to you. I hope you're going to go on helping me during filming. I can't do it without you."

"Yes, and Nonsense, are the answers to that.

"Filming is a slow process. Everything takes much longer than you expect. Just remember to be patient and switch off whenever you can. You're the star act, which we know is harder, because you're on your own, with no-one for you to react to."

"I'm used to being on my own."

"Poor Will. You won't be alone. We'll be there to help you."

"Does it surprise you that I feel nervous? And dependent?"

"No, it's usual. Some actors never get over having first night nerve attacks. Or first day on a longer project, a film, whatever. You could take a beta-blocker, if you're terrified. I don't recommend it. But it's been done."

Yes, I'd tried it once, years before, for a recorded concert in Germany, and I thought I played like something out of Paradise. When I heard the playback, it was more like something out of Oz, the one with the Wizard. Automatic pilot. Not really bad, but programmed.

"No. And how've you been since I last saw you?" I did want to get this conversation on to a local level.

"About the same as when I last saw you a couple of days ago. I've been talking with the director. I have one or two ideas. I think I know your potential better than he does."

"What do you think my potential is?"

I looked her as full in the eyes as she would let me.

"I don't entirely know. But I'm working on it."

"Do you ever stop working and let go, when you're with me?"

"Yes and No. I do let go when I'm with you – you're that sort of man. But I am working, because you're my work, and I need to get this job right. I'm not a successful pianist, or actor or director, and if I want to be anything, then I've got to get a move on. There's a lot riding on this for me."

"Day after tomorrow," she said. "Sleep well."

**

Well, it was something. I went home alone to Schubert. There are difficult moments in this sonata which have to sound clear, sensible, not too emotional – they need to be there to balance the music. It's quite a lot longer than the Beethoven, and it needs pacing, not in speed, but in its musical journey, in its emotional journey. Finding out why the music is repeated, and how to come at it in a different way to show why it's repeated. Schubert will suddenly do something so beautiful that it makes you catch your breath and want to dawdle over it, underline it, instead of letting it be a surprising view of eternity, for which you allow only as much space as it needs in its context. Beethoven reminds me of what I could be. Nobler? To suffer the slings and arrows? Schubert seems to know what it's like to be a human being in need of humour as well as consolation and love.

The filming – Day 1

The 'day after tomorrow' turned out to be quite a day.

A taxi picked me up. Taxi all the way, no changing trains or waiting for a bus. They wanted to make sure I was in full working condition. It made me feel special. Normally I go on public transport to my city concerts, or I drive elsewhere if that suits.

It was my first time in a studio that wasn't just about sound. I reminded myself that I was used to the odd camera peering over my shoulder or looking at me through the piano lid at public concerts, and although I deal with that by basically ignoring it, I knew this wasn't the same thing. Not at all the same thing. Nothing like the same thing.

It was uncanny, almost as if the taxi driver had doubled back. I'd come to the place I live in. Or a bit of it, planted into a larger space. My living room, my Steinway piano. Beyond that there was a lot of equipment, monitors, cameras, lights, wires looking like spiders waiting to catch me in their web.

Josy welcomed me.

"Will, love, good to see you. Good to see you looking so well, lovely even. Very suitable."

He introduced me to Joe, assistant director, who took over.

"Let's get you settled in, and we can have a word or two about how it'll work for you."

He took me up to the spare bedroom upstairs in the house-school.

"This is where you'll spend your time when you're not on parade."

It was a nice room, wooden floor, and pretty rugs in keeping with the taste of the owners, I imagine. It had a small bathroom with a shower over the bath, *en suite*, as they say in the hotel ads. There were tables on which I could put whatever I needed to put on tables: drinking water, glasses, plates, food, non-bedroom things which wouldn't have done the rugs much good if they fell off, so the floor was covered with some sort of transparent plastic sheeting to protect it. The bed, too, was made up for resting, not sleeping as such, though there was nothing in my rather generalised instructions that prohibited me from napping.

A mirror or two, of course, but out in the studio the unit would be watching me, like nature's patient, sleepless Eremite, every face a mirror with a brain. The windows had blinds which I could close. My make-up, designed to make me look as if I wasn't wearing any, would be put on here and checked downstairs. My 'costumes' were hanging on a frame, with labels saying when they were to be used. They had asked me for my measurements, including my shoe-size. I brought my own concert clothes.

"I'll get us a cup of coffee, and give you some idea of what's going to happen. Please don't be offended if I tell you things you know already, but Jane, your agent, did say this was your first film."

I unpacked what I needed; I'd got my usual bag, with the spare things I take with me on my travels – mostly clothing to get into after a hot concert session.

Joe came back with the cups of coffee, and a selection of non-fattening snacks.

There was a lot to remember…

"It does look rather complicated down there," I said.

"It's the truth. Everything that has to happen happens in the same area. We're a tight little team, all carefully chosen.

"You saw how crowded things are. Digital desks, machines, screen to show what the cameras see, other screens, some big, for the digital images which will be added later. No microphones in the studio unless they're suddenly needed for some reason. Loudspeakers to play your recording back for you for filming the piano. and for you to fit your acting to if that's needed. Especially if Josy wants you to dance."

"I don't think I'll be doing that. I've not been practising any steps."

"The wires on the floor aren't all attached to the ground where they lie, because they'll be moved around. But don't worry; you'll be conducted to where you need to be – where the lighting will be set up ready for you.

"We've got things sorted for the piano sequences on the lines you talked about with Rob. Which will start each section. After that, there'll be a lot of arranging equipment, moving lights, measuring distances, changing camera positions. It all takes time, but that can be useful for you to think through what you're about to do. You will be watched by cameras: one which has to move smoothly on tracks, one which goes on a shoulder. We have other small cameras which don't move. This is to make sure we have a lot of choices for the final mix. It means that there need be fewer takes and retakes."

"Sounds good to me, as the new boy…"

"Old boys and girls like it too."

"Just tell me what to do, and I'll try. I've had a couple of advance warnings that a lot of hanging around is normal. And I've seen odd films which include studio scenes."

"Well, they give you an idea, but the reality is much more long-winded. It shouldn't be so bad here because you're the only person we're interested in."

"Bit scary."

"We're here to help. And we'll send you off up here as often as possible."

"That's good to know."

"Come on down and meet the team. It's small by usual standards, because of the budget, so people multi-task if necessary and there's only one actor."

"Me."

"We're really looking forward to this. New stuff. Breaking new ground."

**

I knew Rob, Director of Photography, because we'd kicked leaves together in Burnham Beeches. Janice Stevens (Janny) was Rob's assistant. I would get to know her because she would be dealing with the finer details of the lighting, as well as being a sort of ring-master, to keep things in order.

Eddie (Edmund) Williams was there with a movable camera on wheels, so I was to get used to him advancing and retreating.

Victoria shook her earphones at me and blew me a kiss. She would be looking after the pre-recorded sound.

Then there were the runners.

"Chris, Alice, and Flip. Work-experiencing young people from Media Schools. They help out, you might say. You'll see that Chris is about your size."

Chris waved.

"He'll be your stand-in. particularly when it comes to setting up the lighting, because that takes time. You'll have to be there in person for the fine-tuning. And for getting the special light – the eye light – exactly in place to show in your eyes; that can only be done with you. Janny does that."

Alice was a very pretty girl and discreetly attached to Chris.

Rob said, "Flip is Philip. He's just about to qualify as a cameraman, and he'll come in handy."

Marty was there as he'd promised.

"Hello, Marty. How are you and yours?"

"Maria's just got home from the Amazons and it's good to be out of the salon while she calms down. So I'm looking after your make up and dabbing at the sweat that you're going to sweat. Just for the sake of your beautiful eyebrows."

Ellen came over and kissed me on the cheek.

"I'm Josy's special assistant for this project," she said, "that's what it says in my contract."

"You'll be there to help me in my hour of need."

"No need involved…just believe in yourself. You have plenty to believe in. You're a highly adaptable performer taking on a few more tasks. And…remember to breathe!"

Josy patted me on the back.

"There are some new things for all of us, don't you know? Everything starts with you as you play your piano. Is the central thing. Then we have fun making pictures."

Rob took over, bringing Chris with him.

"We've got the piano set up, and the cameras set. Lights are in place, but the ones for your face will need to be adjusted. So we could be getting you to play the pieces twice. Or part of them. Somewhat unusual territory for us, because of the limitations the instrument brings with it, like its lid, which has to be open on the stick."

I sat at the piano and tried it. None of what I was going to play would be heard in the final film, but I wanted the feel of it under my hands, so that I looked at home.

"Small point: can you give Chris a piano lesson, so that he can double for you at the keyboard?"

"Chris, have you ever played the piano?"

"No. My fingers are the wrong shape, I think."

I gave him lesson number one. How to sit and how to put your hands on the keyboard, how to look into the distance through the lid.

Victoria came to tell me about how the music side would work. I was glad to see her. "It's good to see familiar faces. I don't mind admitting that I feel like an explorer without a map."

"Let me give you directions. I've worked out a system to get the visual 'you' and the recorded 'you' into close proximity. It's a bit basic, but that's an advantage.

"We'll play part of the complete track on the loudspeakers for you to catch the mood. Then it'll be faded, and you'll get two bars of a metronome clicking, and then you start to play for real for the cameras.

"I'll be listening on my phones just in case you get madly out of sync. Which I don't expect to happen. I'm not worried if it's not a complete match all the way through the piece. Everything will be edited. Magic time."

"Sounds OK. It's good we're starting with the Bach which has a constant tempo."

"True enough. But what's filmed at the piano is only part of the deal. You'll be moving about too. So we might play the music for you to act to."

"Like a silent film actor."

"The music won't always be needed. You'll be doing things for the cameras."

Alice came to tell us they were ready to go.

I took my place at the keyboard, Marty checked my face, and Janny checked the lighting and fine-tuned my eye-light.

Joe had something to say before we got under way.

"One final, very important thing; we will be calling for silence and that we're going for a take, but – big 'but' – don't do anything until you hear the word 'Action'. It comes from silent film days but it still exists. We'll be using that formula here.

"And the best of good wishes for our film."

A lot was depending on me, the innocent one. With experienced people on hand to make it easier, wipe the sweat from my troubled brow, make sure I looked the same, my clothes too, in retakes.

There were moments when I had a severe loss of nerve, like a nightmare in which you go on stage, sit at the piano, and the orchestra starts to play a concerto you don't know because it hasn't been written yet.

**

The First Real Action

I suppose starting with the keyboard was the best way.

This prelude by Bach is one of my favourite pieces. It has a built-in sense of joy, though it's in a minor key which has a reputation for looking at the dark side of life. Not this one. It's in three-time and it dances, it swings, it plays games, it makes me smile, almost laugh. I play it like a piece written for the modern piano, but clean of pedal. There are no instructions in the score, only in the music itself, which invites your involvement.

I sat at the keyboard. The lighting had been done with my double, and it had to be checked out with me on the piano stool; this was what was going to happen with all the items. I was filmed by the camera overhead for my hands and the one gazing into the piano. Then, after another visit from Marty and a check on the light for my eyes for the camera whose job it was to see to my face.

I couldn't believe how simple it was to do.

I was sent upstairs to put on my first costume: a loose fitting shirt, a towelling dressing gown and slippers which weren't going to be seen, since they didn't fit. We went across the playground-that-had-been to the outhouse. I wore a long raincoat, because it was raining, and runner Flip held a big umbrella over my head. I wasn't allowed to hold it in case my fingers got caught up in advance of the close-ups. I accepted that I wasn't to be trusted to do much of anything that I normally do.

Bach for getting up to. Running water, beginning of the day. Like my fake living room, my fake bathroom stood in the middle of the area. The shower – a generous size, standing out from the wall, as mine does, with the same decorative patterns round its middle – was in working order. Wash basin too. Loo, obviously, because you can't show 'my' bathroom without one; I've no idea if it worked. There was a blank green window. I supposed they would find something to put on it, since my window at home has frosted glass.

Joe explained more. "Everything we want for this scene will be filmed here – that's the general idea – and we'll leave some of the lighting in position here until the end of our time filming.

"We don't want to be bringing much across in the rain, and this location will be ready in case the director decides to do more shots here when the rest of the film is in the can. After-thoughts, or re-thoughts. Don't be surprised. They will be for close-ups – of you shaving – that sort of thing."

There wasn't a lot of room. This was supposed to be early morning in what should look like a happy day dedicated to seven pieces of music. Rob was to be mobile with the camera, once we started, and he'd been rehearsing the shots with Chris, the runner-cum-stand-in for me.

Josy appeared.

"All happy, dear boy?" We were Hitchcock now, it seemed. That figured; after all, this was a sort of post-shower scene.

I had a question.

"Can I just clear up one thing? I am not in the shower, am I?"

"No. This is after you have your shower. You will come out of the shower getting into your gown."

Ellen was with him.

"I'm your dresser. Strictly non-union in a real film – you can't be a coach and a dresser and a special assistant to the director. You're not a union member, are you?"

"I belong to a society, but I don't remember any rules about these things."

She shook the towel dressing gown out.

"Are you going to dress me, nursey?"

"Behave yourself," she said. "And remember in theory you're not wearing anything under this towelling gown."

It was an odd feeling. I had re-invented myself, in the aftermath of my sunken marriage, and was still at odds with my outward and visible appearance, and now it seemed as if it was to be detached from me. I was a commodity, not an 'artist'. Could be fun. Be a clown? Be a clown with L-plates.

The shower was run to cover the glass with droplets.

Josy went off to watch on the monitor in the school house.

Janny took over. "You will have ended the shower – we shall hear the sounds of the water splashing, which will be put in afterwards to mix with the music. We will see you pulling your dressing gown about you – only the top part of your body. You will turn, take a towel and put it round your neck; you can touch your face with it."

Marty cut in. "Remember you have make-up, so no crude rubbing if you don't mind."

"Yes. No rubbing. Then you'll get to shave."

That's what I had to do There was to be a swirl of dressing gown between me and the camera. This needed rehearsing to make sure that the gown really was between me and the camera. No sight of the jeans or anything else I wouldn't wear in a shower was to be allowed.

It seemed a long time after I was all set and ready to go that the magic word 'Action' was called. No sound was being recorded, although everyone was quiet, which made it easier for me to concentrate on getting things right. Several takes were needed as I got better at swirling my way into my towelling while the camera watched.

Then my gown was fixed so that I could do the shaving in it, with a contrasting towel for the face and hands. It was all very logical and in the right order.

"Now you shave."

Ellen said, "When we're ready Marty will put your shaving cream on."

"I don't use it. I use gel."

"White cream for this. It photographs better. Be pleased it isn't beaten-up egg white, which is what they used to use."

Basin, water, razor, mirror (a round one on a trellis thing), all in position. All away from the wall so that Rob could get behind them. I was positioned in front of the basin, which had warm water in it. The lighting was checked, and Janny made sure that the eye light was visible in my eyes. It took time. Marty flicked my hair around a little, added some wet-looking gunge.

"It's supposed to look as if you've just had a shower, and not just got in from the hairdresser's. Close your eyes while I put the shaving foam on. Can't have it making you blink."

"Or clogging up my contacts."

"You're not wearing your lenses, are you?"

"Have you ever seen me without my contact lenses in?"

"Oh my, I thought you'd never ask."

I shaved three times, no blades in the razor, each time splashing my face with water (eyes, tightly shut), towelling. The water had to be drained out and replaced each time. My shaving cream replaced, make-up checked each time.

Then there was a silence. A long one. Total.

"Did I do something wrong?"

"No. We did."

Josy's voice on the speaker: "It does not look good."

"You don't surprise me. I've never shaved for other people before."

"You make faces."

So I did it twice more, trying not to get anything in my eyes, while keeping an expression of neutral bonhomie throughout. Another silence.

"Would you walk to the shower, wait a moment, and then slide the door open? As if you are wishing to have this shower more than anything else in the world. More than making love."

Why not? I'm an obedient man. I did as I was bid. Wearing my towelling robe, since we'd already done a bit of me getting out of the shower.

Since there was no sound track involved, Josy called out instructions like a silent movie. We went through various water-related exercises.

When I finished, Ellen patted my face.

"Josy has just decided to modify this morning to night thing. Keep the water image; you out of the shower, splashing your face, cross-cutting with water images and pebbles, and all that."

"So he's hardly using my re-created bathroom. Money wasted."

"Not at all. You have a bathroom that's all yours when you need it. Just use it. It'll help you to relax between takes. Better than the one upstairs."

True enough.

"We've spent more time on this that we expected, but it's given you a bit of a run-in."

I ate next to nothing for lunch, though it had been recruited from a well-known local restaurant.

**

So to the afternoon.

I was wearing autumn clothing for autumn. *Automne* by Cécile Chaminade.

A loose blue pullover, cuffs turned back so that my wrists could be seen. Trousers a denim blue. Nothing green, so that I wouldn't disappear if I got near any of those green screens which were going to be used for putting in the clips from Burnham Beeches. Trainers.

We did the music-performing bit. Lights already set up. Now adjusted slightly.

The outer parts of the piece are melancholy, and the central bit is the storm. All good stuff for a proficient pianist. My grandmother made quite a good fist of it, though she cooked it – tactfully leaving out some of the notes. Gran would have played them if she'd had time to practise, and hadn't had to look after Grandpa and my mother, until she took off to be an actress. And then me…

We did this in three separate bits, each cued in by Victoria.

Hands OK. That bit of the acting wasn't hard. I am not a showy pianist. I make playing the piano look natural, although it doesn't go into the same drawer of natural behaviour as walking or eating. I'm not against the odd histrionic gesture, but only if it takes me that way.

The body language throughout the piece had to be autumnal, but not without energy. Autumnal sentiments that become distant memories as time washes away the traces of the separated lovers – the *amants désunis*. I know about disunited lovers, so it was easy to go there.

Once I was freed from the keyboard, they put me on a chair in front of a green screen, with one camera, just for my face. Josy wanted me to look dreamy, as if I was listening to the music, not playing it. Communing with it, he said. Then I had to look dreamy as if I were watching leaves. Not leaves doing anything, but just being leaves. Yellow leaves, if I liked. And then leaves moving in the light autumn breeze which turned into a storm. The leaves would be added later, when I'd imagined them.

OK, perfect sense. A doddle for an undergraduate at any acting school you care to name. I'm sure they do it all the time, watching leaves turning yellow on trees and then falling off. My acting schooling had been very good, thanks to Ellen, but limited to the last couple of months. I seized up and I forgot all my lessons at once. Mental leaves. I found that too hard. Yellow leaves? One yellow leaf?

I asked for my coach. Ellen came over.

"Remember the poem? The long sobs…? We could play it back now and you could lip-synch it straight to the camera. Are you up for that?"

"I'll give it a try. Play it to me a couple of times while the lighting is done."

"You know it from memory, which should help. One final suggestion…do it very simply, as if you are murmuring the words to yourself."

So Verlaine rescued me with autumn's sobbing violins: "*Les sanglots longs des violons de l'automne,*" I said, and the languid feeling of those past times came into my mind, and into my eyes, and stayed there.

They changed the lighting, and we did it all again.

"The important thing," Ellen said, taking me by both hands, "is to remember that we are the ones who will do the worrying and choose the shots; you just keep your thoughts and feelings going. The way you feel the music. Or the poem you just said."

For the storm in the middle, a wind machine was pointed at me – a little one, like a big hair-dryer. But my hair was so gelled that all that happened was my eyes watered, not a whisker of hair moved.

I bathed my eyes.

Change of lighting, so that they could film me full length. The music was played to me and I reacted with whatever I could think of – anger, fear, resentment at the evil wind in a bad-temper, trying to blow me away, while I was fighting back, and not winning.

By now, I'd given them blocks to construct something I couldn't see. There would be lots of cross-cutting and cross-fading. This was like recording a sonata a bar at a time. All the same I had to do it, and I did.

There was a general feeling that I had done well, that by the time I was processed, the camera angles manipulated and the shots intercut with real images of autumn and the sequences with me in Burnham Beeches, they would have something very special.

They sent me home early, to make sure I got a good night's sleep. I hoped that didn't mean I have a tendency to look tired. It happens, they tell me: it's as if your face says enough is only too likely to be too much.

Josy said Goodbye. "You're picking this up quickly, boy, and we'll get used to what your best angles are."

I left it to him. I trusted him. It was the only possible way.

I spent the evening reading a book, and then thought about what I had to do for the next session, with Liszt and his feux-follets. Not the calmest of pieces to go to bed with.

Filming Day 2

Liszt at his piano study best. Hardest. *Feux follets*. Will o'the wisp. It's not the sort of 'study' that's meant to help your technical development, more a sort of challenge for the composer as well as for anyone who plays it. Here you are in hand-to-hand combat with Liszt the pianist. It's not just about flashing fingers, but flashes of light. I imagine a tiny demon (called Will) running around setting things alight but not dealing with the consequences. Liszt gives this untrustworthy light some sweet moments, jokey moments, graceful moments as well as energetic ones – these are his instructions in the score. And there's a little musical figure, unstable, could be unhappy, running through.

My costume was dark, loose top with white patches sewn on with glittering thread.

They filmed my fingers dashing about the keyboard. The keys waiting to be attacked, the works inside the piano – the dampers on the strings rising and falling – rippling effect. They would certainly need Victoria on hand when they put the whole act together, because marrying the fingers you could see with the fingers on the sound track wouldn't be easy. I suppose a little mismatching would be hard to spot, but we wanted it to be as near as possible. I'm a pianist, not like the actor called Sam who can't actually Play It Again in the *Casablanca* film – I'm expected to play the right notes.

Liszt's marsh lights tempt, intrigue, disappear and reappear. Sweet, tranquil, they leap among the drifting mist; every now and then they tease, coming at us from all sides, glittering, with a tiny recurring theme that means – nothing? Is it meant to pull us alongside it, then pursue us with their moments of glory, none of which will last? I kept in mind the lights of the River Weser that drew the children of the town of Hamelin into the waters to join the dead rats the Town Council wouldn't pay him for.

I stood against a large screen, and did a series of paint-by-numbers expressions, made to order, practised at home; reactions to the foolish, leaping parts; looking surprised, shocked by the unexpected, scared, darting my eyes from right to left, and back. I started out with the best Will in the world; a feeble joke meant to cheer me on. But all this looking around made me feel as if I was having my eyes tested, and I began to laugh. And once that happened, I didn't stop.

Sympathy at first from the controllers, but it didn't last.

Josy got a bit stroppy. "Come on, Will boy, every time you laugh costs us."

There was muttering.

Ellen's voice: "Josy has another idea. Scrub the last remark; don't be offended by it. We can make use of the laughter we caught. Are there some points in the music that could move you to that level of delight?"

"Yes – brief, but one or two. Victoria will know where they fit in."

**

184

We took a break for lunch. But they hadn't finished with it yet.

A new idea. A light like a tiny torchlight would lead my fingers around the keyboard in the first and last bars of the piece and intermittently throughout. A pencil torch appeared from somewhere to give me an idea of how it would look, although the light would be added at a later stage. Getting the torch and my hands into the right relationship was tricky; but if I played as if I was playing a duet, it would be possible. Victoria came in to move the torch. It worked well enough to give an idea that could be extended in the editing. Then the cameras were reset, and it all took time.

I did the keyboard bit again, Victoria with the torch, and then without Victoria with the torch. But with me playing and watching my hands as they went to the top of the keyboard.

"We can cut that together. We need you in front of the screen again. New thoughts."

Ellen brought out a black opera cloak. "Josy's idea. Put this on, and think Dracula."

Hard, because I've never read Bram Stoker's novel, and never knowingly seen one of the Hammer horror films, or anyone else's, but I tried to look like someone who sucked blood for a living. There were two cameras in action, one behind me, and one in front. I stood absolutely still, my arms slightly outstretched, while the light in front of me darted and flickered as I'm sure it does in Transylvania. They took the cloak off and shot the whole scene again. I didn't know what to make of that.

And finally, we referenced the Pied Piper more closely; I moved, almost danced, to the music, smiled at the children as I led them to the Irrlichte waiting on the River Weser.

And so ended the second day.

Day 3

Ritual fire-dance day. Although this is a dance number from a ballet, there had been no talk of dancing. Mercifully. If the dance works, the evil spirits will go away – that's what it says in the score. I did the easy bit first. They filmed me playing the piano. Which meant four times, with gaps in between for me to be wiped – carefully, because Josy thought it would be good if I glistened with sweat.

When the great pianist Arthur Rubinstein played this piece, he used to do big forearm movements up and down at one point, giving the keys a good hammering. A hint of violence which fits with the idea of dancing round a fire. Burning someone, as like as not. I never saw him do it – he's before my time – but I've seen him on film, and it's impressive. It has nothing much to do with playing the piano, but it looks dramatic, and risky, because there seems to be a strong chance he's going to miss the notes. He doesn't. It's actually quite easy to do once you line yourself up. I didn't imitate him; I didn't want to look as if I was beating the flames down in my ritual fire, but creating them.

This is really an orchestral piece, so I'd put in extra notes from the orchestral score to beef it up. Victoria had wanted me to add even more extra notes on an extra track, so that she could over-dub it and make it sound even bigger. A gimmick, but a good one, since it's music to dance to, music for the theatre, and I thought about it. Bit more fire for the ritual. Only problem is you can't play it to live audiences afterwards, because you don't have the backing tape with you. So we didn't do it that way.

This was going to be massively red. In fact, a lot of the redness was going to come from those magic green screens, afterwards – flames and sparks and such. Time was spent on the lighting so that my face would have some human colours in it as well as the red hues that came and went with the flames. Post-production could do most of it but the details of my sweaty face and flesh had to be visible. Chris stood in for me as much as possible. And the 'eye-lights' were more tricky…

My outfit was sort of toreador-ish. A shirt, white with short sleeves and a red embroidered waistcoat without buttons, which wouldn't have done up anyway, since there wasn't much of it. Trousers, which I wasn't measured for, but since they were made of some elasticised material, they fitted, believe me.

We moved on to the bigger images: two views of me, one with a camera watching my back, then another camera, on someone's shoulders, aimed at my front. I was watching a fire, and the red flames were leaping, gradually growing into bonfire size, and a few token flames, equals red lights, coming and going to make it simpler for me. Than what? I found that quite hard to do. I had to reach my hands out as if I were controlling the fire, drawing it up. It took a few times before it looked right. My first attempts looked as if I was warming my hands at a log fire. I thought of one or two conductors I've worked with who dramatize the music with their arms and hands. I found something there.

Then I had to see figures dancing around the fire. Ritual figures, with a couple of evil spirits mixed in. Someone was supposed to die at the end of this spell, and it was important that it didn't look like me... An advanced improvisation challenge, I thought, with only a green screen to look at, and the little red lights coming on and off like part of a traffic system. Fortunately Ellen and Victoria didn't belong to any union; they came in and started moving about in time with the music. Off camera. Ellen did it brilliantly; that was par for the course. Victoria was more surprising. I had no idea that flamenco dancing was part of the academic studies she took at Cambridge. She looked very convincing. And so, apparently, did I. Josy was pleased with the whole thing, but wanted more shots of me after the lunch break.

**

I really needed to rest for longer than an hour. This time I took my lenses out and dozed. Then splashed my face in the en suite and put another set in.

After that, small conference. Josy explained.

"Will, baby, would you do me a favour? Two favours. We would like a few more shots of you just standing there, light flickering on your face. Open your eyes big, big, big till we can see the whites. Lovely; just like that."

"Second favour. I want to see you like without the shirt. Just the waistcoat and the trousers. Your torso looks good, and maybe with this primitive music we need a mixture of the sophisticated clothes, and something basic: the red waistcoat against the skin on your chest...It could be like dynamite."

"I have to tell you something, Josy. If I take my shirt off, you won't see the waistcoat against my skin, because..." I took my shirt off to show him.

He was surprised. "You have hair on your chest. You want a job in a circus?" I've never been terribly bothered one way or another by the way nature decided to cover my body, but what with Marty the make-up man, and now Josy, I was beginning to feel rather defensive.

"I'll keep my bleeding shirt on if you don't like it."

"Forgive me, Will baby. You are a guy that plays all that civilised music. You should be smooth underneath. This is primitive, animal stuff from a civilised person."

"Forgive me, Josy, but music can be primitive animal stuff too. It's about real things, about survival and feeling good and bad, and about feeling better."

The primitive animal bit suited Manuel's fire-dancing music, so I agreed to do the thing without my shirt. But with the waistcoat. Why not? The light was pretty dark, and red, and I thought I didn't have to do much, except be photographed.

I was wrong about that. This time he wanted me to do shoulder movements. Disco movements, with teenage memories when my extra flesh didn't seem to matter as long as I was in time. Ellen reminded me how to arch my back like the famous Spanish dancer Antonio Vargas in the Australian film 'Strictly Ballroom', and after I got the hang of that, the music was played into the studio and off we went for another batch of takes. Male preening. Ellen danced for me out of shot, just to make me respond, and it was like Carmen dancing. Very tempting, and I wished we'd had a chance to rehearse this bit before. Several times before.

It was hard work. Short takes, and rests.

We persevered, until I had to call it off. My back was sending danger signals: muscles unprepared to be used for a long period for things like dancing, however modest, and for things like arching, equally modest. And we had two more days to go.

"I could use a shower."

"You can use the one in your bathroom."

"What?"

"The one through there. The shower works."

I knew that, and it did. Privacy in the real bathroom space. Hot water. Shower. The towels were dry. I took my time, and it was a lifesaver.

Day 4

Basically easier. We got two done.

Debussy's piece about the Flaxen-headed girl, the Scottish girl, was first. I hoped Josy hadn't done any homework on it, and think it would be a gimmick to dress me up in some mid-European idea of Scottish.

In fact, they got me up in a hand-knitted Scottish cable jumper and trousers which hinted at the tartan without going there.

I had brought in my copy of the poem, to read to myself, and make sure the feeling was French, that my face was French, even. I'd no idea how many Scottish girls Debussy met when he was in London, but I don't think that the

Aberdonian Mary Garden who sang his songs and his opera looked like anything that you can spot down in the glen.

Josy talked his vision through with me. It would begin with a sight of the words on paper with an olde texture, my voice speaking a line or two until the music creeps in. Colours muted blues and greens.

I did my piano stint. Gentle lighting in keeping with the mood.

Then they played back my recording of the poem, and took a close-up of my mouth lip-syncing it.

Then I had to look into the middle distance. I was getting more and more acquainted with this middle distance, though there was never much to see apart from a few people, machines and green screens.

I was relying on the sexy poetry about tempting lips, long eyelashes and blonde hair to prompt my reactions. They shot me from different angles for the sake of variety. They were going to add shots of heather, and of the wind riffling over the grasses on some bank or brae or other. From a library. But no girl. With no blonde wig. I would have been quite happy to say the words to Ellen: "your mouth has the colours of the heavens, and just begs to be kissed." I wouldn't have minded retakes for that.

I apparently got facial expressions to suit. They say that when you try least you get most. I hoped that was the case.

I took a rest over lunchtime, because I had a love scene coming up, the story of a whole relationship. I had some predictable anxiety about this one.

Liebestraum. Dream of love. As dreamt by Franz Liszt.

Josy and I talked first – or rather he did.

"Ah, you must forget you are English. Be Hungarian, like Liszt."

He'd not been in London very long to know much about the English. That depends on who you meet.

"Would you like to show me how to be Hungarian?"

We gave up on the idea.

"Any lover will do, any country."

I pushed Byron's Spanish Don Juan aside as an example to follow. The young Donny Johnny wasn't much of a great lover; more a 'great beloved-er'.

So here I was, in my concert clothes at the piano. When I play *Liebestraum* for the public, I just look a little quiet. Watch my hands, think about making singing tone, matching the sounds and fingers, balanced, listen to what I want to play at the same time as listening to what this particular piano is playing. This was a harder exercise. Looking like someone in love is something I haven't practised doing. Is it something you practise? I was beginning to protect myself by thinking that I'd never been in love. Certainly not in love the way I think Liszt was, or as often. There's not a huge amount of love-music for pianists to play, as opposed to music to love.

Before I went on set, I re-read my translation of the poem Liszt set for his song. Love, of course, long-lasting love, until death; treasure your lover; don't hurt each other with careless words. Not what I wanted to think about, and yet I had to. Pushed into it by life. Music, distilled from love, and the anxiety which can go with it.

That's what I put into my mind as I sat at the piano and played.

Then, after a break, they found me a table and chair, and I leant my head on my hands looking into the green distance. I murmured a shorthand version of the poem: "love when you can, if chance brings it your way and you can find a partner to complete this circle of love."

Josy came to life. "Listen Will, we have made a good start. I'm sending Ellen to you; can you look at her as if you love her?"

There she was, not to be on camera, as such, although her shadow might well be. I took her hands, and this time she really had to look me in the face. With cameras watching me, which should have inhibited me, but didn't. Her eyes gazed, and looked away, and glowed warm and tender, and I reached out my hands as if to take her face in them, and I thought of kissing her for a long time…until they shouted, "Cut." I've no idea what the cameras were up to during that time.

"Look, you've got footage you can use, I'm sure. But I've been thinking about other ways to come at this. Can I give it a go on camera, please? You never know."

"I'll stay here. Just play the music again. Give me a minute."

I stood and thought about the first bars and the idea of not having love around me just now. That took some restraint, since it was running along parallel tracks to my own life, so I went for 'where did I go wrong? ideas. The sound track started, and I rehearsed my thoughts about wanting to love as much as I may, wanting to sing a song of love that needs love to complete it, as long lasting as we can possibly make it; otherwise the grave will yawn to reveal a parting with no return. Sharing means caring about the other person, making them happy. Watch what you say, or you might destroy what you most want…

What I did was no tour de force, but I tapped into something of myself, with rather a lot in reserve if needed.

Victoria thought it was very touching. The way I could look so loving, so often, so long, in the takes and the retakes.

What a great gift. But what would happen if there are many girls out there just waiting for you and you might possibly want only one? Ellen? Wait a minute – was this me slipping into another version of a situation I just wore out? Was so spectacularly bad at? Had just escaped from? Did I have any idea what the hell I was doing?

Of course Josy had more ideas: Liebestraum is a dream, and he wasn't happy. Love OK. Dream? It needed a framework. A bed was wheeled forward. It had been there all the time ready to be used as part of my bedroom furniture. My heart sank.

"No, Josy, no. I refuse to get into those silk pyjamas which are attractively laid out on that bed. Why has no one told me this was going to be the angle for this bit? Silk pyjamas don't accidentally come from nowhere. I don't believe anyone wears them anymore. You don't, do you, Josy? No, don't tell me, I don't want to know. I've just done all that acting thing about being in love, and I really don't want to get into bed and pretend to do the dream bit."

There was a silence. Just because I was new on the block when it came to making movies didn't mean I was submissive plasticine waiting to be moulded into just anything.

"There are limits. I don't sleep in silk pyjamas, not for anyone, and what I sleep in isn't for this film."

"Aw, come on, Will boy – you 'd look great in these white silk clothes. Not for nothing do they cost a fortune."

"If you've come here to persuade me to take my clothes off and get into this silk, then you've chosen the wrong time."

Ellen took my hand. "No. Don't worry. Not the silk pyjamas, not whatever it is you sleep in."

She was talking to me like my grandmother did when I was a child. And of course it was ridiculous. I laughed.

"I'll lie on the bed, with my arm over my head. I'll undo my shirt if that's what the boss man wants. But that's it…"

And that's what we did. In my working clothes. I took off the jacket, threw myself on the bed, pulled my tie off, undid the buttons on my shirt, and did the business of running my hands over any bit of me that might make me look like your average Romantic lover. Like Liszt himself preparing for a passing countess. Once I got the idea of being Franz in that mood, I rather liked that. So I played him as he must have been when he went to stay at George Sand's place in Nohant, sleeping in the next room to Chopin, all the while with Marie d'Agoult in his arms; I could do that. It appealed to me. Dreaming and loving at the same time. I thought he would know about that.

Then I had an unexpected thought.

"This is an experiment for the library. No results guaranteed."

Back to the piano. A camera for my face. No music playback. Instead I played some of the Schubert sonata I was to record for my CD. Just a few bars from the slow movement, which move me deeply whenever I play them, taking me to the verge of tears. This time I let the tears happen, enough to cloud my eyes.

Then, my face no longer being necessary, I had finished for the day.

The Last Day

The last day. The wettest day. For me.

We had Chopin's Raindrop Prelude to do.

The filming at the piano was easy, and the crew knew by now which shots worked, and I had an idea of where to look. We did the central section a couple of times, with Victoria clicking me in, and then did the final part.

After a short rest, it was playing-in-the-rain with serious water.

They'd been doing shots of rain standing on surfaces, like the paving stones outside the studio-school, to be supplemented with things from a library. They'd been praying for rain, as Josy's peasants did. The prayers had been answered, too, because it had been raining off and on during the last couple of days, and it was raining now. Quite a lot.

"I hope no-one's expecting me to go out into that."

There was a silence. A whispered discussion, so that I couldn't hear. Josy came up to me.

"Look, Will, baby, it will not take long. We have special clothes here for you, so you can get wet in them…"

I didn't answer that.

"Oh please, Will – you will be in a safe street; all we want is just a few shots of your feet walking along. Those beautiful shoes will show up well, and keep your feet dry. We have those special clothes.

"Then in the studio we'll take shots of you with wet clothes. Don't worry, we'll just do single takes. When we finish, you can take a shower to make sure you don't get a cold. Like I said. Safe as houses."

The houses he'd shot in his films were broken-down cottages that the breezes from the Russian plains could enter at will.

I did what he asked for. The 'special clothes' were trousers, of course, of indeterminate kind; and a shirt. Nineteenth century shirt, as in Jane Austen, quite loose.

I braved the rain in Kent in this get-up and walked up and down twice in front of the school-house, slowly, like a man lost in thought, rather than some poor sod getting wet. No one was supposed to know where I was, after all. They did indeed film my feet, thoughtful feet, slightly unsure feet temperamentally, wearing smart new moccasins. Just my size.

They took close-ups of my face, leaning my head back for the drops to strike me, running my hands over my hair, when instructed.

Josy was standing next to Rob, both of them protected by umbrellas held by the runners. The camera and the lights had umbrellas too. I understood the equipment needed to be dry, but I thought Josy might have been more sympathetic and joined me in the wetness stakes.

Now would I be kind enough to walk up the slope in the garden and back? Slowly. No. I wouldn't. I had agreed to a few shots of my feet, and they already had more than that. My feet would remain inside. Sorry.

Consultation, and it was doubles time. Chris was kitted out with the waterproof jacket, unworn so far, and encouraged to walk up and down the hill as if fighting the elements.

I left them to it, took a quick shower, and got warm.

The internal shots were easier. Me at home in a dry version of my shirt looking out of some window, again, watching myself out there walking in the rain. That made me feel better.

For a while, not for long. They brought in a small watering machine, hired for the day, into the studio. It came with its own waterproofing, so that it could be used in the 'studio' without the floor or the walls being damaged. As for me, it is well known that the human skin is waterproof, so I spent the next part of my life getting wet all over again. Only this time really wet. My shirt clung to me, I pulled it out over my trousers, rubbed spots of water off my face, ran my hands through my hair. They took more shots of my shirt, which by now might as well have been my skin. I am absolutely sure Chopin would not have been allowed out in this weather. His lady took very good care of his health.

Being an artist brings suffering as well as joy, but this wasn't art, I told myself, it was commerce.

After that, I had another shower with water I was actually in control of. Very consoling.'

**

Lunch and a rest.

That left Bach. I was in a white T shirt.

"Let's get you playing the piano for real first."

"I've done it already."

"Let's do it again. Now that you are experienced. The usual trio of cameras is in place."

Marty checked my face and eyelashes, and I took my place at the piano.

Shuffling around of cameras and checking of lighting, and then they took shots of my face, amused, delighted at the sheer effervescence of the music.

"That's great. Let's take a break. Let's talk."

A period of brainstorming. Josy, Ellen, Victoria and I. Thinking on our feet.

Josy spoke first. "This music speaks to me of water, a river with stones."

"Brook would be a better image."

"Yes, little river. Like Bach's name. But we need your hands. Splashing."

"Splashing. OK. Can I wear an apron?"

This question was ignored.

"Rob will take his camera and come with you over to the bathroom. Just the two of you together playing around with the water. Hands on piano, hands in water. Some library scenes of a brook and a little waterfall. Yes, that will do it."

I put on my raincoat and hat and walked over with Rob to my pseudo bathroom, hoping for the best. This was the last bit, my final appearance in a starring role.

There was only one basin in this place – the second one in the bathroom at home wasn't used any more. There was no bath because I don't have one, so we couldn't use that to access more water. Rob brought his hand-held camera. We ran some water, and I splashed about a bit.

"Hard to get an angle on this. I keep getting the taps in the frame. Looks naff."

Josy's voice. "Can you just get close-ups of his hands under water?"

"Doing what?"

"Moving around, turning over. Splashing as much as possible."

With absolutely no confidence, Rob and I tried to make something of it.

That was the last we heard of Josy. He'd run out of steam.

Rob took over.

"I think we'll play it our own way now. There's no microphone in here, so there's no sound being recorded.

"Take your hands out of the water, and shake the drops on to the surface. Can we turn the tap on to fill the basin and you can use the running water?"

"I'm getting rather wet," I said. My T-shirt was indeed wet.

"OK. Just to give us shots of you, looking happy with your wet hands."

Me in a wet T-shirt was no big deal…after the morning I'd just spent with Chopin.

I did what I could with that. Thought of the music, and followed it through physically.

"Hold your hands up to the camera."

"Which way? Palms?"

"Both ways. OK. Now play with the water as if it's your friend." Rob was rather better than Josy at prompting movement.

"Can I get out of these soaking things? I want to take a shower. Do you mind?"

Rob said… "Of course, do that. Would you mind if I film you from outside the shower…very discreetly, of course…I'll move slowly round you. You can spray the glass with as much water as you like before you get down to the showering bit and there are decorations in the glass at the right level to preserve your modesty…"

"I'm not sure I have much modesty left at this stage. Go ahead. Why not? But no full frontals, or anything like that. I may be a man on the market but I'm not doing advertisements."

Rob busied himself with his camera while I got into the shower and ran water over the glass. Then I showered. The Prelude takes about three and a half minutes so I took my time, going over the music in my head all the while. Acting out the music in the way we might use to describe how things might sound for our pupils or fellow musicians. I felt a sense of release.

**

Back in the school, clean and dry, and dressed in my going-home clothes – jeans, shirt, with a sweater over my shoulders – I asked if we might take the piano lid off for me to play some of each piece, a minute at most, in the order it had been filmed while cameras looked at the action the instrument was taking. Victoria made notes while I played them.

**

This was the last day of my involvement in the project. The next couple of days had been kept free in case there were any retakes.

None were asked for…but before I took off, Josy wanted some more pictures of my face, for them to use whenever they liked, and Ellen suggested some of me to go with the closing titles.

"Are you up for this now?" She asked.

"Is my face up for it now?" I asked. "It's been a very wet day for me."

"Marty is still here. He can give you a going-over."

Marty came and looked closely.

"You'll do well. You've got used to the cameras peering at you, it seems. All you need from me is a bit of sprucing up, and a tweak or two of your hair."

Ellen came over.

"Just think the thoughts you have before you play. They won't necessarily be moving pictures when it comes to the point; we can freeze the frames we like. Just a last reminder: keep it simple – it's the eyes that matter."

"What shall I wear?"

"What you feel comfortable in. What you're wearing now. It's your face we want."

I suggested going through the programme piece by piece.

"Good idea. And some shots of you just being you, happy to be here…happy to have pleased us over the last five days."

By now, they had got a green background for me, and a camera in place. I sat on the piano stool, doing my breathing exercises, while the lighting was got ready for me.

So I went through, putting a label on each take – just in case I wasn't making it clear enough with my face. Tenderness, rueful with a touch of anger, dreamy, falling in love, mischief, magic, gaiety. That's what they set out to be.

Then the publicity gestures. All the time straight to my friend the camera, the smile when taking a bow, or welcoming my friends the audience. Anything that came into my head.

By then, I really was tired.

The team were happy. They applauded, which was gratifying.

Before I went home, there was one thing I had to make clear.

"Rob and I did some work with me taking a shower. I was probably on a sort of high about all the physical things I've been doing on camera for the last few days. I meant it only as possible additional material, in case I get cold feet about it. It was very personal, as you'll see, and I really want to see how you use it. So could you make two versions of the Bach item – the one with me in the shower and the one without the shower, please?"

"No problem…Of course…We wouldn't want to take advantage of you…"

A chorus of reassurance.

I thanked everyone for their help and understanding, kissed and hugged them all indiscriminately, and patted the piano. Victoria made a joke about actually getting to touch a sex symbol. I said, "I'm not a symbol, I'm the real thing."

There wasn't much to back that up.

Definitely time to go home.

That was it until the results. I had no say in the final editing, except an option to veto, which was in my contract. Which was in my contract, wasn't it? Surely?

Once away from the studio, I felt flat. I'd enjoyed being part of a team, and now it had gone away, and left me on my own.

**

CD work

Next day an email from Jane:

I hear it went fabulously well. Sorry I wasn't there. Josy is over the moon, and thinks we're going to get something so out of the ordinary, and yet so honest, that we should get an award for it. There's a lot of post-production work to do, which he says is a good thing, because they have so much material it's going to be hard but exciting to make up the mind, as he puts it.

Do you want to choose your piano for the CD recording? You've got a couple of months to go yet, but let's get in first, since there might be a problem of availability. It's the usual Steinway at the studio – a good one, as you know from last time, but you might have something else in mind. I know you can get a good sound out of almost any piano. I remember one of your early concerts in Bedfordshire when the pedal went wrong and the secretary of the club had to lie under the piano holding it in place. Luvya. Jane.

To jane@curzprod.com

I trust Martin with the piano. The CD really needs to be good. It might be a turning point, and I might need it as a counterblast to what is going to be a downmarket film, let's face it. The critics might well not like that. Or more importantly the public. If anyone sees it. I don't mind being flesh as well as spirit, but in the long run it's what I do with the music that has to please the world out there with ears to hear.

Talk again—Will.

**

Any time you play a major work it's like putting down a marker: this is where I am on the way to eternity. I had the facts Beethoven left behind: what he wrote down on the page. I've played his concertos, and I've been happy for years playing his Moonlight sonata; there's a public performance built into that music (more than one, depending on how slowly you play the first movement) because Beethoven played it. He'd given up playing in public when he wrote op 109 and left us instead with something private to share with him. I had a look at some of the very intense comments people have written about this sonata. They are intriguing, but also personal to the writer. They don't 'explain' Beethoven for me. I can only do that in sound. There's a lot of drama, and a lot of beauty, and a lot of thought, intellect, if you like. The beauty I knew how to do, because I was taught to make a piano sing by my first teacher. The drama? Could I find something more intense and more subtle? Ellen had helped me in the obvious music I've been filming. Would she let me act this out to her? With no picture to paint, or story to tell? Would it work with more abstract music? Is there such a thing as 'abstract' music? Discuss.

I decided to call her.

Her answer-phone asked me to leave a message, so I rang off and rang her back when I'd worked out a suitable message; not explicit, but asking for help.

She phoned back. I tried to explain what I wanted.

"Can you come and listen to me play this Beethoven sonata I'm recording? I've got a bit stuck with it."

She sounded bewildered.

"I'm not a musician, you know – I've not listened to music much, until I met you. But that's about it."

"I think you owe it to me…"

"Sorry? Owe it to you? How?" She didn't sound cross, which she might well have done. It was an impossible thing to ask, and it was beginning to sound too phoney for words.

"You surely don't mean because I spoilt your style? Tried to make you think like an actor, and stopped you from thinking like a pianist? Made you want to change your career? You really think that?"

"No, of course not. I couldn't stand all that rain all the time. But you challenged the way I set about my work. Somewhat."

"OK. I'll accept that. So…if you think I can help…I can see it might be a good idea, professionally, to watch you play, without having to wonder where the camera is. Make sure we've been playing fair by you."

"Yes, that's right. Absolutely it."

I really hadn't much idea where we were going with this, and I don't really think she believed anything I said, any more than I did.

A message from Victoria

Victoria rang.

"I'm getting a new portable minidisk recorder, so it would be easy to take up that idea of coming round to record those sonatas. First impressions, important, and we have the time. Or I have, if you have. I'll bring the technical equipment round to your place, hear what you do on the piano that knows you. Save time in the studio, maybe."

I wanted the music to be between me and the composer, to make it like a drama on radio or television, with no audience. I hadn't played it to anyone in its current state.

Victoria would be the first to hear it – when I recorded it.

But I didn't want to be an Icarus trying to fly to the sun, and having my wings fall off because the wax melted in the heat of a recording studio. Playing it to her privately, on my own piano, would be more than just a dummy run. She had all that academic training in Beethoven, after all, and listened to hundreds of performances for her degree. She could well take a wider view.

"Good idea. Can we leave it until closer to the time? I've got a couple of dates now. Being in front of the public after the camera has been peering at my inner soul should shake some of the movie-star-dust out of me."

**

Ellen comes to tea and I play to her

Ellen came to tea a couple of days later.

She'd been catching up on the work on the film. She was having a lot of input.

"Of course, it's Josy's show, and he's made his mind up about how he wants it to be. Not the same as when he started, but that's par for the course. It's to do with how you look in individual shots."

"How do you do that?"

"Ask questions. Does it look true? Real?"

"Sounds like the psychiatrist's couch."

"Sort of. But not very seriously. That would be a much longer project, the psycho bit." She smiled. "I would have needed a much bigger fee for that."

"Or no fee at all, maybe?"

She went on smiling.

"Are you allowed to tell me how the film has worked out? Will I do?"

"You really are being over-anxious. We've caught you. It's you on the screen. You look amazing. The camera, as they say, loves you. You will break a few hearts if they're up for breaking."

"Breaking doesn't interest me much – making them feel better is more like it. What I'd like to know is, do I speak to you through the camera?"

"Not easy for me to say. I believe so. Like when you play the piano. You make it sound natural, though it must be one of the most complicated things to have going on in your head – and your hands."

"I'll accept 'natural' as one of the best things anyone has said to me."

"Your natural way of expressing yourself."

She patted the piano.

"So will you show me more of that? I was looking forward to hearing you. Or I wouldn't have come."

"Would you really not have come?"

"Play the piano, Will."

I did. Beethoven. I played her the first two pages. And asked her what she thought I was saying with the music. There was silence. A bit daunting.

"I have to say that this is the first time I've knowingly heard music by Beethoven. All I can tell you is what goes through my mind." So I played all of the first movement of Beethoven's sonata. She listened, never moving, watching, I think, though I didn't look at her, or think about her either.

At the end, I turned to her.

"That'll do. Most people who listen to what I play don't tell me anything. They applaud instead. If there are those who didn't enjoy it, they don't come and tell me. I hope there aren't too many of them."

"OK. If you'd asked me to do an improvisation to that music in a movement class, I would have started with something sort of happy, but restless. Which didn't last. How long was the bit at the beginning?"

"About a quarter of a minute."

"Quarter of a minute, then suddenly this huge sub-text would come welling up, to push it off the scene. Question is: has it taken me by surprise, or has it been there all the time, and I've not admitted it?"

I'd been hoping that this session might lead to something not directly connected with music. But she was wise about something else, which I hadn't suspected.

"You know I don't know much about music. I couldn't tell you if you're playing the right notes, or going at the right speed."

"When I go to the theatre, I don't know if the actors are getting everything right, in the right place. But I know if something's happening up there on stage. I should be able to have the same effect with music."

"How do I know if music's making sense?"

"You'll know. See how this strikes you."

I played her the slow movement of the Schubert sonata. With feeling. With much feeling for every note I played. As if I was trying to tell her I thought I could fall in love with her. Poor Franz Schubert would have collapsed under the weight of emotion I was heaping on his shoulders.

This little experiment was beginning to backfire.

She expected me to play some more, since that's what I'd got her round for, I'd said. True enough. So I played the last movement of the Beethoven. The variations pleased her; the idea of exploring something in different ways appealed to her as an actor, she said. Like in life, she added.

I stood up, went to the kitchen and put the kettle on.

"It's tea-time."

She came to watch me do the tea ceremony.

"I must keep an eye on the time. I've got to make sure Josy isn't doing anything terrible. The great thing about modern technology is that it takes a lot of determination to destroy anything, but it can be done, and I don't want him spoiling anything before I've looked at it again.

"But tea from that teapot you're waving at me would be a new adventure."

"My grandmother's carefully preserved tea service, almost complete. Tea made with real tea leaves."

"And tea-biscuits. You spoil me."

"Naturally, because you deserve to be spoilt."

I poured the tea out through a silver strainer and offered milk from the milk-jug.

I said, "We've come to the end of our official time together, I know. I wanted to say how much you made it possible for me to do what I did."

"I'll tell you how much you made it possible for you to do what you did. You were an innocent who didn't know what to do in this strange land, and you let me get insights into you, your way of thinking, and your life. You're a complicated man. In a complicated part of your life."

"You found that out."

"You wanted me to find it out, didn't you? That was good. For the film."

"Always the film."

"This afternoon has been a chance to hear you play as you really play. Long thoughts, I mean, not short pieces for a film. I like what you do. It's not that you make it sound "easy" – that 's the wrong word, since there must be a lot going on in your head just to remember it, and in your hands. You make it sound as if it's the right way to express yourself. An element of nature."

"That's high praise. Can I use it in my CV? A great notice."

"As long as you don't give me a credit.

"Look, Will, I really must go. Shall we meet when everything is in the bag, and we can talk through the result?"

She left, with a kiss on the cheek, from a warm friend you can safely kiss when no one else is there.

Library and teaching again

Conservatoire again, with nothing except a note from Sir Greg saying that my agent had said that I did have a window for the flag-waving concert, but that she would have to talk to me, and talk about what they wanted me to play. She thought the Paganini Variations of Rachmaninov would give the orchestra a chance to shine, knowing it was one of the pieces scheduled in my diary around that time. He agreed.

I was able to give my students more attention, which had been somewhat scattered in the winds of filmmaking. They had been given time to consolidate what we'd been working on. Of course you hope there will be moments of amazing revelation for them as you guide them, but if there are too many revelations on the journey, the road to Damascus might lead them to Bluebeard's Castle. Yes, you open doors for them, but if you push them through too many, they'll end up on the other side of the building.

I enjoyed my tomato sandwich, and nipped up to the library to see if they had a book of Rachmaninov's letters to give me a slant on these Paganini variations I was going to play. There was nothing. Someone had taken the only copy out. And had had it out since before I was a student. The library had been more disorganised in those days. This young librarian took a lot of trouble.

"There should be something somewhere." He tracked down a story that Rachmaninov found the piano part difficult and used to drink a slug of Chartreuse before he went on to play it.

"I don't know if you want to do that," he said, "although there's no harm in being authentic."

"Makes him seem more human. He looks in some of his pictures as if the Russian snows haven't melted yet."

"Are you thinking of playing it at the circus?"

"The...?"

"Sorry. No animals will be maltreated. Only students. The road show, the concert.

"A hundred and fifty years of anything is impressive, I suppose, even if Sir Greg is the one at the helm. All that teaching and learning. Got to be good."

"Of course. Education is a blessing."

"I believe so. I'm still not sure that Sir Greg knows who I am – and I'm a member of the staff, for Goodness' sake."

"Who are you? Sorry – that sounds rude. Who are you? I can't think of any other way of saying it."

"It's OK. I'm Tom. Tom Jordan. D.Mus. of this Institution. Four years on. For what it's worth."

"That's a bit of a put-down for an institution going on a hundred and fifty years old."

He made a face.

"I didn't mean to do that. But you still need work at the end of it. It's not the ticket to romantic places, just the door to the ticket office to see if there are any tickets going."

"You're a librarian."

"I like books."

"So you came to a music school."

"I like music too. In fact, I write it."

"Ah...this is the holiday job."

"Yes. Even though this is not a holiday. It's a good job. I have unlimited contact with scores, and musicians. I like that. And there's the music I write. Afterwards."

"Anything in particular?"

"Whatever comes into my head."

"Anything I could hear?"

"There could be. Don't look too hard. No CDs."

"You should push it. You have to doubt and believe at the same time. You should give people a chance to get to know what you do."

"I'll remember. I'll play at street corners."

"You could do worse, so let's assume I'm a street-corner. When you write something for the piano, let me see it. Make it short, if you can do that, and I'll look at it and see if I can tuck it into a programme."

"You mean it?"

"I'll pay you."

A very business-like rest of the day with my students. Sorting out finger-patterns, checking levels for the dynamics, balance of the hands and the fingers – the things you do when you're making sure the vehicle's ready for sophisticated usage.

My Japanese duettist students were being too respectful. Not of me, which I don't mind too much, but of each other.

"You're taking your name too seriously," I said to Hiroshi. "Hiroshi – generous, tolerant man? Isn't that what it means?" I hoped my internet connection had got its translation right. I hadn't upset him, so it seemed fine, and I hoped he knew the English words.

"When you play two together, you equal partners."

I actually said that, even though there was absolutely no point in trying to sound like a translation from a language I didn't know. I translated it again.

"In a duo, you must be equal. Hiroshi, you give way too much to your wife, Misouki." Misouki, beautiful moon, the internet said, but I couldn't think of any way of working that into the conversation.

They smiled very nicely, and got down to putting it right.

Gary had been doing some preliminary work on Ravel's *La Valse*.

"I hope you don't mind – I didn't clear it with you first."

"I'm not a censor, you know. But... "

"But you don't think I should do it? I love it."

"Right. It's not really just a piano piece, but a complete sketch Ravel made to play to Diaghilev for a ballet."

"It's a great competition piece."

"True. I doubt if there's a piano competition in the world which doesn't get it from one of the pianists. Or two. Or more. But..."

"But you don't think I can play it."

"I didn't say that. But I wouldn't advise you to play it. You're up against people who could play this on a dummy keyboard in their sleep."

"How do you mean?"

"Fits their fingers, if nothing else."

"You don't think I'm up to it."

"I think it would take time better spent on something else. Some Chopin. Make the piano sing a more Romantic song."

"Oh yes, that would be good."

OK. So I told him to learn the second Scherzo. Not too romantic, but truly Romantic.

Felicity was rather restrained. When I teach women students, I am well aware, as a married man – as a former married man – that there might be times when things go on physically which we should take into account. Or not, depending on which school you belong to: the one that 'understands' about cycles or the one that ignores them.

She looked upset, so I had to say something.

"D'you want to skip this lesson?"

"No. Why?"

"You seem out of sorts."

"It shows, does it?"

Of course it did, or I wouldn't have said anything.

There were tears around, and I'm not very good with tears, except my own, because they are rare, and I treasure them accordingly.

"You don't need to tell me." I meant it.

"It's home." A relief, because what went on at home wasn't here.

"My parents aren't speaking to each other."

"Is that unusual?"

"No. Not really. They don't talk a great deal. When they do, I think it's mostly to exchange information. I don't think they interest each other very much now. No surprises. But I think there's been a sort of surprise, one which they didn't tell each other about. Or Daddy didn't tell Mummy. It probably wasn't the sort of thing he would tell her anyway. Not if he could help it."

I assumed he'd been found out in some sort of sexual philandering

Felicity went on. "Of course, you might assume that it's some mistress she's found out about: I should think she's given up looking for blonde hairs anywhere on his clothes. He's a man of the world. And she's not an idiot."

206

So was it Lady Chislehurst, with her careful vowels and her ventriloquist lips, coaching her tennis coach?

"It's money. That's the only thing that seems to get them going. I shouldn't complain, because it's been a great help to me. My mother told me she was going to make a new will, and she wanted me to know that she intended to make a few bequests here and there, and that she wanted to make sure that Granny would be well-protected if she went first. If Mummy went first. I hate talking about these things, and I didn't pay much attention. But she said that when she got her lawyer to look into it, some of the shares she thought she owned had been transferred to Daddy."

"Isn't that illegal?"

"I suppose so. But she couldn't remember signing the transfer. Or not. It's quite a lot of money, and it was hers, from her godmother. Anyway she's not talking to Daddy, as in putting up silence like a wall for crashing into. It upsets me, because I crash into it too."

"Have you got an aunt you could go and stay with for a mini-break?"

"Well, yes, but that would mean I couldn't practise."

"A couple of days wouldn't matter."

"But I don't like to let you down. Make you think I don't care…enough about the piano."

"Well…" I stopped. And started again.

"I was on the point of saying that the practice you do when you don't feel all's right in your world may not be so good. But I've thought better of it. Practise, concentrate, and the other bits of your life will fade into perspective. Believe me, I know that's true."

"Was that what you did when…" She tailed off.

"When I hit a wall of silence?" Big grown-up smile. "There was no alternative. I had dates in the diary. Concert dates. And yes, it helped."

She was on the point of following up with another question, but this wasn't a thing I was going to share. Vulnerable girl, recently in tears, looking for parenting, possibly, though just as likely to be what I was looking for. Definitely No.

Bach to sharpen the feelings and the mind.

"Let's start with the English Suite in A minor."

I hoped that her father hadn't siphoned off some her mother's cash to pay for my film.

Victoria and the recording machine

I did my concerts; from home, this time, no travelling involved. One in a National Trust mansion – or rather, in the ballroom they had built behind it in the nineteenth century. The other really was local: in a school music block nearby. Audiences make a difference, because of the sharing thing. I felt like my own self again without the cameras. The encore was the Ritual Fire Dance, each time. Two ghosts eliminated again.

Now was the time for the test recording. It was close enough to the real thing, but still with enough time for a rethink if I wanted it.

Victoria. With her recording equipment. I have a perfectly good set of my own, but it would be quicker to let her use her new gear; she'd know how it works and I don't have to remember the details of my own machine.

She arrived mid-afternoon. Tea in mugs this time.

" I know you've done a detailed survey of the way Beethoven's been played."

"Yes."

"Did you enjoy that?"

"I did, although it took a long time, and some of it was rather dull. It's detective work. You have to be patient, look for clues. From the man himself down to the present day. The things people thought Beethoven would have written if they had been possible on his keyboard. Lots of editions to look at, in libraries, also online."

"Impressive. Did you ever wonder whether you were getting researcher's fever?"

"You mean…?"

"Getting to know more and more about less and less."

"That old one… But couldn't you say the same thing about playing an instrument or singing? You have to be sure you don't get bogged down in technical details"

"True. Wood for trees."

"Anyway, it got me more years at Cambridge."

"Seriously?"

"I had this relationship with one of the dons; I moved in with him, and he supported me to some extent."

"D'you mean he funded your research, so that you could be together?"

Victoria made a face. "I suppose so…Kept woman status. I had a good subject for a thesis, and I had to work hard. Doctorates don't fall into your lap in that neck of the woods."

She paused.

"Charlie wasn't even in the same field; he's a scientist. Aerodynamics. We lasted just the length of time it took for me to get my PhD."

"That was neat."

"No, it was planned. I learnt that from my mother."

"Not at your mother's breast?"

"My mother was at Cambridge in the early seventies, and she had a fabulous time, hurtling towards an ordinary degree, no class at all. Then she pulled up short and decided she wanted a doctorate – more useful to her future; so she concentrated on someone who might stimulate her in that direction."

"Do you think you've taken after your mother?"

"I think I may have some of her genes."

"Your father worked for the BBC you said."

"Yes, he was a sound engineer and he moved on. I learnt a lot from him."

"Parents can be useful, if they leave some useful genes behind."

I didn't explain.

"You did the media bit afterwards."

"Short course, and then I attached myself to a small recording company: half secretary, half assistant producer." She paused again. "With no strings. Only cables."

After that, we got to the business with her CD recorder, and the two microphones she'd brought; she took a couple of tests to get the level right.

"Shall we make a recording?"

I played opus 109 from end to end.

It was marginally awkward, playing to her. Almost like being in an examination room.

"Astonishing. Hearing you play at such close quarters."

We took a break.

"Don't you still hanker after playing the drums?" I asked.

"Sorry, you lost me there."

"You played them in that Emperor Concerto at university, you said."

"It was an accident. It was never meant to be a job for life. It's a bit gender-led with a few notable exceptions."

"Didn't you want to be a practical musician, then?"

"Yes, and No. There are too many. If I had my way, I'd put iron bars on the doors of all the college and university music departments, and only let students have a music education if they can find out how to break in. But I can't complain; here I am working with someone like you. For money, even. It's great."

"Someone like me?"

"Of course, there's no-one like you," she said, indulgently.

"You know, we've never talked about the details of this CD. How long it lasts…"

"I suppose you could say it's on the short side; if people expect their typical CD to be running at seventy-five minutes or so. I think our masters at Pythagoras Records would like more."

"I've been playing Beethoven's Bagatelles – opus 126. I can add them to the parcel."

"I'm happy with that. Let's do Schubert."

We went back to work. Schubert.

When you put Beethoven and Schubert next to one another, you have to find a different sound. These two sonatas were written in the 1820s, about eight years apart.

Victoria said I could imagine I was playing them on different pianos.

"Nice idea," I said.

"I can't take credit for that; it was something I picked up in a master-class. Can't remember who the master was, or if it was a master at all. But it was useful, and you grab anything going past."

"Were you playing in the class? Piano?"

"Sort of. It was a learning exercise. I certainly wouldn't play when you were in the same room. Definitely not."

"Do you keep up with your academic work? Any more projects for research?"

"No. I just wanted the degree. That was enough for me."

"I must say, you don't look anything like a Cambridge Doctor."

"You mean I don't look like a blue-stocking, with heavy glasses and my hair scraped back? Rather an out-of-date picture, don't you think? How many women academics have you met?"

"None, to tell you the truth. I live a quiet life. When I'm off the platform I spend a lot of time practising for another platform. I read quite a bit. I'm on my own a lot. A man apart."

"A man apart from what?"

I changed the subject.

"Let's listen to the recordings."

I made some notes on my score.

"Shall we leave the Bagatelles?" Small pause.

"Glass of wine?"

"Small one."

Then I changed the subject with an obvious crunch of gears.

"So how was the filming for you? It's the first time I've ever done such a thing."

"It's the first time anyone's done such a thing, I would have thought. Shame there weren't any visuals like that when I was researching Beethoven performances. I did watch films of pianists playing from the olden days. But they were filmed playing as they normally would. On scratchy film stock."

"You don't think it was a mistake, the film? I keep saying that this is why I want this Beethoven-Schubert CD to be good. Deep, full of understanding and feeling and fire, and intelligent, too. Just be honest. Oh God, I'm giving myself advice."

"I'll keep an eye on you. It's what producers are for. Enabling."

" I've been going on rather a lot about how I want these recordings to be as good as I can be…as they can be. I'm being boring about it. I'm sorry. But you will point things out if I miss them in the heat of the moment."

"There'll be plenty of heat, you can be sure of that. You can hear it in those little pieces you just filmed. You generate it, and it served you well for the Beethoven we did together in Cambridge."

"Thank you for that. All the same, Beethoven is a taskmaster. All those marks on the score. This sort of thing – you know…"

By now, we were together looking at the score as it lay on the piano.

"The problem is to make them sound big when recording, and not brittle. James, who'll be looking after the engineering, is great. But I really need your expertise. Your ears. What do you think?"

"About James, or about the black marks on the page?"

Victoria was very close.

"About keeping me on track."

She turned and touched my ear with her left hand. My ear. It was so intimate that I nearly lost my breath. I kissed her. Hardly sweeping a girl off her feet. She had made the gesture that defined the situation.

"You understand," she murmured, "this will make no difference to our working relationship."

I wished she hadn't said that. It deflected me from my path.

"Compartmentalise," she said. "I'm a past mistress at it."

I wished she hadn't said that either. She was right about herself, presumably because she'd done it before. Perhaps Charlie with his aerodynamics had injected something into her soul.

But how could I be sure about me? I'd never had to put anything like this into a compartment, had I?

Of course I could concentrate on Beethoven and Schubert. Of course I could. But it would be better to wait. Wouldn't it?

"Victoria," I said.

"Yes, Will."

"I'm going to ask you to go."

"Go where?"

"I'm sorry to say, I mean it. I'm not going to let us do what I hoped we were going to do."

She laughed.

"You're not playing hard to get, are you?"

"No."

"It's not that you're thinking about someone else? Your former wife? Ellen?"

Ouch. Ouch.

"No, definitely not. I'm not a complete fool. It's just I want to, but I can't."

"You're not about to tell me something I don't want to know, are you?"

"How?"

"Well, that there are problems…"

"No, if you mean what I think you might mean, and yes, if you will understand that I've got to rein in. We're working together in the studio; you say you can deal with that. I simply don't know if I can. I've never had to."

"I thought you used to play sonatas with your wife. And presumably you…"

"Not the same thing. Part of a long relationship, which conspiculously failed on both counts. Music-wise and relationship-wise."

A pause.

"Ah well, I was looking forward to that."

But she smiled. No hint of disdain, or dismay, or disgust, or any other dis- I could think of.

"Don't worry, Will. I know where you are. And now I know where you live. Some other time – soon, I hope, when we're not turning music into a memorable CD – I'll come back. Yes?"

"Oh yes. That is, if you want to, after what I've just done. After the work's finished."

" I really do understand how important this work is to you. As it is to me."

She took her recording equipment and went. Amicably.

The CD recording

Life went on, teaching, and a couple of concerts taking me up north for a few days. Then we moved into CD mode.

This wasn't the small studio at Cricklewood where we did the film music. This was larger, with its own personal acoustic. It had been a church, and now wasn't. Not big, but with a feeling of space, and with an accidentally good shape – two cubes next to each other – for sound.

There's a control box from which the team can see, and wave, if they don't want to use the intercom.

I felt at home here.

The piano I'd asked for was lovely, like a friend, and Martin was on hand to keep it in order. James was there, moving microphones about. He could take all the varieties of sound I try to get into my playing.

Victoria, with photocopies, offered no hint of anything that wasn't to do with recording. She gave me an admirably cool peck on the cheek, but shot a sharper glance at Felicity, who'd come to turn the pages, if I needed it.

I decided not to use the score. I knew what I needed to know, and I wanted to be on my own. Felicity went into the control room.

We started with Beethoven.

"I'll play it right through, to get used to the piano and the acoustic."

Let them balance, but not record, I thought.

When I stopped, the studio speaker came on and Victoria said, "Would you like to listen to that?"

"You recorded it after all?"

James's voice came through.

"I've done a couple of slightly different balances, using a couple of new mics, which I like very much, but I want you to know what you sound like."

It takes some concentration to listen to the sound of the piano, and not the sound of the music. Both balances were good. Slightly more depth to one, maybe a little less definition. Not much to choose. Not enough difference to make or mar my playing, I thought.

"Can you do both? Use one for the Beethoven, and one for the Schubert? Look, I'm going to leave it to you. They give a good BBC sort of sound, rather than one of those over-etched ones you can get from abroad."

Down to work. Beethoven's first movement went well enough, and yet...I wasn't happy. Victoria got me to listen to the playback. The sound was good...very good... and somehow...

"Do you mind if I tell you what I think? You can ignore it if you like."

That was what she was there for. To offer advice. To be taken or not.

"I think I can hear you thinking a bit too much. All those pianists who've recorded this stuff. Look, it's only Beethoven. Not God. Go back and do some of it phrase by phrase, rather like the way you did when you were filming. We'll record what you do and see where we get to. This is not a final take. Go and play around a bit, let your fingers guide you, and then we'll do another take of the whole first movement."

This was unexpected advice, but it helped; I got happier and happier with myself. I work well when I'm setting my own limits, but being challenged also helps.

Then I did a complete take. The whole sonata. Twenty minutes.

I alternate between thinking that recording should be just a one-off job, like the real Venus coming out of the sea, complete, new and fresh and all in one piece, and feeling that it should be like Botticelli's Venus coming out of the sea brush-stroke by brush-stroke. I usually compromise by settling for a broad sweep followed by such replacements as are necessary. And trusting your producer. Never forget that: be nice to the people with your sound in their hands. With your hands in their hands.

I talked a little with Victoria over lunch, straight, harmless gazes, with a little friendly affection. No suggestion of anything more.

Felicity spent our lunch break with James.

In the afternoon, we were ready for the Schubert sonata.

Schubert must have known he was dying when he wrote this and the two other great piano sonatas. Writing them for no reason I know of except that he felt he had to. Is there a better reason for writing anything? It's not important to know these personal details; it shouldn't change the way you play, or you get sentimental – a "Farewell to the World" – and turn everything into a jar of honey.

A funny thing happened. I couldn't get Beethoven out of my fingers. Three pages into the Schubert and I stopped.

"Let's do the other pieces. The Bagatelles." Late music, almost as if Beethoven was making up for his sterner image.

We were pleased, and called it a day.

CD Day 2 and Felicity

On the second day, it flowed. Schubert's sonata is longer by quite a few minutes. It's a wonderfully constructed work, each movement like an act in a play, with the curtain falling in between, and the next act picking up an idea or two from the one before, but without flagging them up. I decided to record the shortest one first. This is the scherzo, the comic relief. I wanted to do it first because it asks you for brilliance, and its middle section blossoms into beauty. You have to get the speed exactly right so that the two sections come from the same impulse: it's as if Harlequin dances, and then declares his love for Columbine.

The last movement is a rondo; it opens with a charming invitation to dance, an invitation which is renewed, subtly different each time, with some acrobatic gestures, and some almost acerbic ones to propel the music onwards. At the end, Schubert doesn't seem to want to let his melody go; he makes it fall silent, and then lets it scurry away, grabbing a fragment of the theme as an excuse until it's firmly dealt with in a final flourish.

We had all day to do this sonata, and I was happy to leave those movements, since they had come out with a feeling of immediacy, just as you might want them to be.

The first two needed a closer relationship with the piano. It was a lovely instrument, but not my own partner, and I wanted the most beautiful sounds I could tempt from it for this music which is so close to my heart. Beautiful and yet clear, as if two or three individual players were bringing their own colours to the complete whole.

215

James wanted to explore his slightly different set-up, so we spent the rest of the time before the lunch break exploring. Martin checked the voicing of individual notes, if either of us was unhappy about any detail. I played, using as little pedal as I could, making my body take full responsibility, and not just my fingers.

Then we had an early lunch break.

Victoria had some tidying up to do – the more notes she made, the better, she said, while her mind was full of what she'd been doing.

Felicity and I went for an Italian meal. At a restaurant nearby.

I made polite enquiries about her father and mother.

"I haven't seen Daddy for a few weeks."

"Is that because of the family thing?"

"Which one was that?"

"Are there so many?"

"We're a family."

"The bonds thing. Your mother's bonds."

"I think it's blown over. I'm not at home much."

"Really?" I said, "You didn't tell me."

"There's not a lot of time in my lessons to do much but work."

"So – are you going to tell me now – or am I going to guess?"

"I've got a place of my own. Well, actually with someone."

"With someone special?"

"I hope so."

"And are you going to tell me who it is?"

"It's not a secret."

"Someone I know, then?"

"He's a conductor."

"A real grown up conductor?"

"What do you mean by that? I'm grown up too."

"Yes, of course you are. I didn't mean to suggest anything else, just because I came back to your school with you."

"That made you think of me as a schoolgirl." She laughed.

"Not exactly, but – well, maybe a bit."

"You're wrong. Otherwise you might well have found out if you'd noticed I had serious feelings for you." She looked at me seriously. "How was it that you didn't see I was really deeply in love with you? Seriously?"

216

Very easily. I have no experience in this subject. I don't know the signs. A woman could be Dido, and I'd sail off in my boat to Rome thinking she was sending me smoke signals to wave me Goodbye and then going back to run the country instead of wading into a funeral pyre.

"I wasn't ready to take anything like that on. I didn't look for any signs."

"Wouldn't you have liked to?"

"Don't get me wrong. Felicity, you're a great girl, you look great, you have a fine talent. But you're the daughter of my patron, you're not much more than half my age, and I think there are rules about that. I never even considered it. Now you have a real grown-up conductor as a boy friend?"

"Oh yes."

"Not a student? Which is what I meant."

"No, not a student."

"Your father doesn't mind?"

"No. Daddy is modern minded. Mummy too. Anyway, he's not the first."

I was amazed. This girl that I had been teaching, and off-and-on fancying, was not the hands-off girl I thought she was. Pedagogical honour, such as it is, would have kept me pure, as far as she was concerned, but it might well have been harder to keep to it if I'd known what she had just said six months earlier. Not the first? How did I not know this? On the other hand, why should I have known?

"I thought you wanted to know who it is."

It wouldn't do any harm.

"Michael Aaronowitz. Do you know him?"

Wasn't that the man I'd worked with in Scotland a few months earlier? Who asked me to call him Aaron? The man with the wife who rang him up to find out what he was doing in Glasgow, apart from making music? So his name was Michael. Perfectly good name, I would have thought, though he billed himself with just the one name. He struck me then as a loose cannon, but I'd no idea he could be as loose as this. What about the wife? And the children she regularly tucked up in bed? He was older than me, which I supposed made some sort of sense, considering what she'd just confessed about me. And I suppose he wasn't as old as all that – not like the sixty-plus conductors who get a new lease of life when young flesh is ready and willing to stimulate the slowly aging hormones.

"Can I ask if you're making it a permanent sort of arrangement?"

"I've no idea; I'm just playing it by ear."

I wondered how they met.

"At a party Mummy gave in one of those entertaining suites at the South Bank. Some charity or other. I was there. You never know what contacts you might make."

"And you did. Make contact."

"I meant for my career."

She was already making contacts. I knew nothing about her.

I was dying to ask if she knew he was married, but didn't.

"Of course, he's married, but it's all in the past now, you know."

I did know something about that. But my marriage was more in the past than his was. If his was. Still, I could only wish good luck to them both. She was nineteen by now. She was to go on studying, and she had a piano to practise on. And quite honestly, if he intended taking her round with him as his soloist, then it really might be a good thing.

Her 'deeply in love' feelings for me had vanished very thoroughly indeed. She was able to talk about them in the past tense...a plupluperfect tense if there is such a thing. It was a sort of insult and a relief at the same time. My interests seemed to be getting engaged elsewhere. Victoria. Ellen. How much more growing up do you have to do when you're thirty-five?

It distracted me from thinking about the recording for a while.

**

Back in the studio, we took up with Schubert again.

Traditionally the first movement of a sonata has the deepest thoughts and intellectual prowess. We learnt about how such things are constructed in our theory lessons at the Conservatoire, and then dealt with the fact that the great composers bent the 'rules', as great dramatists did with the old formula laid down by Aristotle.

I played the first movement complete. Strong chords to begin, arpeggios to lighten the impact of these opening bars. To lighten and strengthen. The music led me along its familiar paths that seem fresher every time I take to them. There's a moment very near the end where the notes become a momentary doorway to Paradise. You have to let them take their time, but not over-indulge them, before they disappear into the final bars.

I walked around the studio, moving on in my head to the second movement. You can't play this beautifully enough, until you accept that most of that beauty isn't of your making, but of your willingness to let Schubert play through you. Be grateful.

The left hand makes the lightest sounds playing notes as if they were written for a double-bass and a cello while over them a heart-breaking melody unwinds. The central part takes off somewhere else, as if to say that you can't have heaven without being aware of hell; then the opening music again, with new voices taking part, soul-searching.

I played it twice, complete, and trusted Victoria and her team to detach themselves and decide which was better. If I got involved with critical listening, I would end up re-recording until Doomsday. I had done what I wanted, and was content to leave it at that.

Gary

It's important to admit that your pupils get better because they practise, and not because you pump them full of everything you know. They need to find things out for themselves, with guidance where it suits. I was lucky to have a bunch that did just that.

Gary told me he was filling in a form for one of the big piano competitions. What should I say? That he wouldn't win? That he wasn't ready? You can't always tell. I didn't know if there was a competitive streak in him that would bring out elements that don't come out in lessons. And there have been some surprising decisions in the past. There was always a chance he might win the audience prize or something, nice, confident American that he was with a big smile.

My own competition win came as a surprise; most of all to me. I went in for it as a career move to kick-start a career which didn't seem to be going anywhere much. Pats on the back, at that point, but not many engagements. When I came across the Endenich Schumann Competition, I thought it might be worth a try. Whoever heard of the Endenich Competition? Endenich didn't seem the ideal place to have such a thing, since it's where Schumann ended his days in a lunatic asylum. Once you knew where the money was coming from it wasn't such a bad idea. Some American businessman had left a huge fortune and a widow who loved music and pianists, if not in that order. She earmarked a sum from his fortune to set up a one-off piano competition. She looked for a special slant.

What better than one centred on one of the world's greatest composers for the piano? One who, like her husband, had to deal with the tragedy of losing his mind? She fixed on Schumann, and since Endenich isn't far from Bonn, that's where she did it.

Once only. In fact, we had to have the main part of the competition in Bonn, but we were taken to Endenich and photographed outside the place where Schumann spent his last days. It attracted some media attention, of course – almost impossible to avoid – so I'm not quite sure what her motives were.

Mrs Howard Everding was her name. She came to all the stages of the competition and sat just behind the jury. Amazing-looking woman, plastic to the tips of her fingernails (except that they were gold), looking nearly the same as she must have looked twenty-odd years before. She had a sense of humour. I think she was working something out on her husband's ghost. And on the Mexican pianist who came with her. He had a moustache, I remember, and he gave a recital, which all competitors attended, naturally. Good photo opportunity. I've still got the picture in some drawer or another. You can spot me in the back row if I ever find it. There are about fifty of us in front of the house where Schumann thought his last thoughts. Mrs E looks glamorous, rather like Marlene Dietrich, her hair pulled back, and her face with it. The Mexican is lowering (as clouds do, though the other sense could be applied to him too, if you're talking about standards; his recital was probably as much of a strain for us as it was for him). He's been a husband and a widower since then, and now he gives concerts for fun with Mrs E's husband's money, or what's left of it.

The prizes were generous. They brought a serious contingent from the other side of where the Iron Curtain used to be, which still had some relevance in the half dozen years since it was raised. There were rumours of fixes among the jury, and the British member went public, when she was safely back at home, about threats. In the old days, it used to be bribes – much safer.

There were three of us who were first equal, one American, one Russian, and one European. All men. It looked like a fix, and it quite possibly was, with Mrs Everding's real gold fingernails leaving their marks on it. I was without question the least photogenic of the winners, which made me value my first prize even more. The press had a field day on their Arts pages; headlines had 'mad' or a variant of it in the title.

It still gives me a lot of pleasure to remember that feeling when I won. It wasn't quite as spectacular as it might have been, but a British musician winning these continental things at all was still enough to bring attention, and then there were those hints of scandal. It got me my trusty agent, Jane Curzon, who made a major story out of it back here in the press, and there I was, spiralling gently upwards.

It was also a challenge in my first professional years. I had to live up to the publicity, and then live beyond it, or else I got dismissed as stuck in a time-warp: "William Winton, six years on, must realise that he can't go on playing the same winning card all the time; the game changes, and the cards and players too." I really did get a review like that. Fortunately it was in an obscure newspaper in the West Country. No one saw it, except the kind friend who sent it to me. It hurt, and I'd have liked to ignore it, but in the long run, it made me think.

Now there was Gary. He had to be talked to and I had to take my time to tell him what I thought.

Yes, Gary.

"I've filled the form in for a modest competition, and I wanted to give you as a reference as my current teacher. Would you do that?"

Of course I would. I wasn't obliged to write a testimonial in advance. Ours is a competitive profession, even when you're giving a solo concert – but you're on your own there because the other pianists are playing somewhere else. You may get compared with whoever the audience can remember. Or your own recordings, which can be worse. That's the way of the world. But to be in direct competition with a lot of other pianists, one after another, in front of special people on a jury, each with their own opinion of the music you're playing? And at the final round, a prize given by the audience which knows what it likes, and doesn't always agree with the jury, because they haven't heard all the earlier rounds and formed a more complete picture of the talent on offer. It adds another dimension. Or takes it away, because really the music is the tape against which you should be measured, and here you are being considered not in relation to the person who composed it, but to people from the East and the West.

People love competitions – the greatest, the best, the fastest, the biggest, the cheapest. It's a risk. I thought Gary could well get into the second round. That was the thrust of my intended argument. And since I thought it would take quite a long time to put over, and I didn't want to hurt his feelings, and since he'd come from the U.S. of A specially to sit at my feet, I said we needed time to talk.

I was thinking of taking him out for a meal to do that, but he wouldn't have it. He asked me to his place. I was surprised.

"Kitty will provide food, and drink – she's good at that. That's to say, she'll fix it up with one of those meal companies that deliver the whole thing. Very American, I guess."

An expensive girlfriend? I just hoped she would let us have time to talk.

"We can talk much better if we're not in a restaurant."

He was quite right, and I wasn't in the mood to do entertaining at my place.

I went. That was a surprise. It wasn't so long since I'd been a student, and I expected a bed-sit, maybe a bit bigger since he was American, and whatever happens to the economy over there, they still seem to have more money than we have. But that's not what I found. This was an apartment built in a converted warehouse that once housed tea from China, and probably a few of the other substances which didn't end up in packets with labels on shelves in shops. I wouldn't have minded the place myself.

Windows at each end, view of the River Thames. Grand piano, of course, black, but everything else rather unstudent-like, in other words, white and pale grey.

I looked around for Kitty. No sign.

"It's a fabulous place you've got here."

"I'm lucky. Kitty spoils me. Probably doesn't trust me otherwise."

"She's not here?"

"She'd like to be. But there are things back home she's got to do. My stepfather can be rather demanding, and she has to back off from being a mother to please him."

"Just let me get this right – Kitty is…"

"Mother dearest."

"And she's in the States?"

"She would love to be here, of course, but that isn't how it worked out."

Kitty must be another multi-millionairess, probably second or third time around. And that was leaving Gary's stepfather out of the equation, who was never mentioned, but who may or may not have come into it financially. Should I expect the people I meet to have been divorced, unless proved otherwise?

I gazed out of the window.

"Very nice," I said. "Big place for one person," I said.

"Well, yes and no. I don't live here alone."

Not that you would have known. There wasn't a single sign of another person's presence or personality in what I could see. In fact, there wasn't much sign of anyone's presence or personality. Like the meal, I guessed, it was something Mother had ordered complete, out of a glossy promotion magazine, maybe.

"Very nice," I said again.

The table was set for two.

The flat-mate he shared this place with was absent.

"D'you share it with another musician?" I asked, and thought what a fool I was to pursue something which was nothing to do with me. Curiosity stalks large and long in our profession. In any profession, I guess, but in ours you can justify it: it's slightly important to know who's with whom, or you might say something wrong, either hurting the other person, or even your own career.

"He's an American I know from back home – a distant relative, so Mother's quite happy about that. He's not a musician. We were, you know…close."

I let that one pass by.

"Can you practise as much as you like here? There must be neighbours."

"Well-sound-proofed neighbours, fortunately. Two ways, up and down. Above is just God and the aeroplanes, mostly friendly, we hope, and underneath is an actor who has parties when she's out of work, which seems to be quite often. She's friendly too, but we don't hear them really. Soundproofing is one of the things we pay for. Nothing through the walls, either."

"More soundproofing?"

"No, just no-one there."

They had the whole floor. Why did Gary want to go in for a competition? His mother could have bought the Festival Hall for a night, and an orchestra to go with it, just like that. But it's not about that, I know: it's about making your own waves.

Gary uncorked some champagne, which was good, and we talked about New York a bit, and how he thought London was, and why he had wanted to come here when clearly he could have afforded the best tuition in the States. I wasn't angling for a flattering reply, just curious.

There were reasons, he said.

"I wanted Europe, and I don't speak any other language. Anyway I was getting German-type teaching in the States, and France and the US don't speak often at the moment except to leave messages on each other's answer-phones. And then there was you – you play impressively, if you will let me say so, and you studied in France, which takes care of that bit. I heard you play here in

London when I came over with Mom a couple of years ago. I felt I could learn from you. Studying with you and practising, of course." He laughed. "And now, well, now…It's amazing that you're actually here…"

"Just us, tonight, then."

Gary didn't answer, but told me how his mother had insisted on deciding what we were going to eat, (calorie controlled, but tasty, he said) and that the champagne was part of it, and he was to give me her thanks for looking after her favourite son.

"You have brothers?"

"No, but she still calls me her favourite son. I like it, because it's illogical."

He disappeared, and came back with food on plates, and we started to eat. I asked about his family background, asked him to remind me how long he'd been playing the piano. I should have remembered, because it was something I'd asked him last year when he started to study with me, but had forgotten. He told me again: there he was, sitting on his mother's knee playing the piano by putting his hands on hers as she played nursery rhymes and Danny Kaye songs (The Ugly Duckling, I guess) and then she was guiding his fingers as he began to play real things on his own piano. He was under five, remember. A privileged childhood, and a mother who did no pushing, just bestowed warm praise if he did things right.

Maybe he had that extra something he could access if his life depended on it. Gary had moments, I'd noticed, when I could tell that playing the piano was his survival kit. Maybe the competition might give him the chance to throw carefulness to the winds.

I agreed to be his referee.

We talked about the view from the window, about the concerts he'd been to, and where he lived in New York, and about Kitty, who was now a film-producer in partnership with her new husband. How they got on. And nothing was said about his father. We got through the meal pleasantly.

Then there was a pause. After a very light, calorie-controlled (I hoped) main dish, microwaved to perfection, there were strawberries in a light spun sugar jacket. They didn't look as if anyone had been counting calories when they spun them into that.

"Oh I'm so sorry. But it really is very low in calories. Considering…"

I could deal with the diet consequences later. He hadn't finished what he wanted to say.

"Can I say this, while we're talking calories?"

"It depends on what it is."

"You look very different now from the way you looked when I saw you playing here in London a couple of years ago."

"I don't think I've changed in any other way."

"Oh please forgive. I didn't mean that."

"I think you've come a long way in the last six months, here in London. But if you have competitions in mind, I think you should go and get some extra sessions with…" and I suggested a couple of famous pianists who would not just take his money and spend the lesson playing to him themselves (just to show you how it goes, boy, this is how I play it). One of them was likely to turn up on the jury at almost any of the competitions Gary had in mind. He wouldn't be able to vote for him, because he was a pupil. But the rest of the jury would know that this candidate was from his stable and that could well make them vote differently. After all, you can't suggest that your esteemed colleague's pupils are junk. Gary was shocked.

"But you're the only teacher I want. You're the one I need."

When I looked into Gary's face, I thought I could see something I should have known all along. He was trying to conceal something he actually wanted to show. So I tried to look encouraging and discouraging at the same time.

"Can I ask you something personal?" he said.

No, Gary, you can't, I was going to say, but by the time I got round to it, it was too late.

"The girls are saying you're a single man now."

"Well, that isn't personal, it's common knowledge. And this is a great meal. Did your cookery messengers send any cheese, by any chance?"

Gary leapt up. "Christ, I'm not looking after you."

There was some cheese, and it looked as if I was going to eat rather more than I intended, all with a view to softening the blow which hadn't yet landed. More champagne, sweet this time. The talk got to cooking, which he did, and did I cook, now that I was alone?

"It can be an emotional thing, cooking. One of Mom's protégés is a New York cook, and he says there are times when it's all he can do to break an egg without feeling he's breaking into his sainted soul."

I felt something of an expert on eggshells, since I could feel a few of them under my shoes. "I don't entertain at the moment. I'm thinking a lot, reading a lot, too. All the things you might not do when you're sharing your life with someone else."

"I like being alone too. When Mike's away, it leaves me space, you know."

Looking round, there didn't seem to be much shortage of that. I said so.

"No, I'm lucky that way, but I meant, you know, space for me, and for what I might want to do, or broaden my experience."

We seemed to be heading in some direction I knew next to nothing about. Now that Gary had virtually opened the door to it, I would be careful that we didn't go too far.

But he wanted to talk about it.

"Things can get a bit difficult, especially if my emotions get involved elsewhere. And if that involves a member of the Conservatoire staff…"

This door had to be closed at once, since it seemed to me to be getting too close to home. Cheese cutting filled in the gap, and changed the subject.

"Let's talk about the music you might play. Of course it will depend on what sort of thing the competition wants."

We short-listed some things.

Safe territory. He got his laptop computer and we went on sitting at the dinner table, making a list of repertoire he might offer.

He'd cleared away but there were still glasses glittering, with the colour of the wine to set them off. I got up and went to the window. The lights down the river were very picturesque. All that area which used to hum with commercial and industrial activity now turned into pretty lighting displays.

I leant my head up against the oak window frame. Gary came over.

"We can go out on to the balcony; it's not exactly pollution-free, but it's fresh and it's worth a couple of brandies on its own."

The window was one of those huge ones that seem to be operated like a lock gate. The air was fresh, and once the window was open, the sounds of London's traffic came up and down, depending on whether the people on the move at this time of night – eleven o'clock, perhaps – were on the ground or in the air. Trains, several successive police cars, and a late plane bringing Sharon fruit from Israel as like as not for Tesco or Sainsbury or Waitrose. Important enough to disturb the night air. I'd just eaten a good meal so who was I to take an attitude?

I looked over the balustrade of the balcony.

Gary grabbed my arm. "Be careful, it's a long way down."

Of course it was, and I knew that. It was a good idea to give up the balcony scene.

And go home.

"I've been enjoying your hospitality rather too well, Gary, and I think I need a taxi to take me home."

"You could stay the night if that would help…"

"That's kind of you. But I want to wake up tomorrow in my own bed and begin the day from there. So a taxi is the way."

"The offer still stands; there's plenty of room if you change your mind."

"No. Thank you. I'll be fine."

He got on to his mobile.

"If you show me the bathroom, that would be a kindness."

We walked past the chairs and the white sofas facing one another, through a bedroom of the most unremitting white. How did these two men live in such whiteness? It was like being in a laundry.

The taxi announced its arrival – it was obviously hanging around in the neighbourhood. Gary took me down to the front door.

I thanked him again for his mother's hospitality and got into the taxi.

About twenty minutes it took, getting home, with a driver who had plenty to say about what it was like to drive a taxi through the rubbish systems some American had made to make London's traffic move more freely.

He had plenty to say, too, about the London Mayor who was behind all the problems taxi-drivers faced. Quite a range of language he had in his vocabulary.

The next day

I thought it best to play down the whole of the later part of the evening.

When I next met Gary, I'd say, "Look, Gary, I'm sorry I left rather abruptly."

We'd slap each other on the back and be friends, and he'd move on to some European teacher, pleased to go, because he'd have to move on now, wouldn't he?

When it came to the point, that isn't what happened.

He came into the room and put his music down.

I smiled, and looked civilised. "I've been thinking more about those competitions you want to do. I'll recommend you to Johann Kurzmacher. He's just what you need. He has a more positive attitude to them than I have. There are ways of setting about winning, and he very likely knows what they are.

Naturally, you must feel you can come back and play to me if you want to. I'll write to your mother and thank her for the meal, and explain how things could be."

That should have been that. It wasn't.

Gary looked me straight in the eyes.

"I understand what you're saying. I thought about it after you left – about going to someone else; I decided that what I would like to do is go to a summer school and work with the guy you suggest, while continuing to work with you. I don't think you've taught me anything like as much as I would like to learn from you, do you?"

"Well, no. If you think that on a personal level, that would continue to work…"

"We get on, don't we? It was great you came to dinner, and we got a chance to talk."

"It was a great meal. I enjoyed that."

He laughed. "Perhaps I was on the point of telling you a bit more about me than you expected, but I didn't. I mean, you know I'm gay. I make no secret of that and I'm easy with it. After all, it makes no difference to our relationship – I regard you as a friend, if I can put it that way."

"I must admit you threw me a bit when you mentioned my divorced status…I did wonder where you were going with that."

"Oh I'm sorry. I just intended to be sympathetic. I know what it's like to have a relationship come to an end, and I'm heading in that direction again."

"It's not easy, especially if you don't spot it in advance. Thank you for your kind thought."

"Then I let slip that I had feelings about a member of staff here. There was no reason to tell you that, but I felt comfortable and probably over-stocked with wine. Anyway, it's true, and I could tell you who it is, but I don't know how well you know him, so there's no point."

I laughed and sighed at the same time. "I thought you might be sending me a coded message."

"No, never in a hundred years. Don't get mixed up with your teachers That's a cardinal rule, if you want to make progress."

"That's a relief. So we can just go on as before. I think your solution is right. I would like to keep on teaching you. And for you to sign up for some sessions with Doctor Kurzmacher."

"Ja, and I can come back afterwards and we can go over what I thought I'd learnt from him."

I would now get down to finding ways for him to get deeper into the music.

After that

Pythagoras Records were keen to get my CD turned round as soon as possible. I dare say Jane had told them of the untitled film I'd made, and if that was going to attract the attention it was meant to, it would be a good idea to get Beethoven and Schubert established in their own right. Very soon.

Email from Jane Curzon To *will@williamwinton.co.uk*
I haven't seen you for ever, and propose to put that right by arranging a lunch date with Kerri Burston. Do I need to remind you that she's the mezzo-soprano from the States who's going to be your partner at the Festival in Bellagio in October this year? The one who OK'd you from the photograph I sent her? and I think someone played her some of your film soundtrack CD, so she wants to talk programmes when she passes through London next week. I see you're free on Wednesday. Will confirm. J

The lunch happened on the following Wednesday. Jane was there, along with Kerri's agent, whose name I didn't quite catch.

I'd never been engaged on the strength of a photograph and a CD before, and there was a sort of deep-seated hope (not too deep), that if she was all glamour and a singer, then she might be used to a freer life-style which could prove interesting. Or something. Nothing substantial or in any way lasting.

Not a chance. We met in a quiet restaurant in Kensington. I think she was staying locally, but I never found out.

Nice food, though we didn't actually eat a lot. Or rather, Jane and the other agent did eat quite a lot, but Kerri and I didn't; we were both on diets, though for different reasons. Mine was for weight preservation. Hers seemed to come from some way-of-life religion. I didn't ask for details. It involved rejecting most of what arrived on the table and adding something to what stayed there.

Apart from that, she was absolutely breath-taking in every way. She looked as if she'd just come straight out of a fashion magazine, straight off the press. Not a fault in her make-up, hair, clothes, figure; and her modulated speaking voice sounded like a voice-over, or as if someone else was prompting her via a hidden earpiece. It was uncanny. She was incredibly glamorous. She was a package put together for the paparazzi. But that was about it. I think you could lust after her on the printed page, but faced with the reality, that didn't happen – she just wasn't real.

She was interested in me alright. As a commodity. She was openly measuring me against my photograph. "I'm glad you look as good as your last picture," she said. "And you play the piano too…"

Her manager was a woman. Wisely, because any man who got too close to her would be looking for trouble.

Kerri was very confident, very charming, said the right things, smiled by opening her mouth a little and showing her teeth – no pretty laughter lines were going to get to the surface. I wondered how she managed to sing without spoiling the picture. Could she let herself go for those few minutes? She didn't seem the sort of artist who had grown from her art and her love of it. More like a kit to be assembled at home, in a theatre or on a concert platform. It occurred to me that maybe I'd been going through the same process, until I remembered that I'd been made of baser materials in the first place. I didn't find her in the least attractive. Nor did I feel her stir with interest for me. Perhaps the two things were connected. We were a partnership made in a publicity office.

A huge rapport wasn't necessary for this one. This was to be a trio of concerts made for the tourists in Bellagio. Wealthy tourists bussed in by an international firm, which in this case meant American, with some oil-rich leavening, so there was money, serious money, globalised money. They'd lined up one of the big houses around Lake Como; not the Hotel Grande Bretagne, which appeared momentarily in that film 'Rocco and his Brothers', since it was still in a state of disrepair; the money voted by the government to reconstitute it seemed to have disappeared into the waters of the lake. So not there. Nor any of those where the film stars might live.

This was a Belgian prince's house which has a large salon, so that you can do very expensive things there. Two recitals with a small chamber orchestra, one for her and one for me, and then a joint one as a climax, with some operatic bits from Kerri, a concerto from me, and then the grand finale – an aria which Mozart wrote for someone he was in love with, giving himself an important part in it for the piano which he would play like a declaration of love.

"It's really for a soprano," breathed Kerri, "but I have such an amazing range, and my voice gives it such character."

She almost giggled, although her expression didn't change.

These exclusive events make me uncomfortable. Playing at an expensive school for one of my pupils is one thing, but this didn't have the same appeal. The fee Jane asked was huge by my standards, and we would stay at the Metropole. Lake Como, they said, is fabulous.

"It's just wonderful. Did you know that the singer in one of Willa Cather's novels drowned in that lake? I think it's hilarious. I could use it as publicity, don't you think? She drowned. I walk on the water. That's a joke." I wouldn't have known.

Well, if she didn't actually walk on the water, at least she seemed to be unsinkable – all surface, no substance. Of course, we would only find out when we worked together. I didn't tell her that in 'Lucy Gayheart', it's a baritone and a pianist who get drowned.

Sir Greg and Felicity

A couple of weeks later I was at the Conservatoire again.

Sir Greg had sent a note through the post. Email was not in his area yet. "*Matter of some delicacy, you know,*" (this was hand-written, presumably to by-pass his secretarial staff) "*so on your next visit, which I see is booked for tomorrow, would you be kind enough to call in? I need your help. GJ*"

I had no idea what it could be, but I rang to make an appointment with Margaret, his secretary, who sounded somewhat surprised. She had been his secretary for some time, without seeming to change. She looked much the same when we were students, swaying more when she walked in those days; we thought she was Sir Greg's lover. Greg's Peg. I hope she enjoyed it, if she was, because he smoked a pipe almost non-stop in those days, and it must have taken determination on her part, and opening his windows whenever possible. We were advised to wrap up warm if we were going to his office, but since few of us ever visited him in his office, this remained a largely untested, unproven theory, a Con story.

Margaret said I was lucky to catch him.

"I didn't even know he'd written to you, so he must have posted the letter himself."

She showed me in.

"Good of you to come. Some delicacy, as I think I said. Wrote."

"You did." But he wasn't ready to talk about it, whatever it was.

"We're agreed about the concert in the summer, aren't we? I think your agent has fixed that, and we've managed to get a spot of sponsorship to cover your fee, which is – er – acceptable. I had no idea such recent alumni were able to earn so much, even if it is what your agent lady said was a specially reduced rate, on your instructions."

"It just goes to show how well you prepare us for the profession, though, don't you think?"

"Now this little matter. It's about Felicity Smith." Of course it would have been. But I had no idea what exact line he was going to take.

"I don't know if she's spoken to you about it. She's – how shall I put it? – living away from home. Which, of course, is part of the business of growing up. But, unfortunately her mother isn't too pleased."

That wasn't exactly what Felicity had said when she had told me that her mother was modern minded.

"In fact, Lady Chislehurst's really worried. She's been in touch with me, which surprised me a little. It seems that her daughter has moved in with a foreign conductor. Never heard of him. Aaronson, or something."

"Aaronowitz…" I corrected him.

"So you know him? From Estonia. I rather think Felicity's funding the flat they live in together, with money her great-grandmother left her. Lady Chislehurst is a wealthy woman, as we know, but other bits of the family money passed her by and landed in Felicity's lap."

"And passed her grandmother by, too." I remembered the lady who was or wasn't a lover of Picasso's.

"You know more than I do, William. Well, Lady Chislehurst is worried that the money will just disappear in the direction of Estonia, leaving nothing for Felicity. Especially as it doesn't seem to be absolutely clear that Aaronowitz is a free man."

"By which you mean unmarried?"

"By which I mean divorced. I ask you this as a colleague who has the good of the girl at heart. After all, she is a student at this institution. You know him, you said. Do you know anything much about him?"

"I did a concert with him in Glasgow."

"It would be a great service if you could find something out. Maybe from Felicity. You're her teacher, and teachers often get to know more about their students than their parents do."

"I have to say that I think it's her own business," I said. "But Lady Chislehurst is a nice woman, and I'll do what I can."

That seemed a reasonable get-out clause. So I got out.

Felicity and I ate our sandwiches and drank our fizzy water in my teaching room – strictly forbidden by the Con rules, totally ignored by most of the staff. It's a chance to recover from teaching without the noise of fellow-eaters taking the edge off your ears.

I gave her vague 'how are things?' leads. Got nowhere. So I asked her plainly how she planned to continue her studies.

"With you," she said. "Micki has a very high opinion of your playing. You could almost be an Eastern European pianist, he says. I think he means it as a compliment.

"Micki as in Aaronowitz?"

"He's good for me. He's got a job in America next November – an assistant, deputy, conductor-in-waiting, whatever it is, and he plans to have me do Mendelssohn's First Piano Concerto there. I think I could do that, don't you?"

I did. I could help her find the right way to find that. She had enough power to be heard with an American orchestra and an Estonian conductor, provided they got the style right. There was plenty of time to set her up and she had the motivation. And he?

I asked her if she was in love.

"Oh yes." She looked doubtful, and then added, "Well enough. He's a bit unsophisticated, you know, and that reminds me of mio babbino caro, my beloved father."

I could see what she meant.

"He's good for my self-confidence. Keeps telling me he can't believe he's so lucky as to have me."

That figured too; after what he'd been after in Glasgow, he must have found it hard to believe his good fortune.

I asked her if she intended to stay with him just so that she could play concertos.

"I don't know. We'll wait and see. He's talking to the orchestral people over there. There should be a contract soon......"

"A contract?"

She shrugged. I think she'd changed rather a lot in the last months. Or maybe she'd been like that all the time and I hadn't noticed, in the same way that I seem not to have noticed a lot of other things about her.

Later still

It was March. I rang Ellen. The answer-phone answered, so I stuttered a question about how the film was going. Had they got my recording laced up with the images, and would she like me to come to the next session to help, because I have a couple of days floating at the moment? I'm not good with messages, I always feel they're being taken down to be used in evidence against me. The ones that tell you your message can be re-recorded at any time don't help, because I dread I shall get locked into a search for the perfect message. Stammering is better.

Ellen rang back soon. "Are you alright? You sounded as if you were in some kind of trouble."

"It's just my answer-phone technique. It never fails: it's designed to get the person at the other end so anxious that they ring back."

"A quick update, before you tell me what you want to tell me. We're doing OK. We have Victoria on hand to match your fingers and the notes. She's good at it. She says she's enjoying the images too. As well she might."

She agreed to meet me for a drink after she'd finished work. A loose arrangement, because there are no office hours for our sort of work. A quiet bar, early enough.

"I hope you don't need any re-takes." They obviously didn't, since it was more than two months since we finished. No answer to that.

"OK, so I'm nervous. I'm not actually looking forward to it; I know how to deal with my playing when I'm making a recording, and I know what to listen out for. I'm a complete novice when it comes to cameras, so I've no idea. Even with you to help me the way you did."

"I understand that, but believe me…"

"I hope you have plenty of editing tricks to make up for my inexperience. I'm not an actor. Or one of Josy's farmers."

"We have everything we need, and you photograph well."

She even patted my hand. Like the mother who never did.

She said, "When it's all over, can we have a proper meal together? An evening; go to the theatre, a concert even, or would that be like work if we did that?"

"I'm grateful for the way you helped me with Beethoven, you know."

"I did nothing. But I enjoyed hearing you play just for me, as you might say. That was quite something. I don't have experience of classical music, but you give off something – I don't know exactly – star quality?"

"Star quality? What are you talking about?"

"Something that's powerful close up on the screen."

"That's kind. Someone to listen to me is good, and someone innocent like you is better."

"Was it alright in the recording studio? How was Victoria?"

There was a moment when I wondered if this was a sharp question, but it wasn't, not that I could see. Not the slightest flicker of subtext in her eyes.

"She's the real thing, as a record producer. She's young at it, but she has ears and an instinct. And sympathy in the right way, as if she knows what you want and helps you do it. A midwife, sort of."

"Sounds good."

"Right. That's why we have a producer. I've been lucky, though sometimes they can get in the way."

"I'd no idea you need the sort of build-up that actors need."

"Pianists are solitary souls. So it helps once in a while. It's not to do with your ego, it's to do with your psyche."

"Which means?"

"We don't want to be admired, we want to be appreciated, and a bit of truth helps."

Which is a wholly different area.

We had only half an hour, but I felt better. I couldn't analyse what I felt, or would have liked to feel, about Ellen. To be closer to her. I still had the memory of kissing her in the context of the filming, and I couldn't help wondering if there wasn't more for me there. Something more than duty, or paid lip service.

**

If Ellen wasn't interested in me when the cameras and the lights were switched off, and the editing complete, then I had to take stock.

Patti going off with another man on the back of nearly fifteen years with me wasn't proving at all easy to get over. I thought I was finding the way to be balanced about that, breaking a habit that I didn't know I had, realising how little our marriage had come to mean. So little that we didn't even talk about it.

Now I think that we could have talked about it. She might have said, "Now we're settled and in our thirties, do you think we might start a family?" Choosing to forget my ardent protestations against fatherhood. Instead she chose someone else to father her child.

She had fallen in love with him, hadn't she?

The Ellen thing was not working the way I hoped – but maybe it was as well. What did she want? What did she not want? A permanent relationship like the one I had just got out of? Which she didn't know the details of? Did I want to talk to her about it?

No more Patti, please…especially not if she was going to be called Ellen.

The photographer

The record company asked for some new pictures. Jane had been banging on at me, ever since I'd been made over, to have pics done to keep up to date. In our profession, many of us have expensive photographs taken years ago, making it look as if we have discovered the secret of eternal youth. Some people's photos would be recognised only by their mothers dead these last twenty-five years. The new me had to be promoted.

I sent an email to Sir Greg at the Conservatoire saying that everything seemed to be under control as far as Felicity was concerned. "She's a young woman who's grown up very fast, and knows what she's doing. She doesn't want to upset her mother…" Vague reassurance.

I didn't tell him that when she came for her last lesson she had a completely new air about her. I could only suppose that whatever Aaron brought her was more than just what he could do in bed. I suspected that what she wanted Aaron to do for her wasn't really about bed, anyway. I didn't see how it could be.

So I don't know why it surprised me that Felicity was actually playing the piano better than before. The answer was simple: she was about to start her career. She had been practising. I didn't know how much work Aaron was doing before his contract in the USA started, and I assumed he was having to nip back to Estonia to deal with the wife he'd left behind him. If indeed she knew he'd left her behind him. But what he was doing with Felicity was having a good effect on the way she played. Muscles can be trained, but not spirits – or at least not so obviously, and it's possible that sharing a flat with a man with a contract in the United States under his arm provided the spur. She was very likely to do an admirable Mendelssohn concerto for his concert in November. Being Lord Chislehurst's daughter was also likely to give a slant to the publicity with those democratic audiences – in fact it might have been useful if she'd been an Honourable, but he wasn't that sort of lord.

**

So, the photographic session.

It was a new experience – in the past I made do with a High Street photographer, who'd done wonders with my unphotogenic look, and managed not to get any reflection in the glasses I insisted on wearing. This time I had to have my hair styled in Bond Street in the morning, and I wasn't allowed to touch it afterwards. It was spiky, but not gelled. I liked it, I must say; the odd spike escaped forward across the hairline, which I'm thankful to say, is absolutely firm. One of the staff streaked in a few blond bits, and I looked like someone on the way to being photographed.

Not the High Street this time. A mews off Kensington High Street. Modest-looking from the outside, a garage underneath, which housed a Maserati, and a door made of heavy glass with a sort of montage of heads etched on it so that you couldn't see the staircase inside. It shouted success in an inaudible voice. Inside there was leather everywhere. And lights on stands, or hanging from the ceiling, once you got upstairs. God knows how they had got them up the stairs.

"There's a balcony, and we bring them in through the window. I know you didn't ask me how we got them up here, but most do. So I saved you the bother."

George, the man with the camera. He smelt of Bottega Veneta, or some such. Like oculists might like to wear so that when they come close to change the lenses in those metal frames they don't make you blink too hard.

He was small and wiry. His hair was tied back, with bits coloured red. He wore dark glasses, which surprised me.

"It's alright; I take them off when I need to."

Marty from the make-up firm was there.

"How've you been, kid? Seen the result yet? Just as well I was there, with all that sweat you give off. A bit of sweat turns the ladies on, they tell me, but not my little lady back at home." That must be the little lady who went out to deal with the Amazons.

"I'm glad you were free to do it," I said.

"I wanted to make sure my make-up was worthy of my name."

"It was a relief to have to sit still and let you do your work."

"That's why I'm here now. So sit still and let me look at you. This one is the serious one, isn't it? Classical CD stuff, so no green eye-shadow this time." I hoped this chatter wasn't going to go on too long, and indeed, it didn't. It was just his prelim to the serious business of making me look good but real. Smooth skin, making sure no eyebrow made a bid for freedom.

A very light powdering down? Don't want you shining too much in the wrong places, or it alters the shape of your face.

"Behave yourselves while I'm away. I'm off to get a sandwich, but my mobile is on."

Marty went.

George came and inspected me.

"He's done a good job. You look the way you looked when you came in. Natural. We'll start with the serious pics for your CD stuff. Head and shoulders.

"Was it your idea to be wearing the dinner jacket? I suppose it goes with the job."

"I've got some informal clothes as well, and my agent is keen to have some relaxed shots. You know, to look like someone who's being welcomed into listeners' houses."

His assistant lit me swiftly.

"The lighting will change from time to time. If you've been making a film, you'll be used to that. And we'll take the odd break where necessary.

"We do good coffee here. Would you like some now?"

"I'd like to get started if that's OK."

"This music you play on your CD. It's by..." George picked up his notes, "Beethoven. I looked at some of his portraits on my computer. Brilliant. Great."

"He sat for several artists – he was a famous man."

"And this other composer. Schubert. His pictures show a much more ordinary man, somehow."

"He was only thirty-one when he died. His really big success came afterwards."

"Tell me about the CD."

"It's serious music but with a broad range of feeling. If I go over some of the music in my head, we could see if the expressions on my face look good. I had to practise doing this for the film I've just made, and you can stop me if you think it's over the top. Shall we give it a go?"

"Suits me. I'll just take a couple of 'getting ready' shots."

Then he did the serious work.

"Let's take a break."

We had some coffee. George was right. It was good.

I asked George who he'd photographed. I'd heard of most of them.

"So it's glamour portraits you do?"

"Yes and no. Depends on who it is. I do nudes too. I've had some exhibitions in America and Rome."

"With the nudes."

"Yes. And the other images I do."

"You mean like landscape stuff?"

"No. Like documentary ones. Pictures of kids in the Balkans."

He showed me some. Quite different. Grim. Cartier-Bresson stuff. Reporter material. Impressive.

"How can you come back and do this sort of thing after you've done that?"

"Different hat. One pays for the other. And I do like looking at lovely things. I don't like the other things, but someone has to draw attention to them.

"Now, let's get back to you."

Change of clothes. Casual. Hair uncoiffed. Shirt. With buttons to undo.

"Right, we've got all the time it needs. I only do one sitting a day.

"So tell me about yourself a bit: what you do when you're not hunched over the piano keys…that sort of thing. Drive fast cars? What's your love life like? You know, the things that you do every day."

I told him a little, but I made the rest of it up. I thought imagination might photograph just as well as truth. He snapped me as I talked. It was quite easy.

"That's lovely. Now let's go for a different angle…"

He got me to sit in a metal and leather chair. Gave me a book to put on my knees.

"Right. Read the book a bit."

"I can't read this."

"I know. That's why it's in Japanese."

"I'd have brought one of my Japanese students, if I'd known."

"I'm glad I didn't warn you."

I started to read, going along the lines, instead of up and down.

"Now look up, as if you're going to explain what you've just read."

"I don't understand what I've just read."

"That's the whole point. If it was in English you would start judging it.

"Believe me, this works."

So I did. It made me look intellectual, engaged, George said.

"OK. Now some other things, like I do with the models. The professionals. Just look into the camera as if you're coming home. That is, if you like coming home.

"Right, now as if you care about it – the camera, I mean, and you're about to touch it as if you love it."

Nothing happened, obviously.

"No? Well, OK, think about chocolate cake? Smouldering for something you shouldn't eat. Good.

"Now can you look as if you are trying to seduce me? No? Oh go on, I'm not that bad-looking, and I could give you a good time, I promise you."

That made me laugh, and then the laughter wouldn't go out of my eyes, which was great, George said.

"Look like that, and I think you could sell any music you like to name, whoever wrote it."

Then the gaping shirt.

I was used to this undressing routine by now, and accepted it as part of the new look for classical musicians, part of my image.

"This time, imagine I'm a green screen, like the ones you get in the film studio. Put your own pictures up there and don't tell me what they are."

When it was over, George said, "I think we've got something here. Your face should come over direct, purposeful, sensitive, artistic, but like a bloke. I can just see you doing a concert with the West Side Story man – what's his name? – Leonard Bernstein."

"I hope not," I said, "he's dead."

"Oh well a bit of necrophilia never hurt anybody, in moderation, and with some people you mightn't notice the difference. Believe me."

And that was it.

He saw me down to the glass door.

"Shame I didn't get you sooner – I could have put your picture in there too."

"I would've been honoured to be turned into a bit of glass."

The CD

They sent me a proof of the CD. Somebody said that you should record your pieces over and over again; like painting the Forth Railway Bridge, you freshen it up, although the structure remains the same. Not like the Forth Bridge in the future, when it won't need a coat of paint for decades to come; so that's the end of a useful symbol.

The sonatas had the mixture of head and heart, repose and excitement that I was seeking. An arch from start to finish. I was pleased, and was rather proud of them. There were one or two things that I hadn't planned that surprised me, and seemed to give the performance an element of immediacy. Victoria had done an excellent job when she edited it.

James's microphones had caught Schubert's moments of tender humanity, as well as the sound of Beethoven in his arching Olympian mode. With the Bagatelles, an affectionate farewell.

Pythagoras had started making noises about Chopin, about having things in the cupboard ready for the bicentenary. Other pianists, more famous than me, would be issuing or re-issuing their complete take on Chopin. I wasn't keen to do one of those comprehensive things, putting down every last note a composer wrote, even the ones left on the back of an envelope or at the bottom of a drawer. Recording a couple of discs on the piano I had just used for Schubert and Beethoven, with the team that had made me sound so good – that interested me. And I thought we might mix Chopin with other composers: the French who inherited his music – Fauré, Debussy, Ravel.

**

The CD came into the shops on May Day, a Friday, to catch the weekend customer.

The reviews came at odd times according to how often the papers review classical music. The *Telegraph* thought my playing had style and quality and that touch of educated, unscheduled wilfulness without which no young artist could be taken seriously; that my Schubert discovered extra voices not usually heard in other performances. That pleased me greatly, because I think my acting lessons were a help. A serious by-product. The *Guardian* liked the freshness and immediacy of my view, and felt that my playing of Schubert had a magic mix of drama, delight and love. That was nice. The *Evening Standard*, having welcomed my last CD, the one with the film music, printed my latest photograph, said that purchasers would be in for a surprise if they bought it: these sonatas were serious pieces: Beethoven concentrates a lifetime of genius into twenty minutes and Schubert travels from the depths of despair to the highest joys of living. The *Metro* published one of my latest pictures with a caption about the CD.

France begins

From *jane@curzprod.com*

I'm so glad the notices are good. We haven't got the specialist magazines yet, and I don't know if the Beeb will put it on their list for a one-off review; they did one of their 'best buys' programmes on opus 109 not so long ago, so we missed that one. Luvjane

Email to Jane at *jane@curzprod.co.uk*

Just as well we missed the library one on Radio 3. I don't want it to be compared with all the great artists who've been recording it since they flattened wax cylinders out into discs. I'm a new boy, really, in spite of my age.

Could you check: I've not got my tickets for France yet. If you remember, we agreed I'd go by land, and not fly. Two concerts. Nohant before Lyon, and it's much easier staying on the ground because I like to look at the countryside. I know it's not always very interesting, because France is so big, but it soothes me, and the TGV eats up the boring bits very acceptably. It comes out of the fee anyway, and I'll save money by staying with my old French professor. He's sure to be happy to run through the Lyon programme with me, especially as I'm doing Ravel. No problem with someone I trust as much as I trust him. It'll give me the chance to speak the language too, which helps with the musical idiom.

Will

Eurostar first class is nice. London tunnel, stop at Stratford (East), under the Thames and into Kent, which flashes past and it's great not to be overtaken by the cars on the M20, the way you can be by cars on the A1 when you're on a train going north.

I spent some time looking at the notes of the Ravel, to top up. *Gaspard de la Nuit* was one of the pieces I practised so thoroughly when I first learnt it that it's stayed in my fingers like a second nature. Up to a point. It doesn't change, but you do. I played it in the concert in the Barn near Aberdeen last year, which was fine, but I spotted a couple of details I'd misremembered. Easily done, but better not done. Henri would notice.

Henri Samain. He didn't know it, but at one time he was my pseudo-father. I had money to study with him for a year and a half in Lyon, just after I finished at the Conservatoire. Specifically a scholarship to study with him in Paris. He lives in Lyon, and took me into his house there.

Patti came out to spend time there when she could; she needed to be in London for her lessons, and she was beginning to get orchestral work as a deputy, which meant she had to be available at the drop of a hat. Anyway, we'd decided that our careers would run in tandem. Looking back, I can see it didn't work; you can't have a tandem going in two directions at once. The visits got less frequent. None at all in the last six months. Not surprising; each time she'd come, I was more into French life, more a member of the Samain family. They made her very welcome – she was my wife, after all, and we were young and that touched them.

In Paris, I took a taxi from the Gare du Nord to the Gare d'Austerlitz, then a train to Châteauroux, a journey of about two and a half hours. I got out there, because en route for Lyon, Henri and Jane had got me a concert at Nohant.

**

Nohant is a favourite place of mine. I went there for the first time as a student living in Lyon. There was a bus tour, a round trip in a day (a long day) from Lyon, to see the house where Chopin wrote much of his music. I knew nothing about Nohant, except that one of the more romantic bits of music history had taken place there. This was where Chopin stayed for seven summers with George Sand. I could have told you how many Polonaises or Nocturnes or Ballades Chopin wrote, and something about how they differ from one another, but his private life was private to me. I'd never paid much attention to their romance, and if you'd told me about it before I looked into it, I'd have assumed that Chopin had an English sponsor called George, because that isn't the way the French spell Georges. George Sand was really Aurore Dudevant.

At the centre point of France is 'L'invisible province', Le Berry. It's an interlude going south before the land heaves itself up into the extinct volcanos of the Massif Central. The countryside has curiously English features, but on a larger scale. Hedges and trees, and streams and rivers in rolling land. Most of the traffic through France goes either to the west or east of it. Norman Foster's new bridge across the Tarn valley near Millau on the way south will make no difference, because people will still be on their way to places closer to the edge of France's hexagonal.

Le Berry is good if you want to find somewhere to have a quiet life. The cathedral in Bourges is one of the most beautiful I've ever seen. It has five naves. In the outer ones you can almost reach up and touch some of the stained glass windows.

Visitors to Nohant are dedicated people, for the most part, like the busload I joined at Lyon. It had been organised by some women's group or other, but it wasn't full, so it had been thrown open to any students who wanted to come. For nothing. Not many were able to leave what they had to do. I turned out to be the only one.

These serious ladies knew about Chopin, but it was George they were really after: George, the heroine of the independent Frenchwoman. A trailblazer. The woman next to me in the bus was very full of George, brushing Chopin aside as little more than an episode, although their relationship lasted for nine years before it came to its bitter end.

Once he'd left her, Sand did some brushing herself, sweeping him out of her life, and out of her house too, which was just what any practical woman would do. Why keep a room for a man who will never use it again, either because you've broken up with him, or for the perfectly honourable reason that he's dead, and you need the space? She filed him on the shelf with her other longer incidents, alongside Alfred de Musset and Alexandre Manceau, her last love, all three of whom she managed to love and to nurse, sometimes not making much distinction between the two, while running her property and making it pay, and writing about seventy-five novels and some two dozen plays. And enough letters to keep a cohort of postmen busy.

My informant in the bus told me about Sand's family. Her great grandfather, King of Poland twice, was supposed to have had at least a hundred and seventeen illegitimate children. Imagine having a hundred and sixteen great-great aunts and uncles. Her grandfather was a general, so I'd expected her château to be something much grander, with a drawbridge or the remains of one. In reality, it's more like a smart farmhouse where the occupant isn't afraid to get out there and swing a scythe with the land workers, and then get into the kitchen and make jam.

244

It made me happy just to stand on the floor where Chopin stood, to look out of the window he looked out of, and reconstruct his room in my mind's eye as it might have been, with a double door onto the staircase to minimise the draughts. I imagined him walking around, struggling to remember the notes his fingers found on the keyboard and get them down on paper.

**

This concert was an oddment. The normal concert season is in June and July: anniversaries of Sand's death and birth, in that order. But my teacher Henri Samain had good contacts in Paris, and knew an agent who was looking for a chance to promote one of her actors with something unusual. She had arranged this gig on location. Her client would play George Sand in an event put on for the locals, and for her pub. Publicité, that is. She needed a Chopin, and that was to be me. We would do a two-hander: I'd play and she'd read bits from George's memoirs, diaries, letters, novels, whatever they fancied.

I arrived in a taxi from Châteauroux, and settled down for a couple of nights in Nohant.

The curators let me wander about the house which Chopin had visited, and which brought him some health, if not a cure for his TB. In the salon where the company would have had their after-dinner entertainment, Chopin acted in charades, and improvised at the piano to amuse the guests. He had his own piano upstairs in his room. He took it back to Paris when they split up.

They had separate rooms, but they must have slept together sometimes. Did Chopin call her George? No, he called her Aurore, the dawn. It must have been like the dawn of a new life for him, when they first were together. Later more like a sunset. Their physical relationship went on to a back burner pretty soon, apparently. He was poorly much of the time.

She wrote too much, and I dare say she didn't have much time to be critical: she had deadlines to meet that meant money. I'd brought a couple of her novels – a short one about a country girl, *La petite Fadette*, set in the countryside around Nohant – and *Lucrezia Floriani,* which became controversial because Chopin's friends were convinced she'd used him as the model for its principal male character, young mal-adjusted, sickly, Prince Karol. It's one of the reasons some musicians can't bear the thought of G. Sand. She was the woman who 'destroyed' Chopin.

The concert in Nohant

The concert was in the Bergerie. Where they used to keep sheep. It was like a larger version of the Barn Hall near Aberdeen – what is was good for the animals has been made good for us. There was a useful audience space kitted out with scaffolding with plans for a more permanent look. It has its own character and hasn't been sophisticated into a concert hall such as you might find almost anywhere. On the whitewashed wall to the left of the stage, there's an enlargement of one of the pictures of George – the prettiest, an early one. The platform was shallow, front to back, but enough for two people and a piano.

I stayed in the hotel in the square across from the house. Settled in. Very comfortably.

I went over to the Bergerie, which they unlocked for me, and switched on a working light. I wanted to introduce myself to the piano. It was a Steinway, voiced rather in the French style, slightly brighter than I am accustomed to, but I had my study year in France to thank for being able to come to terms with it. I put the piano through its paces. And then I played two of Chopin's preludes, a lilting one in A flat, and its follower, short and more fiery.

At the end, there was applause. Single applause. One pair of hands. A voice. "Bravo." From the doorway at the side of the concert room. A woman came forward into the light. I got up and went down the steps that led from the stage.

"On m'a dit que vous êtes ici, and I've come to say Hello. Hélène Caplet."

"William Winton. Enchanté." It was an understatement.

It was the first time I had been close to a woman like her. There isn't a woman like her, which is why. She was beautiful, breathtakingly. Her voice too…This promised to be a very good date – professional engagement.

Our rehearsal was scheduled for the next morning.

"I shall leave you to your piano, and go and look at my script. À demain."

She left. I wouldn't have minded a professional drink and a meal together, but she was more professional than I was, with her eye on the performance.

I dedicated the Nocturne in C sharp minor that I played next to her instant memory. It has the most beautiful opening bars, the melody creeping up from minor to major in its first two notes; the passion comes later. A love affair in essence.

I had ordered a meal in my room, and opened the packet containing the script, which Hélène had left at the desk for me. It gave me a very clear breakdown of how the evening would go, what each of us was doing, when.

The next morning we met to rehearse. There was much to do. We had to gel as a public event. Hélène was reading some of what George Sand wrote in the house just over there; I was playing some of the music "Chip-Chip" wrote there; some Bach too, because he loved Bach's music. The mixture was predictably successful. You could hardly go wrong.

There was a very discreet photographer called Christophe who took unobtrusive pictures after the local technicians had set the lighting up. He would do the same at the odd moment during the actual show, and afterwards. A photo opportunity for Hélène, and for me too.

We were going to remain on the stage the whole time to give it continuity, and not make it look like two separate performances which happened to be taking place concurrently. With an interval, naturally.

The lighting was simple, but theatrical; they have had other actors performing in this venue. We did a proper run-through. Hélène read all the words, and I played all my notes in the rehearsal.

"I have listened to them all, you know," she said, "but it's not the same when you are actually close to the sound source. I want to catch the mood."

We spent time arranging how each would behave when the other was performing, because there was no complicated lighting plot; we were in view all the time and we acted as our own director.

"Perhaps you would look at me and watch me when I'm reading."

"I don't think I will have any trouble doing that." I felt schoolboyish. She laughed. "You won't be seeing me full face, you know, so don't hope for too much. It will suggest that we live here – together. Would you mind if when you play your first piece I stand with my hand on your shoulder? In a way like the picture Delacroix nearly finished of the two of them. The two of us. She's actually sitting behind him, but it's close enough."

"Let's try. The first piece is some Bach."

Her touch was light, but she lightened it even more to make sure it didn't inhibit my movements. In this F sharp major Prelude and Fugue by Bach, there isn't a lot of movement, and it's quite short.

At the end of it, she crossed over in front of the piano to where her desk was, not like Hélène, but as George.

We decided I would sit listening, not trying to 'react'. The mechanics of the performance were easy enough; I knew how long each narration would take, and I had a short prompt sheet to give me my cue.

247

"Would you like to speak a few words? You know, Chopin was good at imitating an English Milord. Your French is good, but you could make it more English."

Imitating Chopin imitating an Englishman abroad in Europe for laughs was beyond my reach. We didn't have much time anyway, and I needed to spend it with the piano, to make it play his notes under my fingers.

I couldn't help thinking that something might develop after the concert.

After Hélène left the Bergerie, I stayed on to play, and talk to the piano tuner, Viviane, who arrived from Paris. She enjoyed the chance to get out of the city, especially as her daughter lived in La Châtre, not far away from Nohant.

I left her to her work and went out into the square. I slipped into the church. George and her family are buried in the church grounds – well, nearly buried there, because the cemetery has railings to keep them out. I've no idea what she believed in, but she didn't fit into any of the church slots, I'm sure. All the same the church is so near that she can't have ignored it.

Palpably silent, dark, a country church. A good place for someone about to do a concert. As my eyes adjusted to the light I saw that Hélène must have thought so too. She was there, sitting, not kneeling. She probably wanted something from the stones, from the history of the congregations, just as I did. I sat peacefully somewhere else.

When she got up to leave, she came to sit next to me. She took my hand. A gesture of fellow feeling – two artists in a special situation.

"I don't think this is the first time you've been here. You seem to be at home."

"In this church?"

"No…in Nohant."

"It's a holy place for me. I can breathe the breath of genius."

She squeezed my hand. "We can breathe it together…"

She looked at me a moment or two. She leant towards me and kissed my cheek before she slipped away. Nohant is a memorial to a great love story, or at least a great relationship. This woman had it in her to bring George-Aurore to life. I am much more solidly human than Frédéric but I work with my fingers to bring his soul back for a while. A happy reincarnation for one evening.

The show itself was a live reflection of the two people who had lived here. Words, music, place, all together at the same time.

"Nous ne nous sommes pas trompés l'un l'autre…We were not wrong, we had no doubts at all, we gave ourselves up to the wind as it went past and swept us away, the two of us, into another region. Yet we knew that we would have to come down to earth after heaven had embraced us and taken us up to the greatest heights. Poor birds, we have wings, but our nest is on the earth, and when the angels' song calls us upward, the cries of our family call us back."

The opening words Hélène read were from a letter written by George Sand at the beginning of their relationship in 1838 to a close friend of Chopin, uncannily predicting what would happen in the next years. Those family cries would play a major part in the end of their affair.

My music kept on the short side: the longest was his third Ballade, which takes about seven minutes. In the Nocturnes, there is so much that accesses the darker side of night among more traditional reactions to its atmosphere. That was where I found most to say. To end was his blockbuster polonaise in A flat.

I learnt more about George Sand. And something more immediate about Hélène. She was much too beautiful to play the character to the life. I've never been close to someone so beautiful, and it's difficult to say what it does for you, just to look. Her voice had a range of expression that sounded as if it was always telling the truth as it is at this moment. I believe you can fall in love with people you work with; that's what happened in my first marriage. What you share is something of yourselves which you didn't know was there, and sadly might not be there at all, because it's in your work. I could fall in love here and now, I thought. Romantically in love. Nothing to do with the concert. I'm not easily distracted from my playing, but I think there was some element of distraction in my performance this evening. Did Chopin want George's approval when he played to her? She had musical skills herself, although she would never play the piano when he was around.

After it was over, there were well-wishers outside. We were photographed by Christophe, for the archives, and by some of the fans, for their own purposes. We held hands, as if taking applause. Close – or as close as you can be when you're being photographed by the public. It felt good, and I hoped that what had started in the church might yet be the special baptism I was hoping for. We split up to deal with those kind people who wanted to tell us how much they had enjoyed it. I had a couple of local fans who had heard me when I was in France before. One of them even had my black and white movies CD to be signed.

Hélène was surrounded too; she waved and kissed her hand to me. I was feeling tremendously happy.

Until I saw the Alfa-Romeo waiting, and the driver sitting in it. A young man, blond, expensive-looking, like his car. He didn't look up much when she got in and that made it even more like a long-term affair. Affair was what I was afraid it was. It seemed only too likely. There could be no shortage of suitors.

I didn't try to conceal my disappointment. There was no one to conceal it from. The kiss Héléne blew to me as she left was no consolation for the kiss on my cheek earlier. Obviously. It had raised hopes which were now being scotched by the Romeo in the Alfa.

After Nohant

Maybe I should invest in one myself. An Alfa Romeo. I was thinking along those lines when two hands gripped my arms from behind, and forcefully turned me about. There was only one person who would do that to me, and when I turned, there he was – Henri Samain, my teacher, my pseudo-father.

"Mon Dieu! I didn't see you…"

"That doesn't surprise me. You have eyes only for your co-star."

It was true enough.

We embraced.

"You came over here specially from Lyon for the concert?"

"Surely. To do some research on Hélène."

"You came all this way to see a TV star?"

"Only to see if she was as beautiful as the camera says. She is exceptionally lovely. As you have noticed. Perhaps."

He laughed.

"It was a bonus; I came to hear you, because I was part of the team that set this up. And to see if you are playing well enough for the concert you are giving for us. And to take you back home with me. Now."

I looked around for Mariette, Henri's wife, who was usually his transport. "It's a long way from here to Lyon, and you don't drive."

"Mariette's not here. Listen, I know you don't sleep immediately after a concert, and I'm glad your co-star has a boy-friend – even if you aren't – or I might have had to stay in the hotel myself, waiting for you until tomorrow. Discreetly."

He had hired a car and a chauffeur, and by and large it was better this way. The hotel was understanding about my sudden departure. Perhaps it happened all the time to the visiting artists, and I said my Au revoirs to the Nohant staff. The car was comfortable, and Mariette had provided food and drink for the journey.

France is criss-crossed by good roads, and once we hit the open road beyond La Châtre and even more when we were on the autoroute south of Bourges, we moved. According to Michelin information the journey should take just over three and a half hours, Henri told me. Maybe my watch stopped, but this expert driver made it in much less than that. The car was big and comfortable by any standards, and Henri was right, I was wide awake most of the way, and there was enough to talk about: the concert, with Sand's words carefully implanted.

I told him about my divorce.

"Oh! I liked Patti, although I didn't get to know her very well. She didn't come often, and not at all towards the end of your time with me."

"These things happen, you know."

"Quel dommage," he said.

"You disapprove?"

"No, not at all. Divorce is common enough in this country; we are not an officially religious community, you know, not since the Revolution. We have a new divorcée in our family – and one separated from her husband. Mariette's nieces. A good Catholic family is not without such things these days."

"My divorce was my fault, you know."

"No. I don't believe that. Unless you had a mistress and your wife found out."

I shrugged. As audibly as I could.

"I thought not. And I don't think it could have been your fault. It needs two to marry, and two to divorce. Did she have a lover?"

"A husband now, I believe. To replace the husband I wasn't."

"You are too modest."

"No it's true. I was speeding towards middle age and taking her with me. I was thirty-four and I looked forty-four or more, and worse, I was behaving like fifty-four. No, divorce has been good for me. You will have noticed I look different."

"Yes, I noticed there was something different about you, but I couldn't decide what it was."

How like him: here I was, kilos lighter, spectacle-less, hair short and spiky, clothes more fitting in both senses of the word, and able, however momentarily, to attract the attention of the most beautiful woman I've ever seen. And he'd noticed almost nothing.

"And you – have you a companion too, une copine?"

"No. Je suis seul, quite alone. But let's not talk of that. I'm so pleased to see you."

This man had changed my life as a pianist. I can get my head round the notes of a score fast, with my fingers close behind. My memory is quick and reliable. I'm lucky, though I work hard to keep everything in place. Even now, any critic running out of words to write me up can always fill a line of print about my facility. When I first came to Henri, I had discovered very little more than that.

"It's a gift from God. But you must develop it to make music. You know exactly how to construct the house according to the instructions left by Ravel, or by Chopin même; all the details are correct, every nail and screw fits, the house is habitable – but you have to move in, inhabit it yourself, bring its personality to life, don't you think?"

When we arrived in Lyon, Mariette saw the difference in me at once.

The first thing she said: "You are not the same man…"

"Do you mind that?" I asked.

"Is it really you, Guy?" Mariette always called me Guy, the French short form of William and I like it.

"You're transformed. Like the Beast in Cocteau's film of the fairy story. Perhaps you were never as ugly as the beast, but I always thought there was a prince waiting to get out."

I was back in the only real home I have known since my grandmother died. And that includes my own.

In my old room, too.

My bathroom was shared this time, with female presence clearly visible in it and odorously sensible.

I slept until lunchtime, by general agreement.

There was time for me to play my music to Henri. I get a frisson of nervousness every time I play to him, as if part of me doesn't want to forget my first lessons with him. We have a rule not to make huge criticisms when a concert is imminent – as in the tempo of a whole piece, or such. The opinion afterwards is more useful. At this stage, we only do the sort of thing you could do at an orchestral rehearsal on the same day as the concert, or for a retake in a recording studio.

Henri had little to say, except to praise. He thought my Ravel had taken on some more humanity, some more humour, things which the composer admired, while keeping well this side of sentimentality. I went to the concert confident.

Henri had got me a full house. He'd drummed up plenty of people – it wasn't the first I'd given there, so maybe some came without being drummed up. They were warm and welcoming. The idea that the French are cold and unfriendly is rubbish. It helps if you speak some French, more still if you like their music, and their books and their cinema. Art, too. I feel European when I'm in Europe. I owe my living to Europe, to the composers of Europe. For me, nationality is only part of being a human being. When I play music, I get the mind-set of a common heritage. Humanity itself.

The concert hall in the conservatoire is virtually black, and the audience is well tiered. It's a conference place as well, and this part of the building is named after the composer Varèse – very modern, multi-purpose, very suitable. I liked the audience, and they liked me. I suppose it's a matter of degree. I always play well. You have to – you can't afford to be off-form like some tennis stars, lose a match and make a comeback next time.

There was another full house back at Henri's. It's French in the old-fashioned style, with wood, and the smell of French polish. Flowers with scent. Splendidly modernised plumbing that had caught up with the twenty-first century. It was wonderful to spend some time with Mariette again. She wanted me to stay longer, and I decided to fit in another day, and since I was travelling first class, there was no problem about the ticket. Why not stay, after all? There was no one to go home to. Mariette didn't mention Patti, so I guessed Henri must have told her. Perhaps I should have told them sooner, but since I'm not sure what the rules are in the etiquette of divorce I'd never got round to sending out cards.

We had a really late meal, with well-wishers, and some family. My French 'siblings' were mostly away. A family of six children: a good Catholic family, though not as formidable as the good Protestant family J. S. Bach had. I'd not been there for what? How many years? And nothing had changed. Change is less likely if you're outside Paris, which is where you go if you want the action – if you want promotion, for that matter, because the 'real' jobs are there. Or people think they are. None of the five who had left home had gone into the music profession; it wouldn't surprise me if Henri had seen to that. Much more secure jobs. And from what they said, jobs in banks were still more secure than they are in England. Not loved, I dare say, but profitable if you're in front of the right computer screen.

Michèle, the only daughter left, was engaged to be married, and her fiancé worked for the council. A witty young man, who wrote a column in the local newspaper from time to time and reviewed concerts, even. I was nice to him, though he said there was no need. It's hard meeting your critics socially, hard for them as well as for you. Distance is the best way to keep your head cool, both of you.

The house is big, and there were others staying. Mariette's sister and her husband, and their grown-up twin daughters. I knew the parents, but not the women, because they were in Paris when I did my time here. These were the divorcée and the séparée, making their lives all over again, and coming back to Lyon for a break. Attractive women, so their husbands must have been looking for something other than looks. Or looking for them somewhere else.

They were clever, cynical, sophisticated, Parisian. They were going to be around on the next morning, so they offered to take me to see the old town and the amphitheatre.

They were particularly interested in my divorce.

"Marriages are made in heaven, and maybe they're better left to the angels," said Nadia. "And my husband wasn't one of those."

"But he was handsome, which must have been some consolation," said Cécile.

"Yes, when you saw him. Not so much when you couldn't." They both laughed at that, so I didn't ask more.

"Are you still friends?" I asked, thinking of myself.

"Not after he saw the account from the lawyers. But he paid up, and we both drew a line under it."

Cécile smiled. "I think Nadia secretly wants him back. He's part of her life, you know."

"Yes, true. But not on his terms. The memories are sweet if you go back far enough. But the more recent ones make it hard to go back that far. It's only now that I think it would be nice to be with someone else."

"But you're a man, so perhaps you know what it's like. You have your life to lead, your career to make, and that makes it easy to walk away from the past and from your wife, perhaps?"

"I had no choice. My wife – my ex-wife – has a career of her own. She plays the violin in an opera house."

"And that is enough for her? She tunes her violin, draws a bow over it in time with everyone else, puts it in its case, and feels all the better for it?"

"I think she likes doing that."

"More than being married to you?"

"I don't think that being married to me mattered any more."

Nadia touched my knee. "You look nice, like my husband, but much more sympathique." Nice French word, that. The others were talking elsewhere, and no one was listening to us. I had these two attractive women sitting one on each side of me, and maybe it wasn't only the wine that was affecting my post-concert mood. The French wear perfume differently, and their faces are so different, especially when they deliberately shape words with their mouths.

"Of course, my husband is still my husband," Cécile said. "But at a distance. He goes his way, usually in the Middle East, where he sells engineering things. Best not to ask who to. We have grown apart, though in his case, I don't think much growth was involved."

"It's difficult to believe that you have husbands who would leave you."

"It's difficult to believe that you had a wife who left you."

"It's not how I see myself."

"But you are alone, and need feminine company. It's not natural."

My God, that was true. But faced with two women with defaulting husbands, I hadn't the courage to admit it. It might be a good idea not to get too involved with them – first of all because they were Henri's nieces and maybe because the husbands had good reason to be absent. One failed marriage is an accident in any family, two begins to look like it's hereditary.

"Have you any children?"

"Non," said Cécile.

Nadia said, "Yes, I have a son of fourteen."

"Is he here?"

"No. He's in Paris with his father and his new mother."

"One of many new mothers," said Cécile.

"Maybe. I don't ask," Nadia went on. "my son Philippe occasionally mentions one, but he leads his own life." She paused. Then went on.

"I think he could be gay."

"Your ex-husband?"

"No, my son."

There was a pause in which both sisters lit new cigarettes, and I tried to look as if I didn't mind the smoke that gets in my eyes; and fortunately that made it unnecessary to say anything much to follow that remark.

"How do you feel about that?"

"Nothing. It might even be better for him, make him more independent. I don't know. I don't have an attitude. What d'you think, Cécile?"

"Perhaps Jean-Marie is teaching him to be gay. By having all those women you can't establish anything with except a physical relationship."

"I don't want you to think that Jean-Marie had so many lovers while we were in the serious marriage business. He had me, you know, and I am more than enough for any normal man." It seemed very likely.

"All the same…"

Time for me to say something.

"You don't look old enough to have a fourteen-year-old son."

"I'm so glad. It costs me something. Or rather it costs Jean-Marie something to keep me the way I was when he first decided to marry me."

"And you, perhaps you have children." This was Cécile, turning to me.

"No. I have been too busy."

They gurgled. "Il ne faut que dix minutes to become a father, you know. Ten minutes."

"Or even less, if you lack the finesse."

I blushed. I really did.

"So you are alone, of necessity a bachelor. Without wife; without what you call a relationship?"

It was true.

"I can't believe that. A talented man like you, who has the whole world in his hands when he plays the piano, who can be a lion or a lamb, soft and feminine, or firm and masculine. All done with the fingers."

"And is so good-looking. Our uncle and aunt didn't tell us they had a young man like you staying with them, did they, Cécile? No girl-friend? Not even for the moment?"

"Well, it takes a little while to get over a long relationship, a marriage. I had got used to my wife. I believed in her. She filled just the right corner of my life. It's quite difficult, you know."

"Perhaps you need a little help, do you think?"

"Well…well…it's not easy…"

"Oh, I don't know. I think one might come to an arrangement."

I had no idea what Cécile meant, or whether she was just making conversation.

**

My bedroom was next to the sisters', with the one shared bathroom between, fitted out with the usual locks. Well, there's a formula for that, so it wasn't a problem. There was a certain amount of calling from room to room through open doors to make sure the bathroom was free. It was late, and we all wished each other a good night.

I went to bed, pretty tired, as you can imagine, but happy, on a sort of low energy high. A good French bed, wide, roomy, and I stretched out with pleasure. Success in the music, and the family affection I felt all round me, the love I'd not felt for Goodness knows how long. It all fed into the sense of well-being and happiness. I'd showered after the concert, before we started socialising here, and now I was smiling to myself in the darkness, my body relaxing. The door was closed but not à double tour. Drifting off, phrases from the music I'd been playing haunted my mind. And then Ravel's version of the conversation between Beauty and the Beast came into my head, because Mariette had said I was la bête transformée. It reminded me of Cocteau's film, *La belle et la Bête*, and the way that Beauty is brought to the Beast's palace and mysterious hands appear from the walls bearing candelabras.

It was really dark, and there were the usual creaks a house allows itself as it goes to sleep, and shrinks back to its preferred shape. Some of these creaks had nothing to do with shrinkage, because just as I was touching the edges of sleep, I began a half-dream about the moment when Belle arrives at the Beast's castle, where she is welcomed by gentle hands holding candelabras from the walls.

Gentle hands, indeed, with no such intention, were bidding me welcome. I didn't move, not sure what to do. Except to enjoy, and play the part I might be expected to play. It was enough to feel the sensation of my skin being touched, the muscles around my neck being persuaded into a neutral gear in which almost anything could happen. These hands knew the places where a pianist aches after a concert. Where any man might ache when he gets into bed. On his own.

It was amazingly silent and purposeful. If I say I lay there passively, I think I might need to qualify that. Physical contact with the soft warm skin. No words, no voice, just gentle breathing, whispering without words. Orpheus with one Bacchante, who hadn't come to tempt and punish, or to destroy in the end, but to…do what we did. One glorious improvisation, followed by disengagement, with nothing said, only the gratitude of a body elated and relaxed. Within an intensely short time, I was alone again. All in the dark, no name to put to a brief encounter.

**

When we all met next morning, we behaved amicably. I knew perfectly well which was Nadia, and which Cécile, but not which of them was the one with whom I had had a relationship.

"If you don't mind, we'll defer that visit we'd talked about to the amphitheatre and old Lyon until the next time. That is till the next time you visit Lyon." That was Nadia.

Cécile smiled too. "There are memories which one does well not to weaken with others which are less serious."

"Surely, and perhaps keep to oneself. For the winter nights when one is alone, perhaps."

When they left after lunch, they both embraced me warmly, kissed me on both cheeks, and pressed my hand. And laughed.

Just as well they went back to Paris.

How far was I expected to go in my search for a new life?

I didn't feel unmanly because I had no initiative in what happened. I was like the young Donny Jonny…one who benefitted without having to strive for it. As Byron knew.

Return to London

My upcoming film had been on the list of things I wanted to talk over with Henri, so that he wouldn't be surprised, but it slipped my mind. I don't think he would have approved anyway. He was still too much of an idealist to think there might be valid new ways of engaging with the public. Instead, we talked about the bicentenaries coming up. I must go back soon and play to him. A pianist needs a sounding board, apart from the one built into the piano. Even the greatest

258

have to get out from under themselves. Perhaps it might be a good idea to choose a time when I know his nieces won't be there…There are limits, if you want to work.

**

There was an email waiting for me when I got back to London.

From *Hélène@villeprod.com*

Chéri, A short note to say how much I enjoyed that evening at Nohant. Chopin and Sand – they had a rapport which I believe we created all over again. You made me listen to music as I have never done before. I hope that when you heard me reading the words of George Sand, I conveyed the feelings they felt in a similar way.

If there is a chance of another collaboration in the future…it was such a special event. J'attends ta réponse…

Hélène

I copied that and saved it into Word, to read again at leisure. I wanted to enjoy the memory and the rapport she spoke of.

Perhaps I should go and live in France? It seemed the land of opportunity.

I answered at once.

From *will@williamwinton.co.uk*

Dear Hélène

I was so happy to share the evening with you. I loved the sound of your voice, the nuances you brought to your text, and although I couldn't see your face when you were reading, your whole bearing was one of sympathetic identification with the ideas and emotions of the words.

I would love to share another such event. I wonder if one could create something from Sand's novel Lucrezia Floriani, which many people have thought presents a fictionalised version of her relationship with Chopin. Spread out over seven days, one for each year that Chopin was in Nohant, it could be an attraction as well as an opportunity for us to work together.

If you agree, we will need to check the dates that fit at Nohant, because there will be celebrations for Chopin's bicentenary!

Tous mes vœux

All my best

Will/Guy

She answered within the hour.

From *Hélène@villeprod.com*

A marvellous idea! I will ask a director friend of mine if he will think about it. It's not a long novel, and very much about the theatre as well as an actress's life. I'll alert my agent to find out how things are at Nohant.

Tous mes vœux de bonheur.

Hélène

**

The Film

In the afternoon of the next day, the film arrived. It had a name. 'Fire and Water'. After all. Well, there was some of both in it, so it was as good a name as anything else. A hint of the Magic Flute and Masonic ritual about it to give it depth, dignitas, maybe. It came in a package, special delivery, to my home. To be signed for. They didn't want it wandering around untracked.

I was enjoined to view it on my own. Completely on my own. It also came with a warning which made me wary.

"We recommend that you watch it with a completely open mind."

I had no idea of how I would react, watching myself playing the piano, moving around, alive, acting in front of cameras intent on making a commercial product.

I drew the curtains and made a cup of tea.

I watched it. Trying to do that in the way I listen to my CDs, from outside. Regarding it as an object. I'll try and describe what I saw, *a prima vista*. It's over-the-top, I know, like scraps of the essays I used to write on Sundays in my schooldays.

OK.

This film is a series of piano pieces, all fleshed out on screen to make them into a visual experience as well as an aural one. Fine, so far. In principle.

It starts in silence and darkness. Then two titles follow each another: 'Sight and Sound' and 'Fire and Water', then my name is etched slowly. As the faint sounds of a piano begin, a third title, 'Yellow Leaf', brings in a distant montage of tiny excerpts from the seven pieces of music, overlapping, sometimes making sense, sometimes not, like an ill-defined universe in chaos. Black and white piano keys fade up, at changing angles, overlaying one another, as if they were an orchestra tuning up visually. Patterns like veins fill the whole screen, and turn into those of a yellow leaf. Through them a man appears, his head bent, as if seeking fallen leaves on the ground…

He looks up slowly as the title '*Autumn-Automne*' brings with it a gentle voice murmuring '*Les sanglots longs des violons de l'automne blessent mon cœur…*'

The broad tune of Chaminade's music begins. A love song from the past, maybe, with moments of serious passion, which clearly were not built to survive. The leaf in the background is dissolving into more leaves, floating leaves, the colours changing from yellow to shades of burnt sienna, to fading green: a keyboard lies behind them; hands playing the notes on the keyboard chase the leaves away to show a man walking in an autumnal wood, his movements uncertain, telling of an affair which was all-consuming while it lasted. A storm breaks out; as passion turns in the direction of anger and despair the music grows, the leaves swirl, and the colours change, now flashing with brighter autumnal lights, yellow, red, even a hint of silver as if frost were threatening. The man among the swirling patterns kicks the leaves into the air and punches them as they flurry past, as if they had brought the deception that his love has cost him. Now there are two men, and then three, yet always the same man, in perspectives that shift until they coalesce into a screen filled with leaves of all colours. The last ones float down with Chaminade's calmer thoughts of autumn, the copper strings of the piano overlay them, yielding in their turn to the pianist watching the keys, then slowly looking up, thoughtful, shining with distress at the end of the affair. Behind him the picture fades into a single leaf and then into darkness and silence; he almost whispers *qui m'emporte de ça, de là, pareil à la feuille morte.*

Silence, a luminous screen with no image.

The title of the 'Ritual Fire Dance' flashes up in brilliant red; hands appear on the keyboard, transparent, in multi-images, on the darkened screen. The music begins with trills matched by small, busy flames, growing in size, leaping and falling back. A figure emerges, his back to the camera, his embroidered waistcoat brightened by the reflected fires, one arm behind his back, the other persuading the flames to rise, as the theme of the ritual dance plays around. He spreads out his arms, clenching his fists. The fire dies down. Crosscut to the keyboard for strong but quiet chords, hands moving up and away from the keys, as if they contain the secrets of how to banish bad spirits. The magician charged with this task is all the while there, but now he looks us in the face. It's as if the fire is our fire, and we must play our part. Strong arm movements, alternating with gentle rhythmic stepping, zapateado-like. Smoke envelops him as the fingers at the keyboard cast their own spells, to bring him slowly back, his face and arms sweating with the heat, his body moving slowly, his face twisting with a shadow of a smile, exercising his power over the spirits. His music summons up angular shafts of smoke and fire. Primitive fire. Fire for exorcism – hell's flames challenging the sun, joining up with powerful sound, dramatic, compelling, sudden, now loud, now quiet. The camera is as restless as the rising smoke, pulling back to show the sorcerer – motionless, eyes dark, hair glinting, expression sombre, the music pressing onwards like the wind. Columns of fiery light define his features, the Spanish dancer's clothes outlining him, his waistcoat undone. Lightning flashes of light grow brighter; there are yellow flames among the red. He does not move, he stands triumphant.

Smouldering cinders obliterate the image, sending up plumes of smoke. The whole thing erupts into an eye-shattering red, as the final chords blaze, and the piece is over, fading into nothing but silence.

Silence, yes, but there's no pause visually. The darkness mutates gradually from a deep red through to deep purple, slowly lightening into the colour of a field of heather. A soft voice murmurs as the title comes up on the screen: *La fille aux cheveux de lin. The girl with flaxen hair.*

Leconte de Lisle's verse is there, printed on linen paper in an ancient font; the voice continues, very light…

Ta bouche a des couleurs divines,
Ma chère, et tente le baiser!
Sur l'herbe en fleur veux-tu causer,
Fille aux cils longs, aux boucles fines?

Music takes over from the words while the screen keeps its linen look. Beyond it is a field of flax; its pale blue flowers dip and rise as a gentle breeze moves over it, like a mirror for the music's warm chords and solo lines. Hands lightly touch the key-board, replacing the image, and with great gentleness seek out the sounds of Debussy's 'Flaxen-haired girl'. The fingers stroke the keys, as they might well seek to touch her hair, her face. Black keys fade and cross-fade at right angles, delicately driving each other away. The dampers on the piano's strings rise and fall, making patterns to catch the light. Through it all there is the player, his eyes shining in soft-focus with expressions of tenderness for the girl and her music, the girl always beyond reach, the girl with her Scottish voice, hinted at as a woman's shadow slowly and gently crosses the face of the dreamer, and then blots out everything. It's been an interlude, cool and soothing.

From green to dark blue, nearly to black, bringing in the title *Feux follets* – *'Will o' the Wisp'*. A spot of light appears in the top right hand corner, crosses the screen diagonally and then over to the right, dragging into view a piano keyboard and hands playing a laughing swirl of music. The fingers run so fast and so close across the keys that they appear little more than a blur of movement, out of which come tiny specks of light, glinting and prancing, as Liszt's 'Will-o'the-Wisp' scampers through the night. The spot of light goes on dictating the music for a few moments, until in the changing shadows it gives half-glimpses of deceptive fire, unreliable, shimmering, dancing, leaping, teasing, calling for attention, then avoiding it. Images of the piano's action appear fleetingly, eclipsed by a figure who could be a Piper, his face trying to understand and keep up, amused, bemused, as he watches the lights sweeping up and down. Do these lights suggest the face of a puckered witch on a Sabbath outing, looking for somewhere to warm her hands and chafing feet by the blue-marsh-hovering flames? The shadow of the Pied Piper leads us, as he did the children of Hamelin, past more uncertain, tremulous lights, until they persuade the pianist's hands over the black and white of the keys into a fading pageant of night and silence.

Grey clouds move lazily; 'The Raindrop Prelude' begins and the keyboard comes into vague, unfocussed view. The insistent notes that run through the music are tranquil, like the gentle rain from heaven; drops fall on pools, on leaves, which shiver and shudder beneath their weight. A man leans his head against a doorway; he reaches out his hands to catch some of the water. He walks into the open, among the dancing raindrops; he seeks to put them on like some soft bejewelled coat. The camera swings slowly round, the picture widens out into the rainy shadows of the countryside; in the distance, he moves up the hill towards the trees, slowly, picking his way with care. The repeated notes of the music seem to encourage him onwards through the cold bleak air to the brink of despair, then bring him downwards as his first thoughts return, more lyrical, like a hymn to rain and to man. He walks towards the house, as if he were taken over by nature and the thoughts that come to him through the music. Passing grey clouds return to engulf the scene.

The clouds slowly clear.

Liszt's *Liebestraum* is a dream; hands touch the piano's keys gently. A man lies stretched out on a bed. He stares at the ceiling; he drifts drowsily into sleep. The images in his waking dream begin to suggest themselves; veils, barely visible, float, almost hinting at the erotic with their sensuous, lazy movement. Mingling with them is the piano, lights glimmering on the wood and the strings. In the moonlight, a lover looks out through the window, seeking the girl he wants there in the shadows. The man on the bed slumbers on; he turns about in some anguish; his thoughts are unhappy. The shadow of a woman is in the frame. He looks at her with an expression of tenderness and love, reaches out for her; as he leans forward to kiss her, his face disappears into the darkness, leaving only the figure lying on the bed. The strain begins to show in his body, as if his dream has been an act of will…the crossfade to the piano takes its time, as the pianist watches his hands playing the last chords, and slowly looks up, tears in his eyes. Silence for what seems a long time with a blank screen.

A stream bubbles over pebbles, silent, but lively, and Bach's name comes forward, 'Prelude'. Cut to the piano, fingers scurrying about the keys.

Running water in a brook sparkles and jumps for joy; fingers skip over the keys, hammers make patterns on the strings as the water changes to the tumbling waters of the Falls of Feuch in Scotland, where the salmon leap in the many smaller, temporary, streams that the burn creates over rocks to reach the river Dee lying in wait in the valley. After a while we become aware that we are looking through a glass screen covered with droplets of water. The outline of a man appears, delighting in the water that showers over him, twisting and turning happily at this close contact with its elemental power in the sophistication of his own personal place. The camera moves round slowly and pulls away to show him moving for joy in the pleasure of nature, his own and that of the world around him. The movement freezes with the last chord and disappears in a shower of water.

This first version of the final piece ends.

An alternative one appears. It focusses on the piano's keys, the pianist's hands and his smiling, happy face, washed away by splashing water.

More images supervene: a running stream pouring over the Falls of Feuch, a man in white watching the salmon leap among the rocks, reaching out at times as if to catch them or help those that do not seem ready to make it to the higher reaches. We see his hands splashing water, cross cutting with them playing the piano.

Then a final wave of water washes out the whole screen.

After a few moments, the 'Songs Without Words' by Fauré begin, charming, delightful, like a fond farewell. The credits come in at once. 'Water and Fire'. 'Fire and Water'. With an album of portraits of me, changing for each item, serious, thoughtful, smiling, full-face, profile. No piano in view.

This slightly overblown description of the film tries to explain what I saw. The pictures to be seen aren't part of me, I am part of them. The person in the images could be anyone brilliantly photographed, but it was me, as I'd never seen myself. The Ritual Fire Dance is brilliant: it doesn't ask much of me, and I have my quickly absenting father to thank for my physique, which the visits of the personal trainer Frances Macbeth have sharpened up. She did a good job, I could see that. I looked like someone I'd be quite happy to look like. The time I spent making a new self had been well spent, for the sake of…well, for me, as it turned out. And now for anyone who watches the film.

My murmured French was evocative; autumn, with its sad and angry thoughts. Debussy's blonde girl and Liszt's magic fire were delicate and sparkling respectively. You could believe I had it in me to fall in love, and to play round with the idea of a being a Pied Piper.

I'm not against the rain in Chopin's prelude; he didn't call it the 'Raindrop' but the music could well suggest that. What we get is me, getting wet… Still, if a wet shirt could be fitted into Jane Austen's 'Pride and Prejudice' for a television film, then I had to admit I look fine in this context. I felt a faint wisp of uncertainty as I watched myself, somewhat surprised to see that getting wet has a sort of evocative maleness. It took me aback, could well give me an exaggerated idea of my impact.

The dream of love? Uncertain love? My acting pleased me well enough because Ellen produced a good performance from an amateur. She had brought me to the stage where I could make the emotion I feel when I play take over my whole body. It's a new route for me to follow, the hoped-for dream.

And me on the bed. It was a good idea not to do the silk pyjama bit that Josy had wanted, because I don't actually know how to wear them. My gestures suggest a search for an imaginary reality. Love, I repeat – important as it is for me, a man without it…Judging it as dispassionately as I could, it was a romantic dream, strongly conceived, and I hoped male viewers might identify with me. What female viewers might feel is not quite the same thing, but then Liszt would have known about that. The tears which come to my eyes are real, and right, though another composer had prompted them.

Then there's Bach. I have to say that the second version, with water and rocks, is good, but it undermines the whole thrust of the film: music personified in the person of the man who plays the music.

The first one catches the energy and spirit of water and the delight of the music. The shower scene is splendidly edited, and the figure on the screen looks amazing, discreet but powerful, animated by an enjoyment of life, of joie de vivre, Lebenslust. Frankly, it works.

It's harmless enough, isn't it? Dancing to Bach is not unknown. Dancing to Bach's prelude in a shower is an interesting concept, normally done in private, if at all. Naked, yes – but how to explain this? – there is no real nudity. This is a male body in the service of music and drama.

You can justify it like that, if you will.

**

I rang Ellen.

"I thought you might be ringing about an hour or so after the special delivery was scheduled to take place," she said.

Followed by silence.

"Well, are you going to speak to me?" I asked.

"Well…where do you want to start? General opinion? What did you think of the finished product?"

"Well…"

"Listen," her voice was soft and caring, like a speech therapist, "we won't get very far if all we say is 'Well…' so ball in my court. Most of this is what you might have expected, yes?"

266

"Yes. Maybe not quite, but it looks good, very polished, the sound is good, and at first glance everything ties in correctly. I look as if I'm playing the notes you hear in the finished thing."

"True. It's been lovingly prepared, no short cuts. And…"

"The final scene is…well…"

"Yes…"

"Choice of two."

"Your choice. Do you want time to think it over? Or do you want a discussion?"

"The second one is very nicely done. But it's hardly the finale you might expect, is it?"

"Go on…"

"I suppose you could move the Magician to the final spot, and rejig the order of the others…"

"Yes, you could."

"I suppose you could. Look, it's obviously me in the shower. There's no way anyone is going to think that they got a body double, is there?"

"No. It is you, and that's what you thought it would be when you agreed Rob should film it."

"I was worried that I had got carried away with my physical self."

"A bit late to do that. Do you want to go on talking? Would you like me to tell you what I think?"

"Right."

"First, I think it's a very fine sequence as a whole. I think it's the right finale. There's no disrespect for the music, and there's no disrespect for the performer. It's not as if you are just a Muscle Beach man flexing his muscles. You are acting, presenting yourself as the music, not just as a man with the hands and mind to play the piano. It's all of a piece with the leaves of autumn, the flames of the fire, the fields of flax. It belongs."

Short silence.

"Call me back," she said.

I knew what I wanted to say, but had to rationalise it. Would it do my career any harm? I'd given that a great deal of thought before we set out on this path. The last scene had some of that primal energy that runs through this music, of going somewhere with a sense of movement and direction.

I did watch it again. I couldn't play the innocent, could I?

I rang Ellen.

"Let's go with the shower. It's the right way for the twenty-first century. Talk to you later."

Post film

Email from Jane

jane@curzprod.co.uk

This film is sensational. It should find a good market, because it is artistic like nothing I ever saw. It's entertaining. None of the pieces goes on too long. Very involving. There are bits I think people will want to see again and again. Disney's Fantasia huh! You are a star.

We're doing a cover for it...picture of you, golden strings and a suggestion of Fire – as in Ritual Fire Dance – and Water – Falls of Feuch. It looks very marketable. Trust me. We can get it under way straight away, now that your CD is already on the market. Jane

Email to Jane

will@williamwinton.co.uk

Sensational in more ways than one, there's no doubt about that. You might have told me that Josy had got part of his reputation, whatever it is, making this sort of movie. I am an actor, that's all I set out to be, and I owe more to the direction and the editing than to much native ability. I play the piano well, and the sound is exact, the camera seems to like me—remember what I was like a year ago? My body is in good nick, except for my feet – they are cold. What seemed a bit of fun looks set to change my image so much that I wonder if, even if I have a success with Beethoven and Schubert on CD, anyone will treat me seriously.

Signed : Anxious pianist.

Phone call follow-up to Jane:

"Listen Jane, you didn't really tell me everything about Josy, did you? Those boring continental films with farming and sheep being milked – they were only part of his output."

"I never made any secret of that. They're the ones that get into the art-houses."

"And few go to see. Alright, only serious people go to see. So he has to make his money doing more commercial things."

"True. I'm sure I told you he is on his way to more important ground."

"Have you ever seen one of them, these commercial things he's doing on the way?"

"Not as such, but he came very highly spoken of."

"By whom?"

"Well, by people in the know. You know…"

"I just wish I could feel comfortable with it."

"Listen. I've seen the film. It's part of my job, what my clients do for money."

"Yes, yes, I know that. You do realise I am not wearing anything in that last bit. Well of course you do, how could you not?"

"There are shadows, and patterns on the glass. No. Wait. I can put it better than that. You're like Catherine Deneuve in *Belle de Jour*."

"Oh come on. I'm nothing like Catherine Deneuve in *Belle de Jour*. I'm clearly and obviously a man."

"In principle you are showering – modestly showering."

"Modestly? How do you take a modest shower if you want a shower?"

"As you did. What I mean is, we get the fabulous sensation of a man in touch with the music, because there's nothing keeping him away from the sound. Music is like water; it flows, and water is elemental. This really is artistic. Intellectually artistic."

She added that last remark rather quickly.

"Obviously I want to believe you."

"It all has great joy, and freedom, and élan, and imagination, and newness of concept. No-one has done this before, and you are going to triumph."

"You're over-egging the pudding. I was just beginning to believe you. Can you try it out on more people before it's released? Haven't I got an approval of artist clause in my contract?"

She didn't answer that.

"I'll get Ellen to ring you."

"I've spoken to Ellen and I can't make out what she really thinks. She's too closely involved in the project."

"I'll get her to ring you again."

"Tell her to come and see me."

"Ring might be better." She'd obviously begun to notice about Ellen. "It's just I know she's very busy just now." She hadn't begun to notice about Ellen.

Ellen next

Next day Ellen rang.

"Did you get my card?"

I didn't.

"You are wonderful. You did all I could have hoped for and more."

She was my teacher.

"What's so good is that you give exactly what you would hope to get from an actor. Nothing false. It seems to be real life. We see you as you are, or, if you don't think that's the case, at least we see you as you could well be, a living creature of imagination. It's a gift, and you've got it."

This threw me rather. There wasn't going to be much room to talk about my doubts. Yet how could she be totally dispassionate about it? Goodness knows how much of what I saw was initiated by her rather than by Josy.

Of course, I didn't mind being told I've got gifts. Who wouldn't?

"But this…this product and me? I don't know that we belong together. I worry that what you see gets in the way of what I do. You know. Music is about hearing, isn't it?"

"Of course. But the moment you go out in front of an audience wearing your best clothes, you turn it into something visual as well. Don't you?"

"Yes. But in one of these scenes I'm not wearing any clothes at all. Not wearing anything draws attention away from what I'm doing."

"You could say it adds something…something about life. I think what we see on the screen is you: aspects of you. Your nature. Your soul."

Again, how could you mind being told that?

"You're making it hard for me to ask what I want to ask."

"How d'you mean?"

"Is it alright, what I did? These physical things…wet shirts…showers…they seem to swing the spotlight away from me the pianist, on to me, the…well, the body. It's as if what is there on the screen isn't anything to do with me."

"But don't you find when you perform really well, it's a special aspect of you that you don't bring out every day. Isn't that the best way?"

"So what I see isn't me exactly?"

"Yes and no. It's you releasing yourself. Being yourself, perhaps more than you ever knew. Joining up the way you look, the way you think, and the way you play."

"I think we'd better meet. I need some counselling."

It wasn't counselling I wanted, at that particular moment. I wanted to believe what she said about me being released. Being released was OK.

The first reactions

The first thing I heard when I picked up the phone was a man laughing.

Then the voice said, "Well, what do you know?" to which there seemed no obvious answer, especially as I had no idea who it was. It would have made sense to put the phone down.

"What do you think I know?" I said instead.

"It's amazing," he said.

It was Lord Chislehurst. I didn't know what on earth to say to him, and he didn't seem to have anything else to say about it.

"It's amazing," he repeated. I thought that was the end of that.

So I asked him about Felicity, and that produced another burst of laughter.

"She's booted that Estonian out. He hadn't really told her the truth about his wife. I dare say he doesn't tell anyone the truth about his wife, but it doesn't make the poor woman go away."

"Yes. Felicity knew he was married, didn't she?"

"Oh yes, but he was intending to get a divorce. Well, you'd know all about that, wouldn't you?"

I was rather offended at being compared to that man. The reason for my divorce was completely other.

"Well, his wife wasn't having any," he said. "I don't know if he even asked her. Anyway, there are rather a lot of children. She also seems to know several things about him which might not matter if he were a better conductor, but probably will matter in the States where he goes next."

"I suppose that means the end of Felicity's Mendelssohn concerto next November?"

"She's not my daughter for nothing, you know. In fact, nothing doesn't come into it. She costs me quite a lot, in spite of her great-grandmother's money. But she's no fool, and she signed a contract for the concerto, so you can expect to go through it a few times with her. But that isn't what I called about."

And he laughed again.

He obviously did want to talk about the film.

"Let me guess. It's about your investment in me?" is what I said.

"Well, son, I think as investments go, it's one of the best I've ever made. It's likely to bring a good return. *'Fire and Water'*. It's a good title, but don't you think it's too clever?"

"How do you mean?"

"Well, one cancels the other out."

"I think it's meant to show how elemental music is."

"Oh. Your man Josy has sent a copy of it to some firm in the States, and they're interested."

But I hadn't OK'd it.

Obviously it didn't matter whether I did or not.

"That means a lot. Nothing goes on too long. And I have to say I'd no idea you could act the way you do."

"It's the brilliant editing that does it."

"Look, you mustn't get into the habit of saying that. Just smile and look modest."

Hardly the appropriate word.

"You don't think it's over the top?"

"The film? Good God, no. Or rather, yes it is. Who cares? It looks like a guy enjoying himself with music. I must say you've made me think about losing a bit of weight and getting down to the gym myself. It might help with the women."

"I don't suppose you're intending to appear on camera, promoting your produce, are you?"

He laughed again.

"You're an interesting man," he said, "you've been hiding from us all this time."

"No I haven't. It's called wearing clothes. Anyway, until last year I didn't care how I looked. It's the end of a marriage that did it. Changed my life. I can recommend it."

"I think Lady C would take a dim view of that."

"I was joking. It was the best thing Patti ever did. She's got something that she never got from me: a more focused family life and a child on the way, so I heard."

"They'll be after you for a classical music based movie."

Oh my God.

"Do you know something I don't? I've got concerts to do, a broadcast; there's a Prom."

"No, I'm just guessing. What I do know something about is entirely centred on business and politics. We must have a party for you soon. A promotion party. A launch? Somewhere smart. How about the National Gallery?"

"And put me in direct competition with all the rest of that naked flesh? Much better than mine, because an artist invented it. No. A modern gallery would be better, although you have to watch what you stand next to for the photo opportunities."

Rather a sweeping remark, unresearched too, but I didn't want to do it. In fact, we never did. I think Jane had a word in an ear or two.

We agreed to keep in touch.

Next visit to the Conservatoire

When I next went into the Conservatoire, I put on dark glasses, trying not to draw attention to myself. Then I remembered that the film hadn't been issued yet.

Felicity was already in the teaching room, practising her Mendelssohn concerto, when I opened the door. She stopped, and ran her hands over her thighs before looking round at me. It's not an unusual gesture among pianists, and usually has no significance whatsoever. She was dressed rather differently; her clothes looked more shaped to the body, and the upper and lower garments didn't meet in the middle by some distance, though I didn't really look.

"I've seen your film. It's fabulous."

"Thank you. It's hard for me to tell, as you can imagine."

"Imagine. Yes. That comes into it, alright."

Oh well, this was what I'd laid myself open to. Musical talent and looks don't come in exclusive packages. Either/or. Even tenors don't have to be fat and plain, though there's an old tradition that they do. George Eliot chalked that one up in her novel *Daniel Deronda*.

The man you see while Bach's music is playing in the shower scene isn't by any means really clear, and you could say it's better directed than the shower scene in Hitchcock's 'Psycho', because nobody dies in my shower. It would take more than that to kill me. Or Bach.

"That was Mendelssohn you were practising. It sounds good."

"The concerto, oh yes…" Her eyes were wide-open now.

"Business side going smoothly, is it? Have you got a date for it?"

"Oh yes and a contract. Whoever ends up conducting it."

"I thought that was all signed and sealed. Aaronowitz. Michael Aaronowitz, isn't it?"

"It might not be. It depends."

"I thought he had a contract with the orchestra for the whole season."

"Yes, he had a contract. But Daddy has lawyers. In the States."

"So it might not be him? Conducting."

"True enough. There are others."

She looked at me.

"I think Daddy told you: I've broken up with Micki."

No point in denying that.

"I knew it wouldn't last, of course," she said. "The age difference for one thing. But he might at least have meant what he said. Or at least a part of it. Do you know what? He had no courage. He just couldn't deal with it. A wife back home, and who knows how many children? He ran up huge phone bills talking to them. My phone bills."

"Why did you go with him, then, if you knew the odds?"

"Oh. Pure sex, really. It was after the concert Mummy was connected with. He'd just been conducting the orchestra, and he was sort of glowing with strength and something or other. So when he asked me to have a late drink with him after the reception thing, I said Yes. And somehow that was the word I used for the rest of that evening. In fact, it's my favourite word in the right circumstances."

"Listen. If you're going to be a professional musician, I can tell you that No is an even more useful word. Stops you taking on too much."

"Then there was the bit with the concerts in America. He did hear me play, you know. It had nothing to do with pillow talk or with Daddy's millions."

"I believe you, because I know how you can play. Anyway, your daddy's millions aren't a very well-kept secret."

"OK. I know that. All the same, he said he liked the way I play the piano, as much as the way I…"

I stopped listening.

"…as the way I look. Anyway, it's all over."

She didn't look very unhappy. She continued after a moment.

"He wasn't very good in bed."

"I don't want to know anything about that."

I might have guessed, though. If what he'd been after in Glasgow was anything to go by, "good in bed" didn't come into it.

274

"I wasn't a virgin, you know. You can't have it tattooed on the fingers of one hand… All the same some men can tell whether a girl is or isn't."

Some men, indeed. "I'm not one of them."

"You know now. Does it make any difference?"

"To the way you play the piano? I don't think so. Being a virgin doesn't really come into playing the piano. Imagination and good muscular control. And don't make anything out of that."

"I want to tell you something. Micki wouldn't have happened if you'd treated me as a woman, and not as a talented girl just out of school."

I couldn't have this. I wasn't going to take any blame for what she chose to do. It was bad enough trying to work out the Patti thing.

"No. I don't think that's right. I'm responsible for your musical education and beliefs. I've told you before."

"You might like to know how it ended. Micki has decided to take his wife and kids to America with him. She'd been watching television, of course, since that curtain came down, or went up, whichever. So she thinks America is the answer to everything. He wondered how I would feel about being his sort of unofficial mistress.

"I told him I was OK with the girl-friend situation, but not with the mistress stuff."

She seemed to have some fine definition of the difference. Based on money, probably.

"They must be seriously stuck in the past where he comes from. If I was going to be a mistress or a kept woman, or whatever, I think I could do better than him, don't you think?"

"I'm sure you could." I was wondering when we were going to get to Mendelssohn.

"Of course, there was the concerto in the States for me. All the same, I was practically keeping him in the end."

"Not too many concerts for him to conduct, then?" That wouldn't have surprised me. He didn't seem much more than competent, once you took the theatrical gestures away.

"No. That's not quite fair, but not many. All somewhere in the future. So talk of the divorce went away. And so did I. Or rather he did, since it was my place we were living in. I wanted him to get a divorce, really. I don't think I would have married him, not once we'd been living together."

"Don't ask me about divorces – I'm the one who's been on the receiving end of one. It wasn't my idea." There was a silence.

"Well, I would have thought the advantage of a divorce is that you're a free man, aren't you? Although after the film is released, you might not be as free as all that. I wouldn't know, but that's what Daddy says."

"You're talking about me like that behind my back?"

"Not really. Or rather, yes. It's a very beautiful experience in its way. Your film."

"I hope it is. That's why I made it," I said.

Then I thought I ought to take a more positive attitude about it. After all, it wasn't just my film. Other people had an input.

"It's very professional, and I think it's a very good way of giving music a visual dimension." I sounded like a professor.

"The dimensions look very good to us Smiths. Especially in the Chopin and the Bach. Very good."

She thought I was losing this skirmish, so she made up for it. Generous in victory?

"We also love your CD. The Schubert and Beethoven."

"You've listened to it, then?" Stupid remark. She obviously had – she was there when it was recorded.

"I find the Schubert very moving, very young."

"What?"

"As if it's happening now and as if it's saying the truth about him, and me, in a way. And it's a great performance of opus 109. I can recognise that, even at my age. Full of heart and mind."

She was quoting the review in the 'Times'.

She smiled: "Heart and mind. And some body, too. Bit more body in the film, though. It's like a personal statement made visible, my mother said."

My heart sank. Yes, it's good that women like Lady Chislehurst were listening to Bach. I have no idea if people imagine anything when they listen to music, so what goes on has nothing to do with me.

She went on. "I have too. Watched it. You know it's quite difficult to sit here, and try not to imagine you in...the...shower. Tell me, how do you tell your teacher you fancy him?"

She got up and walked towards me. Fresh, innocent, except of course it wasn't. She put her arms round my neck.

I removed them. Very firmly. Even roughly.

I pushed her away. Tactfully. Or at least what was meant to be tactfully.

She didn't think so.

"How can you do that? Have you no idea what I…"

"Stop right there. Listen. Do you want me to tell you that you remind of my former wife when she was your age? The age we got married. That you remind me of her? And I don't want to go there again."

She backed off pretty fast. It wasn't at all true. If Patti had been like this, I think I might have had trouble fitting in the practice I needed to do.

"I'm sorry. I had no idea. I got that wrong didn't I?"

"You're a lovely girl, possibly with a taste for older men. I'm pretty well twice your age."

"You aren't, because I know how old you are. You're fourteen years older than me."

"Sixteen. And you're a student at this place, and there is no way, there is just no way…"

I stopped.

"I'm not a child you know."

"I can see that, and I know that, but this one really isn't on. I'm deeply touched by your interest in me, but that's it."

It looked as if I should have to get rid of her sooner than I had intended. For her sake. As a pianist.

Further Reactions

'Fire and Water' came out and Jane was right. Even the serious press was amused by it, and took it seriously because of my CD, Jane said. There's nothing like Beethoven and Schubert for making people think you're serious.

Email from *jane@curzprod.co.uk*

Fire and Water is selling like crazy. Great reviews. I don't normally send them to you, but knowing how your mind is set at the moment, here are some of them.

Two of the Dailies print pictures of you, and talk about the silent majority at last being catered for, without wasting Government money on subsidising the arts. The Guardian is amused: "The elements are all here – not only fire and water, but also earth and air – as Chaminade, Liszt, Falla and Debussy saw them through their own coloured glasses. If we are going to watch music made flesh, then Mr Winton's flesh is as good as flesh gets." I think you've got an invitation there if you want it: it's a woman critic. The man in the Telegraph takes an age-old view: "William Winton's recent CD brought such instinctive experience and freshness to these two sonatas so close to the last words for the piano for each composer. In this product, he sounds equally at home with these little miniatures, which can sound tired – it's time you went home' music. The whole exercise surprised me and William Winton has never sounded better. Listen to his playing and watch what the camera makes of him. You might even close your eyes…" That is one of his jokes; not a bad one, considering the context.

The Sun prints a rather smudgy picture of your shower scene with a complaint that it might have been more clearly photographed. All the same, how's this for a quote for your CV? Another woman writer: "Forget Mr Darcy, sexy Will will make you want to go for a walk in the rain; forget Psycho too, this is _the_ shower scene for this viewer. Buy it, guys, turn the sound down and be standing outside the shower with your towel in your hand, ready to rub him down." The headline is 'In The Buff For The Music Buffs…' I think they could have done better than that…

And one of the classical music magazines picks it out for attention in its editorial : "We said about his Beethoven that it 'gave a view from the other side of the bridge. Many pianists wait for obvious maturity (that is, the maturity of artistic age, say at fifty) before tackling this great music. William Winton, by being young, gives us the eternal youth and vigour that makes Beethoven a man for all seasons. And his new bouquet of extras, encore music, basically, Fire and Water, shows us the man he is during all those seasons." That's racy, for them, don't you think? There's more about the Schubert sonata too, which I will leave you to read. Perceptive, which is a plus.

The TV channels are making a few noises about having you on a chat-show, or chat-up show, depending on the host. I suggest you leave them alone until the dust has settled, or the raindrops have stopped falling, because the conversation might go in the wrong direction, and, if you'll forgive me, you've not got much experience in taking command of an interview. Radio is different, provided it's a serious show.

Keep smiling for the cameras.
Jane

The Con tour

I had a call from Sir Gregory, asking me to meet him in his room for lunch, if I wouldn't mind re-arranging my pupils, which actually meant only Felicity, since the others were before lunchtime. I was trying to avoid lunch engagements because of my diet, but Sir Greg's meal, with seafood as the main part, was alright. He'd obviously got some decent food from somewhere or another. Maybe he did it every day. Fruit and avoidable biscuits came afterwards. Even good wine from the Con's small but classy cellar, which had benefitted from a sizeable gift from one of the benefactors in the days when the Con was thought to be a safe place to send your daughter to finish off her education nicely. It meant you could keep an eye on her if you didn't want to take the risk of sending her to Switzerland, where she might get finished in a way you weren't planning…Way back in the pre-war years, you understand, when the place was very proper, with different staircases for the men and the women.

I took a polite glass.

Sir Gregory, who followed no noticeable diet, was affable. Congratulated me on the Beethoven sonata recording.

"It really gets to the heart of that poor and wonderful man," he said. That was a real compliment, because, whatever you might think of him as a Principal, he is a good musician, and he had good mentors versed in the old traditions. Not back to Beethoven exactly, but there was almost a line there. Schubert too, so full of aching truth and effervescent delight.

"And the Bagatelles have the right mixture of thought and charm that would have pleased the composer, I am sure. No heavy German psychoanalysis behind it."

All good to hear, even if psychoanalysis is Austrian rather than German. Or Swiss, if you want to include Jung. I appreciated what he meant, and was grateful.

We skimmed on. A little bit about the world, the loss of some of the Con's earnings from Japan, because not so many students were coming now, and they hadn't made a replacement hit on China yet. He didn't say whether that was because they were going elsewhere. I was beginning to wonder when we would get round to the business I assumed I was here for, the rehearsal schedule for the concert. And that was when we did.

"You know, William, I'm very proud of you. You're one of our most successful products. You have everything you need to be one of our greatest artists. The CD proves it."

I began to suspect what was coming.

"We're a great institution, with a history of one and a half centuries now, and a great reputation for all-round musical education, and we teach skills which transcend mere note-bashing, or note-writing. We take students from all over the world, and some of them are very young. It's easy to overlook the fact that we are a religious foundation, in the sense that there is always provision on the Council for a bishop of the established church and one member from one of the non-conformist, evangelical organisations."

Now it was obvious why I was there. Oh dear, oh dear, I had blotted my copybook in the eyes of the bishop and the non-conformist evangelical organisation. He went on.

"I think you may have guessed by what I've just said that I am faced with a small dilemma."

There was no reason I should help him in his task.

"I'm sorry, I don't follow your train of thought."

Sir Greg cleared his throat. Slowly.

"You see, your little film…"

"Yes?" I said, "My little film – the film, *Fire and Water,* you mean?"

I didn't care what this man thought of my little film, but I began to feel defensive about it. Aggressive, even.

"We had a Council meeting yesterday, just before I phoned you, and we talked of those concerts we've scheduled for next year. One of the members of the Council brought up the question of the publicity surrounding your little film. I have to say that I personally hadn't seen it, which put me at a disadvantage, because clearly several of the others had. In fact, I found out that they'd been ringing round one another to make sure they did watch it."

"But you've seen it now?"

He waved to the desk. And the screen on it.

"Yes. If I may say so, I found it just a little surprising, but then I find that with much that happens in the world these days."

He stopped, sighed, picked a strawberry and a finger of cheese, had a sip of wine. All very sophisticated, but a way of playing for time all the same, so I tried to move things on.

"Don't you think that anything new is surprising anyway? What about Beethoven and Wagner?" I thought that wasn't exactly what I wanted to say. It wasn't exactly as if Beethoven and Wagner were wet shirt people. "If you see what I mean…"

"I think I do. Changing world and all that. Well I thought your little film perfectly clever and not disrespectful of the music, although the Bach at the end does challenge one."

I wasn't going to tell him about my own doubts, so I let him be challenged.

"You had to chair a discussion about a product you didn't know?"

"True enough. That's how it was with some of the others. Our politician hadn't seen it, but then he's got troubles in his constituency, and troubles of a different kind here in London, which we're not supposed to know about. I'm sure that wouldn't stop him from having a view. It's part of the charter that politicians sign up to, I would have thought – having views on anything they're asked about, except their expenses. Or offshore investments. All absolutely legal, of course."

He knew more about the world than I expected.

He went back to the subject.

"It's only fair to say that the general view of the council was that they had no problems with it, those that had seen it."

"I'm pleased to hear that." I thought I had made a mistake after all, and I was home and dry, and we could move on to rehearsal schedules. But Sir Greg cleared his throat. Twice.

"Unfortunately that's not all. We have a problemette." Which meant nothing of the sort; it was a major problem, and he was too embarrassed to use a known English word for it. Or a known French one, either.

"It was one of the women councillors. I don't know if you know Natasha Archbold."

"No. I think I'd remember a name like that, don't you?"

"Archbold is a north-country name; she's from County Durham. She tells me the name is from the Normans who came over with William the Conqueror. Doesn't sound like it, but there's no reason not to believe her. She's a musician, Edinburgh music doctorate, a couple of years post-graduate work here at the Conservatoire, composes music, in particular for engaging the unpractised listener. She plays cello. Chamber music. Small orchestras. She is a right person for the Council, especially as she's the only woman at the moment. We're working on that."

"Can I ask how old she is?"

"I do know, but I'll only say that she's about your age."

The direction of this conversation had made me feel that she was older.

"And she has an opinion about it?"

"She said she'd seen it, and was amused by it, thought you looked amazing, as well as playing so beautifully."

"So she's not got anything against the 'Fire and Water'."

"She's a sophisticated lady."

"I'm pleased to have her opinion."

"You should be. She thinks it will be good publicity for music in this century."

Right. At last, I was going to find the reason for the free lunch.

"I need to explain that every year we have an event for our alumnae. Female gender, because some of the women who trained here didn't go into the profession, but went away and made money or married it. They loved their studies. Some still turn up at the official alumni concerts or cocktail parties. Very old, they are, but very polite, mostly widows with rather loud voices and money – old money. With some knowledge of music to show that they had passed the right exams.

"We feed and wine them, give them a short concert, and talk to them. We need them, because we ask them for their money."

"I understand that. I get requests once a year for contributions, and I'm not an older-generation woman."

"Council members try to fit it into their schedules. Natasha is invaluable on these occasions. She's lively, funny, and successful."

"I'd like to meet her."

"You will. You're doing a concert later this year in Durham, she told us. She's on the committee that's organising their little Festival, and she says she's looking forward to meeting you too. Especially now, she said."

Good to hear. And now for the crunch.

"She feels that the attitude of these valuable members of our community is much more fixed than we might wish. They will have views."

"Views ...?"

"About what goes on here."

"In these hallowed halls? Quite a lot does go on here. That's what we're for. Isn't it?"

"Yes, I know it does. But she wonders if they…these hallowed old ladies…– might think we're going too far."

"…if you're featuring a pianist who doesn't mind his body being looked at by all and sundry."

Silence. There was no more eating going on. The coffee was poured but it had been sitting in its thermos pot for much too long.

"When we were founded, the founding fathers didn't trust musicians much, so they put a series of checks and balances in, to make sure we kept respectable. Not like those girls' schools in Venice, where they learnt to sing, and play musical instruments. And possibly other things in case the music didn't bring in the money. In Casanova's time, you know."

"I didn't know, but I can imagine."

"She felt particularly that since we take young girls into our conservatoire, many of them barely eighteen, it might be thought by valued members of our school diaspora that they should not be seen to be in close association with a man who looks the way you look in certain circumstances."

"I see. So you…"

"She wanted to make it clear that she had no objection to watching you getting wet. There's nothing immoral about being photographed when you're damp."

"I am very discreetly shown on screen."

"I'm not putting this very well. It's just a safeguard. I hadn't thought of it until Natasha brought it up. I know our girls are modern in their outlook. I've got teenagers of my own, and I'm sure they are not unaware of what goes on in the world these days."

Well, well. Teenage daughters. Who would have thought it?

"But it made me nervous. I have to admit."

"You don't want the funds to dry up. Because of the shower. I understand that."

Sir Greg sighed.

"We can't afford the risk."

"Yes."

"I can see you might bring in more of an audience."

"We don't know that yet, do we?"

"Exactly."

"And you quite properly want to put the emphasis on the young players in the orchestra."

Small silence. I knew what I was going to do, but I didn't want to put myself at risk.

"Can I just ask what level the publicity has reached? I'm quite happy to withdraw, if that's what you're building up to, but I don't want it to look as if I'm withdrawing because I couldn't face the public."

"No. We're OK on that score. It's just a Conservatoire thing. No details released. It's not until July next year, so few people know."

"Fine. I'll withdraw."

"You do understand, don't you? We don't want to offend you – such a valuable member of our staff."

That was it. They got one of their prize-winning pianist students to play, the Dame sang her Last Songs and there was a celebration overture by the recently graduated composer Tom Jordan, now in the Library, which pleased me. A much better programme.

BBC Radio Interview

I recorded an interview for a BBC radio programme. They wanted me to go in and do it live, just before nine o'clock. That's not a good slot really, because sometimes there's not much time for anything when they've finished trying to get answers out of the usual suspects – and not just the politicians.

Jane pointed out that although it's a radio show, there could be spare cameras lurking around the building. We had to stay in charge of this if possible. So she told them I would record the thing in Broadcasting House. About midday.

I didn't know Broadcasting House very well. The days when the Concert Hall in the centre of the old 1930s building was used for live music broadcasts had already gone when I was a young pianist looking for dates.

And now the building was being updated.

I listen to the radio – enough to keep up to date, and have a ready hand on the off button to deal with the moment when I begin to get depressed by the way the people in power are dealing with the world. But I needed to get a handle on how to make sure I said what I wanted to say, even if the questions didn't seem to be going my way.

Jane and I talked it through. I needed to be prepared in case my interviewer was going to be serious or flippant or both.

The interviewer was a man, and since we were recording we had time to get to know each other slightly more, and not be influenced by the people he'd been talking to about the banking crisis, or whatever, if we'd done it live.

"Is there a way in which your film appearance might make those of the public who know you as a serious performer – not that you're not serious in the way you play on the sound track, of course – feel that you're taking risks with your chances of impressing those who love your Beethoven by playing people like Chaminade and appearing in a sort of film-star role like Colin Firth and Hugh Grant rolled into one, with a touch of one of the Latin lovers added for extra value – do you accept that it's a tricky career move?" He was trying not to sound as if he was reading a prepared text. I felt a bit sorry for him, but there really was only one answer.

"Yes."

A silence followed (it was edited out of the broadcast) during which it became obvious that his question was supposed to prompt a longer answer from me. And of course we couldn't leave it at that. So I said something about the changing face of classical music, that we're nearly a decade into the twenty-first century, our need to appeal to the young and win back the not-so-young who'd somehow not come in our direction as much as we would like.

"Of course there are limits to what I can do when I'm playing the piano. You have to keep in contact with the keyboard. And, as you can see in the film, I'm not playing the piano all the time. It's much more to do with atmosphere, and imagination, and good film editing. If I say I'm pleased with it, it's not because I have ambitions as an actor, or much conceit, but because the people who made it knew what they were doing."

And so on. I was quite pleased with myself, although it sounded as if I was also reading from a prepared script.

"You're down to do a Prom, I see from the prospectus. What sort of reception do you think you'll get from the Promenaders, who are always given to pulling people's legs?"

"They've always been good to me. I expect they'll tease me, but I'm playing Ravel's piano concerto and somehow I think they'll be more interested in the music than in anything else. They're mostly young people, and they're used to the modern world. The BBC itself is deeply into the latest developments, as you well know. So maybe a flight of harmless imagination like 'Fire and Water' isn't going to get in the way."

"'Fire and Water' being the name of your film. I've seen it, and I must say I liked it. And the people over there on the other side of the glass there seem to have liked it too."

I wished I was as confident about the Prom as I made out.

**

Ellen comes for a meal

Ellen and I had the scheduled evening meal together. At my place. She had made a condition – she had to leave early, because there were important new contacts to be made tomorrow. Everything was ready, keeping warm, or just needing last minute touches or a final blast. A good white wine I'd got from France through Henri.

It was to be a quiet, informal evening, and yet, when she arrived, she'd dressed up for me.

"My…you look fantastic. Smell nice. Was it something I did?"

"Well, yes in a way. You seem worth dressing up for."

"That's kind."

"I owe you so much. The film already looks as if it will be good for my career. Sounds commercial, that, but I wanted to get it out of the way."

"I'm glad you think it might help."

"This isn't business, though, coming to see you when I don't actually have to."

That was better. At some point, I meant to ask exactly how they'd been able to get my Bach prelude to look the way it did. The question was whether I wanted a discussion, or a relaxed evening with a woman I liked.

We had a preparatory drink. She asked for dry sherry, which surprised me, I don't know why. Then, after she'd looked at my books, noticed that some of them were plays, we got round to the film.

"It works, doesn't it?" That was me.

"You had a great deal to do with its final shape, I imagine?"

"If you mean the sort of visual ideas, the cutting and all that, well, yes, quite a lot of that was me. Josy was very adaptable, because he felt a bit out of his element with the music. I'd kind of got to know the music, and I'd got to know you. All I had to do was put you together."

"I'm taken aback by it."

286

"Perhaps you should be. You found out something which you perhaps hadn't known since your schooldays. How to make an effect, just by being there. I wouldn't say I know what makes you tick, but I know a bit about your strengths and your weaknesses. My job is working with actors, and that's what you are here. You have real talent."

Naturally I demurred.

"Yes, but it takes years to make an actor, in the colleges and academies."

"If you have talent, you develop the appropriate skill. Techniques for the theatre are one thing, but for a close-working camera it's being prepared to go with yourself, really. Remembering to breathe."

We left it there for the moment. The food was ready. The wine needed to be drunk respectfully.

She admired the cooking – said she had no idea about that, that she didn't have much of a housewifely streak, that she felt she lived like a permanent student.

"I would hate you to see where I live."

So that was out of the picture, anyway.

"I have no time to do much to it. Glad to have it to myself, of course."

That was good. No partner, it seemed. She continued.

"I have to say how much I've enjoyed working with you."

"I couldn't have done it without you," I said.

"You'd have done it with someone else, believe me. There are others out there who can do what I do. It's what we get taught at drama schools."

"But not the way you do – did – do."

"OK – I'll accept that."

"We were right for each other."

This was proving hard work. A new angle…

"Would you like me to give you some piano lessons?"

Ellen just laughed.

"I thought I'd like to return the compliment. You taught me how to act, and I thought I might teach you about playing the piano."

"You'd get to know that I have no musical talent whatever. I like music, but the woman who was supposed to teach us singing at drama school thought I might well manage without needing to sing. She said I was tone-deaf."

"There's no such thing."

"You lie very well."

"No, it's true."

"Honestly…if you want a nice relationship like ours to end abruptly, the quickest way is to get me to sing to you."

We went on eating.

"It's been good, over the last eight months. And now?"

"I know what you're asking, William. Give me a little more wine, and I'll tell you what I think. We worked and we were close. How close we can be without work is another thing. It's like shipboard romances used to be: the sea does it as much as the people. Propinquity, you know."

"We've not landed yet. Perhaps we can just go sailing on."

"Be serious. You're not long divorced. What does that mean? Apart from not having a wife."

"It means I'm a second-time bachelor."

"How does that feel?"

"Strange. I'm still getting used to it."

"Can I ask you how much you knew about your ex-wife?"

"I never thought about it. We lived together for a large part of my grown-up life. Not a lot, I suppose…Not a lot, I see now."

"How would you have to feel before you cast yourself in the part of a married man again?"

"Do you think I should get married again? Really?"

"I'm not saying that. But for some people you're on the market."

"But not for all? Shop-soiled, I guess. Return to marriage-maker."

"I didn't mean that. Coming out of a marriage is more than coming out of a relationship, do you think?"

"I've no idea. I thought I had both. There's more unpicking to do, I think. It was certainly a big job for us – nearly fifteen years of communal acquisitions. It did mean I was free of the things I had to be polite about."

"Like?"

"The things you don't like but she does. Or her mother gave her, or reminded her of something you know nothing about."

"Big adjustment."

"I'm having to find out what it is to be available."

"What do you mean, available? Lots of people are available. Quite a lot of the men I meet are available. Only too available, some might say. No strings. Or at least no visible strings. Is that what you mean?"

"Well…" was all I said. Because it was what I meant. But I also meant something more which was proving difficult to put into words. So we got on with eating and talking about the food.

At the next glass-filling natural pause, she made it clear that she had come with a definite purpose in mind.

"Do you mind me asking why you got divorced?"

"I'm not entirely sure. It came to an end rather suddenly. Patti had a completely different view of our marriage from mine. We'd lost touch."

"She's with someone else, then?"

"Yes. Married to him. And surely expecting a baby."

"Ah."

"What does 'Ah' mean?"

"Just that. Ah."

"I could say it was because we grew into an affectionate disbelief in one another."

She laughed. "I like that – affectionate disbelief. Though I don't think it means as much as it sounds as if it means."

"It's true. Patti and I didn't know one another any more, if we ever did."

Ellen waited a moment. "We all have a past, you know. It's just a question of how much of it we want to face up to, and how much we want to forget."

"I don't see any point in trying to forget what's happened. There was no infidelity. I was never encouraged to commit it. The women I met back then used to shake hands, ask for my autograph, and then look at what I'd written, rather than me. Surprising what a difference a serious diet and exercises can make."

"Ah, now I see. This is William Mark Two."

"It says on the label."

"You almost told me about that a little while back, and then you decided against it. It explains one or two things you've not admitted to."

"What things have you in mind?"

"You might be surprised to know that we had bets in the studio about you."

"Who won?"

"No-one, because we were right, all of us."

"Like how?"

"One view was that you really did know that you were good to look at. That you took trouble to look good to look at. Another was that you really didn't believe it. Victoria said that."

She hit that on the nail.

"That was backed up by the fact that you had no sense of humour about it."

"Which did you think?"

"I'm not saying. Once you were up and running, you got on with the job."

"No real problem, because I didn't have to relate to anyone else, except for the moments when you helped me out off camera."

"You just had to tap into what you have when you play the piano. You can make delicate sounds, and then turn into a sort of tyrant when the power comes out through your fingers."

"A Hitler of the keyboard."

"Of course not. Don't send me up. You know what I mean."

"It's not just me, you know, it's the man or woman who wrote the music I play."

"Without you there would be no music. Just dots on a page, locked in silence."

"There are other players."

"Yes, of course there are, and they're doing what you're doing. Life support to composers who are dead."

"Those that are."

There were some table things to be done. Ellen watched me take a small piece of cheese after she had taken a selection.

"So the diet is permanent?"

"Oh yes. Would you like to see a picture of what I looked like when it wasn't?"

"Seriously?"

I don't keep pictures of myself all over the place, like some I know. With Royalty in the background, or Sir Michael Tippett looking approving as you get some award or other. But I do have one from my study days in France, living with Henri and Mariette. We're all laughing and happy. It's been promoted into a more prominent position since Patti left.

She whistled. "Which one is you?"

She knew well enough.

"I see how you've changed. Remarkable. Under that flesh and behind those glasses and neglected hair there was you."

"There still is, behind the contact lenses, and the styled hair and the whatever you call my body now. Except that now I'm at a loss, as you can be when you know you've done something badly wrong in your life which affected someone else. We're getting serious. How about some coffee? I'll brew it while I fill your glass again."

Ellen came with me into the kitchen.

"You know these sessions we worked together were just that – working sessions. I'm surprised I didn't get even a hint of what goes on in there." She pointed to my head, and I thought for a moment she was going to touch me. She didn't.

"You picked up the acting you needed very quickly."

"If so, I expect it was because of some small amount of inherited talent. My mother is – was – whichever it is – an actress."

"Would I know her?"

"I don't think so. I don't. She went to America thirty-five years ago, and apart from a few cards in the early days, I've not heard of her since. She may be doing a TV thing, but it's certainly not been done in 'Frasier' or 'Desperate Housewives'. Or maybe it was, because come to think of it, I wouldn't recognise her. Just think, I might have watched my own mother in something without knowing it. To be honest, I would like to think she had some talent for me to inherit, but I think what there was she really needed for herself."

"Oooh. She hurt you, did she?"

"Only when I think about it. I had lovely grandparents. And before you ask, no father either, except on a postcard or two."

"You're quite a package. No wonder I like you. I usually get ones you can see right through."

I took a breath. "You mean like Jolyon?"

"Jolyon?"

"The actor in the pantomime. The one I met at your Christmas party."

"That's when they do pantomimes."

"In Dartford, it was."

"Funny you should remember that."

"It isn't really. He got a bit nasty with me – thought you and I were lovers, and got aggressive about it."

"He's around. And that's not his real name. Which is John."

"I just wondered if you still saw him. He seemed to think you two were close."

"I dare say he did. But that was his take on our friendship. It never was anything more."

Coffee time.

"I would have expected you to be more aggressive about your appearance. It's a triumph. It's what you intended it to be."

"You mean I created myself, like an Identikit."

"In a way. Does it make a difference?"

"Yes. People look at me as well as listen to me. It's a two-edged sword, of course. How I play is what matters, and I'm the same struggling artist inside, regardless of what I look like on the outside. And…" I stopped.

"And…?"

"I haven't got used to it. I get, well, some offers."

I was going to say something about walking away from them. I didn't.

"Don't tell me. Did you expect me to make you one?"

Pause. How to answer that?

"I could say that I hoped you would. I've still not got the hang of asking for myself. If I asked you, would you?"

"Would I what?"

"Take any notice of it."

"It depends on what it was. You know, I used to smoke – a lot of actors do and not just because they have to in their work – all those thirties and forties plays and films. There are times when I really could do with a cigarette."

"And this is one. Doesn't sound like a good thing."

"No, but it shows something about this evening."

"OK, before I send the butler out to get a packet of fags, let me tell you a bit more. I'm risking a lot bringing you here, because you make me sort of hope that a relationship could happen again. It has to be a better one, when it happens…I don't want it to be like the last one, and that's asking a lot of myself…I'm getting muddled up. I didn't ask you round to bundle you into bed."

"I know that. I can recognise the signs that go with that one."

I'd got this far. She wouldn't have come, would she, if she hadn't wanted my company? I was deliberately silent. I took her hand.

"Am I getting anywhere with you?"

"I don't know. I don't want you to think I don't notice. We've been close because I've been looking into your eyes while you were being a fireman or a waterman or a dreamy lover."

She squeezed my hand and I let hers go. She had more to say.

"There's a lot I haven't found out about you. And a lot that you haven't found out either. You're most likely going to need time to find it. In a way, it's typical."

"I'm not sure that I want to hear that. Typical?"

She continued. "The marriage that failed. You obviously feel you came out of it badly. It's pretty close to the surface still, or it is when you're with me. I know something about relationships that fail – not marriage, but near enough. I don't want to be destroyed again either."

She went silent. Sipped the empty coffee cup. I thought that was the end of what she was going to say. But it wasn't.

"You are in the wrong place. Like me. I think you're attractive, and I don't just mean the way you look, and I think you have all the potential for something between us. I don't want an affair, because the way I feel just now it would uncover some pain, and I'm not big enough for that. I think I would enjoy being in your bed, but not now. Not until…" She stopped.

After a moment, she took my hand. "We're not ready to get out of the wood, yet."

Companionable, it was, and it had to be. And still she hadn't finished.

"If I tell you I could fall in love with you, that wouldn't exactly be the truth. There's a chance I could love you. But you need to be certain it's not going to end up in a divorce courtroom. Relationships are hard to end too, for reasons, and each one is different. It's best if you go around without me for a while, but I want you to know that I'll think about you. That's it for now."

"I understand," I said.

"And, as you know, I have an early start tomorrow. I must go."

And that's where it ended. Apart from a brilliantly managed goodbye kiss which said exactly what she had just said in words. Warm, tender, not cold, but leaving things as they were.

**

Email from *jane@curzprod.co.uk*

Sit comfortably and read this.

"For a long time now, with the growth of the inevitable power of television and the internet, the visual aspect of the serious performance of music has developed. Listening is conditioned, in many cases, by the eyes. Women soloists have long known the advantage of their appearance. Even if nature has been somewhat ungenerous with her gifts, some of them do their best with a glittery dress and some earrings, unless they're playing a violin, and give their audiences something to see as well as hear. They could well do yet more. Have instructions in sophisticated make-up. Men are encouraged to acquire a more casual dress-style. Artists must relate to their potential audiences and not be stuck in the realms of the past when the audience dressed up almost as much as the people on the platform. We must look for more ways to market our younger clients. The older ones may well not need it, or agree to it. We cannot afford to let the market for classical music die under our feet for lack of keeping up to date with the world around us."

That excerpt is from the chairman of our agents' association. It represents what we are having to learn to do. We don't want to find we have fine artists and no fine concerts to put them into.

Fire and Water will do you nothing but good. No-one is suggesting that when you appear at the Proms you'll be wearing a T-shirt, but knowing that you are a man of the moment will not get in the way of their listening to you; in fact it is likely to add a dimension. Liszt himself had huge sex-appeal, Paganini so much that they thought he was in league with the devil. You know all of this. Relax.

Signed; Jane, your devoted fan and your agent

PS

Plenty of serious enquiries for your services: Edinburgh, Berlin, the USA with masterclasses as well as concerts – on the strength of the Beethoven/Schubert CD those are.

Oh, and an enquiry from a film-producer who wonders if you might be interested in making a movie. He hasn't worked out the plot, but you would be a pianist who likes playing the piano while playing the field...plenty of action and opportunities to make the most of your acting abilities and appearance, especially as it showed up in the last part of the film. Should I ask for more details? J

I think she was sending me up.

Victoria

Victoria had left a message on my answerphone.

"Can we meet? I'd love to know how you are, and how you think we did in getting you into 'Fire and Water'. Good title, don't you think, since there's a significant amount of both, one way and another. I'm a bit busy at the moment – you know how it goes. I've got sessions not far from home. Would you mind coming up to Notting Hill, where I live? There are plenty of good places around to have a meal."

I called her back.

"I think you're worth the price of a meal to thank you for editing my playing so brilliantly for the soundtrack of the film. And maybe talk about some future ideas. For CDs to follow Beethoven and Schubert."

"Thank you for the compliment. It was totally new for me. Not easy, exactly, to make the sound and vision really fit. We worked as a team getting it right. Yes, I'm pleased with the result."

"I'm truly grateful because the music part is the only thing I can be sure about, and you made me feel at ease."

"Let me know what sort of meal suits you and I'll book somewhere quiet."

**

It was small, very much family-run. Not smart as in luxurious, but smart as in French with good food, and a good wine list.

We talked about work.

About how far a woman can get in an industry which has been male-dominated; about trying for a job with the BBC, not radio – television. She loves the radio, but she thinks the only interesting programmes of the future will be like the old ones her father remembers. Mixed output, with news, drama, music, some comic shows – really funny ones. Broad broadcasting. Surprise the listener.

She wonders how much future there will be for a full-time music network. Some time or other it will be sacrificed to a pure web-site issue, with people programming their own listening to suit their own tastes.

She wants to take Pythagoras Discs down that road, and once the present boss is out of the way, I dare say she might try for his job. The CD market might well not go on for ever, but recordings will, beamed up to the clouds. She plans pre-packaged programmes, like Chinese restaurant meals for those who know what they like, once they've got to know it, with some unexpected dishes too. Alternative visual versions, perhaps.

"Wait a minute: – this is my career you're talking about: live audience, live me, out for the evening – an event. Not just something you get by remembering your password."

"There's no worry there. Being in an audience with other people adds another dimension. But you must admit it can be costly to go to concerts: seats aren't all that cheap, and in this dicey financial age, when things are run for profit, who can know how long it might be before going to a concert is only for the rich?"

"There might always be audiences who would pay up for that. But people like me don't just travel around grabbing eye-watering fees. I have an adjustable rate, depending on where the work is."

"I think they might come to see you in person, after having seen you on film."

"Nice. And I hope they'll come again after having heard me in person."

We spoke about the food, about life in London, about anything really.

"What happens now?"

"To me? Pythagoras have decided to keep me on a small retainer. They're waiting to see what sort of form I can deliver. Basically, until they see how your CD does in the long term."

"The reviews have been alright. Jane sent me a résumé."

"Good reviews help. They really do. Especially for those of us behind the desk or the camera."

"Did they teach you that on your short course?"

"It was part of the syllabus. How to turn reviews to our advantage."

"Is there part of the syllabus that tells you how to deal with pianists who are satisfied with your recording techniques?"

"No. I don't remember a lecture on reciprocal satisfaction."

"If they tell you that there seemed to be some unfinished business between you…"

"No. If they did, the protocol would suggest that questions should be asked."

"Like what?"

"Like, exactly which sort of business is it? The sort you don't mix with pleasure, as in making recordings, or the business which didn't happen the other day? For business reasons."

"We're getting closer now."

"There are no dates in the diary for other work now."

"Are you saying that as long as there's no date in the diary, there's no business to mix with pleasure? Except the unfinished business I was talking about just now."

"We're playing word-games, aren't we? Are we ever going to pass GO on this board?"

"The time will come, if we keep throwing the dice."

"You'll prefer to have coffee at my place, I think."

We were advancing to GO.

I took her back home. Her home. Small but with character. An upright piano, not too large a TV-screen, many, many books, and rows of discs.

The coffee was deferred, because I kissed her. The woolly jumper she was wearing last time had given way to something much more approachable. No doubt deliberately chosen, but now was no time to think about choice of clothes.

This was joy, like listening to a good record is joy, like, I guess, writing a thesis, and not having to defend it. What am I saying? It was nothing like that. She had no plan, she was open to anything a comparative novice to the subtler ways of love might think of.

This carefree relationship might have had something to do with my playing, which she admires, and which she had done so much to capture on disc, or my body and my increasing interest in love-making which made her willing to share a little time with me.

We lay for a while, warm from contact, from delight.

"You know," she said, "there's one thing I've been wanting to tell you."

"Will I want to hear it?"

"Maybe. I think you'll agree that you've changed rather a lot since you came to play the Emperor concerto with us? I mean in the way you look."

"I had to do something to bolster my personal self-esteem."

"I'm not complaining, believe me. But…well, it may surprise you to know that I would have hopped into bed with you back then, if you'd have given me the smallest encouragement."

That certainly did surprise me.

"You mean with that plump bespectacled guy who accompanied me?"

"Yes. It was nothing to do with the way you looked. It was to do with the way you played. You sent out beams when you played, and they warmed me."

I said nothing.

"You know what women like most in a man?"

297

"It's pretty obvious that I don't, or else I wouldn't be spending so much time alone."

"It's the man himself. That's why I was keen to be your recording angel when the chance came my way. Then when I saw you again, I thought my memory was playing me false." She stroked my stomach. "I like you being flat, but until you actually started to play, I thought I'd made a mistake, and got you mixed up with someone else."

"A mistake?"

"Not as you might think. Believe me, I've had a great time. I didn't want to discover that you'd become obsessed with your appearance and lost what it was you used to have when you came to play the piano concerto with us. It's that 'you' I wanted to be with. Not what you look like."

Au fond, it seems as if it doesn't matter what I look like. That's a shame, if it's true, because my appearance was the raft I'd been clinging to after my shipwreck of a marriage. My wife had gone, and I had to accept part of the blame for that. As she also had to. Definitely.

It didn't seem to be a good time to think about it, just when I had decided I was getting a sort of handle on this extra-marital sex thing. Post-marital sex thing. But there it was: what I didn't want to confront. My big makeover was intended to stop me analysing what was really wrong. If what Victoria was saying was what women think, then Patti didn't go because of the way I looked. And she wouldn't come back because of the way I looked now. Not that I wanted her to. In all our years together, she never said anything about slimming, or contact lenses, or about the way I looked tonight, or any other night. In hindsight, it was almost as if she didn't give it a thought.

Victoria didn't know the real me either, only the one who can be Beethoven's Emperor, with or without new clothes. I'm beginning to enjoy the man I can see in the mirror. "I love me" is a joke, but it's not a bad line for someone who parades himself in front of the public. It's an invitation to other people to love you too. And it partly explains why you're there.

"I have no complaints. A bonus, maybe."

Victoria got up and put on a dressing gown. A reminder that she was a working girl, and I'm a busy man. The bed was ideal for what we did, but sleeping in it wasn't.

It wasn't part of my plan to start something that we both couldn't manage each in our own fashion, and it looked likely that I had succeeded here by unmentioned mutual consent.

And further on still

The interview at the BBC had made me a bit nervous. I had the Promenade concert to do. and I knew there might be some teasing going on. I thought I could deal with it, but it was my first appearance after the film came out.

I rang Ellen.

"You know about the Promenaders, who stand where the stalls would be if there were any seats there?"

"Yes – they wear hats and conduct and things. The ones with flags on the Last Night."

"Ye-e-es. They're a very good audience, and they've always seemed very happy with what I've done over the past few years. They listen – they're a good thing in capital letters. But they're no respecter of persons, in the nicest way."

"That makes you nervous?"

"Wouldn't it make you nervous?"

"I'd be nervous having to play the piano for a start."

"OK, OK. But wouldn't you?"

"Just think of the music. It's your reason for being there."

This was true enough.

"You're right. Keep thinking of the piano…Thanks."

Victoria was out when I called, but she rang back almost at once.

"Will, you sound worried in your message."

"I didn't say much."

"I can tell, all the same. Musician's ears. What's up?"

"I'm throwing a bit of a wobbly about the Prom next week. You know – after the film."

"Don't worry. They might send you up a bit, but it'll be affectionate. If you asked them, they probably admire you for going where the others don't. Ravel will take care of the rest. Trust…"

"Yes. Are you going to be there?"

"Yes. Do you want me to get there early enough to get a position in the very front row? I used to stand through all my first Proms. Not in the front row."

"No. I'll get you a seat. On the right hand side of the stalls, where I can spot you between the movements. Sounds crazy, like a small boy wanting his mother where he can see her. Except you're not my mother."

Something of a give-away, that. Victoria didn't notice. All she said was Yes.

The Prom

Two summer months of concerts in the Albert Hall in Kensington, as well as others nearby. It's not surprising that the Proms have been called the greatest Music Festival in the world.

The Hall is huge. Full of people listening to music. I was first taken to a Prom as a ten-year-old. We sat in the Amphitheatre directly opposite the orchestra. It was exciting, not just because we were a long way up, as well as a long way off.

From the stage, it looks even more impressive, the British Empire pushed into one building in memory of Prince Albert. Still relevant even though we have left the Empire behind for good – for everyone's good. It's too big really, and you have to know how to play on a big scale and a small one at the same time. Like a Greek actor in an amphitheatre. With no mask.

This year the planners had put me with a French orchestra with a fine reputation, and recordings to prove it. They were stopping off in London, so to speak, en route for the Edinburgh Festival. Once there they would join up with their opera company to do Poulenc's opera *Les Carmélites.*

At the Prom they were doing two pieces by St-Saëns – an overture and a symphony – and then I would join them for Ravel's Piano Concerto. After the interval they would play the second symphony by Henri Dutilleux.

I met the conductor, Jean-Philippe Chalamet, on the day before; we had the big music studio at Maida Vale to ourselves for a piano rehearsal. He played the orchestral part himself on another piano – very well, in that way that some conductors have – sometimes a bit splashy, but with a feeling for orchestral detail.

He'd been to the concert the night before and although he knew about the Proms, he was still surprised to see so many people standing.

"It's almost like the old theatres where you stood in the parterre."

He meant the audience that stands in the Promenade part, within spitting distance, and which can be in a very jokey frame of mind. The way the groundlings behaved between items – lively, noisy on occasion – had surprised him. He'd only heard broadcasts from the Festival Hall or the Barbican, where the behaviour was much more proper.

He felt a bit nervous, too.

"The British reserve – I know it from concerts I've heard – is not the same as in the football stadium, of course, but you know – the old entente cordiale, which is good on paper, is like a dog and cat..."

"Don't worry. They will love the St-Saëns, and the Ravel, which is popular, and they will listen carefully to the Dutilleux, which is an exciting and marvellous piece.

"They will be very enthusiastic. They will shout something when the piano is brought to the centre for the concerto. 'Heave – ho!' Or even 'Hissez, les gars" and then laugh. It's like a party but with serious intentions.

"Unique. And they are the youngest audience we ever see at a grown-up concert."

"This must be good for the music in this country."

"Yes, it is, but they don't appear in these numbers until the same time next year. No-one seems to know where they go, all those people standing in the prom...To be fair to them, the prices can be much higher elsewhere."

On the day, the rehearsal was a joy. The orchestra and I got on like old friends. They were good to work with, and mine was a concerto they knew well. I had more time with them than usual, because the rest of their programme was fully prepared – it was just a matter of finding out how much they were all going to hear of one another in the Albert Hall. They hadn't expected me to rehearse in French, and the rapport the pianist needs with the cor anglais in the slow movement was easy.

I stayed on and listened to the Dutilleux which they'd decided to play straight through, then make any adjustments needed for the acoustic afterwards.

**

It was the Prommers I first saw as I walked up the slope on to the stage.

When I made my entrance, I looked to my left, and caught sight of Victoria, in her seat by the gangway, and very kindly wearing a yellow dress. I didn't do a 'Hello Mummy' gesture to her, but I sent an energised smile in her direction. In fact, the Prommers did nothing. They had heard the overture and the symphony, which they liked, especially since it was a very high-class performance. Then it was me and Ravel's sharp and beautiful concerto. The groundlings made their usual nautical noises when the piano was moved into the middle, and they gave me a good welcome…I'm one of the Prom babies who's grown up over the last years.

The performance was one of the best I've done. I'm sure of that.

Afterwards…The first call was OK, just about the performance, very good applause, and a special vote of thanks to the solo cor anglais player. The second call was strong enough for an encore. There was a microphone for me to pick up and announce that I was going to play Ravel's Toccata from his suite *Le Tombeau de Couperin*, wonderfully flashy and every phrase with Ravel's name on it.

When I stood up to take the applause for that, there was a little pantomime. In the front row. The orchestra was amused by it, though they can't have had much idea what it was about. A small gang had brought a shower attachment each, and waved them at me, calling 'need to freshen up?' Harmless enough. So I laughed and made a special hand-on-heart gesture saying, "I surely need to. Thank you for bringing me the equipment." They didn't hear it, because the mic was off, but I think they got the idea. Goodness knows what they said in the broadcast. Depends on whether the presenter was filling in time by reading from my official CV printed in the programme, or just introducing an interval programme about the orchestra. I never heard one way or the other.

Victoria came round. She knew the pass-doors.

"You see. You were marvellous." She stepped back to let other well-wishers appear. It was the interval, and they didn't stay long.

"It was alright, wasn't it? I was happy with it."

"Yes. More than alright. The music was great: Ravel with your human heart beating inside it. Some players play him like a clock-maker. Not you." She kissed me on the cheek.

"They're right," she said. "You could do with a shower."

"Do I smell?"

"No, you don't, but you're damp."

"The Albert Hall isn't my favourite place for a shower. "

"Come back to my place. Notting Hill. Have a shower there."

"And then I'll take you for a meal."

"We'll see," she said.

It turned out not to be what we thought it might be going to be.

When we got to her place, she had guests. Her mother and father. Unexpected arrivals. God knows why she let them have a key.

"Vicki…we tried to phone. We did a matinee at the National, went for a meal with some friends we met at the show and missed the train home. To be honest we didn't know you'd have a guest." This was her father.

Her mother was different.

"I hope we haven't got in the way." That remark was meant for me. Obviously. Her wild days in Cambridge had not been buried. And then she said another right thing: "I love your CD; especially the Schubert sonata. Anyone can play Beethoven if they're serious enough, but Schubert needs love, too, delight, yes, and a sense of impending tragedy."

That went a long way to smoothing the situation out.

"Will's been playing and needs a shower more than anything in the world."

"I'm sorry we're in the way." Mother again.

After my shower, Victoria and I went out for a meal. Plenty of places in Notting Hill. Having done French last time, we chose for Italian. I can't quite work Victoria out. We had that swift and pleasing encounter – not exactly Brief, but not Prolonged, either. Sex as part of friendship, maybe. I had made a mental note that the evening might end that way. Was my sexual success going to be on the occasional snack side? Grazing, but not eating much grass.

"You could come back," Victoria said, "my parents will have gone to bed by now."

I thought about that and decided against it. I didn't fancy making love while Victoria's parents were in the spare bedroom. On a put-you-up bed, even, judging from the size of her apartment. I've not had much experience in that direction. I don't mean the bed, but the confidence in how to deal with the afterglow.

"You've already given me a big lift by coming to the concert. I'll go without the extra one. We'll put it in the savings account."

Durham

I spent the rest of August and early September learning new pieces, and going over my old repertoire. I took a break to go down to Cardiff and play a couple of dates with David and his quartet. That was like a refresher course, rehearsing and playing with people who played in symphonies by Brahms and Schumann giving them experience in a wider range of musical sound than mine.

303

In the last days of August, I had a concert in County Durham as part of a mini-festival taking place in a local school in holiday time. It was to start on Sunday with a brass band, and end with a choral concert on the Saturday. In between came my recital, and performances of a new play, crafted on a summer course for drama run by a local man who had made a name as a TV director. There was, all the time, an art exhibition: pictures, objects, some old, some newly created by local talent.

The secretary of the arts society, Dr Robson, met me at Durham station, gave me time to admire the spectacular view of the cathedral and castle, and took me to my hotel on the outskirts of the city.

"I'll leave you here to have lunch. Then you can put your feet up, or I can take you down to the hall this afternoon to try the piano. Whichever you prefer. Call me on my mobile. I'm free."

I called him after lunch, and he picked me up.

"It's a good piano – it's being lent to us by a concert pianist who's had to give up playing because of arthritis. It sits in his house, unused. He says he can't even enjoy playing for pleasure, which is sad."

"That's one of those things we save our money up for, the sad times," I said. "Insurance firms don't usually cover fingers and joints."

"I'm his GP, and believe me, it's been tough. He finds it a bit hard to get around, so I don't think he'll be in tonight. Otherwise, he's managing; he can use a computer to dictate his memoirs."

"Can be a bit tricky writing memoirs. You can't always tell the truth about the people you've worked with."

"I don't think he cares a damn. He says if this is the way people behaved, then they deserve what people write about them. The truth is elastic, anyway."

We drove on a little.

"I'm making a small detour to show you the site we're hoping to occupy fully in due course."

He stopped outside a disused railway station with one platform.

"There used to be a flourishing coal mine in this village. It was worked out long before the chimney came a-tumblin' down after the blitz of the Thatcher-Scargill war. No development of any importance has happened here since then. Those two rows of cottages were built by one of the Stevensons; they were dilapidated, so we've got them, and we're making them into art studios, and study rooms. The drama company is going very well. People come out from

Durham to take part, and once we've got the chance, they'll use a bit of the station – the bit that's safe – as our main place to rehearse. And when the time comes we'll make an arena using the station platform as the basis for the 'stage'."

"Where will the money come from?"

"We do the usual things. High-pressured coffee mornings. A spot of money from the National Lottery. And we've done DIY work on the cottages. So we've got started."

"When you think of all the money the owners took out of these places, it must make you wonder."

"It's what people did in those days. You know – North and South stuff."

"North and South divide?"

"Mrs Gaskell's novel. Not just that. Rich and poor. It still happens."

"I'll put it on my list."

"Someone's had the idea of looking into the estate of the last owner before nationalisation. She was Canadian, the last bit of a Scottish family. She was a woman of principle, and curious about what she'd inherited. She never came here, but did some research, and ended up knowing more about our history than we did. She saw how many men and young boys were killed in the pit over the century it was working, while her family was pocketing the money; so she tied up some money into a fund to be used to settle her family's debt to the place. It's taking time, but we've got good local minds working on it. And the European Union is showing interest in giving us a grant.

"Meanwhile we use a modern school out of term-time."

He drove me over.

"Look, I'm going to leave you alone now. Natasha Archbold is going to come round to say Hello and she'll take you back to your hotel. She says you know each other."

"We both do things for the Conservatoire in London."

Dr Robson started to leave, and came back.

"I forgot to ask. Would you mind doing an interview for the local paper? You don't have to do it, but it won't last long, because they don't do long interviews with classical musicians. If any at all. It can be done after the concert. Reporter called Kate Garbutt."

"Surely. It'll fill the time before I go to bed."

"That's great. It'll give their readers an idea of what important things we do with the money we got from the lottery. Also it would make a break from their usual 'personality' interviews which are short on both interview and personality."

He left me to the piano. A lovely instrument indeed, one of those which needs no cajoling before it will play with you.

After a while, Natasha Archbold appeared.

"You really make the piano sound as if it's loved."

"It deserves loving."

I hadn't known what to expect after the business about the Conservatoire's concert tour. Something more severe. Not the case. She was good-looking and her voice was low, with the sort of vitality that doesn't need to bounce off the walls.

"I'll run you back to the hotel when you're ready. Meanwhile I'll look at the pictures."

"Twenty minutes should do it."

The journey didn't take long. My carefully chosen hotel made it unnecessary to negotiate the streets of central Durham.

She had things to tell me.

"I put on events up here, my native heath, which are meant to bring newcomers to classical music. Your film seems to show you have a mind to do the same. Maybe we could collaborate on a missionary journey. I know that you take reduced fees if you're interested in anything new."

"I do some outreach events. So, yes, this interests me."

"I write music for them to play and listen to. We could maybe join ideas up. At least, kick ideas around a bit. Let's meet. Keep in touch. I come to London to teach and for Con meetings."

"I come up north for concerts. I've not got my diary, but I've a date to play in Richmond, followed two days later by a concerto in the Usher Hall."

"I'll come to Edinburgh to hear you if I'm free. We can take it from there. Or you can come and spend a day with me on your way back to London, if you're happy to do the journey on train."

"I like trains."

That's where we left it. It'll happen.

**

The concert itself was a typical, old-fashioned, even, programme: Baroque, Classical, Romantic, French. A mixed bag. I could, I suppose, have promoted my CD ("get your copy after the show at a discounted price…") by changing the programme to include one of the sonatas recorded on it. But I didn't.

A Bach English Suite, in G minor, the one which I plundered for my shower scene; a complete coincidence, because I'd finalised the programme with the society well before the film happened the way it did. Now it would act as proof that I needed no water to do a convincing presentation. Haydn's sonata in A flat: the slow movement is one of the most ravishingly beautiful things ever written. Chopin selection with no rain on this parade. Debussy's *Cathédrale engloutie* and *L'isle joyeuse*, about Cythera, the island of happy lovers. Rather extrovert love, public love, according to Watteau's painting of the place. *La campanella* with Liszt showing he could be as spectacular as Paganini had been when he wrote this bell-music for his violin.

As an encore, Liszt's wisping wills.

Well-wishers afterwards, autographs, Natasha and Dr Robson.

I had to meet Kate, the interviewer who would now be my lift back to the hotel.

Kate. I was ready to greet a teenager who would ask me how many notes I could play with each hand, and did I play the piano all the time, and what sort of music I really liked.

The Kate I met wasn't the one I'd expected. In her twenties, very attractive, and she'd taken trouble to dress up for the concert, discreetly, but very suitably.

"I don't know how you are after a concert, but if you want something to eat, I have food in my fridge, and I live just round the corner from your hotel."

The school would be happy to close up for the night as soon as possible. I accepted the offer.

She drove more wildly than Natasha, but she knew the road and didn't hit anything.

She did live round the corner from the hotel. A pied-à-terre is a good thing to call it, and certainly good for a face-to-face interview.

She put the food out – tapas-style with biscuits, some cheese. She had a bottle of New Zealand Sauvignon Blanc; she poured out a glass each, and we started to eat.

"Just to put you in my picture. I'm covering the whole of this local arts festival on my own, and if I say my normal interviews are mostly with footballers, that's because my editor reckons that hits the right spot with his public. This time I asked him to let me tug on the lead a bit. I belong to the drama group doing the play that's happening this week. I was part of the improvisation behind it. So I have an insider's view."

"Tell me about it."

Kate laughed. "Don't let me forget I'm supposed to be interviewing you.

"We're excited about our piece. It has a Punch and Judy show for a framework: 'Maggie and Artie'. You can guess what it's about – still an issue round here. People don't forget easily. With other characters and episodes. Quick changes. A woman in a posh gown in a sketch with a man in a suit talking about nationalisation. Two policemen in fish-net tights, one of them a woman (I play her), with Cockney accents, up from London with a couple of batons."

"It sounds fun."

"It's meant to be. Serious fun."

"Isn't that the best sort?"

"Finale with all the cast, including Punch and Judy, wearing miners' hats with lights, turning them out one by one."

"I'm sorry I won't be able to see it, but I have to move on."

"I'll send you the programme, if you like."

"I would. I'll give you my agent's address and email."

"Fine. I've got a couple of pictures of you on my phone, but I'll get him to send me a publicity picture."

"She's a she."

"Ah! D'you like working with women?"

"I like working with people I like. There are many women in my profession and I don't find that a distraction when we're working."

"Can we do that little bit you just said with the recording machine on?"

She switched it on and asked the question about working with women again. I said more or less the same thing.

She played it back. It never comes out the same the second time when you try to catch your first thought. It wasn't quite so good. What I said. Still, this wasn't a broadcast, and she could use the thought itself. Back to recording.

"OK. I want to ask you personal questions. Will you go with that?"

"Fine. If any of them get too personal for me, we can stop the recording."

"You're in your mid-thirties, and you're terrific when you play the piano. I'm not an expert, but the audience thought that. It's hard what you do, is it?"

"It's not easy, but it's easier the more you work at it."

"Like being in a circus."

"Yes. A mixture of talent and showmanship. A sense of risk at times. It's a public event."

"Circus people often come from circus families. Is that what it was for you? Musical family?"

"My grandmother brought me up. She was a good pianist – not a professional, but she played seriously for the sheer fun of it. As a kid I was always going to the piano, exploring it, I wouldn't leave it alone, so she fixed me up with proper lessons. I never stopped."

"Your grandmother looked after you. Were your parents away a lot? Can I ask you about them?"

"I never got to know them. I was a selective orphan. They left."

"Did that hurt?"

"No, not really. More the idea of it. It's hard to miss what you never had. Almost at once. Mother was an actress, maybe still is, and Father was a sailor. Somewhere else. But they left some of the DNA behind, and that was probably the best they could do."

"You look like an actor who could sail a boat. Did you play sport? Football?"

"No. I was always on the heavy side – like fat, eventually. Anyway football would have taken up too much time. I was never put into teams at school. They used to let me go running, and I did physical exercises. I tried tennis, but it wasn't good for my right forearm, so I didn't do that either."

"Did you mind?"

"I don't think so; Saturday was a busy day once I got into the Conservatoire Junior School."

"Were you a sort of music swot?"

"I suppose. But I was in the school play and I was good at French."

"Can I ask a personal question?"

"Try me."

"Did you have time for love?"

"As in sexual encounters? I wasn't the sort of guy anyone pursued."

"I find that hard to believe."

"You're kind."

"The way you look. Even if you were heavy…"

"Wearing thick glasses."

"You got married, it says here in my notes."

"Yes."

"And now I'm unmarried."

"And not fat."

"And wearing contact lenses."

"Tell me how much time you spend practising? You couldn't play the way you do without working out – on the piano I mean."

"It varies. Depending on what I've got coming up in my schedule. 2010 is a big year for pianists. It's the bicentenary for Chopin and Schumann and the year after for Liszt."

"Two of the composers you played tonight."

"Yes, Special concerts."

"What's the happiest moment when you're out there in front of the public?"

"All of them. In different ways."

"Do you get nervous, thinking of remembering all those notes? And hitting them in the middle."

"Not about that. There are moments when I have to concentrate extra on the geography of the keyboard, but it's all part of a big deal."

"Is it emotional for you? You get different reactions from audiences?"

"Yes. It changes depending on where you are. Some London audiences are very international. The Promenade concerts in London are an experience of their own; the Albert Hall is so big. But what you work towards is for people to be able to enjoy the music in whatever way pleases them. The silence that follows the last notes you play at the end of a quiet piece is very gratifying."

"Like after the Cathedral piece you played. Before the noisy one for the Joyful Island. The island for lovers – Cythera. Those lovers sounded as if they were really having a good time."

"I think it's maybe about the journey on the way there as well as the load of noisy sex acts. But it's about what the music says to you."

"You said you were unmarried now. Do you want to expand on that?"

"I'm alone, through no wish of my own, and commitment is difficult after divorce. I'm a single man, enjoying meeting more women than I ever met when I was married. I'm getting myself a life, you might say."

"Right."

"And what about you?"

"I'm on my own. I'm after a career more than anything. So I don't side-track in any permanent sense."

Short silence while I looked at her. She smiled and made no move to switch the recording off.

"Did you see the film I've made?"

"Naturally. I told my boss that it would be a good idea to follow it through. See what you were like in real life – you know, whether you were as good in concert as you are in the film. So I sat in two different seats. One so that I could see your hands, and one so that I could see your face."

"And?"

"I used to think classical musicians sort of protect themselves with their music. They wrap themselves round with it. Not like rock stars, who use the music to strip themselves off. Well, you're not afraid to show the real you. I like that."

"As in stripping off? In the film? You just caught sight of a man in a shower."

"Is that not you then?"

"Oh yes it's me."

"Who did you make your film for?"

"For people like you who listen as well as watch."

"It spoke to me."

"I'm glad. I'd die a happy man if I thought I'd said something to you, and to everyone who buys a copy."

She switched the machine off.

"I've got plenty of material there."

"Send my agent a copy when you publish, and maybe she can use some for my publicity handouts."

"I'll just make a random check on the recording."

"...*meeting more women than I ever did when I was married. I'm getting myself a life.*"

I wasn't entirely sure what to do next, still too much of a novice.

I looked at my watch.

"It's getting on for eleven, I see."

"You'll have time for another glass of wine. Is there anything else you'd like?"

Could I say 'It depends what you mean by anything else?'

311

My birthday was a month away. My recent love life, such as it was, had been conducted on a rather passive basis, like my hero the young Donny Johnny – in the poem. Just wait until the woman makes the move, and then don't dodge.

"This is a nice flat you have."

"Believe it or not, it goes with the job – that's to say I get it for a reduced rent. The newspaper owns it."

"Do you interview all your interviewees here?"

"No. Some of them would take it as an invitation over and beyond the calls of journalism if I did."

"I can see how they would."

"And you, how do you see it?"

"I'm trying to work that one out."

"Can I just say that I loved the way you looked on film, and you live up to it? Does that help?"

This woman knew what she was doing, so I went to help her pour out the wine (how much help do you need for that?).

What followed was great. By which I mean that I proved that making love after a concert, with a lovely journalist with a mind and a sense of humour, is something I could do. It felt both committed and uncommitted at the same time. And it was something I initiated. Or, on mature thought, that we initiated together.

"You're really real," she said at one point. She couldn't have said a better thing. My re-construction job, without an architectural plan, was working.

It was a short walk back to the hotel. It was late when I got there, but the night-porter didn't mind. He went back to his TV screen.

Short break in Scotland

My house was in order. My dates were far enough away, and term wasn't due to start at the Con till after my birthday. I had concerts in Germany in view, and the Chopin and Schumann year soon to begin, some broadcasts, and a peppering of solo concerts around the British Isles. Probably something in France, maybe the US. I scheduled a couple of catch-up sessions with personal trainer Frankie.

I needed to go somewhere for no reason at all. I texted Eleanor Gordon and reminded her that when we last met at the concert in the Barn near Banchory she'd issued an invitation to stay with her. She answered with an email.

312

"Lovely to hear from you. Yes, of course you must come and spend a few days. Just tell me when it would suit. My two sons have just gone back to Edinburgh and their work there, so I'm here on my own. We have a good microclimate and we don't get the rain in such amounts as others do. No guarantee. You should be able to see the Falls of Feuch that appeared briefly in your film, and you might spot some early-bird salmon practising their leaps. Eleanor."

We fixed a date. I took the train to Aberdeen, picked up a hire car, and drove to her place.

Eleanor's is a lovely house, not far to the north of the Barn. Solid and stone-built. Modern inside, comfortably brought up to date.

I'd spent most of the day travelling, and was pleased by the smell of the meal she was cooking.

I suggested I take her out for a meal later in my short stay.

"That's very kind of you. There are pleasant enough places to eat round here, but none of them provides food as good as mine. We'll go out to tea instead, with real Scottish scones."

"Perhaps I can help you in the kitchen…peel things or stir sauces. I cook for myself, you know. With recipes."

This was the beginning of a few days of a complete shutdown for my problems, real and invented.

Every day I would drive to a central point, park the car and walk a circular route, with a packet of food in my pocket, and my water bottle full.

The weather was good for my visit to the Falls of Feuch. They were much more exciting in reality, because of the sound the water makes as it takes different routes over the rocks to get down to the River Dee not far away.

A few salmon obliged me with their presence, one or two having to make several attempts to get to their Promised Land.

Other days were a bit mixed, but the sun shone bravely enough and I saw a partridge or two which had possibly been shot at by some member of the Royal Family taking a break from duties up the road in Balmoral.

Eleanor told me she was a distant relative of Lord Byron.

"Gordon is a common enough name around here. Byron was one of us, and lived up here until he went south into England. I was actually born a Gordon too. I don't know how many cousins removed I was from Alexander, my husband, who died before you and I met. He was a wonderful man, and we had the two boys."

"You were never tempted to re-marry?"

"I was a young widow and there was no-one else who could replace Alex."

"I remember something you said when I was up here last year: Being alone is no bad thing, once you're used to it."

"It's true for me. Did you find it a help?"

"I try, but it gets hard at times."

"Things not perhaps so good?"

"Yes and no."

"After your concert here, you seemed to have a new life-style…to judge by the woman in the car."

"That was part of the not so good bit. My first time away from my customary life-style. And it didn't work. I'm not used to dating, and I'm hamstrung by the fact that I don't want to get into another Patti situation. Patti walked out on me, because she wanted something I couldn't do for her. I think she made the best move for her."

"That's a very generous way of looking at it."

"It's the reason I changed the way I look. And a way of assuming complete responsibility for what she did to me."

"It's an improvement, that's for sure. Makes a woman look twice, and not just at your film."

"True, but I have to be certain that any woman I go with is not looking for anything permanent. It sounds very casual…"

"It's the way of the world. My two sons brought temporary girls up here before they got married. Nice girls, not fly-by-night floozies. I've had offers myself – none recent – from men who should know better. If I said No, it was because I owed it to the community I live in. Remember that women are equal now with men, and they have the right to choose their life-style.

"If you ever find someone you want to settle down with and have a family with, you'll know. As the auld Scots Grannie said, 'Whit's Fur Ye'll No Gang By Ye'. Do I need to translate?"

"No, I think I get the idea."

Well worth travelling so far to get advice like that, and a sympathetic ear.

When I left, I felt better, much rested, and calmer.

The day before my 36th birthday

September 20th.

Ellen's phone was in answer mode, and Victoria was away producing a record in Germany. Put that together and it wasn't likely to lead to much. But of all things, Patti rang.

This was the first time we'd spoken since the day she took her last supper without me. I still had that image of the biscuit crumbs on the plate and the milk in the glass that she drank before she left.

"I hope you don't mind, but I've been thinking I ought to be in touch."

I hadn't thought of it, because – well, it had been different for me.

"Yes, nice to hear your voice…" It had taken a moment to recognise it. Was the tone rather professional, or had I forgotten her sound in my ear?

"How are you doing? Baby behaving?"

That was a bit of a wild guess, with perhaps a touch of malice. It could have been wrong. It wasn't.

"Kicking like mad. So I'm out of the orchestra for a while, at any rate. I'm only paid for one person…playing a solo instrument."

"Seems fair."

"We've seen your film. We were going to watch it in a spirit of…what?"

"Mockery?"

She laughed.

"No. No. Curiosity. Plain and simple nosiness. We heard you'd changed a bit. We wanted to see for ourselves. You know: 'What the hell is he doing? Anything to make a wave these wicked days.'"

Careful plurals, I noticed. She went on.

"I have to say it's good. And you didn't look like this when we were married, you beast."

So that was to be the tone of our relationship, even though I know that looks can't mean all that much to her, or she wouldn't have married Keith. Not the Keith in the photograph of the orchestra. Or me in the first place.

"You're happy to be a mother-to-be?"

"Yes, yes I am. And I'm very pleased for you; you seem to have discovered something about yourself that you never did with me – better for your career. Charismatic might be the word. You could say."

"Thank you. I was worried that showing more of me than usual might set me back. Turn me into media fodder."

"Nothing wrong with that, if the circumstances are right. And in this instance, I think you're justified. I must say, when Keith watched it he was amazed. Couldn't understand how I could have left you for him."

"If he has any doubts about that, you can ask him to talk to me. I think I've sort of worked out what I failed to do for you, while he obviously succeeds. It was nothing to do with the way I looked, was it?"

"I suppose not. No, it wasn't anything to do with that. You always looked fine to me. Yes, somewhat overweight, and I had to nag you about having your hair cut. But I don't know if I could tell you exactly what went wrong."

"We didn't try to put it right. We never talked about a family after we were up and running professionally."

"You said you didn't…"

"At the beginning, yes, because of my parents. But after years of what I thought was a successful marriage, we might have talked it over."

"It wouldn't have been sensible to have a child when I knew we were fizzling out. Not to give us a sort of shot in the arm. That would have been disastrous. Children as glue."

"True. Anyway it didn't occur to me then. You're happy now, which is what matters."

"It's good to hear you not being bitter. Finding your own way."

"I'm still looking for my way but I'm getting better at it."

"We were very young when we got together. Probably didn't know who we were."

"We could have managed it better than we did. Grown up together."

"Like two flowers on the same stem."

"What?"

"From Gounod's opera Faust. I do sometimes listen to the operas I play in. But it didn't happen."

"I suppose not. It's just that I didn't notice."

"Maybe that was it."

"Yes, maybe it was."

"So, is the film selling?"

"I don't know. I wait to be told. There's too much else to think about."

"Have you got a new…No. I don't need to know that. Though I think I might feel better if I did."

"No. I haven't got a new anything."

"Apart from appearance. There were one or two rumours about. You know how kind people tell you things they think you ought to know. But I had no idea you were this man kicking leaves or lying on a bed thinking of Liszt."

"Not to mention the other things."

"Not to mention them. Absolutely."

I wanted her to say something more. I wasn't sure what. I'd thought about Patti quite a lot since we divorced. Even more about me. Only to spend my time wondering if I was getting it right. All the same, her voice was now stirring memories of a sort of security, although it was nothing of the sort.

"Funny. It was like watching someone else. Someone I didn't know."

"Someone invented? A celebrity?"

"Oh no. Celebrities don't play the piano the way you do. You play the way you always did: truth in music, like it comes from you with nothing in the way. You didn't invent that. It was always there. How you behaved, how you looked, was something that could change."

"I didn't want to change. I was where I was and I thought I knew where that was."

She changed the subject. Slightly.

"You don't mind me calling you like this?"

"No. Let's be grown-up about it. Be good friends. Let me know when the baby is born. I'm not going to offer to be godfather – I think there are limits. But you were a part of my life. And, to be honest, you were the reason I did what I did about my appearance. Pathetic, in a way. Do you think I could have got you back somehow?"

No. I don't think so. We'd gone into separate compartments, really. Two different careers, which meant we were two different people."

"It needn't have been like that. But it was."

"I imagine the way you look has altered your life somewhat."

OK, there was no need to let her know what I was going through.

"Only when it comes to having my picture taken for publicity. The lighting is different."

"And the photographer, I dare say. Mike in the High Street didn't try very much."

"I think he thought you were a natural, and I was a no-hoper. A passport photograph would have done for me, just to make it easier to make sure the right man came on stage."

"Well, enjoy it. It will be a subject for chat when I go back to the orchestra."

"It doesn't affect Keith?"

"I don't think Keith has problems. If the other brass players say anything to him, it's more likely they'll show respect for a man who can replace you the way you are now. Hidden talents I think they might think he has."

"It's my birthday tomorrow."

"I know. Happy birthday."

"Listen. It's part of a birthday poem:

    "'Tis time this heart should be unmoved,

    Since others it hath ceased to move;

    Yet though I cannot be beloved,

    Still let me love!"

"Interesting."

"It's what Lord Byron thought when he was going to be thirty-six tomorrow, and it rings a sort of bell."

"Rubbish. That's about him, not you. Keep an open mind, and you'll find someone, if that's what you want."

We said goodbye. Somewhat formally.

Tomorrow, I'd begin to learn Beethoven's opus 110.

THE END